I0709369

Books by S.C. Giedzinski

Nights They Forgot
Island Rain
Nine Million Marshmallows and More

A Novel by
S.C. GIEDZINSKI

NIGHTS THEY FORGOT

Illustrated by
MIF RODRIGUEZ

SEE THE FUTURE

Nights They Forgot is not suitable for younger audiences. Its story contains explicit and sensitive written material in many forms. For a complete list of content warnings by chapter, use your camera to scan the code below. You may also navigate to https://giedzinski.com/nights-they-forgot/content.

THE MAJOR ARCANA

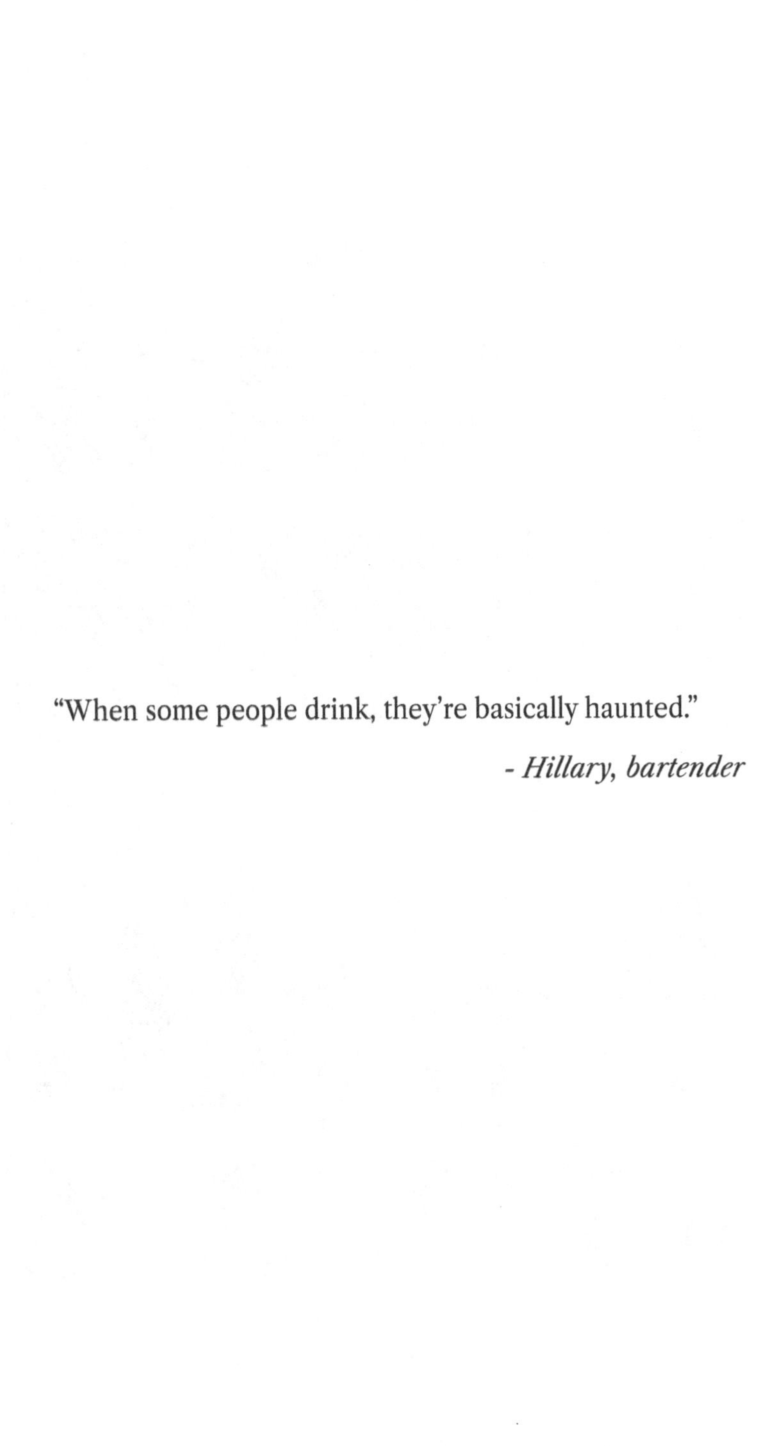

"When some people drink, they're basically haunted."

- *Hillary, bartender*

THE FOOL

0: THE FOOL

One more night fell, and the blues darkened to black over downtown. Northwest of the bus terminal, four empty lanes squeezed any rare foot traffic into single file. Andy faced backwards, leading Levi and Ellesandra down the concrete sidewalk.

"It's not *all* about the beer. It can be spiritual. It's about how the space makes you feel!" An untrimmed branch whacked the back of his head, so Andy faced forward again. "Shit, okay, Leader Avenue *is* more walkable, but it's for tourists. All those hip new brewing companies do is repackage and rebrand the same pale ales with cute names and pretty cans. Then you've got the places that pretend to be clubs, you know, charging cover to the clueless university kids. Levi, *you* know that shit worked on us. You two, though? You've been here long enough to drink with the rest of the locals."

The three waited at a crosswalk. Ellesandra kissed Levi's hand.

"Gross," Andy sneered.

Levi shoved him, not quite into the street. "You sure this place is actually here?"

Andy pointed to a low building ahead. It hunched forward, its dim bay windows angling over the sidewalk. Thick velvety curtains blocked the glass from inside and pressed a small neon *Open* sign against one pane. Long, black-painted cinderblock walls framed the streetside facade. At a side parking lot, two metal doors flanked the structure, constricting the music that seeped through them.

"Sounds open to me!" Andy spun around to walk backwards again. Levi grimaced at the vaultlike building, and Ellesandra rolled her eyes.

"Okay, one drink, then we call it a night." She made sure they both heard her and squeezed Levi's hand for good measure.

"It wasn't even that far," Andy derided, circling an orange pin on his phone's map. "I can't *believe* you guys haven't been here yet."

Levi craned his neck and pushed his wavy hair away from his eyes. "This place looks like an evil strip club. What's it called, again?"

Andy moved into range of the thrumming music and couldn't hear the question. A small sign above the double side door answered it, and headlights from a passing car lit the sign's stenciled white letters: *ARCANA*. When Andy pulled the handle of the stickered steel door, reddish light beamed a Hollywood carpet onto the asphalt. It beckoned them into the embrace of 80s surf-punk guitar.

"Wow," Ellesandra muttered. A mid-30s man with a tall red mohawk rose from behind a tiny table in the entryway. His lips spoke through half a dozen sharp silver piercings:

"Got y'all's IDs?"

Andy produced his first, and the bouncer scanned it with a tablet under a goose-necked lamp. Ellesandra held Levi's hand while Andy tried to calm their nerves. "I love this! C'mon, this is sick."

"Agent Orange is the fucking shit," the bouncer affirmed, bopping his head to the song. Clueless, Andy nodded at man and his mohawk. "*Bloodstains*. Their first hit? That's early 80s hot sauce right there."

Andy reclaimed his ID. The bouncer took Ellesandra's next. He held it under the lamp, dancing in place while focusing the tablet's camera. Meanwhile, Andy charted his course to the bar. He found an opening between a fur-coated man in a metal chair and a wooden pole wrapped in fluffy pink fabric. The awkward, ill-placed pink structure left just enough space for Andy to lean over the heavy block bar top and catch the attention of a lone bartender with pink glitter around his eyes.

"Three shots tequila reposado."

Levi and Ellesandra tried to make themselves comfortable on a small, red-patterned couch across from the bar. Levi stuck out his tongue when Andy returned from the bar with three salt-rimmed golden shots and lime wedges.

"Oh fuck, is that tequila?" Ellesandra scrunched her nose.

Levi squeezed her hand. "Ah, shit. Andy, it's—"

"Can't beat the classics!" Andy set the shots on the coffee table at their feet. He forced his way onto the couch with them, next to Levi, who shuffled closer to Ellesandra to make more space. Andy opened one hand, beckoning towards their drinks.

"What? This isn't your go-to anymore?"

Levi shrugged. "*I* can do it."

"If it's gotta be tequila, I go blanco," Ellesandra said. Andy tutted and slid her glass mockingly away. She laughed. "I'm sorry! I should've said. It's okay, though. I can handle it. I'll do it."

"Wait! I can go grab a blanco." Andy stood halfway, but Levi pulled him back down by the back of his fitted T-shirt. "You sure? Both of you?"

Ellesandra lifted her glass. Next, Levi claimed his, then Andy. He held it like a precious crystal between his fingertips. "Levi knows, a lot of interesting nights in college started this way."

"Cheers to one more, right?" Levi tapped his glass to Ellesandra's, and the couple took theirs first. Andy drained his shot in one quick gulp, catching every drop, but something in the liquid struck him from within.

An electric wave of dread and panic rocketed through Andy's body, too strong and irregular for even the shittiest tequila. His head emptied like his glass, crashing his train of thought and vaporizing its debris. Secrets, worries, hopes, desires, and all their memories washed clean from Andy's consciousness. He reset like a digital clock from a blackout, flickering alone in the swirl of barroom activity. Outside, nothing changed about Andy. Inside, only flashing zeroes remained of whomever he was.

In his place, in his body, THEY began THEIR life.

The man next to THEM—whose name THEY failed to recall—ditched his glass and bit his lime wedge. The woman swallowed, gagged, and sprang up from the couch. THEY blinked at her, the stumbling stranger.

The man spit out his lime. "Elle, you okay?"

"Mm!" She dismissed him and chased after a hand-painted *Restroom* sign above a side hallway. He started up after her, but she waved at him again to let her go. THEY lowered THEIR empty glass to the coffee table, leaned back on the couch, and set THEIR eyes on the unidentifiable man to THEIR right.

"She'll be fine," he assured THEM. THEY stared at him, uncomprehending, as Andy's smirk faded from THEIR mouth. THEIR shoulders bent inward. The man beside THEM stiffened. "What's that face? Are you freaking out right now?"

The warm liquor spread its way throughout THEIR chest, awakening four unfamiliar limbs. THEIR attention drifted to the room around THEM: the bouncer, the bartender, the countless points of colorful light across every dark surface, like rainbow stars in a planetarium. Beginning to accept THEIR own permanence in this nameless space, THEY cleared THEIR throat. "Is this a dream I'm having right now?"

The man cocked his head. "Fuck off. You think I should go check on her?"

"Who?"

THEIR question seemed to stump him. "Elle. You saw. She just went..." He squinted. "Are you *good* right now?"

THEIR curious hand wandered to his dry glass, then the coffee table, then to the ripped denim on the man's knee. He knocked THEIR hand away. "Not now." He sat further forward on the couch. "You're *not* doing this now, okay?"

"What am I doing?" THEY recoiled and touched THEIR lips— a reflex alien to THEM. THEY blushed with embarrassment but not fear. THEY felt the sudden loss of something inside THEM, but THEY also lost any sense of what it was. This life sprinted onward.

The man's eyes narrowed. "Save it."

"What was I just—?"

Interrupting THEM, he threw one arm around THEIR shoulders and lassoed THEM close enough to speak straight into THEIR ear. "I actually *care* about her, okay? I really fucking do. And if you *meant* what you said last month, don't *try* shit. Don't say shit, Andy, just let last month, let three years ago, let it *all* go. It was what it was. Don't say *shit* to Elle, okay? And don't act like this isn't hard for *me*, too. Chill out. *Fuck*." He leaned away and squeezed the bridge of his nose.

Andy, he called THEM. Now alone at THEIR end of the couch, THEY repeated the name in THEIR head. Who was Andy to this man? Did THEY need to be Andy? A simpler question erupted from THEIR throat: "Do I *love* you?"

"Not now," he exhaled.

THEIR dismay expanded, rippling with the buzz of alcohol poisoning THEIR blood. This noise of the bar planted seeds of stress in THEIR skin. As a million more unanswered questions stacked between THEIR ears, fear took root. THEY needed to escape the red couch by any means. THEY shifted Andy's unsteady body from the couch towards the restroom sign and into the short side hallway, away from the bar.

A woman walked straight into THEM.

"Sorry," THEY said to the stranger, before remembering her face from a minute ago. *L*, the man called her.

"You good?" She stopped THEM as THEY passed. Over her shoulder, the man on the couch shot daggers from his eyes. *Don't say shit to L,* he warned. THEY wondered what the letter stood for.

"I'm good. Just, restroom." THEY hurried past her into the small, blue-lit sitting room beyond the hallway, then picked the closest of two poster-coated restroom doors. THEY fumbled in the dim chamber for a light switch, then for a steel latch above the loose doorknob. The small single restroom boxed THEM between four walls of graffiti. It even spread across even the sink and toilet. *GOODBYE JOC*, said a wavy red message on the wall. *Fuck off, Oren,* said another, in bright golden script on the bathroom mirror. Behind the words on the glass, a young face in the reflection studied THEIR clean jaw and misty blue-gray eyes for the first time.

Alarmed by THEIR own frantic glare, THEY patted THEIR pockets and scavenged for a wallet, which THEY dropped. It fell open on the floor, revealing an ID. It matched the person in the mirror in the tight gray heather shirt: A man named Andrew, or *Andy*, as the guy on the red couch called him. Still, THEY felt no more kinship to that name or reflection than to the names scribbled above the toilet.

THEY steadied THEIR breaths and replayed every memory THEY could. During THEIR messy conversation with the man on the couch, he seemed to know THEM. What was *his* name? *He...* that guy wanted Andy to hide something from L, the woman coming from the bathroom. Before that, all three of them sat together, with three empty glasses on the table. THEY still tasted the tequila, but THEY couldn't remember raising a glass to THEIR mouth. *That* was the dividing moment between the known and the unknown world. Each time THEY racked THEIR brain to glimpse what happened before the empty glasses, THEY drew a blank.

The fool in Andy's body asked a simple, futile question into the mirror:

"Who the *fuck* is Andy?"

No time for answers. An unseen hand rattled the loose handle of the bathroom door, then knocked twice. THEY shoved Andy's wallet back into a back pocket and flicked the door's latch open.

"Let me in," the man from the couch insisted, wrestling his way through the half-open door, accompanied by two bars of a staticky grunge song. He relatched the door behind him in one quick flourish.

THEY backed away into the paper towel dispenser, fishing for more answers against a roaring tide of nothingness. "I don't think I know who you are."

The man leaned on the door, fixed his eyes on the ceiling, and took a deep breath. THEY held THEIRS, waiting for another rant, insult, or out-of-place comment from this man THEY couldn't name. Instead, he said nothing. He softened his tense shoulders and stepped closer.

THEY tried one more time. "I don't know who *I* am, either."

"Andy," he shook his head. He wrapped his cautious arms around THEIR back and kissed THEM. THEY let THEIR fingers float up his neck and brush the warm roots of his wavy hair. The man's eyes shut before THEIR lips connected, then reopened when he pulled away. "I'm Levi. You're Andy. And yeah, I *do* love you."

THEY breathed. So, his name was Levi. "I think... I love you too?"

Another hand—someone out in the sitting room—bashed on the door. Levi ignored it. He perched on the tank behind the toilet, one flat-soled shoe balanced on the plastic seat. "This isn't how I wanted tonight to go."

THEY rubbed the back of THEIR neck. "She loves you more than I do, doesn't she?"

Levi laughed once, so loud that it echoed off the bathroom walls over the thumps of music outside. "It doesn't fucking matter. Who knows when I'm gonna see you again after this, anyway?"

Andy's phone vibrated in THEIR pocket. THEY slid it out, and a notification emerged:

HART AIRWAYS: Your flight to LaGuardia (LGA) is ready for check-in. Tap to open app...

THEY swiped the notification aside, unveiling a blurred wallpaper photo of Andy and Levi, grinning and running up a flight of stairs. THEY locked the phone and hid it away again. "You're never gonna tell her about this, are you?"

"*You* asked me to move on," Levi asserted, although THEY couldn't remember. "Why would I tell her, when I'm moving on from you as fast as I can?"

"It's too hard," THEY groaned, massaging THEIR temples. "I don't know if I can remember who I am without you."

Outside, a fist pounded again on the door. Levi ignored it. "New York was *your* fucking plan, and you knew I couldn't afford to move there with you. Unless you forgot that *some* people actually use *loans* to pay for college."

"Levi, wait, that's not what I—"

"*Now* you pretend we could be real, like you need me?" Levi jumped back onto his feet and strutted towards THEM, backing THEM into the door. He pressed his hands to the wood on either side of Andy's head. "Actually, fuck it. I *would* go with you, but you'll never ask. We both know what it would do to her, so spare me the hope. Let's both admit it's easier for us to *pretend* one more time, like last month. And then I'll say it's the 'last time,' one more time. You and her get to cut me up and take your pieces of me, and I love you *both* enough to let you."

"Stop!" Cornered against the door, THEY braced THEIR palm on the chest of Levi's buttoned paisley shirt. "From when we took those shots, before that, I *literally* can't remember anything about anyone, not even me."

Levi held THEIR hand on his chest and hesitated. "What the fuck are you talking about?"

A scraping object jostled the doorframe. Next to Levi's head, the thin plastic corner of a credit card shimmied up the edge of the door and popped the swing latch free from its bracket. The door wedged partway open. The bouncer, holding a flashlight in one hand and a credit card in the other, shone his light inside.

"You boys illiterate, or what?"

Levi stepped aside to let the door open fully. The bouncer patted a stained paper sign, fixed to the outside of the door with packing tape: *One person at a time, losers!*

Levi raised his guilty hands. "He was feeling sick. I had to see if..."

The bouncer clicked his flashlight off and holstered it in a pocket of his patch-covered leather jacket. "Buddy, I ain't a fed. Love is love, but rules is rules." He raised his chin at THEM. "You good, 'sick' guy?"

"Feeling better now," THEY lied, and the bouncer retreated towards the main entrance.

As THEY and Levi stepped out of the restroom, a group of three people in the sitting area stopped talking. THEY wiped THEIR lips and tried not to acknowledge those prying stares, tugging like harpoons in THEIR skin. THEY followed Levi through the narrow hallway back to the bar, where L waited on the red couch, zoned out on her phone.

"I'm gonna get some air," THEY told Levi. He ignored THEM and joined L on the couch. She continued on her phone. He whispered something to her, but she didn't react.

Approaching the open front door, THEIR heart almost stopped. The gentle outdoor air washed over THEM like a tidal wave of every unknown thing beyond this space. The heavy music, multicolor lights, monochrome posters, and dark-clothed strangers filled THEIR mind to its brim. It hurt to think of a whole world beyond this small space, beyond THEIR intricate memory of the past few minutes, but what choice did THEY have? After a few seconds sitting with L, she'd know *something* was wrong with THEM. THEY stepped outside, letting the building's cinderblock wall separate THEM from her.

A few black picnic tables lined the parking lot along the wall, covered by a long beige canopy. Smoke and spinning pink disco lights swirled under it, where three people chatted at the middle table. At the far end of the open canopy, a fourth person rocked from one foot to the other and sipped the last drops from a can of light beer. THEY snuck behind the trio and lowered THEMSELF onto the bench farthest from the door.

"I waited in the car like ten minutes!" One stranger with a pink buzz cut emphasized to the other two. She gripped the table like the handlebars of bicycle. "The pharmacy didn't even *have* it."

"Wait, wait," another interrupted, "what was he even looking for?"

"I don't fucking know! But we had to go to *another* pharmacy. And there's like—"

"And y'all are already in what, fucking Chesterville?" The third person mumbled the question through a beer can, sounding half robotic.

"Chesterville, yeah! So, the next pharmacy is like ten minutes further west. And at this point... Yeah, yeah, I went. Shut up, I know I'm a dumbass, shh! I was already late for work, and I didn't want to argue with him. So, I take him there, and he gets his fucking *whatever*, and we go."

The second stranger groaned and spun an empty ashtray. "You were way, way too nice to this man."

"Yeah, the guy I drove around for two days who didn't even *act* like he wanted to fuck me? I wanted to strangle him at this point, but he was *so* pretty. Did I tell you he had that one piercing? You know, the double-thing?" She mimed something, tugging her ear.

"Like that?" The third stranger in the group pointed to the fourth one, at the end of the canopy. "Industrial piercing? Like what they have?"

She turned to the stranger with the cheap beer can beyond the last picnic table, who noticed the collective attention and wandered closer. She leaned forward to see them, behind a torn flap of the canopy. "Hi love! Can I see your piercing?"

The fourth stranger stumbled under the tent and sat across from THEM. "I think I missed what's going on here."

The girl laughed. "We were admiring your piercing."

The late arrival shook their head, slurring, "I have a piercing?" Pink light glinted off their right ear's thin black bar. THEY smiled, glad to no longer be the most clueless person at the table. The other three laughed, and the one with the piercing did, too, but not convincingly.

"I'm Oz," said the girl telling the story. "Nice to meet you. Over here, we got Georgie, Saint, and..." she landed on—

"Andy," THEY borrowed the name. "Nice to meet you all."

THEY meant it. The quick glimpses of their world, even as fragments of a story, lifted the weight of imagining Levi and L on the other side of the wall.

The newcomer with the industrial piercing crushed their hollow beer can against the table. "You have names. I have a name, too."

"Ah, playing the *mysterious* card?" Georgie forced a laugh.

The stranger shut their eyes. "Just one... a second. I can't remember."

Saint elbowed Georgie and whispered to him, just loud enough for THEM to hear: "They're cut off, right?"

Georgie nodded. "A-Bomb's seen them by now."

THEY waited for the stranger's head to roll back in THEIR direction. Two hazel eyes wobbled up to THEM, framed by curtains of straight blonde hair. THEY hoped to keep them awake. "You look like you've got a story to tell."

They sighed, and it smelled like beer. "What you see is more than I am."

"On the bright side," THEY redirected, "you've got nothing to weigh you down."

They picked at THEIR crushed can and shrugged. "What about you, Danny? Or, uh, Andy, yeah. What's your story, then?"

The attention of Oz, Saint, and Georgie shifted THEIR way. Instinct begged THEM to deflect and say anything to avoid seeming as drunk as the blonde beer-crusher. THEY knew Andy's name, but what beyond that? THEY imagined the shock on everyone's faces if THEY explained THEIR deceitful connections to Levi and L. THEY barely understood the truth THEMSELF. Andy left few clues to the bigger picture, so THEY fabricated the rest.

"It's not a good story," THEY admitted. Saint hummed and leaned in to listen.

"Good stories are no fun," Oz encouraged.

"So, I'm visiting here from New York," THEY began, "visiting my friend from college, and his girlfriend. They're inside, somewhere. I know, that's not the whole thing. It's complicated. My friend and I, we knew each other better back then. A couple years ago, I guess." THEY lingered on that detail for a moment. "Anyway, I think I was the luckier one. I could afford

New York after graduation, so I kinda left him behind. That's probably how he'd tell it. He stayed here, and he's with his girlfriend. They're doing well, I think. It's hard to know, really."

"Did *you* meet anyone?" Oz asked. "In New York?"

THEY winced. "I don't know, yet. Maybe."

Georgie took the ashtray from Saint and repositioned it on the table. "So your friend and his girlfriend live here, and they took you out to *this* place while you're in town?"

"Yeah, basically," THEY assumed. "It's scary. I mean, cool, but scary."

Saint nodded. "Scares away the right people."

"The *wrong* people," Georgie corrected. "And if the wrong person does show up, A-Bomb keeps them in line." Georgie gestured at the front door, where the bouncer with the red mohawk adjusted a loose strap of the beige canopy. So, *he* was A-Bomb. THEY tried not to stare, wondering whether getting kicked out of the restroom made THEM one of the *wrong people.*

"College," repeated the dizzy stranger across from THEM. "Friends. Anyone you met? You *do* have stories. You remember." A light breeze pulled the strands of blonde off their face, revealing small black studs in their dimples as they rubbed their neck.

THEY imagined how Andy and Levi might've met. Were they roommates? Co-presenters for a project? Or were they drunk together at a place like this, or at a grungy party, sitting together by chance at a table in the dark?

"Yeah," THEY said. "I met someone in college, then I guess he met someone else."

Saint clicked their tongue, and Oz downed the last three sips of her drink. "The fucking worst."

THEY worried THEY'D said too much. "I'm over it. Feels like it didn't even happen."

"I need another one." Oz scooped up her empty glass and pointed at THEM. "You too?"

THEY stood to follow Oz, and so did the stranger across from them. Georgie waved the beer-drinker down, and Oz dismissed them too: "Nah, not you. You remember your name, then we'll talk about another round. Andy, c'mon."

Oz took THEIR hand and led THEM back into the noise. The 80s punk tracks gave way to heavier, newer goth rock. Someone turned up the volume on the speakers, and at least a dozen fresh faces populated the fray. Over on the couch, L chatted with Levi. THEY tried to read her lips.

"Hey!" Oz spoke close to THEIR ear, and THEY jumped. "What are you drinking?"

"Anything but tequila," THEY told her.

"Tequila?"

THEY shook THEIR head.

"Oh, I thought you said?"

"It's okay, just anything else. Thanks, Oz."

"I got you," Oz winked, then pushed her way up to the bar beside the man in the fur coat, just in time to catch the bartender returning someone's credit card. THEY hung back near the entryway, just far enough from A-Bomb for THEIR comfort.

"Who's she?" L asked THEM, suddenly standing at arm's length. Levi remained on the couch, typing on his phone. THEIR comfort evaporated.

"Hey," THEY choked. "That's Oz."

"Hope she knows she's out of luck, buying *you* a drink."

Andy's phone buzzed in THEIR pocket. THEY lifted it, welcoming any diversion, but the text message from Levi was unwelcome: *Elle knows something.* Was *that* how she spelled her name? THEY hid Andy's phone as casually as possible, but Elle stayed on THEM.

"So, like, did you think I didn't see it?" Her question sent THEIR mind spinning.

"My text?"

"No, earlier." Elle stepped closer and cupped her hand over THEIR ear to whisper: "Coming back from the bathroom, you wiped your lips."

THEIR heart rate doubled. Of course, she noticed, but what else did she know? In a race to deny or dismiss the allegation, THEY froze for longer than planned. Looking confused wouldn't dig THEM out of this hole. THEY needed an excuse.

"Oh," THEY forced a laugh. "I, uh, puked."

Elle pouted. "Aw, are you alright? I was worried."

"Oh, fine. I'm fine now. You? Are *you* alright?"

She bit her lip. "I'm great. But for a second, I thought my brother tried to fuck my boyfriend again."

Brother. She said *brother*.

"What?" THEY didn't mean to look straight at El's eyes, but even in the low light, THEY recognized them. They were hers, but not hers alone. In a terrific flash, THEY saw the uncanny resemblance to THEIR stormy blue irises in the bathroom mirror: Andy's eyes, those same two open windows that his sister saw through in an instant. Elle made a fist, aimed for the space between her brother's eyes, and punched THEM in the face.

"You lying *bitch*!" She shouted as the blow rocked THEM backwards into the man with the fur coat. THEY grabbed THEIR nose. Sharp pain spread across THEIR cheeks.

"Ellesandra, stop!" Levi jumped up to THEIR aid. So that was what *Elle* stood for.

She stood firm in his path. "Sit your ass! You're a fucking liar, too."

A-Bomb cracked his knuckles and trained his flashlight on the scene. "Take that shit outta here!"

Elle paid him no mind. "But *you* didn't stop, did you, Levi?"

"I tried to tell you, I—"

"And your 'work trip' to New York last month? Was that just *him*?" Elle kicked a wild heel in THEIR direction. Oz pulled THEM clear, and A-Bomb formed a wall with his body before Elle could take a third swipe at THEM.

"Let's go!" Levi yelled and pulled Elle by her waist without luck. She elbowed him in his gut, and he retreated clear of her next swing.

"Am I asking *so* much?" Elle wailed, eclipsing the music. "Am I *insane* to ask my *brother* and my *boyfriend* to keep their hands off each other? Cause for two people who say they love me, neither of you seem to give a *fuck* how I feel about any of this shit! I'm literally standing right here. I'm here for both of you, all the fucking time, and I'm alone!"

Half the people inside the bar clutched their glasses and peered around one another to track the action at the center of the room. The discreet half pretended not to do the same.

"Out!" A-Bomb ordered Elle and Levi back towards the exit. "If you're gonna have a bad night, go do it on Leader Avenue."

Elle marched off alone, not waiting for Levi. THEY waited for him to say something or lead THEM out of this horrible place, but Levi followed Elle without a hint of a goodbye. One at a time, the spectators returned to their murmurings. The constant soundtrack from the rafters reigned once more. Only Saint and Georgie remained on guard in the entryway, conversing in whispers. The drunk blonde stranger with the pierced ear and dimples floated past them both, past A-Bomb's unattended post, and back into the bar. They fixated on THEM and gawked at the blood dripping from THEIR nose. "What'd I miss?"

Oz pulled a cocktail napkin from a stack and wadded it up. "Here. Fix yourself, Rocky." She also slid THEM a small glass of something beige and cloudy, keeping another for herself. "Then, drink."

THEY dabbed THEIR upper lip with the napkin. "My *sister*," THEY hissed. "I never even realized. I didn't know she was..." THEY stopped THEMSELF, "...gonna do that."

"You're shittier than I thought you were," Oz admitted, "but, whatever. I already bought you a drink, so enjoy your buttery nipple."

"My *what*?"

"Butterscotch schnapps and Irish cream. I didn't pick the name."

Before Andy could accept the tiny glass, the nameless drunk from outside snuck between them, stole it, and sucked down THEIR drink in one sip. They smacked their lips and blinked a few times. In a glimpse of apparent sobriety, they returned the glass to the bar with a brief complaint: "Wack fucking aftertaste."

Oz sighed and slid her own glass to THEM. THEY frowned at it.

"You sure?"

She shrugged.

Napkin on THEIR bleeding nose, THEY drank to forget what little THEY gathered from a night of pain, embarrassment, and confusion. After forgetting THEIR name, the bar's name, and even THEIR own sister, how hard could it be to forget one awful night?

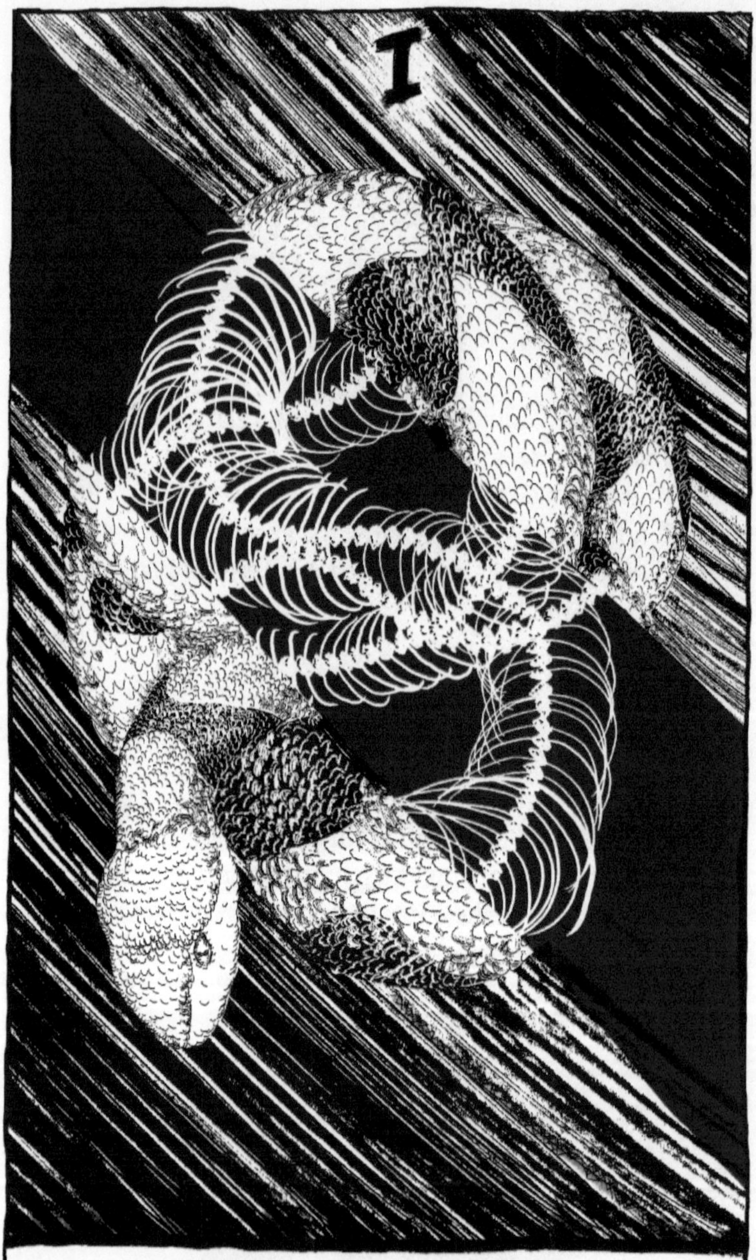
I
THE MAGICIAN

I: THE MAGICIAN

The lights dimmed to red. The song cut straight into the middle of a muffled, dark electronic track. Molded black ceiling tiles replaced the open rafters over the barroom, but this wasn't the barroom anymore. A fresh new flavor of disorientation arrived.

"Oz?" THEY glanced to either side, but she was gone. THEIR voice sounded unlike Andy's but felt no more like THEIR own. THEY clutched THEIR nose, which no longer hurt. An empty highball glass replaced the shot in THEIR other hand. Everyone else at the bar vanished with Oz, but so did the bar top itself. One full gulp of that butterscotch drink transported THEM to this gothic, sparser space. A few lone figures lounged throughout the room at a lone cocktail table, near a yellowed fainting couch, or on a reclaimed church pew. Two others played cards at a low circular table, surrounded by red-upholstered seats. In the middle of the long side wall, the broken ivories of an old wooden organ console opposed the church pew, flanked by two mismatched sconces. A mirror in a champagne-gold painted wood frame hung above the two tiers of keys. There, in THEIR own reflection, THEY saw Oz.

"What the fuck?"

THEY squinted at Oz, at *THEMSELF*, and brushed THEIR fingers through THEIR buzzed pink hair. THEY set THEIR inexplicably enlarged glass on the organ console. The last bubbles of some unknown cider ran down its inner edge, and its sharper sweetness lingered on THEIR tongue. A quick scan of the quiet room showed no sign of Andy. Here THEY stood, one second after *being* him, now with only the memory of his bloodied nose.

Despite THEIR dreamlike relocation into a new place and body, THEY remained unbearably conscious, remembering THEIR whole evening as Andy up to now. In Oz's body, as with Andy's, none of her memories shared space in THEIR mind: None of her stories, her friends' birthdays, her childhood fears, or her dreams for the future. Only the aftertaste of her fruity draft cider rendered THEM a stranger to THEMSELF once more, walking in Oz's shoes and wearing her face.

"It's your turn," Saint said. THEY ditched Oz's glass and spun around.

"What do you mean it's my turn?" THEY tilted THEIR head up to meet Saint's confused eyes, unaccustomed to standing a few inches shorter than before. "Do you know what's going on with me right now?"

Saint laughed. "Uh, karaoke? One does not simply say no to June."

THEY examined Saint's salty gray trench coat. "When did you change clothes?"

"Oz!" A voice called from the other side a curtained doorway. "The great, the powerful! Where'd you go, angel?"

The black curtain swept open, and Georgie's face hovered above three stairs that led to the next room. THEIR heart raced. THEY approached, ascended, and emerged... back into the main barroom. It showed no sign of the brawl just moments ago. A different bartender poured a row of green tea shots for some college students. A young woman in a green hoodie sat in the place of the man with the fur coat. A-Bomb stood at his post, far more concerned with taping up a torn poster than breaking up a scuffle. No one whispered gossip about the recent fight, leaving THEM to question whether Levi, Ellesandra, or Andy even existed.

In the corner, along the velvet-covered bay windows, a sleek white projector screen hung in the corner facing the bar. A short pole saddled a microphone between THEM and the screen. A black cable snaked from the mic to the corner opposite the screen, into a box on a table.

"Karaoke?" THEY stammered. "Right now?"

"If not now, then when?" The hostess behind the table asked. She perched on a tall barstool, draped in ruffled tangerine layers of a hand-stitched dress. Her eyes gleamed through fiery drag makeup like the whorls of butterfly wings. She tapped a key on her laptop. "And now, the woman from behind the curtain, Oz! Singing *The Who.*"

The jazzy drumline of some other song faded before THEY even noticed it playing. In its place, a fluttery electronic organ simmered, and a title credit splashed across the projector screen in purple: *Baba O'Riley, as made famous by The Who.*

"Shit. Oh shit." THEY grabbed the microphone, less out of any desire to sing than to avoid letting THEIR hands shake loose at THEIR sides. THEY wrested it free from the stand, which wobbled. From the threshold of the hidden red room, Saint hollered some vague encouragement. Emulating Oz, THEY flashed a hasty grin but focused right back on the blank screen. A slow progress bar marched towards some inevitable lyrics.

Lyrics. The fucking lyrics! THEY already forgot the name of the song. '*Baby...* 'what? Who the fuck signed THEM up for this? Whether or not Oz knew this song before downing her cider, THEY failed to recall a single word.

A piano chord progression joined the electronic organ. Closer now, THEY wished for the progress bar to hurry up. Then, THEY wished for it to slow down, whatever, just stop crawling along without telling THEM anything.

The screen changed. Bars of text flashed. The first piano chord struck. Clueless, THEY let go of the air in Oz's lungs and sang, tracking the tune on instinct alone. THEIR voice met the guitar and drums. The words magnetized to the beat with unreasonable ease.

The hostess wooed. THEY scowled at the mic like it had done the singing for THEM. How else could this be so simple? The next lines scrolled up the screen, and THEY caught them in THEIR mouth, praying the notes were as correct as THEY sounded. The instrumental left no hints of a melody, but even the irregular string of disappearing *yeahs* matched THEIR rhythm at the end of the first verse.

During the next interlude, THEY caught THEIR breath. At the end of the bar closest to the screen, a few heads nodded to the beat of the track. Some smiled. In the corner over THEIR shoulder, Georgie filmed on his phone. THEY tried not to think about any video of this horrifying moment being captured forever. Only Georgie's casual thumbs-up suggested maybe THEY'D done alright so far.

When the lyrics resumed, THEY withheld THEIR next note out of uncertainty. Still, when it came, it sounded fine. THEY allowed THEIR arms to loosen. For the first time, THEY mouthed the next words before the screen revealed them. Some instinct guided THEM like an invisible hand, as long as THEY let it take control.

The remainder was a dance. THEY breezed through the final verse. Hearing the song for the first time from THEIR own lips gave THEM chills. The sense of implicit *knowing*, absent Oz's concrete memory reassured THEM that some real part of her existed beneath the empty, nameless wasteland of THEMSELF. Better yet, that part of Oz could carry a tune.

THEY belted the last line, and a few spectators cheered.

"Yeah!" The queen at the computer shouted over the song's lengthy outro. THEY stuck the mic back in the stand, and THEIR hands resumed shaking. The faint subliminal guide rails of Oz's instincts slipped away. Georgie put his phone down and filled a paper cup with water from a big orange cooler. He handed the cup to THEM, along with another glass of hard cider. THEY took one big sip of the sweet cider and sighed.

"Thanks, Georgie."

"Killing it up there," Saint told THEM as they led the trio back into the quieter room behind the black curtain. "It's one of those big-event songs, you know?"

"Like a halftime show song?" Georgie scoffed into a beer can, licking its last drops from the rim.

"It's more like a homecoming dance in an 80s teen movie. Who's the guy who did all those movies? Not him. John Hughes! Like a John Hughes movie."

THEY wondered if Oz or Andy ever saw one of those.

"Well, it never gets old," Georgie said, "which means Oz will *never* pick a new song."

"Hey!" THEY took offense on Oz's behalf. "I like that song. If I forgot who I was, I bet you anything I'd still remember those words."

Saint laughed. "Then why do you still look at the screen?"

A clever point, but Georgie redirected Saint. "Hmm, but you know every word of *Baby Got Back*, and you're never getting through that song if you make eye contact with... I dunno, *Chris?*"

"Shh!" Saint turned up the collar of their coat and hunched forward.

"C'mon, I can say his name. He works here! I didn't say anything about you, him, his *body*, the two of you—" Saint pulled Georgie into an angry bearhug.

"Shh!"

"Hey! Don't crush my shoulders."

"Don't crush my *crush*!"

"Deal!" Georgie wailed, and Saint released him.

Someone in a matte black windbreaker entered through the curtain. In the gold-trimmed mirror, THEY glimpsed long blonde hair and industrial ear piercing. The drunk stranger from the picnic tables floated past the church pew, keeping a can of beer close to their face. They stopped at the back wall, near the slender cocktail table. While Saint and Georgie chatted about some obscure 2000s punk album, THEY snuck away towards the familiar face.

"Hey," THEY started, "I thought you left."

The black stud piercings in their dimples rose. "Oh, hi. Sorry. We've met, right?"

THEY blushed. "Yeah, earlier. At the picnic tables?"

"Huh? I mean, I just got here. Maybe I've got a doppelganger?" They spoke ten times more clearly than before.

THEY retreated. "No, I just... Maybe I'm confused."

The stranger plucked the tab from their beer can. "You were here Saturday, right?"

Saturday.

"Wait, so what day—" THEY stopped, thinking the better of asking what day it was. "What, uh, what's your name again?"

"Selene," they replied, without hesitation this time. "They-them. And you're Oz, right? Like the magician?" THEY returned a fast nod. Selene corrected themself. "*Wizard*, duh. Sorry if I was a total bitch to you, or something. I got a little tipsier than I meant to, but I think we talked. I don't remember much, honestly."

"No, no," THEY refuted. "It's cool, you were only a little... gone. But yeah, I'm Oz."

"Pronouns?"

There was a loaded question. What could THEY tell Selene without telling the rest? *I don't know what to use, since I can't remember who I am. I'm not Oz; I'm just pretending to be, and I was a guy named Andy for a while. You stole my drink, which Oz bought me before I became her. I guess I'll use they-them, too. Nice to meet you, Selene.* THEY felt about as secure gendering THEMSELF as THEY did living in the costume of Oz's body.

"Me?" THEY stalled, then fell back on Oz's identity as THEIR cover. "She-her."

"You're a regular for Monday karaoke, right?" Selene's question made THEM choke on a sip of THEIR cider.

"Mm," THEY coughed. "Basically, I think so. Seems like it."

"Nice, nice." Selene radiated concern, but they didn't voice it.

"Yeah, just can't believe it's Monday! You know? Feels like I, uh, time traveled through the whole weekend." THEY took another sip to stop THEMSELF from talking.

"To Oz, the time-traveler," Selene tapped their beer can on the rim of THEIR glass.

Across the back wall, a dozen sheets of thick, jagged-edged white paper hung from plastic clips. Black ink artwork on the papers diverted Selene's attention from THEM—and THEIR attention from the eerie erasure of the past 48 hours. In one large drawing, a swarm of contorted figures and limbs stretched from one side of the image to the other. The blended scratches of dark ink left THEM struggling to discern one subject from the next. Selene pointed to the center of the wide sheet.

"The middle is empty," they said. "Get it?"

"Not really," THEY admitted. "Did you make these?"

"Oh, no. A friend of mine. I think that one's supposed to look like da Vinci's *Last Supper*, but all fucked up. Like a bunch of demons instead of disciples, and no Jesus in the middle, just negative space."

Sharp teeth and slitted eyes supported Selene's interpretation. *The Last Supper*. THEY pictured the fragile blue painting and saw its parallels to the sketch, sensing something much more fucked up: THEY *knew* the da Vinci mural. THEY could visualize all its pale hues and flat layers in THEIR mind, without any memory of where or when THEY'D ever seen the damn thing.

"You hear that?" Georgie's hand landed on THEIR shoulder, startling THEM.

"Hear... the song?"

"Yeah, it's that one you told me about. *The Masochism Tango?*"

THEY composed THEMSELF and played along as Oz. "Oh, *that* one!"

"Someone's singing it up there!" Georgie peered up the steps.

"Oh, cool."

Georgie started towards the curtain but stopped short, waiting for THEM to follow. "You alright?" He ignored Selene, who remained focused on the art wall.

"Yeah, one sec." THEY let Georgie go, then lingered near Selene. THEY hid THEIR hands in THEIR pockets. "You don't re-member someone getting punched in the face on Saturday, do you?"

Selene grimaced. "Uh, definitely not. But like I said, I was kinda *gone*." They waved a finger over their head. "I'm like, actually embarrassed you saw me like that."

"No, no, you're good." THEY shook their head and started away towards the steps. "I was kinda 'gone' too."

THEY met Georgie in the main room, where he filmed two karaoke singers waging war over a disjointed piano track. Their duet bounced from one to the other in irregular inter-vals, each handing off the mic mid-verse and taking it back in desperation. The barebones instrumental challenged both singers to keep pace with the lyrics. One sang a line, then the other sang the line before it. Near the end, the less confident of the duo tried to pawn the mic to the other and escape, but he refused to grab it. Set to old-timey keys, the helpless strug-gle left them both in stitches. Georgie laughed with them. THEY wondered how anyone could smile through a failure like that, in front of so many people.

"Oh God," Saint whispered, rushing up to THEM and Georgie as the song ended. Saint shielded their face from the bar with one hand. "I *talked* to him. What the fuck, why did I *talk* to him?"

"Who?" THEY lost track again.

"Don't look!" Georgie tugged THEIR arm to spin THEM away from the bar. He ushered all three into a group huddle. "Saint, what'd you say to Chris?"

"I think I ordered a G&T, then I complimented the tattoo on his shoulder, but I *might've* complimented his G&T and ordered the tattoo on his shoulder." Saint hunched and wheezed, wide-eyed. The toe of their boot tapped like a terrified heartbeat on the floor. "I didn't think he heard me, but he smirked a little. A good smirk! Unless it *wasn't*. Or maybe I *was* too quiet. Oz, is he looking at me? Don't look, but is he? See, that's the problem: It's *so* much easier to have *you* order my drinks during his shifts. How can you do it? How do you walk up to *him* and talk like a normal person when he looks at you?"

Chris sauntered towards their end of the bar and delivered Saint's drink in a fresh glass. Georgie poked them as a warning, but not fast enough.

"You have a tab open, Saint?" Chris leaned his forearm along a bar mat. Saint puffed out their chest and pivoted from the huddle to face him.

"I'll have a tab. I do, yeah." They picked up the drink and put it back down.

Chris waited. "Last name?"

"Oh, right. No, not *Wright*. It's Perez. Perez, is the one. Yup."

Chris flitted away to the tablet at the register. Saint lifted their drink once more and took a gulp, then another. THEY sipped THEIRS in sympathy.

"On the bright side," Georgie offered, "now he knows your last name."

"And your first name," THEY added. "That's important, too."

Saint drank another large sip and sucked their teeth. "Fuck, that's a lot more gin than tonic. And before you say 'that means he likes you,' Georgie, I'll say maybe it means he wants to *kill* me. Ever think about that, boy genius?"

Georgie raised his hands in protest. "Hey, I didn't say anything! He *is* hot enough to be a serial killer, I'll give you that."

Saint glanced back at Chris before averting their eyes, fast enough that their hair fell in front of their face. "Okay, I'm gonna sign up for a song. Oz, what's something in my range? Something I know."

THEY imagined Saint's vocal range, judging only from their speaking voice. THEY thought about naming a song and hoping for the best, but THEY couldn't name *any* song, no matter how hard THEY tried. With her alleged karaoke experience, Oz would have a track for Saint locked and loaded. THEY had none, but THEY took too long to answer, so Georgie beat THEM to the punch.

"Do something from *Hamilton*!"

Saint pretended to snore. "It's been years! Let it die, I'm begging you."

"You're no fun. But don't do *Baby got Back* again."

"I know, but what else? Oz, you know songs and stuff. Oz? No, wait, what are you...?"

Before Saint could stop THEM, THEY fished a five-dollar bill from Oz's pocket and leaned over the bar top to snag Chris' attention. THEY caught him right at a lull between two groups of college students at the other end of the bar. Chris dumped two dirty glasses in the sink on his way over, then pinched the folded bill from THEM.

"Oz, what'll it be?"

"I'm good, but can you pick a song for Saint?"

Chris smiled and narrowed his eyes at Saint, who pretended not to notice the whole interaction. Chris' fingers tapped the edge of the bar.

"That's tough," Chris contemplated. "I've seen them kill it with Sir Mix-A-Lot a few times now. Maybe they can handle *It's Tricky* by Run-D.M.C.?"

Saint's defenses crumbled, and they looked up at Chris' heartening face. "Yes, I can do that! It's tricky, but... Oh, yeah, that's funny, cause of the song. The title. I'll go over and, uh, sign up. And thanks! Thank you." Saint waited long enough for Chris to walk away before shaking THEIR shoulder, fires in their eyes. "Oz, that was horrible. I loved that. Fuck you. I'm signing up!"

While Saint scribbled their name in a ledger on the hostess' table, Georgie nudged THEM appreciatively. "Bold move, even for you."

"Was it too much?" THEY scratched THEIR ear. THEY imagined the *real* Oz—the one with all her memories, who really knew and cared for her friends. Would that Oz have interfered with Saint's crush on Chris? Maybe THEIR stunt missed the mark, upset the balance, or even crossed some invisible line in the sand.

"I don't know," Georgie said, "but they seem jazzed. Finally broke the ice after what, three months? Since Chris started working?"

"Sure." THEY figured Oz would know that, so THEY pretended to. THEY took another sip of THEIR dwindling cider. "I just don't know if it's my place. Like, if I shouldn't get involved. What if Saint's image of Chris is more exciting than who he is? I'd hate to take that away from them."

Georgie smirked at THEM. He placed his phone face-down on the bar top, maybe encouraging THEM to say more. He bobbed from side to side, examining THEIR face.

"You're *different*."

THEY flushed. "What?"

"No offense, but like, you are on some *shit* tonight." Georgie wrinkled his nose and lowered his voice. "*Are* you on some shit tonight?"

They shook their head, hoping not. "Oh, no. It's the cider talking, I think, if I'm saying weird shit. Sorry."

Georgie hummed. "Mm, no, it's not that. You *look* different. Good! Good, but you're standing different. And your face is like... your face, but something's not *you*."

"My face *is* my face," they joked, trying as hard as possible to mimic Oz's expressions. Not long ago, they stood across from her, as Andy, at this same place along the bar. When they felt their cheeks stretch too far, they abandoned the imitation. "It's not like I can suddenly have someone *else's* face, right? That would be nuts."

"Do you *feel* alright?"

They couldn't remember how *alright* felt. The closest they came was singing The Who, less than an hour ago, harvesting melodies from the air. Only that faint taste of Oz's strength brought any order to their life, and only for those few precious minutes. The rest sucked, so they lied. "Yeah. I feel great. I'm happy."

"You're not doing the *thing* you do." Georgie stuck his hands in his pockets and stepped back, only a few inches. "When you have a problem, you get loud about it, but not tonight. Something new is bugging you, and if it's bad enough that you're trying to hide it, I need to decide how worried to be."

Of course, he called their bluff. Oz confided more in Georgie and Saint than they could imagine. They couldn't fake the generous trust of the Oz they met at the picnic tables. They could imitate her quips and friendly gestures, but those meant little without Oz's heart to wear on their sleeve. As Andy, their failure was a missed connection that blew up three relationships at once. They dreaded a similar outcome for Oz's life.

The chronic ache of THEIR own isolation hurt enough already. THEIR heart sank like a stricken vessel on the ocean floor, wrenching THEIR body's functions to halt. THEY readied THEM-SELF to tell Georgie the truth, no matter how it sounded, if it could spare him the same contagious pain.

Across the room, Saint orbited the mic stand. The hostess tapped a computer key, and an instrumental Run-D.M.C. track cued Saint with only one bar. While Chris pumped a fist in the air, Saint made *It's Tricky* look like a breeze, at least until they ran out of breath. They fumbled the start of the first verse and gasped their way back into the fast, syncopated beat.

"Go Saint!" Georgie cheered, not loud enough to distract THEM. "Oz, were you about to say something?"

THEY swirled the last sip of THEIR cider. THEY lowered THEIR glass to the bar top and leaned down close to its meniscus. The trembling liquid stoked a new fear. The air around THEIR face warmed.

"It's happening again," THEY gasped. "Fuck, it's gonna hap-pen *again*."

Georgie followed THEIR eyes to the near-empty glass. "Should I be scared? What is this?"

THEY covered THEIR glass. "Georgie, on Saturday, remem-ber the guy who got punched? Andy?"

"Saturday? Yeah, the twink with the bloody nose. Why?"

"Okay, so Oz—I mean, *I* bought him a drink. A shot. Some weird butter thing. What happened after—?"

"Buttery nipple?" Georgie took a seat on the barstool next to THEM. "First of all, you are *way* too sober right now to forget the name of your fourth-favorite drink. Second of all, did you just talk about yourself in third person? Cause it came across more creepy than quirky, if that's what you're going for."

"Sorry," THEY rubbed her eyes and sat down, "but do you remember what happened after Andy took the shot? If he didn't just disappear, where did he go?"

Georgie shrugged. "I dunno. He sat down. Then he got kinda freaked out, I guess. I think he blacked out when it all happened, cause he couldn't remember getting hit or anything. You were right there! *You* talked to him. Did he say something to you?"

"Okay, okay," THEY chewed THEIR lip, tuning out Saint's loud rap vocals. "This is gonna sound fucking insane."

Georgie crossed his arms. "Yeah, I'm getting that vibe."

"That was *me* who got punched. I was Andy. Like, I can't remember anything before, and then I was like, *boom*, shot of tequila, and suddenly, I'm this guy, right? And I don't know how I got here, so I don't realize my friend and I are totally into each other. We kiss in the bathroom, and he says he loves me, and I go outside because I'm so mixed up. Then you meet me, and I meet Oz, you know, before *this*. I was Andy, before I became Oz. I wasn't Oz on Saturday. She was. *Oz* was Oz. Does that make sense? I'm Oz now, but I was Andy then. Also, when Saturday-Oz buys me that nipple drink, I stop being Andy. I take the shot, and when I put it down, *boom*, it's today, and I'm Oz. I'm her now. That's all I can remember. It's fucking bizarre, but now I think I know how it works. You see what's happening, right?"

Georgie opened his mouth, closed it, tried again, rested his arms on the bar, then slumped onto them. "But you're you. I *know* you."

"I *don't* know me, though!" THEY clenched one hand and held up THEIR cider with the other. The edge of the projector beam glistened through its bubbles. "I'm not Oz. She's gone. And when I drink this, she'll come back, and I'm gonna become somebody else again."

"So, this is like a drunk-sona thing? Your alter ego is coming out? Oz, what are you trying to—?"

THEY held Georgie's hand. "Ask me where I'm from. Ask me what I like. Ask me about my family, books I've read, why I chose this pink for my hair. I don't know. I'm in this body right now, but it's not mine. It's not me." THEY hoped for Georgie to at least feign some understanding, but his sour frown remained. "Okay, fine. I don't know what's going on. I'm gonna finish this drink. Forget about all of this. Forget I said anything. Just say hi to the real Oz when I'm gone."

THEY raised the glass to THEIR lips, but George sat up to stop THEM. He leaned closer. "The *real* you sang that whole song earlier. I have it all on video. You were fantastic, same as you always are. It was, like, the most *Oz* you can ever be! If you're not her, who *are* you?"

THEY wiped THEIR eye, smearing Oz's neat purple eyeshadow. As Saint's song wrapped up, Chris and a few others clapped. THEY turned to Georgie and raised THEIR glass to Saint.

"Time to find out."

Alone, THEY finished THEIR drink.

II
THE HIGH PRIESTESS

II: THE HIGH PRIESTESS

The glass in THEIR hand lightened and transformed into a slender aluminum can. A harsh synth-pop beat filled the lull after Saint's karaoke blitz. The entire world shifted and morphed itself again, as THEY expected, but the change from sitting at the bar to lounging on a low couch near Arcana's bathrooms rattled THEM. THEIR index finger dented the side of THEIR empty can when THEY flinched. Oz's purple makeup vanished from THEIR fingertip.

"Was that any good?" asked someone seated on an identical black couch across from THEM. His medium stubble looked almost blue in the oceanic glow of the small sitting room's ambient lights. THEY examined THEIR empty can of pomegranate hard seltzer.

"Don't know," THEY said with caution, testing out another new voice. "Wasn't a very memorable one."

The guy with the beard rose from his seat. He reached for THEIR can, and they surrendered it to him. "Can I get you another?"

"Sure. Thank you." THEY wondered if THEY'D ever need to buy THEIR own drinks, at this rate. THEY patted THEIR pockets but found them replaced by the seamless folds of a black yoke skirt. A small backpack with thin pink straps—one worn thin and reattached by haphazard red stitches—hung on the nearest arm of the couch. THEY scanned the empty sitting room for its owner before accepting responsibility for it. The cutesy bag matched THEIR skirt well enough. THEY slung the bag over THEIR shoulder and beelined for the restroom a few steps away.

THEY barely made it to THEIR feet before THEY needed to steady THEMSELF against the wall. Drunk? No, *heels*. Thick platform heels, and longer legs than Oz's. THEY could count the few dozen steps THEY ever took as Andy, Oz, and now someone else. Focusing on walking only worsened the struggle. THEY channeled the same magic trick that saved THEM from karaoke, letting THEIR body do the singing for THEM. This time, THEY let THEIR new body do the *walking*.

Between the two identical bathrooms, THEY picked the second one this time. Flashing back to kissing Levi in the other would distract from the task at hand: learning THEIR new name. THEY shut the door and reached for a missing latch. THEY ran THEIR fingers up and down the doorframe but found no means of locking it. As usual, Arcana left THEM to THEIR own devices.

Fuck off, Oren, read the gold-inked graffiti on the bathroom mirror, same as the one in the other bathroom.

"This fucking bar," THEY groaned. THEIR voice cracked, and THEY cleared THEIR throat. In the mirror, rings of auburn fell just below THEIR jaw, covering THEIR ears. "So, I'm you, now, right?" THEY scowled at the new stranger, her new pupils, and her new body. THEY liked this new voice, at least. Talking to THEMSELF was easier than making conversation with the *real* people outside. "I could stay in here. Want to stay in here all night, you and me?" THEY didn't bother to answer THEMSELF.

Unzipping the tiny bag, THEY claimed a cracked smartphone. It glowed for THEM with a green and purple vertical beam glitching down its center. Its fingerprint scanner refused to sense THEIR thumb or index finger on either hand. Ditching the phone, THEY pulled a dark red credit card from the bag.

"Who the fuck is that?" The card belonged to some guy, not a familiar name. Maybe she borrowed it from a partner, or from family, or hopefully not from anyone who'd miss it. THEY fished around the bag's smaller secondary pocket for an ID: a withered, creased scrap of white plastic. THEY held it up to the mirror, bewildered. The name matched the one from the credit card, and the photo introduced THEM to an unfamiliar man's glum grin. THEY clocked some resemblance to THEIR new reflection. After THEIR ordeal with Elle, THEY wouldn't discount him as a sibling. However, the two faces shared a thin gap in THEIR teeth, a two-pointed eyebrow piercing, and not just similar eyes this time: *Identical* ones.

"Old picture, old name." THEY smiled at THEMSELF, then stowed the ID back in its hidden pocket. "You changed your whole... *self.* Me too, I guess."

Back to the phone, THEY tapped into its passcode screen. Instead of numbers, THEY found a grid of dots. Tracing lines between the dots misled THEM into three failed attempts before THEY even understood how the damn thing worked.

"You jackass. What's your fucking name?" THEY held up the bag in the mirror and traced the frayed red stitches on its strap. "See, I know you can sew. If you're in there, if you're listening somewhere in your head, in my head, our head, *whatever*, why don't you sew your new fucking name on your bag next time?" THEY raised THEIR middle finger at THEMSELF.

Resigned to keep calling THEMSELF *THEM* for now, THEY exited the restroom. The guy with the blue-looking beard waited at the couch with two glasses on the table. THEY sized him up: untrimmed hairs on the back of his neck, dried mud on his leather work boots, and the plain flannel shirt of someone whose elegant beard color was only a trick of the light.

"All yours." He tucked his phone between his leg and the cushion, then presented one of the glasses. THEY sat on the other couch again, across from him. "They had the same seltzer on draft. Thought that'd be better for you."

"Thanks." THEY smiled but took the other glass, from his side of the table. THEY planned to test the waters before blindly trusting another stranger. "What was your name again?"

The question caught him off guard. "Uh, Colton. And you said you're...?"

No clue, THEY kept the ball rolling. "What were you saying before? Sorry, I lost track. What was it about?"

"Right, right." Colton lifted the far glass, now his, and sampled it. "I was saying how scary it is. No messages, no calls from her. I watch a lotta videos about cold cases like this, and a lotta this shit ends bad."

"Yeah," THEY played along, hoping he'd lead the way. "Where do you think she is?"

His knee bobbed. "Same place *he* is, I bet. I don't wanna think it's something bad, but it could be."

The way his tone dropped forced THEM to slow down. "Do you think she's in trouble, then?"

"I don't wanna think that," Colton repeated, shaking his head. "I warned her about that asshole. I keep saying: That Hayes guy, he's bad news, with his big old van, his collecting old guns and shit from wherever. He's *off*. Just a little, at least. Coming from me, you know, she's never gonna hear none of that. And I dunno; she seems happy enough, but I worry."

"About who?"

"About her, Julienne. Duh." He stopped tapping his foot. "Yeah, I mean, you wanna call me a jealous prick, go ahead, but shit, if I wouldn't take her back if she asked. You know, we were nice together. Last year, when I wrecked my bike, I fucked my shoulder up. Still pops, aches and shit. But like, I couldn't work for two months, and she put up with all my whining, hanging around, like *damn*. She made me a pecan pie last Thanksgiving. She cares a lot. I tried to be like that for her, but the hell am I gonna do? She goes and falls for this freak who lives in a van. Maybe we were too good for each other. So maybe that's what it is."

THEY kept THEIR glass near THEIR lips, happy to let him carry on. Why bother probing him with strange questions if he could talk all night? Maybe it was his shameless openness, or maybe it was the tangy glass of cold seltzer, but THEY already tolerated Colton. "I feel like I know you a little better now," THEY said, "but I don't know why you're telling me about this."

"I'll tell anyone who'll listen!" He stared off at the poster of a blue-robed woman on a throne behind THEM. "I gotta find her if no one else is gonna. Julie's lived over in Lakeview her whole life, so I know she ain't far unless something's real wrong here."

"Your ex, then, Julienne is missing?" THEY adjusted THEIR skirt.

"Uh, yeah. I mean, yeah." Colton sat up. "That's the whole *thing*. She's missing for a week or two, now. Didn't I say?"

"Right, sorry. I get it. So, are any other people looking? Police?"

He scratched his beard and leaned back on the couch cushions. "Fuck the cops. I don't know if her family's gone to them or what, but couldn't be me. What are these low life Lewesboro cops gonna do, anyway? Probably dick around in the woods, call it overtime, and shoot somebody who looks at them wrong." Colton unlocked his phone and slid it across the table. "You sure you haven't seen someone, looks like her? This is a few years old, but she looks about the same."

THEY leaned over the phone. The young woman in the photo posed with a graduation cap, wearing a gown. Her face looked the same as every other in Arcana: unknown. THEY slid the phone back to Colton.

"I don't remember seeing her."

"Damn." He locked the screen and took a long sip from his glass. "I thought, maybe, I mean, no offense, but a while back, she posted a thank-you to a girl from here. I've been going back over her posts, and she tagged that girl's art page. I don't know how to say it right, but there's a flag emoji in the page's bio with blue, pink, white stripes. You know? No face on the account, but I thought, I mean, maybe that was you, right?"

THEY felt him look THEM over. Feeling so visible unsettled THEM, but not in any groundbreaking way. The pressure of every eye in Arcana, real or imagined, already tracked THEM from room to room, seeing through THEM and spotting THEM as an outsider. What were another two eyes on this body?

Colton cleared his throat. "I don't mean to assume, but I'm looking for, like, a girl who's, like—"

"Trans?" THEY threw him the word like a life preserver to a drowning sailor.

"Yeah," he exhaled. "I don't know the words. I don't wanna be wrong about things. But yeah, she was thanking this artist with the username 'jadeattackingyou,' and that sounded kinda serious on its own. The stuff on the page was freaky."

Black ink, shadowy figures, and THEIR conversation with Selene rang a bell. "Whoever Julienne saw, what kind of art was she drawing?"

"I dunno, emo shit. Do a lotta people come here to make art and stuff?"

"I don't know. I'm new here too." THEY stood up, taking the pink bag and THEIR drink. "I saw something over this way, on Monday when I... What day is it today?" The awkward question slipped out. Colton checked his phone and huffed.

"Thursday. Damn, I thought it was Wednesday. What did you see?"

THEY led him through the short hallway to the bar. Familiar multicolor lights glistened off the shelves of eclectic liqueurs, a jeweled plastic skull, half a disco ball, and a fake crystal chandelier. Thursday brought only a handful of customers: mostly new faces but a few of the same. The man in the fur coat sat in the same spot where Andy crashed into him. He pointed to a small laptop running the playlist behind the bar, engaging Chris in a debate about remastered versions of a song. Chris divided his attention between the fur-coated guy and a list of open tabs on the register tablet.

THEY sent Chris a friendly wave before remembering THEIR new body. Sure, Chris knew Oz, but not *her*! Or did he know her, too? Even if so, was waving creepy? Or worse, was it flirtatious? To THEIR relief, Chris didn't notice. The man in the fur coat even distracted Colton, too.

"Do you have bat ears or something?" The man asked Chris, who rolled his eyes and laughed. The coat man wore mirrored silver aviators. A heavy, ornate collection of rings on his fingers knocked the bar top as he spoke. "C'mon, it's tiny differences in the sound that nobody can hear. Stuff I wouldn't understand even if some audiophile explained the whole fucking science of whatever and ever. Hang on. A-Bomb? We got this, uh, hey, alright, so *Blue Monday*, tell Chris what's the difference between the original and the remastered one."

"Ah, shit." A-Bomb dismounted his stool by the door and zeroed in on Chris, who shrank away from the whole conversation. "Not even New Order's best song, by the way, and there's no fucking difference between those two. Not anything that matters. I don't care which one people decide to prefer. But the *single* version versus the original? Fuck off. If you can't handle a seven-and-a-half-minute song, you're not ready for any meaningful music."

"Okay boys, for the record," Chris surrendered, hands up, "I don't actually know what song you're talking about."

"Search it! That thing searches, right?" The man with the coat and rings waved at the laptop plugged into the sound system's duct-taped wire. Chris obeyed, and A-Bomb ducked away to his station. The coat man raised two fingers and made a peace sign at THEM and Colton as they passed him towards the quiet room. "I never know what's going on. Don't look at me for computer shit."

THEY pulled the black curtain open. Colton ventured first down the stairs. "Whoa. This place has more rooms than I thought."

"You haven't been here before?" THEY let the curtain fall back into place.

"*No*," he stressed, as if denying a crime. "I used to stick to Heron's Landing, now mostly The Wreck Club." Neither name meant anything. THEY imagined larger clubs full of guys like Colton, walking around in blue jeans and scaring each other with stories of a place like this one. Colton peered up at a square gap in the ceiling, left by a missing molded tile. "What's it mean, anyway?"

THEY examined the back wall, only half paying attention. "What's what mean?" THEY returned to the row of ink artworks taped along the wall, including the parodied da Vinci with the line of demonic figures.

"*Arcana*." Colton pronounced the word with all his confidence on the first syllable. He deferred to his phone. "Guess I'll look it up. You're not a little curious?"

"Should I be?"

"Well, if it's the name of this place, *Arcana* sounds important."

THEY bit THEIR lip. Of course, this place had a name. In all THEIR stumbling and rambling as Andy, as Oz, and now as someone new, THEY never bothered to check the name of the bar. This felt like THEIR entire world; it didn't need a name. Maybe THEY would've learned it on THEIR own, but other issues took priority, not least the ongoing search for THEIR *own* name.

"Secret," Colton hummed. "It's Latin for 'secret.' And there's all this other stuff... What's tar rot? Is that the stars... the Zodiac thing?"

"So, these drawings." THEY ignored him. "Do these look like the ones?"

Colton pocketed his phone. He knelt along the wall of clipped paper sheets. In a drawing to his left, a high priestess sat in shadow between forked tree limbs. Knots and holes on the trunk formed the openings of unearthly, monstrous skulls and wailing mouths. Colton's face shifted from confusion to fear, then to disgust and dismissal. He backed away. "I dunno. She didn't say it was gross like that. Violent-like. I ain't all too religious, but Julie, I... She wouldn't like this. She wouldn't be thanking the artist who made *these*, whatever her name is."

"Jade." THEY read a signature from the paper, tracing a thin line of letters in the bottom corner of the skull tree sketch. "That was the name you said earlier, wasn't it? 'Jade attacking you,' the username?"

Colton inspected the rough-edged sheet and nodded. "This is some weird shit I'm in now, huh?" He pulled out his phone. Its camera flashed, lighting up the whole room as he photographed the wall.

"Could be weirder," THEY muttered. "What do you think this is, really? I mean, what do you think is going on with Julienne?"

Colton rubbed his neck and sat down in a low armchair next to the drawings. "I'm checking everything is all. I wonder if Julie got into something dangerous. Like, I don't know what all kinda people hang out at a spot like this. Julie's a sweet girl. What if this Jade person took advantage of that, somehow?"

"What about that guy, her new boyfriend? What was his name?"

"Hayes. Hell if I know. Hayes is a dirtbag, but he's too big a pussy to seriously hurt... Uh, sorry, I didn't mean that word. I meant he's a coward. Or, I hope he is. I don't wanna think about it."

THEY considered taking the chair across from him, but in THEIR skirt, another low seat would only trade the discomfort of standing in THEIR heels for a different one. "So, you think Jade is involved? More than the sketchy boyfriend, with the old van and the gun collection?"

Colton shrugged. "I didn't say that, but look at this stuff on the wall. Blood, teeth, skeletons, and murder stuff. Everybody's got guns, but I don't know anybody who draws like *that*. Jade might have something wrong, like mentally."

THEY took a big sip of THEIR pomegranate seltzer while measuring THEIR reply. "Look, I'm new to Arcana too. I'm a little bit lost, and a little freaked out, same as you. I know you're trying to be helpful to Julienne, but chasing your ex isn't a way back to her. It sounds like a crusade you're on. It might only lead you to a dive bar, some creepy drawings, and blaming everything on a person you've never met. Why is your first conclusion that a trans person did something wrong?"

"Whoa, whoa," Colton rose and paced along the wall. "I don't care what she is. *Who* she is. That's just what, I mean, *she* put that flag emoji, and pardon my saying, but you oughta know that kinda thing ain't exactly typical around here. I ain't stirring up trouble, okay? I don't wanna hurt nobody." Before Colton could carry on, his phone buzzed and stole his attention away. "Hold up." He screenshotted the caller's number before answering. He accepted the call and covered his other ear with his free hand. If their conversation hadn't ended before, it had now.

THEY tried eavesdropping on the call, but Colton shuffled towards the stairs and departed before THEY could glean anything worthwhile. THEY took another drink from THEIR seltzer, nearly finishing it before stopping THEMSELF. "Fuck. Not yet."

The first two times were easier. Andy and Oz came here with THEIR own trusted social groups, however fragile. THEIR new self chose to visit Arcana alone. Meeting and engaging with Colton kept THEM occupied. Once he left the room, THEIR mind resumed its fight to remember THEMSELF, THEIR name, THEIR past, or anything before those first seconds in Andy's shoes. THEY walked the length of the wall of Jade's drawings, determined not to let another drink, another body, and another night go to waste so soon. THEY saw THEMSELF in the emptiness at the center of Jade's *Last Supper*: an unoccupied chair, surrounded by so many powerful figures in the dark.

THEY returned to the bar, loitering at the end near the big orange water cooler. Chris readied a fresh glass and reached for THEIR dwindling drink. "Finished with that one?"

"Not yet," THEY said. "Do you have a pen and paper?"

Chris grabbed a pen from a small plastic bin in the corner. At the register, he tapped a series of boxes on the screen to print off a blank receipt. He handed THEM the pen and receipt, which bore only the date, time, and *ARCANA* in faintly printed capital letters. "If you're gonna draw me, love, I can pose." He held a pint glass at an angle under one of the taps, pretending to fill it while pouting and arching his back.

THEY shook THEIR head. "What makes you think I draw?"

"Don't you? Unless I'm thinking of someone else."

THEY held the pen over the thin strip of paper. "You don't have to pose, but can you say something? Anything works. Just talk, so I'm not thinking too hard for a second."

Chris put the unneeded pint glass back on the shelf. "A paradox walks into a bar. The paradox doesn't ask for a drink, but they ask the bartender to tell them a joke. So, the bartender says: A paradox walks into a bar. The paradox doesn't ask for a drink, but they ask the bartender to tell them a joke. So, the bartender says—"

"Got it." THEY cut him off and finished writing. "I'll be right back."

THEY carried the receipt back to the art wall, tracing THEIR fingers over four handwritten letters: *JADE*. Despite not recalling how to write, THEIR fingers made those marks on the paper. Those four perfect capital letters transmitted from THEIR head to the receipt as soon as Chris distracted THEM. THEIR body performed another magic trick, like singing *The Who* and walking in heels. It felt as impossible as everything else in THEIR fucked-up world.

THEY held the receipt next to the signature on the skull drawing. From the sharp hook of the *J* to the uneven streaks of the *E*, Jade's handwriting matched exactly between the signatures. THEY crumpled the receipt, shoved it in Jade's bag, and stalked over to the mirror above the organ console. "Of course. Who the fuck *else* was I gonna be?" THEY blew a loose strand of hair off THEIR cheek. "*You* have to be more careful," THEY whispered to THEMSELF, dreading Colton's return from his phone call.

THEY wondered whether Jade knew Julienne or Hayes, or if Colton really dragged her name into this on a hunch. Did the truth matter any more than what *he* believed? The last sip of pomegranate seltzer waiting for THEM to move on and set Jade free, like Andy and Oz. The real Jade could talk her own way out of Colton's suspicions, when he came back. *She* could deal with him, hopefully.

THEY walked back up to the bar again and took the same empty seat at the end, near the water cooler.

"You still good?" Chris asked THEM while adjusting the playlist on the laptop. THEY readied to down the last of THEIR seltzer and leave this body behind, but THEY restrained THEM-SELF once more. If Andy came back with no memory of getting punched, how could Jade be prepared to deal with Colton? If THEY didn't finish what THEY started tonight, she'd be lost like THEM.

"I'm fine," THEY answered Chris. "Where'd you learn that joke you told earlier?"

Chris grinned. "Oh, the paradox thing? I heard it from Malory. She bartended here a while ago, before me, but she moved away last year."

Just outside the entrance, a five-gallon bucket of concrete propped one door open, and the other hung ajar. In the parking lot, Colton pressed his phone to his ear and sat on the hood of a red sedan. THEY waited for his call to end.

"I should have a name," THEY decided, but THEY didn't mean to say it out loud.

"What's that?" Chris raised an ear in THEIR direction. What did he hear?

"A name," THEY repeated. "The paradox. In Malory's joke, I think the *paradox* should have a name."

Chris laughed. "Wait, so the paradox gets a name before the bartender does? Now that's unfair."

"Assume *you're* the bartender, then," THEY allowed, "and you're stuck in the endless loop of talking to this paradox who keeps walking into the bar. If the cycle is gonna go on forever, and if you have to keep telling the same joke to this same paradox, over and over, you'd want to at least know their name."

Chris nodded, but in the detached manner of a trained listener. Before he could suggest anything, the man with the fur coat and glasses threw himself into the discussion.

"Smith," he offered. "Like Agent Smith in *The Matrix*. That's how I picture them, the paradox that keeps coming back and fucking up everyone's shit."

THEY understood nothing of his reference, except that it was one.

Chris seemed unconvinced. "Just 'Smith?' As a first name?"

The man counted on his many-ringed fingers. "First, last, mononym, whatever. If there's already a gazillion Smiths out there, pretty good chance that's already the paradox's name. Plus, Jade, you'll like this..." He spoke her name so plainly that THEY almost missed it. "...Smith, Pamela something Smith, do you know who she was?" THEY shook THEIR head, worried to anyone who knew Jade already. Between her, A-Bomb, and Chris, this regular seemed to know everyone. "Colman! Pamela *Colman* Smith. Like a hundred-some years ago, she illustrated the Rider-Waite deck. Tarot deck, you know, but they didn't even name it after her. They named it after the publisher, Rider, and the author dude, Waite, who commissioned her illustrations, but *she's* the one who made it really popular. *Her* art. Bunch of decades later, this whole place exists in honor of her work. So, Smith is a cool ass name for a freaky little paradox."

THEY liked the name for THEMSELF, too. As a surname, it could be flexible. Andy, Oz, Jade, or anyone else could tack *Smith* on the end, denoting one of many Smiths. A unified surname could encompass the family of all THEIR names and bodies. *Smith* could belong to each one, but really to THEMSELF, the one who borrowed THEIR bodies and remembered doing it. Smith, then, was the one who got punched in the face, who sang *Baba O'Riley*, and who wrote the name *JADE* on the blank receipt. In the words of the fur coat man, Smith was the paradox who kept coming back and fucking up everyone's shit.

THEY—no, *Smith* smiled. Smith pushed their hair back over their ear and let go of the breath they'd been holding.

"Yeah, cool name," Chris scoffed at the coat man. "And now a nonhuman character in Malory's lamest joke is named after a brilliant woman."

The man tapped his rings on the bar top. "If I can name a gnarly fucking dive bar after her Arcana, it's about as respectful, isn't it?"

"Hey, is *this* what you're calling gnarly?" Chris waved his arms over the shelves of bottles and glasses that glistened under red and blue strips of LEDs. "Alea and I run a tight operation back here."

"And I own the place."

Chris snorted. "You *half-own* the place."

"Six of one, half a dozen of another." The half-owner lifted his glasses to sit on his head. Although he spoke as energetically and loosely as Chris, the crow's feet under his eyes told the story of a man twice Chris' age. "Oh, and Jade? That guy out on the phone," he elbowed towards Colton, "was he being a weirdo to you?"

No doubt, the half-owner could dispatch A-Bomb deal with him. Perhaps too absorbed in the excitement of their new name, Smith decided to let Colton off the hook: "Could be worse. He's still figuring his shit out."

"Good, good," the half-owner nodded. "New folks coming in here, I never know what fucking messes they're bringing in with them."

Right on cue, Colton wobbled back inside. He held his phone in one hand like a dead bird scooped from the ground. Colton slammed himself down on a seat in the middle of the bar between Smith and the half-owner. His forearm shook until his phone tumbled onto the bar top.

"Julie's gone," he whispered towards the liquor shelf.

"What?" Smith barely heard. Colton shut his eyes and pinched his ears.

"They found her, Julie. And Hayes. Probably all week she was out there. *Fuck*!" Colton pounded the bar top so hard that his phone and Smith's drink bounced. "His van went off the interstate into the trees. It's all... They were inside. It caught fire too fast."

Chris and the half-owner waited for each other to say something. One song faded, making way for the next. A distant siren howled. The aura of such overwhelming grief threw Smith into a fresh panic. Without thinking, they took the last sip of their pomegranate seltzer, leaving Jade behind to fend for herself.

IIII
THE EMPRESS

III: THE EMPRESS

The drink turned into cheap vodka. A bitter gulp of the stuff passed down Smith's throat. Their new, broader body shuddered as the liquor stung their lips. Their imagination conjured its own terrible vision of a highway ditch, a burnt van, and two trapped bodies. Colton's fears about his ex-girlfriend, however misdirected, weren't so irrational after this terrible news. If nothing else, Smith tried to take some relief in Jade's vindication. As they guessed, she never deserved Colton's suspicions. He got his closure, and she got her body back. For Smith, only a horrid image of flames and the vodka's foul burn lingered.

Smith now stood in a long room with a concrete floor. Cool air wafted under a half-open wooden garage door, and several huge black amplifiers hung from the rafters by steel chains. A DJ with sharp, angular neck tattoos presided over the low stage at the end of the space, pressing buttons and pulling sliders across a heavy controller panel. A pair of black headphones covered her ears, and an iridescent green cloak covered the rest of her. Deep synthetic pulses and rhythms coursed and blasted from the suspended speakers. Throughout the dark, half a dozen bodies swayed and bobbed along to her electronic symphony. Smith leaned one ear on their shoulder and cupped their free hand over the other, gathering their thoughts over the alien noise.

They took inventory of themself: shiny gray basketball shoes, brown cargo pants, and a thin orange sweater with patches on the elbows. Without a mirror handy, Smith couldn't match the eclectic outfit to their new face. They pulled an oversized smartphone from one pocket of their cargo pants. A thin silicone sleeve of cards stuck to its back glass. The first card, a state driver's license, identified Smith's new form as a man named Dorian. After the confusion over Jade's ID, they chose a new way to verify, this time.

Holding up the phone as if to take a picture of the shimmering DJ, Smith tapped the onscreen button for the front-facing camera. Thick strands of black hair half-covered their ears. Between that and a short triangle beard, their looks matched the license photo as clearly as Smith could tell in the low light. Without the real Dorian available to confirm Smith's new identity, they accepted him as he appeared.

"Just another body," Smith said, testing out Dorian's voice. Fast licks from the synthesizers dissolved their words straight out of the air.

Smith left Dorian's rocks glass and its bare ice cubes on the floor in a dusty corner of the loud room. They ducked under the garage door's opening and, to their surprise, emerged into a familiar space. To their left, a few groups of strangers sat and socialized along Arcana's three covered picnic tables. The garage door connected a room at the back end of the building straight to the main parking lot. Smith never noticed the back garage before—not without so much sound bouncing between its walls.

To their right, wisps of serene, smoky heat and spent propane danced upward from an open grill. A woman in an apron rolled over a series of hot dogs with a steel spatula. She lifted two with a pair of tongs and dumped them into an aluminum tray on the folding table beside.

"Is that dangerous?" Smith wondered aloud, eyeing the thin portable canopy over the grill and table. The heat of the grill spilled up from under it.

"What's that?" The woman asked. "Already can't hear shit no more. Too damn loud right here!" She looked to be in her early fifties, at the oldest. Smith stepped away from the garage entry and closer to the grill. "They're five each, hon, if you want."

"I didn't know Arcana did food."

She laughed. "Well, if some city inspector asks, we absolutely do *not*. This was my lovely husband's idea, so naturally I'm the one making it happen."

Smith scanned the picnic tables, unsure who to look for. "You both work here?"

"When we can," she said. "We're co-owners."

Fur coat, rings...

"Oh! Yeah, I just met your husband." Smith saw him minutes ago, but minutes to them meant hours, maybe days to anyone else. After Colton broke the news of the fatal crash, Smith almost forgot the man who suggested their new name. When was that conversation, really? "The, uh, the other day, I mean. I don't know when it was." Smith checked the locked screen of Dorian's phone. "Wow, can't believe it's already Friday."

The woman at the grill peeled open another packet of hot dogs. "What's your name, hon?"

"Dorian," Smith said. "Nice to meet you."

"Twyla. Dorian's a lovely name."

The warm aroma of fresh meat and soft hot dog buns enveloped Smith. In their few hours of life in this world, they encountered many drinks but nothing to eat. Hunger didn't pain them before this. Maybe Andy, Oz, and Jade felt fed themselves better before arriving here. Maybe the sudden hunger came from Dorian's taller, stronger body needing an extra late-night meal. More likely, Smith guessed, they only craved the curiosity of trying food. The idea of a meal felt incomplete without personal experience. They hungered as much for its taste as the ritual of it.

"I don't have any cash," Smith confessed. They thumbed through the silicone pocket of Dorian's phone. The rest of his cargo pants turned up nothing.

"Ah, it's okay." Twyla lifted one hot dog into a bun. "I told Chris he can put them on folks' tabs, so just let him know when you go inside. We'll have a better system next time we run this. Hell, if there *is* a next time."

Twyla slid the paper hot dog tray across the folding table. Smith cradled it in both hands. Steam flowed skyward from the open bread, glowing in the pink disco light from under the larger canopy. Smith wrapped one hand under the bun, keeping their other on the food tray. They took their first bite.

Sweet, salty, and savory notes harmonized with gentle textures of bread and processed pork. The smoke and char of the grill lent an edge of fire and earthiness. Smith needed no further answers so long as they held this truth in their mouth. This revelation of sensory wonder imprinted itself onto Smith's mind. It was the first real, tangible thing that they could call their own. Although Dorian's teeth, lips, tongue, and body belonged to him, the taste of the hot dog belonged to Smith. It meant everything in their world.

Smith turned away. They faced the parked cars and lost themself in the cosmos above the local skyline. The pain, embarrassment, and panic of existence without true form couldn't hurt them here—eating a hot dog in the dark, under the stars. Even out in the open, some brief privacy allowed Smith to cry. The tears came without sobs or aches, only rolling down their cheeks after each bite of their meal.

Left holding only the empty emper tray, Smith wiped their eyes and wandered around the picnic tables to Arcana's main entrance. The Friday crowd matched the one from karaoke on Monday, exchanging familiar faces for new ones. A few long-haired dudes smoked cigarettes outside the doorway. They chatted with A-Bomb, whose chair migrated outside for a change. Inside, a bachelorette party huddled around the coffee table where Andy, Levi, and Ellesandra took their tequila shots. Behind the bar, Chris grooved to the rhythm of a British new wave album as he assembled someone's whiskey sour.

Smith stationed themself in an opening between the fuzzy pink pole and a touristy couple whose lips locked together.

"Hi, Chris," Smith smiled, then worried Dorian might not know him. Regardless, they caught Chris' ear.

"Hot dog?" Chris eyed the empty paper tray and scrolled the register screen.

"Yeah."

"Last name?"

A great question. What was it? Praying Chris wouldn't notice, Smith double-checked the driver's license from the back pocket of Dorian's phone.

"Kipiani."

Chris rang up the five-dollar meal. "Something to wash that down?"

Smith contemplated the list of drafts and cans on a neon-painted blackboard above the register. Individual names of drinks read like incantations in an ancient tongue. At least they recognized each of the categories: porter, lager, seltzer, ale... Why could some words jog their memory, while others drew blanks? Their mind's apparent unfairness offered them the bare minimum to survive. Details, places, and names of particular beers continued to elude them.

"Something cheap." Smith shrugged. Spending Dorian's money to buy themself a drink for the first time felt almost thievish, even if every drop went into his body. The cheaper the beer, the less they stole.

Chris opened a clear refrigerator door and cracked open a sixteen-ounce canned lager. Smith recognized its red, white, and blue label as the same beer Selene drank outside on Saturday, when Smith met them as Andy. The open can frothed.

Smith licked the bitter bubbles, hoping one can of this wouldn't leave them drunk enough to forget their own name like Selene did. Even in that case, Smith supposed, they could always pick a new name again.

"Thanks," Smith told Chris before weaving their way towards the black curtain. They pushed it aside and descended into the quiet room, free from the hollering bachelorette party and awkward new wave beats. Smith sipped their beer and worried they might never reach the bottom of a drink so vile. Maybe they'd remain in Dorian's body forever if that's how this thing worked.

Smith pressed a few keys of the broken organ console. The dead keys rose and fell in silence, save for gentle thumps against their wooden base. In the mirror above, Smith avoided Dorian's reflection. No, they decided: Staying in his body forever wouldn't resolve anything for *either* of them.

Also in the reflection, Smith spied someone seated at the cocktail table in the room's far corner. Jade rolled up the sleeves of her cutoff sweater and inspected a sheet of thick paper. A tiny LED lamp glowed over her and the unfinished drawing. She scribbled with a pen and rubbed fresh ink into the page with her thumb. Smith watched through the mirror until they gathered the courage to walk closer and see her drawing up close.

"Wow," Smith commended, in the way they hoped a stranger like Dorian might. Jade flicked her eyes up at them, but only for only an instant.

"Thanks," she droned, then returned to blending the ink. Smith took in the new artwork: a spiraling, circular void of dark edges, hovering in an empty square room under a dangling lightbulb.

Smith turned the beer can in their hand. "What is it?"

"Trying to figure that out." She frowned at her ink-smeared fingertips. "If you want to flirt with me, that's fine, but I'm gonna be focused on this for a while."

"That's not what I..." Smith blushed, worrying the real Jade might be nothing like the version of her they played. "You did all the other stuff, over there, right?" She nodded. "It's really scary, in a great way."

"Everything is scary," Jade declared, "but most things pretend not to be. I like it better when no one has to pretend."

"Hm." Smith wished *they* could quit pretending. "You mean you like your art to be honest?"

"Like a frilled lizard," Jade compared, waving her fingers behind her ears. "I like when things tell you how poisonous they are."

"Four-point-seven percent alcohol by volume," Smith recited from their beer can. Jade smiled and returned to shading the corners of her new drawing. If she remembered anything of the prior night, of Colton, or of the time Smith walked in her shoes, she didn't let on. Smith returned to fiddling with the switches on the organ console while they worked their way through more of their beer.

In the mirror, someone else descended the three short steps and joined Jade at her table. Selene perched on the chair across from her and swirled a translucent pink cocktail in their glass. Smith focused on the broken instrument and tried not to eavesdrop, but in the stillness beyond the main room, voices carried.

Selene inspected the unfinished drawing. "So, it's been *that* kind of week."

Jade reclined in her chair and shut off the small lamp. "Nothing I can't handle. How've you been?"

"Fucking weird, but getting better. Work's work and all that. Besides Saturday, it's been one of those weeks that'll blend into all the others, like Squidward in the suburbs." Selene lifted their glass but didn't take a sip.

Jade noticed. "You feel okay drinking again?"

Selene grimaced. "Old habits. Or alcoholism, maybe, but it's been nice having a dry week since Saturday. Mostly dry."

Jade scribbled furiously across the page. "You're sure no one got to your beer? You're *totally* sure you didn't leave it anywhere?"

Selene sank. "That's the whole thing with blacking out, right? You miss details."

"Yeah, sure, but not *everything*. And not what happens beforehand."

"I *do* remember." Selene ran their finger along the rim of the glass. "No random redneck dude hanging on my arm or nothing. I remember before, and I remember after. I only lost the fucking gap in the middle. Not a fuzzy part, but a *total* blank. And then it comes back, right back, and I was still here. Here, gone, then here again. Drunk the whole time, yeah, but I can handle *that*." Jade narrowed her eyes at them. "Usually I can, but I'm serious. What I texted you? Yeah. *I* still think I got abducted by aliens."

Jade crossed her arms. "I'm no skeptic."

Selene waited. "Right, but you think I'm deflecting. You think I got roofied and don't want to talk about it."

"We don't *have* to talk about it, but if that did happen, I know you'd see it as some kind of personal failure, and I wanna remind you that's the bullshit they put in our heads!" Jade took a breath. "But I *don't* think you got roofied. Whatever you went through on Saturday, I think... it happened to me, too. Here, last night."

Selene leaned closer over the table. "Shut the fuck up. When were you gonna say something?"

Jade shrank closer to her unfinished drawing. "It's this big, empty void right in the middle of the night. Lasted less than an hour, I think, but same as it was for you: Here, gone, then here again. No clue what happened, but there *was* a random redneck dude hanging around."

Selene kicked their heels on the legs of their stool. "I'll fucking kill him. I'll rip his fucking throat out."

"Easy!" Jade grabbed Selene's eager fist. "I thought our working theory was alien abduction?"

"Fuck off. *This* is real now. If we don't find this fucker and kick his teeth in, he'll try this shit on someone else."

Jade shook her head. "It wasn't the random dude. When I came out of it, he was up at the bar, literally crying about his ex who died. *I* actually bought *him* a drink. Even if he fit the profile, we'd notice side effects, and it'd last too long to explain this weird temporary shit."

Selene caught Smith's curious eyes in the mirror. "Hey. Private fucking conversation, bud."

"Sorry." Smith backed away towards the stairs. They felt more like an intruder than ever before—in this bar, in Dorian's body, and in the private lives of so many others. The crucifying ice in Selene's voice propelled Smith almost to the curtain, where their feet stuck to the floor. An idea washed over them, too strong to ignore.

"Something similar happened to me," Smith whispered.

"What?" Selene glared. "You good, dude?"

"Something similar happened to me," Smith repeated. "I'm sorry. I overheard what you described, and I think I know what you're talking about." Smith beat down the urge to over-explain. It didn't work as Oz, telling Georgie. Maybe in pieces, Jade would believe their story.

"*You* got drugged?" Selene looked Dorian's body up and down.

"No, that's not it." Smith insisted, squeezing their own wrists. "I can explain. Selene, I'm sorry if I made you uncomfortable."

"Whoa, whoa," Selene spun their chair towards Smith and jabbed an accusing finger. "How the fuck do you know my name?"

Smith sat on the lowest step at the entrance of the room. "It's gonna sound impossible. Like, alien-abduction impossible, but I promise I *can* answer that question. Jade, I don't know how else to say this, but *I* have your memories from last night."

Jade pinched the bridge of her nose. She set down her pen. "I hate that. I hate that I'm stupid enough to be fucking intrigued by that. What do you mean? How's that supposed to work?"

"What's the last thing you remember?" Smith let her think. "Don't tell me. Right before you blacked out, you finished a can of pomegranate seltzer. Am I right?"

Selene waited for marching orders from Jade. One more misstep, Smith imagined they'd waste no time summoning A-Bomb to sort this out. Jade slowly nodded. "Pomegranate. Yeah, that's right, but you weren't here last night, so what the fuck?"

From the steps, Smith stared across the room at the wall of Jade's art. "And then, you found yourself at the bar, finishing a *glass* of the same seltzer. That's right, too, isn't it?" They dreaded what needed to come next. "I *was* here last night, but I was *you*."

Jade maintained her poker face, but Selene laughed at Smith. "Are you tripping, dude?"

"Honestly, that would explain this *so* much easier." Smith crossed their arms on their knees. "Jade, do you believe me?"

Jade twisted her bag's strap in loops around her finger. "A true story doesn't need anyone to believe it. You can't prove it, though, can you?"

"Your bag," Smith remembered. "There's a receipt in there from last night."

Jade unzipped her bag and fished out a short, wadded paper. She flattened it on the table and turned the portable lamp back on. Jade and Selene inspected it like an artifact from an ancient tomb. Smith didn't need to see the table to know. "Check the time on the receipt. Do you remember anything from then?"

"I didn't sign this," Jade insisted, sliding the paper towards Selene.

They held it under the light and handed it back. "I don't know what his deal is, but this high key *is* your wack-ass handwriting."

"Okay, leave me alone," she conceded. "So, I wrote it while I was blacked out. I signed my name on a blank receipt. Why?"

"No," Smith shook their head. "When I was you, I had a hard time figuring out your name. Your license is old, and I couldn't unlock your phone. I had a hunch I was... *you* were the artist who drew all those, on the wall. I saw her signature up there, and handwriting is a reflex, right? So, I tested yours. *I* signed a receipt to see if I was really you. Or, in your body. Sorry, that sounds weird. I mean—"

"Muscle memory," Jade interjected. "I get it."

Selene's skeptical attention darted between the two of them. "This is cute. This is real weird. Jade, you're not... you're following all of this?"

She seemed to be. "Dorian, you said that's your name, right?"

Smith curled and uncurled Dorian's fingers. "That's *his* name."

"*Lame.*" Selene rolled their eyes. "If you're both in on some deep-Reddit ARG roleplay or whatever, I can give you the room."

"Hold on," Jade reassured them, still studying Smith from across the room. "You mean Dorian isn't *you*, he's just the body you're possessing right now?"

"No, not *possessing*," Smith balked at her theory. The grim connotation of possession unsettled them, although its raw concept applied in more ways than they could ignore. Smith still resisted the idea, maybe out of dignity, but certainly out of fear. "Whatever it is, I don't want this. I can't control it, either. Every time I finish a drink, I'm in a different body."

"Wild!" Jade beamed, which might have set Smith at ease, but her curiosity rang impersonal. "What happens when you finish that beer?"

Smith wiped condensation from the tall can. "If it's the same as it was with you? Dorian will come back, and I'll be someone else who just finished a drink. A different drink, and then I'll—"

"Fine. Fine, okay." Selene stood from their chair and advanced closer to Smith, looming over them and tapping one foot. "Were you me, too? On Saturday, I was drinking a beer out in the parking lot, then out of nowhere, I was holding an empty shot glass. Tell me that doesn't poke a hole in your theory. Do you have a receipt for possessing me, too?" Their voice lowered, and they crouched down to Smith's eye level. "Or did you make up this psycho supernatural bullshit to cover for drugging both our drinks?"

Smith recoiled. Their neck sweat.

Selene continued before they could deny anything. "Oh, yeah. I bet you used that same sleight of hand, dropping that paper in Jade's bag. Did you copy her handwriting from the wall back there? So, go ahead. Tell me you possessed me too. See if I'm as superstitious." They stood tall over Smith once more.

Smith swallowed another mouthful of their horrible beer. How fast could they chug the whole thing and get the hell out of here? This new, sober Selene brandished a fire and focus unlike the meek, gentle stranger they met as Andy. The Selene at the picnic table couldn't make heads or tails of basic conversation, much less remember their own name.

"You forgot your name," Smith told them, flashing back to their night as Andy. When everyone introduced themselves, Selene didn't. "And then, a 'wack fucking aftertaste.' That's what you said after stealing the shot that Oz bought for me." Smith raced through a series of unlikely connections, even if Selene refused to connect the dots. "That shot wasn't the flavor you expected because, last you remembered, you were drinking a *beer*. You get it, don't you?"

Selene huffed. "I have no fucking clue what you're talking about."

"Of course not. *You* weren't there!" Smith gasped. Selene and Jade no longer mattered. This new possibility was bigger. They jumped to their feet, chilled like a spy glimpsing their tail. Smith glanced from wall to wall, looking for more signs of a pattern. The only other people in the quiet room—a couple in another corner, both on their phones—fit none of the profile. Smith fled back through the curtain into the main barroom.

"Where are you going?" Jade's voice trailed off.

Chris poured a bubbling draft from a tap, same as ever. One of the bachelorettes at the coffee table rambled her way through a story about a flooded bathroom. The others laughed along, interrupting with questions and jokes, each playing their effortless roles. One after another, every patron at the bar sipped or scrolled or chatted or waited with all the dull comfort of a low-budget stage play. Smith rushed along the line of them. They passed an older, bearded man in the hallway, who sneered at them. Even he blended too well here.

The three long-haired smokers lounged in the blue space outside the restrooms, two arguing over a misattributed quote while the third hammered a search into his phone's web browser. None of the three showed any notable awkwardness. A door at the other end of the blue room swung open. Rough, layered synthesizer waves wafted in from the garage behind two girls retreating to the bar for another round. Their confidence never flinched.

Smith dove through the open door into the ongoing electronic show. Silhouettes danced between laser lights and pitch darkness, too fast to distinguish faces. All of them—the DJ, too—moved together. No outliers caught Smith's eye. They hugged the wall and crouched under the half-open garage door once again. The smell of the grill still blanketed the parking lot.

"Not here," they decided, breathless. Everyone fit their clothes, their faces, their roles, and their bodies too well. From the quiet room to the garage, Arcana contained only the usual suspects. Selene's account of their blackout raised an important and frightening question, but its answer escaped Smith like so many others.

Over the simmering grill, Twyla crushed an empty can of pale ale against the table. She flipped it back and forth between her hands. Her shoulders rose, her head bowed, and her hands left the spatula idle.

"Slow business?" Smith asked. She ignored them and surveilled the parking lot like a lighthouse over open waters.

She squinted at Smith through the haze of the grill. "Do you know who I am?"

They wondered how many cans she crushed since they went inside. "Yeah," Smith paused. "You're Twyla, right? You're one of the co-owners. The, like, empress of Arcana?"

Twyla waved away the smoke and evacuated from under the small canopy. She backpedaled into the parking lot, scowling at the building and all its lights. "No, that's not me."

Twyla's aluminum can thumping against the table was the hint Smith needed. They knew that sound, that motion, and that listless voice. These were the telltale signs of a confusion only they recognized. On Saturday, Selene crushed their beer can against the picnic table, exactly how Twyla did. If Selene's blackout began with the last drop of that beer, someone *else* crushed their can. Smith saw that same stranger, now appearing as Twyla. Whoever crushed her can didn't know her name, same as they didn't know Selene's. They acted like another nameless blank—another one of THEM.

Smith followed THEM a few steps further away from the tables. "Hey. It's okay if you're scared; I'm scared too. You feel lost, right? Like you can't remember anything? I've been lost in this place for a while. Maybe I can help you."

"You don't feed a black hole." THEY shuddered. THEY ripped Twyla's flat aluminum can into two jagged scraps and pointed one at Smith. THEY stood THEIR ground. Blood from THEIR palms dripped onto the asphalt. "Don't come closer. I don't know who you are. I don't know who *any* of you are, laughing and breathing and filling your cups. You think I don't realize I'm an interruption? I am evicting creatures like you from your shells, over and over. I want out of this skin, out of this world, *out*. I just want you to give me that drink. I'll finish it, and *she* can go bandage her hands. I'll be gone quick, and just as quick from my next body, and the next, until I feel like I *am* one of you fucking zombies. I'll drink so fast that I won't breathe until I'm who I'm meant to be. Give me your drink. Give me the mercy to stop existing where I *know* I don't belong."

"Okay, but listen." Smith extended their half-finished beer towards THEIR injured hand. "What's happening to you, it's happening to me, too. This isn't my body, either!"

THEY snatched the can. THEIR tense lips broadened into a frightening smile. "Then you should be drinking faster."

THEY tilted the beer to the sky and swallowed as it poured down THEIR cheeks. Bubbles splashed across the ground and mixed with the blood from THEIR hands.

"Wait, wait!" Smith's mind raced. It took so long to find THEM. There had to be an easier way. "Put your next drink on my tab. If it's open, I'm here. I'm *Smith*!"

The last drops of the beer fell over THEIR tongue. Twyla shook back into awareness with a shout. She gawked at the thin cuts on her hands, speechless. Smith ran to the nearest picnic table.

"Help her!" They directed a group of strangers. "She's bleeding!"

The stunned party clutched their glasses, but A-Bomb leapt into action. "Twyla! You try to shotgun that shit? Those cans'll fuck you up."

Smith hijacked one of the strangers' whiskey sours and downed it in a single swallow. They bid goodbye to Dorian and hello to a less lonely world.

IV

THE EMPEROR

IV: THE EMPEROR

Smith entered the new world alone. Their lips parted with an empty silver flask, which slipped from their left hand into their lap. From their last body to this one, there was no jarring shift in taste. Dorian's stolen whiskey sour matched the ghost of whiskey now on their breath. Tonight, Smith sat in a narrow, dark space that reeked of stale incense and musty carpet. Their feet rested on the pedals of a parked car, its lights off, and Arcana's entrance in its rearview. Smith's right hand clutched a tarnished keyring with the car's fob. They rummaged through the car's center console for a driver's license, but the heavy fur sleeves of their coat said enough.

"*This* guy," they realized, now in the shoes of the man who named them. Arcana's co-owner, Twyla's husband, what was his name?

Smith hid the silver flask in their coat pocket and exited the car: a decade-old luxury sedan, kitted with fading chrome rims and windows tinted as black as its paint coat. They tapped a button on the key fob to lock the doors, and the car chirped.

"Who's this shithead?" A-Bomb called out. He leaned against the open door beside the picnic tables. "Bet he thinks he's real cool!"

"Ha," Smith shrugged, the whole fur coat lifting with their shoulders. "Your words, not mine, A-Bomb."

"You know, I scrubbed off some of the graffiti on the bathroom mirrors, but it just keeps coming back. Guess someone really wants you to fuck off, huh?" A-Bomb smiled and slapped Smith's shoulder as they passed over the threshold.

Fuck off, Oren, read the gold handwriting scrawled across both bathrooms. At last, they connected *Oren* to the man in the fur coat. Who but the bar's garrulous co-owner could earn the ire of all its staff?

"Oh, well," Smith forgave A-Bomb, not ready to rib him back as Oren. "You'll get 'em eventually. I guess, uh, be on the lookout for someone who's got a gold permanent marker, right?"

Behind the bar, Chris wagged a gold-capped marker in the air. "You mean like this one?"

Smith tucked their hands in their oversized coat pockets. "Yeah, exactly."

"Sure thing, boss," A-Bomb saluted, stiff-armed, using only his middle finger. "I'll let you know if I see something like that."

Imitating Oren presented greater challenges than acting like Oz. The other night, Oren rambled through plenty of oddball ideas and non-sequiturs without Chris or A-Bomb batting an eye. On the face of it, Smith shared Oren's scatteredness, but they lacked his repertoire of tangents and confident declarations. Faking either demanded intense focus. The sight of Chris, meanwhile, reminded Smith of the issue at hand.

"Chris, I've got an ask for you." They took a seat at the bar, careful to pick the same barstool Oren seemed to prefer.

Chris hid his gold marker and twirled a rocks glass in his other hand. "Does it involve whiskey?"

"If someone comes in, then asks to put a drink on the tab of somebody named Smith, can you, like, point THEM my way?"

"Someone named Smith?" Chris' brow creased.

"Yeah, last name. No first name, just Smith. Remember that paradox-Matrix-tarot thing from the other night? Whatever night that was."

"Right, right." Chris checked his phone. "It's ten now, so I'm closing out, but Alea can take on your secret mission once she's clocked in."

A tall young woman with flared gauge earrings carried a fresh beer keg behind Chris and fixed it into a cabinet under the taps. "Do I hear Emperor Oren declaring the night's wild goose chase?" She closed the cabinet and hoisted an empty keg from the floor. "Let me guess... You need me to construct another dartboard? No, screenprint more Arcana T-shirts with A-Bomb's face on them? Maybe negotiate a better wholesale price for hot dogs?"

Already doubting their convoluted strategy with the bar tab, Smith pivoted. "Uh, I'm looking for... I don't know. If somebody comes up here and says the name Smith, can you let me know?"

"That's all, you're just looking for someone named Smith?"

"Not exactly." They struggled to make the request less absurd without giving themself away. "I'm looking for someone who's *looking* for Smith."

Alea chuckled and surveyed the desolate bar. "Sure, I'll let you know. And I texted you the final schedule of events for next week, but I heard that one of Saturday's bands pulled out to play some festival. Twyla said you had connects on backup acts?"

"Yeah, yeah," Smith improvised. "Always something, right? Nothing goes as planned. I'll talk to some people, but ask me again tomorrow."

"Believe me, I will." Alea stowed the finished keg next to the recycling bin.

Chris ducked under the chain partition at the bathroom end of the bar. He stretched his arms over his head, cracked his knuckles, and slouched onto a stool on the other side of the pink pillar. Chris angled one hand at Alea as if activating her telepathic powers, which appeared effective.

"Coming right up," she said and dug a tall cheap beer can from a cooler. She popped the tab and delivered it to Chris. Alongside it, she poured out a shot of a dark liquor from the lowest shelf.

"Sticking around?" Smith asked Chris. He raised his shot glass.

"Where else, on a Saturday night?" Chris downed the shot.

"Well, there is that *thing*," Alea waved her fingers into the distance. "That event downtown, the fundraiser."

Smith pretended to know. "Probably no drinks at a fundraiser."

"Yeah," Alea grimaced. "I mean, we don't know for *sure* that he was drunk, but that'd be a real fucking awkward way for her family to raise money for funeral costs."

Her family. Smith flashed back to Colton and the news from his phone call: the crashed van off the interstate, the fire, and Julienne and Hayes, both dead. In the stir of Smith's Friday night as Dorian, the horrible tragedy slipped their mind.

"Chris was telling me," Alea continued, transferring a pack of cans into fridge, "that Julienne's ex was in here when y'all found out about everything. That's wild."

Chris downed his shot, loaded its empty glass onto the rubber bar mat, and chased it with several sips from his beer. He spun his stool to face away from the bar, peering out the open door. A crew of college kids lined up to show their IDs to A-Bomb. Chris sighed and turned back to the bar.

"Chris, you alright?" Alea asked. Smith wondered the same.

"Gotta get out of..." Chris trailed off, unlike himself. "A tab. An open tab, there's... *Smith* was the name. If someone named Smith comes in here, just say I got my drink already, and he can leave me alone."

Smith nearly fell from their chair.

"You said *Smith*?" Alea's eyes flicked over to them.

"Chris?" Smith confirmed, grabbing the edge of the bar with Oren's ringed fingers. "That shot you just took, do you remember where you were before you—?"

THEY huffed, drained of Chris' levity. "It's you, again. From the parking lot."

Smith shivered, but they laughed, still awed to discover this other person—another unnamed person, trapped in a relay race between bodies.

"Wow," Smith breathed. "So, you're Chris now."

"Who the fuck is Chris?" THEY asked.

Alea shook her head and leaned back on the sink. "I keep trying, seriously, but I can't keep up with y'all's jokes."

THEY stepped over the chain at the end of the bar and made for the bathrooms without acknowledging her. Beer in hand, THEY disappeared down the hallway.

"Hey, wait!" Smith followed as THEY barreled straight through the door to the garage at the end of the blue room. On the other side, a sea of cold air enveloped both of them. Without the crowd from the synth show, the garage's hollow echo eclipsed even the quiet room. A few Edison bulbs glowed orange among shelves of audio equipment, cardboard boxes, and unarranged decor that toed the line between antique and garbage. THEY planted THEIR feet in the center of the room and sipped Chris' beer. THEY stared at Smith while THEY did it, like a cornered animal bracing THEIR claws in defense.

"Do you remember your name?" Smith asked, but THEY just took another sip. "Don't drink all that. Please, you don't have to leave yet."

"I don't *have* a name," THEY grumbled and sat cross-legged on the rough concrete floor.

"I couldn't remember my name, either, so I picked Smith, that way I don't get confused." Smith pulled over a barstool from a cobwebbed corner and set it near the blue room door.

"Names don't matter." THEY spat on the floor. "You don't know who you are, no matter what stupid name you pick."

Smith deflected. "Oren picked mine, actually. He's... Well, *this* is him. I'm him for tonight."

"You're *not* him," Chris corrected. "You're just wearing his flesh."

Smith's skin prickled at the word *flesh*. "Whatever you call it, it's the same for you and Chris, right? You finish your drink, and you switch to someone new? Unless you have a way to control how any of this works."

THEY shook THEIR beer can in the air. "This *is* control. I have complete control. I drink, and I'm one step closer to finding the real me. When I find my own flesh, I'll know. I *will* remember myself, once you and these nobodies stop distracting me with all your petty, useless talking."

THEIR perspective baffled Smith. "This bar is full of people who know themselves *because* they talk. They know each other, too, and not because they drank themselves into the right bodies. So many lives connect in this place, and I can feel so much here beyond what's happening to me. I know it's weird, scary, and kinda loud sometimes, but I'm learning to make sense of it. Every night begins at the same place, so maybe we can carve out our own lives here, if we—"

"Stop! Alright, stop." THEY got back on THEIR feet and retreated further into the dark, onto the unlit stage. "This is not a 'we' situation. Congrats, you found me, and we're both suffering this drunken prison, but we're not cellmates. You have your flesh, and I have mine. There's nothing between us. Every moment I don't have my own body is torture, so let's not turn the thumbscrews on each other." THEY sat on a bulky, rusted amplifier and picked at the aluminum tab of THEIR beer can. "In the spirit of reducing pain for both of us, I will continue to drink as much as possible, as continuously as possible. Am I clear?"

Smith wondered if that explained how it took so long for THEM and themself to cross paths. "Is that all you've been doing? You suck down a drink as soon as you're in a new body?"

THEY raised THEIR can. "This isn't some leisurely carousel for me. I'm nauseated. I keep pulling the emergency stop: A six pack under a table, a beer some weirdo bought me, or a cocktail left on a chair during karaoke. I stole my first shot straight from the bar! Even before I knew what was going on, I could taste an escape, always a drink away."

Smith tugged a new thread. "What shot did you steal? What did it taste like?"

"Why?"

"Was it a guy you took it from? Gray, bluish eyes? And before that, were you at a picnic table outside? And there were four other people, yes. *I* was that guy, Andy. I got punched in the face."

"Yeah," THEY smirked, "I saw you get punched."

"I knew it!" Smith reveled. "That's why I came looking for you. Somebody else took over Selene's body while I was Andy. You were them when they blacked out last Friday. You're the *somebody*."

"You're fucking confusing." THEY rubbed THEIR eyes. "I was who?"

"Selene. They're friends with Jade, who's one of the—"

THEY pounded the amplifier. "Never mind. I don't care about all the fucking names. It doesn't matter who they are, what they say, or how many times they punch each other's faces. I don't need to know their world. I'm not a part of it, and neither are you. *That's* what hurts. You see how that pain gets worse when you pretend you're like them? Just drink, and you can *almost* remember not feeling that way."

"Fuck that," Smith said, letting the whiskey from Oren's flask do the talking.

For the first time, THEY set down THEIR beer on the edge of the stage. "You want to try that again?"

"Sure: Fuck *you*. If you don't care about names, I'll give you one. Since I'm Smith, you can be Waite."

THEY laughed. "What sort of dumbass is named 'Wait?'"

"There's an 'e' at the end of it. If you *do* care, I can explain it for you."

Waite snatched up their beer again threatening to drink more. "I don't like you, Smith, but better you than all the fucking androids out there."

Although 'androids' didn't sit right with them, Smith empathized with Waite. No connection to anyone else—Andy with Levi, or Oz with Georgie—felt this significant. Like the hot dog, it was *theirs*. Next to that, only hiding alone in the bathroom as Jade brought near the same relief. After finding Waite, how could they be satisfied with avoiding, sneaking, and pretending to know the friends of their nightly hosts?

Waite walked in circles on the stage. "This place smells like rust and old wood. How can you stand it here?"

Smith rode a fresh burst of energy. "We don't have to be."

"What?"

"We don't have to be here. We can leave, probably." Smith left their stool and grabbed a bent steel handle at the base of the shut garage door. It rattled and creaked as they heaved it halfway open, like the prior night. Streaks of moonlight bathed the concrete floor.

"What do you honestly think is out there?" Waite strode down from the stage, under the garage door, and out into the parking lot. Smith lowered the garage door behind them. They pointed over the street and adjacent buildings. "Looks like more of the same shitty world, in every direction."

"It is," said a girl at a picnic table, triggering a round of laughs from her friends. Waite glared at her, less in kinship than disapproval—an expression alien to Chris' face. Smith retrieved Oren's car keys from a pocket of their fur coat and clicked a button to unlock the car.

"Sure, let's just *go*," Waite sneered, wiping a line of grime from the black sedan's trunk lid. "You know how to drive, suddenly?"

"My body should," they assured Waite and climbed back into the driver's seat. Waite set their unfinished beer in the pocket of the passenger door.

"Magic isn't real," Waite scolded, sinking into the seat cushion.

"You've never tried a hot dog, have you?" Smith started the engine. The dash flickered alight. "And if magic is what we don't understand, then basically everything is magic."

"No, seriously, you shouldn't drive," Waite insisted. "You might have a license in that pocket, but it sure as fuck isn't *yours*. And didn't you get here by drinking alcohol?"

The empty flask in Oren's coat pocket pressed to Smith's chest under their seatbelt. They agreed with Waite, but the adrenaline rush of this opportunity dulled their concerns. Smith shifted the car into reverse and rolled out of the parking space. Waite clutched a plastic handle above the door window.

"It's muscle memory," Smith explained. "Every body has some. You've been spending so little time in yours, I bet you never noticed how we can do what they do. Anything they do regularly enough."

The car's rear bumper neared the corner pole of the beige canopy. It beeped a warning signal. Smith stomped the brakes, which squeaked and jostled them both in their seats.

"Fuck!" Waite exclaimed. "You don't know any more than I do. You're arrogant."

"You want to drive?" Smith shifted gears and inched towards the end of the lot.

"I told you I wanted to finish my drink, not go joyriding in some fancy guy's car. He owns the bar? I don't care if he owns the fucking *city*, he... careful. Hey, watch! Okay, you're half in the street. Just go. There's no one coming from the left. Go! Do you have turn signals? You and your muscle memory bull-shit. Smith, the light. The light. *Red* light!"

Smith squeezed the brakes again, smoother than before. "See? I've got it."

"You're a fucking maniac!" Waite cackled. Their laughter stunned Smith. Even from Chris' mouth, the fractured sound welled up from somebody else. Waite let go of the handle and rolled down their window. "Fine. This is fine."

"Where are we going?"

Waite chuffed. "Don't ask me. Punch it."

At the green light, Smith pressed the gas to the floor. The rear tires squealed. The air rushed and buffeted through Waite's open window. The dim sidewalks and dormant build-ings along the four-lane street blurred into a haze. Breathless at the muscle of the whining engine, Smith clung to the wheel. They and Waite charged outward into an expanding universe.

"Woo!" Waite hollered out the window. "I didn't think you'd actually do it."

Smith eased onto the brakes and halted at another red light. The road split around a small park at the heart of down-town. A family in a crosswalk joined a group of several dozen other strangers along the concrete steps of the park's amphi-theater. Many of them held candles, casting just enough light to show their solemn faces. A woman stood at the front of the crowd, balanced on a wooden chair, reading from a paper.

"Fundraiser," Smith recalled. "Up ahead. This must be the fundraiser."

"What?"

Smith traced the conversation to before Waite arrived. "Shit, never mind. Alea was telling you... I mean, telling Chris and me about a fundraiser happening tonight."

Waite leaned with one arm out the window as they drove past. A handmade poster with a website address hung from a table at the edge of the park. On top of it, a plastic donation box faced the road.

Waite read the poster. "Sounds like 'Julienne' had a bad day."

Smith checked the mirrors to confirm, but the park vanished too fast behind them. "They're trying to pay for her funeral. Would it kill you to show any respect?"

"Here you go again, learning names and pitying strangers you never met."

"Alright, enough!" Smith pulled the car into a metered space along the street. They set the gear to park but let the engine idle. "You really think it's useless interacting with anyone? You think there's no point acting like... like you're an actual human?"

Waite shrugged. "You think there is?"

Smith twisted around in their seat to gaze back at the park. "Julienne died in a car crash. And, well, a car fire, I think. Her boyfriend, too. It was his van. The point is, I spent a whole night at the bar talking to this Colton guy who was trying to find her when she was missing. He got the call, and we all found out. I bet Colton's there, with everyone."

"So?" Waite slumped in their seat. "None of that is part of our—part of *your* life, and it's definitely not part mine."

"I left before I finished talking to him. Stay here if you want, but I'm going out there." Smith shut off the car, took the keys, and unbuckled their seatbelt.

"No, hey! Let's keep driving. We started having a nice time, and you want to ruin it with some cry fest?"

Smith exited the car, shut their door, and walked around to Waite's open window. "If none of these people are real to you, don't come with me. Finish your beer, and I'll see you in your next body. How's that?"

Smith started down the sidewalk before Waite could respond. They needed some closure with Colton, whether or not Waite tagged along. By the time Smith reached the crosswalk, a car door thumped, and Waite's footsteps caught up to them.

"What exactly are you trying to do, Smith?" Waite said through their teeth. The *WALK* light invited them both across the street to the park.

"Colton was obsessed with Julienne. He's distraught, and he probably blames himself. Whoever he blames, I bet he'll lash out if he feels ignored. I left when he got the news, and whatever Jade told him afterwards, I owe it to him to finish our conversation."

"'Owe' him? You don't owe any—" Waite stumbled over the curb.

The unamplified voice of the woman on the wooden chair interrupted Smith's briefing. They and Waite hushed to avoid disturbing the attentive crowd. The speaker flipped from one page in her hand to the next. Her fingers shook.

"...That she may find peace with our Lord in heaven. My daughter, Julie, knew Jesus, and accepted Him in her heart. She was a kind and caring example to all those in her life. Your words, your time, and your generosity, would mean the world to her. The horrible and unexpected events of these past..."

The woman, Julienne's mother, continued, but the gossiping whispers of two candle-holding strangers drew Smith's ear away.

"You think any of this money goes to *his* family?"

"Oh, fat chance. You hear what Walt Hayes saw?"

"Saw?"

"Get this. Walt's scanner picked up chatter about the van recovery before it went wide. He rushed out there, saw everything. And he said *she* was the one was driving. Her body, all burned, behind the wheel."

"Oh, lord. Is that true?"

"Can't say. But it ain't the tune her momma's singing."

From the second ring of the amphitheater, Smith read the poster on the table by the candle lights: *Funeral Expenses — Family of Julienne Chord.* Smith surveyed for any sign of Colton in the fray but mostly saw the backs of everyone's heads.

"This is boring," Waite complained, dangling their legs off the edge of the terraced seating. "These idiots should keep their money. No use crying over dead flesh."

"Shh!" Smith nudged Waite's leg. "You can't say *one* decent thing, can you?"

Waite yawned. "None of this is decent. I'm not supposed to be here, and neither are you."

"Whatever." Smith wondered if 'here' meant the fundraiser or the entire world. "Can you at least talk like I do? Less of the word 'flesh?'"

As Smith enunciated 'flesh,' a hand fell on their shoulder from behind. They turned to find Colton, the hood of his gray jacket wrapping his face in shadow. His beard stuck out over the zipper. Smith feared Colton might have overheard, but his reddened eyes lingered between Smith and Waite, unfocused.

"Oren? And Chris, wow. Thanks for being here," Colton droned. Waite failed to acknowledge Chris' name, so Smith stationed themself between Waite and Colton.

"Yeah, of course. Are, uh, how are you?"

Colton scraped the muddy heel of his boot on the stone lip of the terrace. "Crazy day at work, actually. I was up at this site in Rangerville, you know? It's, like, up *there*, an hour that way. Anyway, our crew was supposed to be taking down an old deck at this house. We, yeah, I do renovations and re-builds. But the roll-off got repo-ed cause my clueless boss missed the rental bill. He still won't pick up the phone, and the repo guys dumped half the scrap wood right in our clients' driveway. It's a real, uh, real *cluster*. I gotta..." Colton trailed off and cleared his throat. "I'm sorry, I shouldn't be thinking about that tonight. I'm not even supposed to be here, man. Not invited to her actual funeral or nothing. But Julie would've—I think, I *hope* she would've wanted me to be here."

A silhouette in the crowd of candles caught Smith's eye. "I'll be right back," they promised.

Never mind Colton. Smith dropped from the lowest terrace into the stone courtyard of the amphitheater. Three rows into the crowd, they filled an open space next to her. Without a candle, and wearing Oren's gaudy fur coat, Smith stood out from the modest, mostly black attire of the attendees. Maybe that explained how Jade saw them coming.

"Oren?" She whispered. "What are you doing here?"

"There's *another* one." Smith started, forgetting to reintroduce themself.

"What? Another what?"

"Another me. I'm not the only... Oh, shit, right. I'm Smith, not Oren. I was Dorian last night, and I was you on Thursday. The receipt in your bag? That's me. Stay with me here. Remember how Selene said they blacked out on Saturday?"

A bead of wax dripped from Jade's candle to her thumb, and she flicked it away. "Can this wait?"

"No. I'll be quick. See Chris, back there? Chris isn't Chris right now. That's who Selene was on Saturday. They remember everything, the same way I do, from each of the bodies they've been in. It's happening to both of us! You believe me, right? Jade?"

Jade peeked over her shoulder. To Smith's surprise, Colton stood alone in the back row—no sign of Waite.

"What's *he* doing here?" Jade tilted her candle at Colton. Smith spun in place, frustrated and nervous to lose track of Waite.

"Where the fuck did Waite just—?" They paused. "Did you tell Colton your name on Thursday? Look away. Don't let him see you here. When I was you, he told me Julie tagged your profile, I think. It was basically nothing, but with your art style, plus whatever biases he's got, he was pretty suspicious about you being anywhere near Julie's life. Also, I kind of accidentally pretended you weren't *you*, which probably made things a lot worse. If he sees you now, he might seriously wonder why... you're *here*." For the first time, Smith entertained a few of Colton's suspicions about Jade.

"I never met Julie," Jade said, "but if homeboy's got a problem with me, I'll settle that with him. And for the record, you don't need a permit to be here. Grief is something practiced, like any art, so sue me for being a good student."

At the front of the crowd, Julienne's mother wrapped up her speech. A wave of soft clapping passed through the crowd as she descended the wooden chair.

"If anyone else would like to speak, maybe share a story about Julienne..." She directed the invitation towards the chair. Smith's whirlpool of concerns over Jade drained into a pit of dread. At the front of the crowd, Waite ascended the chair.

"Oh, *fuck* no." Smith ditched Jade and rushed to intervene.

"It's remarkable to see..." Waite began before Smith could reach the front. "...all of you gathered here, contributing to support this family in their time of grief. It is kind, selfless, and verging on illogical. Shouldn't the burden of failing to cover these expenses fall solely on *this* family, which has failed so visibly? Why would they even collect for a coffin, a ceremony, and a burial plot, under the circumstances?"

A few voices piped up in the dark, jeering for Waite to step aside. Smith lunged to pull them down from the chair, but not before their final remark:

"Why bother with a burial, when she's already at *least* half cremated?"

Waite dodged, but not fast enough. Smith tackled them straight backwards onto the folding table, which collapsed under them. The donation box tumbled over the sidewalk and onto the street. It fell open, and wrinkled dollar bills fluttered in the wash of a passing bus. The shouts, gasps, and wails of attendees stampeding to gather the money gave Smith the cover they needed to drag Waite towards the car.

"You sick bastard!" A ragged voice yelled—Julienne's mother.

"You were right," Waite conceded to Smith as they ran. "We *can* leave. We can go anywhere, do *anything* between drinks!"

Smith threw Waite into the car and grabbed their unfinished beer can from the door pocket. "You wanted to drink?" Smith taunted them while pouring some of the beer into Oren's silver flask. They locked the doors. "Now, we're gonna fucking drink, before one of them comes over and stomps our brains out!"

Most of the beer dribbled down the outside of the flask.

"How does that work?" Waite asked, rubbing their back where they landed on the folding table. "Splitting the drink, can we both finish the same one like that?"

"Find out yourself, asshole." Smith threw the flask to Waite, who smiled.

"I like this side of you."

Smith refused to be baited into another fight. They pinched their nose and chugged the warm beer left in the can.

"See you in the next one!" Waite sang.

V
THE HIEROPHANT

V: THE HIEROPHANT

The musty heft of Oren's fur coat lifted off Smith's shoulders, leaving them floating in the dark. Their new feet hardly felt the ground. No, they *literally* didn't feel the ground. Smith hovered in the air, arms at their back, unable to move. Sweet drops of butterscotch liqueur ran down Smith's chin. Someone else's hand held an emptied shot glass to their lips.

"That worked better than I thought. Wow." Smith knew Oz's voice. In front of them, she discarded the empty glass of her signature shot on an empty chair. She inspected something above Smith, reaching overhead. Smith tried to see, but the force holding their arms at their back also kept their head angled down.

"Can you breathe okay?" Oz asked.

"Yeah," Smith could, not without some effort, "but I can't move my arms. Or my legs."

Oz laughed. "That means I'm doing my job right."

Feeling out the extents, weights, and strengths of Smith's other bodies took little time. Without any range of motion, this new body took every ounce of attention and effort to settle into. Smith twisted their wrists. Bands of black cotton rope circled from their arms, over their shoulders, around their chest, everywhere.

"How much do you charge people, now?" Georgie asked, from somewhere behind Smith's field of view.

"Depends," Oz said. "Not enough to pay the bills yet. And good, safe Shibari equipment is *so* fucking expensive. Gonna be a while before I can afford hemp ropes; that's the *good* good."

Hearing Oz and Georgie in the same room, Smith developed a hunch about their new identity for the night. They saw enough friend groups throughout Arcana to sense which factions stuck tightly together. Where one found Oz and Georgie, one could expect to find...

"Saint, you ready to come down?" Oz squatted below Smith's face and smiled up at them.

"Yeah," Smith answered overwhelmed and relieved. Oz vanished aside. The ropes slithered loose, one by one. Smith's ankles lowered towards the ground. Their arms spread outward from behind their back. Stiff muscles untensed. The ropes ran through a metal loop above, dropping Smith from a tall metal tripod. Free to stand, they found themself on the stage of Arcana's garage, opposite an overwhelming and unexpected scene.

Newly rearranged shelves segmented the open space into smaller areas. On the other side of the stage, a short, bearded man wearing a black latex crop top held two lit candles over a narrow table. Someone else lay shirtless across it while he dripped wax onto their back. Behind a shelf of audio cables, another stranger bent over a throne-like armchair, and a tall figure in a pup mask prepared to spank them with a leather flogger. In another corner, flashes of fire... Smith's eyes drifted faster than they could process the unfolding scenes. Shadows milled in and out of even more booths—performing, demonstrating, participating, or just watching the exhibitions—dressed in sharp ensembles of lace, mesh, and leather. The night's fashions bared more skin than Smith had ever seen at Arcana or anywhere.

Otherwise, everybody acted completely normal.

Oz untied two more loops in the dangling rope. "Georgie, you ready to try next?"

Georgie backed away from the metal rig. "Nah, you can... I'll wait. Someone else can go."

"No worries." Oz practiced an array of three knots on the rope while she spoke. "Most people seem more comfortable just watching. There's always Kink Night next month, too."

"This is monthly?" Smith asked before measuring their question.

Oz nodded. "I know, last month they canceled it, but yeah. Didn't I send you the event page? Alea made a badass flier for the Arcana Instagram."

Georgie rescued Smith from answering. "Dude, Saint never knows where we're going when I pick them up. I sent them a link to that punk show, the one last month with the guy... the band where the bassist had a prosthetic leg? *Triggered by Tango*, yeah. Saint liked my message *yesterday*. They might as well not have a phone."

"Well, they did dress for the occasion." Oz admired Smith's outfit. They looked down to raid Saint's pockets but found none in their red sequined briefs. Between the briefs, matching corset, and fishnet stockings, Saint's clothes lacked any hint of storage space.

"It's giving Rocky shadow cast," Georgie adjudicated, and Oz grinned.

"Exactly. Put some respect on Frank N. Furter's name."

Not caring to learn whoever Frank was, Smith searched Oz's corner of the stage for a bag or jacket. "Where *is* my phone, actually?"

"You must've put it down before..." Oz checked along the back wall.

"See? This is what I mean!" Georgie sighed. "I'll go out and check my car. Saint, try not to get lost while I'm gone."

Oz saluted Georgie. "Your watch is ended. I'll keep an eye on them."

Seeing Oz for the first time since karaoke resurfaced a chain of unsolved issues for Smith. How well did Georgie understand what they told him that night? Whatever happened between Chris and Saint after they started talking to each other? Despite the headache of diving back into the friendly trio's world, Smith couldn't pass up the opportunity.

"Did you see the video from Monday?" Smith questioned Oz.

"Video? If you sent me something, I deleted TikTok again."

"No, sorry, the video *of* Monday, at karaoke. Georgie took a video of you singing."

Oz blinked and ducked her head, like the question was a circling mosquito. "Yeah, yeah, I don't know. That night was weird."

"Weird?" Smith knew the rest. "Because you don't remember singing that night, do you? Like you blacked out for a while, but you came back?"

Oz leaned on a metal pole of her tall tripod. She scrunched her face at Saint. "What's up with you? You're boring today."

Smith almost laughed. "Boring? Sorry. It's a lot to explain. I don't want to go through it all again, but I guess I have to. Sorry, I just... You have no idea how many times I've tried to do this."

"Explain what?"

"*I'm* not Saint. My name is Smith. You gave Saint that shot, the butter one, and I basically took over. I'm in Saint's body until I finish another drink. On Monday, I was you. I sang karaoke, so that's actually me in the video. I tried to explain this all to Georgie, but it kinda broke his brain. Does that make sense?"

To Smith's amazement, Oz didn't make more weird faces. She didn't turn away or interrupt. She waited for them to finish, chewed her lip, and set down her knotted rope.

"I understand," Oz claimed. "I mean, *my* part of it. I know what happened with me on Monday. Between us, I haven't talked about this much, but I trust you. Do you know what a system is?"

"System, like generally?" Smith tried. Oz shook her head.

"There are a few ways to say it. I'm a system, or, I'm plural. You know, like, dissociative identity disorder. Used to be called 'multiple personalities,' which is still what shitty movies call it. That'd be how *you* know about it, right?"

"Oh," Smith blushed. Sure, Oz trusted Saint, but in their shoes, Smith felt undeserving of the same trust. Stealing such a private conversation felt dirty. They picked up the empty shot glass and sat on the chair at the corner of the stage. "Sorry, you don't have to say more. I didn't mean to—"

"I don't mind." Oz continued. "We coexist. Alters, I mean. Usually, we're like, co-conscious, but sometimes one might... I dunno, sing karaoke? It's random. It makes remembering things hard, especially in the past, but thank fuck for therapy. Most days are good days, now."

Smith knew better than to question Oz's experiences in her own body and mind, but the phrase *co-conscious* raised their eyebrows. "So, on Monday, were you co-conscious with someone else?"

Oz shut her eyes. "No. Monday was just weird, I guess, cause I've gotten to know my alters pretty well over the years, but Monday felt like someone new. That probably sounds super weird, but I can feel the difference."

If Oz could consciously share her body with alters, living together and forming memories at the same time, could Smith do the same with their hosts? Then again, Oz's alters couldn't inhabit *other* bodies. Jade's possession theory aligned closer with that aspect of Smith's case, placing them well beyond the scope of clinical psychology. Without a psychiatrist *or* a shaman to consult, Smith forced themself to ignore how much they related to Oz.

"It's not that weird," they told her, "but you might have to explain this to me all over again tomorrow."

Two unseen hands from behind Smith's chair poked the sides of their waist. They jumped and spun around to find Georgie.

"Ha! It's in the car."

"What?"

"Your *phone*. You left it on the passenger seat."

"Oh, cool. Thanks."

Georgie scowled at Smith. "What's your deal? You're not being an asshole. Something's wrong."

Smith looked back to Oz, who began setting up her ropes again. A young woman in glossy pink heels stepped up onto the stage to greet Oz, then offered up her wrists to begin another demonstration. While Oz debriefed her on safety procedures, Smith took Georgie aside.

"Is Chris working tonight? I, uh, I wasn't paying attention when we came in."

Georgie's brow fluttered. "Yeah, he's out there. Alea's busy helping A-Bomb keep everything running smooth." He pointed out Alea, standing at the blue room door wearing an orange lanyard and supervising the stations around the room. "You gonna go be brave and order your own drinks tonight?"

Smith breathed as deep as their sequined corset permitted. They flashed back to the fundraiser, where they tackled Waite—as Chris—onto the donation table. The real Chris posed no threat in comparison, so Smith channeled some of Saint's snark. "At least *I* don't have to stand on a chair to get seen at the bar."

"Easy, Frankenslut. And don't—I swear, if you correct me to say 'Frankenslut's monster,' I will give Chris your phone number."

"What makes you think I won't give it to him myself?"

Georgie's jaw dropped. "Look at you, banking some confidence to cash in on Kink Night. Go get a drink. And if you make one more short-Georgie joke tonight, I'm sending your ass to the spanking booth."

Through the blue room, past the restrooms, and onward to the bar, Smith averted their eyes from countless more scantily clad guests of the monthly event. The others, meanwhile, made no such effort to keep their eyes off one another, nor off Smith. Along the chain partition at the nearest end of the bar, Twyla abandoned a conversation with two other women and gasped at Smith. She raised her hands in excitement, two bandages still adhered across her palms.

"Saint! Oh, that corset just shimmers. You're doing Tim Curry proud."

"Thanks!" Smith wondered who Tim Curry was, whether he knew Frank, and whether they'd all crossed paths yet. So many new names, always.

"Drink?" Chris' voice set Smith on edge. Until they met his eyes over the bar, that same voice belonged to Waite. Smith preferred the real Chris.

"The pomegranate seltzer, please." Smith refused to make themself suffer another cheap beer. Saint's bank account would have to spare the extra two dollars, unless... "And Chris, um, *Waite* owes me a drink. Do you know if they opened a tab yet?"

Chris leaned an elbow on a bar mat and cupped his ear. "You said *Wade?*"

"No, *Waite*."

"I can't wait, love, I gotta keep the taps flowing, you know?"

"No, there's someone named... uh, never mind."

Chris fetched the seltzer. As much as Smith wanted to locate Waite using an easy gimmick like the bar tabs, the tactic required Waite's cooperation. That wouldn't come easily,

Smith figured, after the fiasco at the fundraiser. They tapped their fingers on the bar, plotting other ways to track Waite down.

Jade appeared on the other side of the pink pillar. "Nice choice."

"Nice, uh, sorry?" Smith fumbled, unsure when she arrived.

"The pomegranate seltzer's not too popular, but it's my favorite. Have you had it before?"

"Yeah," Smith said. "I've had it once."

Jade narrowed her eyes and hung close along the pillar. "I have *questions* for you." Smith couldn't remember if Jade and Saint knew each other. Across the past few nights, when did the two cross paths, if ever? Being regulars, could they really be strangers? Smith braced themself to roll the dice and play along, but Jade spared them both the trouble. "It's *you*, isn't it, Smith?"

The firmness in her voice suggested it wasn't a guess. Maybe Smith made themself too obvious, if Saint couldn't talk to Chris without making a fool of themself. However Jade knew, Smith skipped any pleasantries. "Okay, I don't believe you showed up to the fundraiser just for the morbid thrill of it. You seriously never knew Julienne Chord?"

Jade flinched, then smirked. "Look at me. An awkward memorial for two violent deaths is an evening well-spent in my book." Her corpse-like eyeliner and miniature sword earrings corroborated. Considering her art style, the excuse checked out. "But I *did* check my mentions, like you said, and yes, she tagged me. It was almost two months ago, when I gave her one of my sketches."

"Gave her?" Smith accused. "So, you were friends, or what?"

"*Sold* her. What's your problem, Smith? Do you and Colton think *I* ran the van off the road? Shined a laser pointer through the windshield? Snipped some brake lines?"

"I'm not with Colton," Smith promised, "but if I don't know you any better than I know anyone else, how do I decide who I trust?"

"For starters, trust the people who can attend a funeral without crashing it." She pointed discreetly at Chris as he scrolled the register screen to close someone's tab.

"He won't remember," Smith assured her. "That was *them*, not *him*. It was a mistake. I shouldn't have brought them with—"

"One of Julienne's cousins took a video, and it got reposted on Reels." Jade tilted her phone up at Smith under the bar top.

On the screen, Oren pushed through the crowd while Chris spoke at the front: "...at *least* half-cremated..." until gasps, shouts, and a dramatic tackle by Oren interrupted him. The video cut off after that. A ticker alongside it tallied fifty thousand likes and a flood of disapproving comments.

"Oh, fuck." Smith rubbed their neck and pushed the phone away. "I left. We both left, we drank ourselves away before... What happened after that?"

"It worked out fine," Jade summarized. Before she could elaborate, Chris delivered Smith's pomegranate seltzer.

"Perez, right?" Chris asked, tapping the register screen.

"Uh, yeah," Smith said, grateful for Chris' help. Remembering Saint's last name took a backseat, especially to the prior night's fallout. Jade's terseness left them unsatisfied. "There's no way it 'worked out fine.' That crowd was gonna come after Waite. Chris, I mean. We weren't... *I* wasn't thinking. I shouldn't have left Oren and Chris like that."

Jade sipped her drink. "Fight or flight. You do what you need to survive. When you two ran to the car, I got ahead of the crowd and told everybody, like, 'hey, I know them, that's Oren and his troubled son, Chris, and they're in a big fight, so, like, Chris was just trying to make his dad angry...' making up something vague like that. I probably shouldn't have used their real names, but it's fine. Half the people were too busy grabbing cash off the sidewalk, but the family was like, 'yeah, leave them alone, we understand.' So, I *am* a shithead for lying to them about all that, but at least Oren and Chris have no idea what happened. Anyway, it worked out *fine*, and you can start here, by the way," Jade finished, chin up, "if you're still looking for who you can trust."

Smith held a sip of their sweet seltzer in their mouth, still processing the thoroughness of Jade's intervention, until they managed to swallow again. "Thank you. Sorry. After Selene called me a liar when I spilled my guts, I thought you'd... I don't know, but you *didn't*. You're the only person who acts like what's happening to me is normal."

"Well, it isn't," Jade confessed and crossed her legs. "To the extent that there *is* a normal, you're not it. Obviously, you're connected to something bigger, but you're living in a body you didn't ask for. Certain people might empathize with that, if you understand what I mean. You *were* me."

"Yeah." Smith recalled their moment alone in the bathroom as Jade, tempted to spend all night hiding away from Colton and talking to themself. "Thank you, again. You're not too bad, for a frilled lizard."

Jade laughed. "You're welcome, again. And after last night, you owe me one, so I'm cashing in."

"What?"

"One favor," Jade pointed behind Smith towards the garage and the ongoing Kink Night event. "I told a friend about you. He has some questions, and a few answers if you're lucky." Jade stood, pushed in her barstool, and tilted back her seltzer can.

"Wait!" Smith rushed to stop her, but she finished the drink too fast. "Jade?"

They waited, eyes wide, ready for Jade to crush the can against the bar top as Waite overtook her body. Instead, Jade placed the can delicately on the rubber bar mat next to the straws. She made the same frilled lizard gesture with both hands at her neck. "Still me. People finish a *lot* of drinks here. They don't all get possessed, right?"

"Yeah. Yeah, true."

"How am I figuring this out faster than you? C'mon, catch up." Jade took Smith's hand. They prayed Chris missed her pulling Saint away down the short hallway. Deeper, slower music seeped from the garage. In the last seconds before Jade dragged Smith back into the dark, Georgie exited one of the bathrooms and shook his hands dry. He gasped at Jade's tall black boots.

"Jade! Okay, step on me? Just kidding, unless?" Georgie winked aggressively. Jade bowed her head and smiled. Georgie redirected towards Smith. "No, actually, step on them. They deserve it, I promise."

"Hey!" Smith couldn't think of more to say before Jade led them into the garage. Through the closing door, Georgie raised both middle fingers and shuffled backwards towards the bar.

"Oh, *there* you are!" A new voice drew Jade and Smith to a tall wooden X-frame, erected flush against the closed garage door. Two metal cuffs from the frame's upper arms bound the pink-heeled woman's wrists above her head, preventing her from turning to face them. A man with a blonde crew cut stood behind her with a riding crop, brushing the flap of its end down the stitches of her corset, lower and lower, to the reddened marks already on her rear. The man, who wore a cherry-red silk dress, leaned close to her.

"More, then?"

She nodded, and he flicked the riding crop. She moaned through her teeth. He continued but lent half his attention to Jade. "Ooh, so *this* is the one?"

"Sure is," Jade confirmed. "Smith, meet Ember."

Smith almost introduced themself, but Ember spoke too fast. "Yes, *Ember*. I know, it suits a *firecracker* like myself, but unlike this grave-faced doll at your side, I can't take credit for my name. Short for 'December,' courtesy of two parents who spent the late nineties smoking shitty weed laced with who-knows-what and meth, but don't let that fool you! I turned out completely normal, as you can see." Ember spun his riding crop inches from Smith's face, then struck the back of his partner's bare thigh.

She stifled another moan, then laughed. "Yeah, the word I was thinking was definitely 'normal.'"

"Shh!" He pressed a finger to his lips. "Natalia, darling, I'll be *conversating* a few minutes. Jade has brought me a fantastic surprise. Can you hang in there for me?"

She nodded. "I'll be patient for you."

"Lovely. Now, to *you*." Ember studied Smith from head to toe. His fierce eye contact threatened to burn holes into Smith's head. "After the ruckus downtown last night, Jade told me *all* about you. Potions, possessions, amnesia, oh my! May I touch your face?"

"My face?" Smith gulped. "Yeah, sure."

Ember cradled Smith's jaw with one hand and posed their head from side to side. "I'll be gentle, for now. How do you call yourself?"

"Um..." Smith glanced at Jade for guidance.

"*Pronouns?*" she mouthed. A great question.

Smith pursed their lips. "Right. I don't know. They-them, I guess."

Ember tutted and seized Smith's palm. He traced its lines, released it, then grabbed the other one. "I know *Saint* uses they-them. I want yours, not theirs."

"You know Saint?"

Ember rolled his eyes, and his head rolled with them. "My good friend June says Saint has the voice of a hip-hop angel. Besides, darling, no one this cute comes to Arcana without me getting to know them. And I don't *only* mean that in the slutty way; I have depth. I think deeply about things, so many things, including you! You're the spirit who took over poor Jade, Oren, Saint, and whoever else. Your aura is steeped in so many tones of the rainbow. Now, how do you call yourself? And I'm asking you, Smith, not Saint. Gender, love, do you have it?"

"Not... specifically?" Smith floundered. "I don't want to make my identity more confusing than it already is. I wear a lot of hats, but it's easiest to just think of myself using they-them."

"Ah! They think, therefore they are." Ember snapped his fingers in excitement. "Jade, who said that? Who thought and therefore 'ammed?' No, not Kant. Descartes? It *was* Descartes! I'm a genius, bitch. Hierophant supreme. Now, Smith, can you control who you'll next become when you finish that carbonated elixir?"

Smith clutched their glass of pomegranate seltzer, having almost forgotten it. "No."

"Ah, wayward spirit! Let me be your guide back to the astral plane." Ember ran one hand down Smith's side, lingering over the cold skin at their waist. "Sorry, I get handsy when I'm high, but the ideas are flowing. My parents, the hippie dirtbags they are, raised me in a whirlwind of new-age eco-mysticism and quasi-indigenous pagan spirituality, in case you missed the vibes I'm broadcasting to your brain right now. You can hear them, can't you? Don't answer that with words. The point is, I had a point. I was venturing *somewhere* with this.

Whatever my point is, if there's any difference between what's real and what isn't, my parents never taught me to distinguish it. My mind is open to believing that what exists is as strange as what doesn't. Your wildest fantasies are no more extravagant than the secrets whispered between two slime molds. Every law of physics in this dimension has a law of mayhem in another, right? But you're not that lost. You're in the same real world as me and Jade. You're not an outsider if we're all here together. Sure, you're stuck borrowing bodies, but everyone has to sleep on couches once or twice. We'll get your body back, won't we, Smith?"

Ember sounded like Waite, only less menacing and more sexual. Smith doubted he could resolve their identity crisis better than Jade or anyone else, but his attention and effort cocooned them in warm platitudes. The unrelated threads wove together, not forming a complete tapestry, but maybe the corner of one.

"I don't need my own body," Smith asserted. They revisited their first moment, when that tequila sank into Andy's body. Smith still reeled from the abruptness of awakening into this frenzy of kegs, kinks, and karaoke, having forgotten whatever dreams came before. They didn't know how dreams felt. They didn't even know the sensation of sleep, nor did they crave it. "Even if I had my own body, it would be wasted on me. No matter how many times I drink, how many bodies I borrow, I'm the same person, starting over, directionless."

"Can't you try to remember?" Jade questioned them this time. "Remember something from *before*?"

"Before?" Smith couldn't imagine.

Ember's eyes widened. "Darling, don't tell me you're a ghost, now. You'll make a necrophile of me, and fuck *knows* I have enough perversions to manage already."

Jade raised one hand and cleared her throat. "*Spectrophile* is ghosts. Necrophile is corpses."

Ember planted his hands on his waist. "My mistake, Jade. Easy for me to forget there's a twisted little fanfic nerd under all that Tim Burton makeup."

"Bite me."

Jade and Ember squinted at one another. This *did* seem to be the venue for one to bite the other. Eventually, Ember snapped out of it. "Smith, here's a new direction for you: Drink."

Smith took several gulps from their glass before wondering why they owed Ember their obedience. Maybe his omnipresent riding crop left an unspoken threat on the table. Smith drank more, careful to leave at least one sip.

Meanwhile, Ember loosed the restraints on Natalia's wrists. She stretched her arms, greeted Jade and Smith, then kissed Ember's cheek. He stood with his back to the wood and set his riding crop upright against the base of the X-frame.

"Ace of wands," Jade muttered.

"Jade, care to do the honors?" Ember lifted his arms. "Count yourself among the lucky few I've asked to tie *me* up."

Jade obliged and fixed the metal cuffs to Ember's wrists. "For the record, Ember, this does nothing for me, but I wouldn't tell you if it did."

"Noted," Ember smirked. "Smith, are you comfortable participating in something experimental? Elemental? Extra-special?"

"Maybe," they figured, glad not to be the one tied up. "What's the experiment?"

"Willpower, desire, and initiative. Freestyle witchcraft with a blindfold and a dartboard, aiming for an unlikely bullseye. There may be a touch of spit play involved, but you'll control the action."

"Hot," said Natalia, watching from the sidelines. "Don't look at me. I never know what he's on about."

Smith stepped up to the foot of the X-frame. "What's the purpose, then?"

Ember looked upwards, into the heavens. "Summoning your friend, the other spirit. Jade tells me dear *Waite* is one naughty wildcard, and that's not just a tarot pun. I'd like to welcome them to the party, if you'll extend an invitation."

Smith took a deep breath, less than eager to summon a total asshole. "We can't control it, the way we arrive. Some nights I'm here, and some nights I'm not. It's the same for Waite, I think. It's random."

"*Nothing* is random," Ember chided. "Now, come spit in my mouth. Yes, really. The last sip of your drink. Take it all in your mouth, then spit it into mine. That way, *I'll* finish the drink, and we'll see if this spell hits its lucky mark."

Smith deferred again to Jade, who shrugged. "Consent is the name of the game. Your call, Smith."

"Who's *Smith*?" Georgie asked Jade, wandering between booths. Natalia pointed to Smith. "You mean Saint? Oh, if this is a roleplay, y'all have at it. No shame, but I don't need to see this go down." Georgie rejoined Oz on the stage.

Smith gazed into their seltzer, raised their glass, and poured its last ounce into their mouth. The last few bubbles sizzled on their tongue, ready to purge Smith from Saint's body. They almost swallowed, but curiosity propelled them to take a chance. They steadied themself with one hand behind Ember's neck, locked their lips to his, and let the sweet pomegranate flavor spill into his mouth when it opened. Smith pulled away. Ember swallowed it all.

VI
THE LOVERS

VI: THE LOVERS

"**D**id it work?" Smith asked. Ember looked up at the restraints on his wrists. His biceps tugged and stiffened, nearly lifting himself off the ground to pull free. Failing at that, he sized up Smith and Jade, but Jade stared right back. She stepped close and studied his sour face.

"Ember?"

He leaned his head back against the X-frame. "I need another drink. Could one of you help me out?"

Smith knew better. "Holy shit. Waite?"

"Fucking *wicked*," Jade whispered.

Smith couldn't believe their luck, if luck had anything to do with it. Despite Ember's scrambled smoothie of conflicting beliefs, his awkward ritual bore fruit. Now, Ember's absence left Smith and Jade without their mad wizard to consult. In his place, an irritated Waite raised their eyebrows at Saint's sequined outfit.

"Smith? I said I'd see you in the next one, but I never thought I'd see so *much* of you." Waite licked their lips and wiped their mouth on the shoulder of Ember's red dress. "I would ask you what the fuck you're wearing, but a better question is what the fuck *I'm* wearing. Okay, say something. You're not still mad about the burned girl's funeral, seriously? I only said what everyone in that crowd was thinking. I can do and say what I want, same as you can. Besides, what's the point of holding a grudge when we can always start over, in new flesh? Now drop your bad-cop act and get me out of this thing."

Smith tightened their fists, tempted by the riding crop and Waite's inability to fight back. Before they could engage, Jade pulled them aside. Natalia took a drag of her vape pen and concealed them all in a cloud of fruit-scented mist. Jade lowered her voice.

"Smith, I don't see how Waite can be such a dick if you're *not* one. I thought neither of you had any memories?"

"We don't," Smith insisted. "Aside from muscle memory, we're blank."

Jade shook her head. "No one's blank, not even you. You're neurotic and anxious for a reason. Waite must be pissy and cruel for a *different* reason, so what's his deal?"

"His?"

Jade glanced at Waite through the vapor cloud. "*Their* deal? *Her* deal? Did Waite ever say?"

Smith shrugged. "I was trying to tell Ember, I don't think we *can* have genders without memories, but 'they' seems a good neutral option for both of us."

"It isn't neutral, actually, but that's a problem for later." Jade tapped her foot. "You've only existed for what, a handful of *hours* you can remember? Somehow, you've already got a pretty clear sense of yourself. You might *feel* like a blank slate, but you're not. Neither of you are, and Waite proves that by being so different from you. That means some part of you existed *before*."

Natalia raised one index finger while inhaling another cloud of flavored nicotine. She let it seep from her mouth and nostrils as she spoke. "I majored in psych, so I low-key know the exact thing you're saying. I *did* drop out, but still, my cognitive psychology professor showed us this tree diagram of memory." She opened one palm and pointed to her fingers with her vape. "If you're only missing *episodic* memory, that's like a branch of a branch of a *branch* on the tree. Without it, you'd have a fucked-up tree, but most of your memory is still there. You're alive and growing, just kinda depersonalized."

"Why'd you drop out?" Jade asked.

"They said I threatened the university president at a protest, but they took my words out of context. Expulsion would've been a worse look."

Arms still locked onto the X-frame, Waite gawked at a woman in the corner as she extinguished flaming drops of isopropyl alcohol on a prostrate volunteer's back. Smith wondered what branches of Waite's memory tree remained, transforming Arcana's soil into such bitter fruit. Maybe Smith lost the nihilistic branch of their memory tree, while Waite lost their curious, empathetic, and hopeful branches. Smith wished for partner who could grow something edible, sensible, and gentle from the same frightening earth. Smith's stomach ached. A renewed awareness warned that only their two legs held them upright.

Natalia backed out of Jade and Smith's huddle. "I'm gonna go for another drink. Do y'all want?"

"Yes, please," Smith decided. "A shot, something cheap."

Jade declined. "Is the shot for you, or for Waite?"

Smith shut their eyes. "Waite can be your captive entertainment for the night, but I'm no use here. All of you know more than me, and I'm too 'neurotic and anxious,' anyway."

Jade groaned. "That was me being an ass. You really don't wanna help us figure out why at the same bar, in the same week, two *spirits* showed up?"

Smith hated that word. "Jade, I'm not a 'spirit.' I'm not a ghost, alien, zombie, angel, or demon. I'm not blackout drunk, and I'm not an alter of Saint or anyone else. I don't need a diagnosis, a new name, pronoun, or the right label to solve me. If I'm a person, don't turn me into the subject of some pseudoscientific study. I want other people to look at me and say, 'that's one of us.' Otherwise, I'm tied to the same wall as Waite, and I'm your magic little lab rat."

"Damn, okay," Jade flinched. "I thought you'd want to learn how to control this power, but sure, go have your drink and let it control you instead."

Smith hoped she'd say more, convince them to stay longer, or at least say goodbye, but Jade let the silence stagnate. It was a coarse quiet, barren of the laughs and smooth music that surrounded them. Natalia handed Smith a topped-off shot glass and approached the X-frame. She smiled at Waite. "You hanging in there, love?"

She ran her fingers along Waite's upstretched arm. They bristled. "Until someone lets me down."

"Unless I hear that safe word, you gotta earn it, baby." Natalia pinched and lightly slapped their cheek, winked, and carried her rocks glass away to find a chair. Waite slumped.

Smith sniffed the brownish liquid running over the small glass to their fingertips. Gold tequila, the first sensation of their life, sent shivers through their body. Even stronger than reflexive disgust, Smith yearned to live again in that night, so naive and desperate to succeed as Andy. His problems were nothing compared to this life. Andy had love, friendship, and plans for the future. What could Smith really claim for themself, aside from one lousy hot dog? Leaving Jade to deal with Waite, Smith longed to be punched in the face one more time.

They let the tequila simmer in their mouth before sucking it down.

When Smith's next pair of eyes opened, the same biting vapors of tequila filled their sinuses and welled the same tears. Smith felt no different, and they questioned for an instant whether the drink worked. The horrific thought of remaining trapped in Saint's body—any body, and living with the consequences—scared them at least as much as the alternative.

To Smith's relief, the drink *had* worked. Although the identical shot glass in their hand reeked of tequila, its clear residue marked it blanco, not reposado. Specks of rainwater tumbled from the flaps of Arcana's beige canopy overhead. From standing inside the garage, Smith now sat at the picnic table closest to the main side entryway. A purple rain jacket crumpled as they moved their new arms.

"On the house," A-Bomb quipped from the threshold. He scooped up their empty glass.

"Really?" Smith's new voice fluttered up to a higher pitch than they anticipated.

"No. But I do appreciate you coming back and talking through all the shit, being civil. Ain't no other way folks get unbanned."

Smith wiped their eyes. "Unbanned?"

"Yeah, else you're not getting in here on some busy night a month down the line, stumbling up from Leader Avenue cool as a cucumber. You wouldn't believe the dudes who try that shit. Last April, maybe May, some poser hippie talking all kinds of California broke the fucking sink off the bathroom wall. Right? He wasn't even up in there fucking nobody. On his own, this shithead pulls the whole ass sink off the wall, bends the pipes and everything. Then he tries to be all, 'it just came off, dude,' like this place is coming apart at the seams. It ain't, not for real, that's just our aesthetic." A-Bomb blew his nose in a handkerchief before continuing. "Anyhow, then we were waiting on Oren's cousin to drive through and fix the sink on his way to Tampa, and that same west coast dipshit comes back a week later. I know! I had to physically turn him by the shoulders and put his ass back outside. I ain't tall or nothing, but I'll make a fucker move. He's *still* banned. Liam... some Polish last name with all the high-dollar Scrabble letters, but I ain't forgetting his goofy face. You, though? Ain't half as serious, not for us at least. Not even a broken glass. But you got some aim, punching loverboy right backwards *into* the bar's co-owner. Oren woulda raised more a fuss if you caught him a few rounds earlier in the night."

Silver tequila. Those last few details pulled Smith straight out of the story. Who else could they be, coming back here to apologize for punching somebody into Oren? They wrote her off after the first night, in the fallout of wrecking her relationship with Levi. Of all the frequent flyers at Arcana, how could Smith expect to ever land in the body of an irregular newcomer like Ellesandra?

"I told you?" They wondered at A-Bomb. "Sorry, I mean, I told you who that was I punched?"

A-Bomb nodded. "If I'd known he was your brother, I might've said something when I kicked the two of them out of the bathroom. I try not to assume too much with new folks. We see plenty of throuples here, and that's just the beginning."

Before Smith could pick through any more of Ellesandra and A-Bomb's conversation, the other third of her story presented himself. Levi exited the main barroom into the rain, carrying a glass of pale brown beer. He sat across from Smith at the picnic table, his soaked wavy hair stuck to the top of his neck. Levi didn't sip the beer, only glared at it like he expected it to boil. Smith could almost see words piling up behind his lips.

Taking the hint, A-Bomb slunk inside to leave them both some privacy.

"Was the tequila blanco any better?" Levi began.

It wasn't, but Smith would've suffered another round to hand the reins back to Ellesandra. Did Levi invite her to talk, or did she invite him? Either way, this delicate encounter didn't belong to Smith.

"Did you read my texts?" Levi finally tasted his beer. "I know the first ones were long."

"No," Smith said, too late to go through Ellesandra's phone.

Levi took a deep breath. "I was thinking, it's been almost three years since Andy invited me to Thanksgiving. You spilled green beans all over your dress, then you wore a navy-blue T-shirt the rest of the night. You told that joke about the traveling nurses and made me spit out my drink in front of everyone."

Smith hid their hands under the table. "Were you his date?"

"No. No, I was his *friend*, I swear. We were never... We didn't call it anything else. Not until he blew up on New Years. You have no idea how bad I wish I'd told you before that night. I didn't think of him as something real. I thought it was over, not just with him—that *had* been over for me and him. After New Years, I thought you'd never speak to me again. You didn't at first. You listened, though, like this."

Smith needed more. "Do you remember what you told me?"

"Sorry. I don't mean to rehash it all." Levi gnawed at his lip. "I told you everything. I *thought* it was everything, back then. Maybe I was in denial about what went on in college. It seemed like everyone I knew was *close* with their best friends. It wasn't one time with him; that *was* a lie, and I'm sorry. You deserved to know when New Years happened. Fuck, I mean, you deserved to know from the beginning! I was fucking scared. I was so scared of losing you—*both* of you. And now that I have, I know I was only ever scared of myself. Of what it meant to feel that way."

"New Years..." Smith tried to imagine the party, the three of them, too many drinks, all the light and sound. When Levi confessed his history with Andy, where were he and Ellesandra standing? What did Andy say to set it off?

Smith picked their next question carefully. "Was that the first time you came out to someone?"

Levi laughed, sniffed, and drank. He pretended not to hide his eyes. "It's not how I wanted it. 'Hey, I love you, I fucked your brother, I'm bisexual, happy New Year' doesn't make for a great coming out story, does it?"

"Well, no." Smith tried not to laugh. "Did I say it back?"

Levi hesitated. "Which...?"

"The 'I love you' part."

"Yeah. You said it back." Levi lifted his elbows off the table.

"If I said it, I meant it, right?"

Levi reached one hand out from the canopy and let raindrops pool in his palm. "If I'd told you everything back then, maybe you wouldn't have. Maybe last month would never have happened. I let myself keep it separate for too long. I think if you let a secret torture you, it spreads like mold, getting harder to wipe clean until you start to decompose. I should've come clean from the start, for you, but I couldn't even do it for myself. Don't just forgive me."

Smith brought their hands back up and laid them flat on the table. "What are we doing here?"

"What?"

"Here. Why are we here together, right now?" Smith meant to sound literal, but it came across as profound.

Levi let the rainwater leak away through his fingers. "You... invited me here."

"I invited *you*." Smith assumed the rest. "All of you. The good parts *and* the shitty parts. I didn't invite you here to pretend you're someone you're not. People do shitty things when they're scared, in case you missed the part where I punched my brother in the face. Being afraid doesn't make you shitty; it makes you a person. You and me, we're both here, in this fucking rain, wet and embarrassed and sad because clearly we both see past the shittiness in each other. I wouldn't drag myself all the way back here for the tequila, would I? Of course

I'm gonna forgive you. If you wanna stop me, you're gonna have to... I don't know, fuck my brother *again*?"

Levi choked on his beer, coughed, and hunched over the side of the table to spit on the ground. When he sat back up, Smith couldn't tell whether the water in his eyes came from the coughing, the rain, or however he felt about Ellesandra. Smith only hoped they said what she might have.

"New fucking York can have Andy," Levi grumbled. "Elle, you know me in a way he never... *cared* to, even in those years when we were closer. Somehow, you don't hate me for it. How can I walk away from that?"

Smith tensed. "Did I ask you to?"

"No, not actually. Like, the hotel was your call, and it's been good to have time alone, thinking about... things." Levi shook his head. "No, it's really been shitty. I hate it there, and I'm gonna hit the limit on my credit card if I stay another night. I know I can't just ask you to let me—"

"Come back with me?" Smith finished. Even without a clue where Ellesandra lived, they couldn't bear to kick Levi out in the rain. They caught him trying not to smile at the offer.

"I have to pack up the room," Levi leaned out from the canopy again, letting the rain douse his face, "but I can check out tonight." The drops fell smaller and slower than before, floating down around the streetlights like lazy fireflies. Walking wouldn't be too miserable.

"I'll come with you," Smith proposed. "After you finish your drink. Did you close your tab?"

Levi nodded and drank the last of his beer. Tiny rivers of rainwater snaked along the edges of the street, distracting Smith from Levi for a second or two. When they looked back at him, he slumped. His eyes drifted across the table, unfocused. Timid and cautious, he mirrored Smith's concern.

"Don't look at me like that," Levi scolded them.

"Like what?"

"Like you know what I'm thinking."

"What?" Smith scoffed, unsure what set him off. "That's not what I'm doing."

"That's what *everyone* does. They can tell I shouldn't be here. They can tell I don't wanna be. They can tell..." Levi stopped playing with his empty glass. *His empty glass.* "Are you... Smith?"

"Waite!?" Smith slammed their arms on the damp table. All the meaning and care and sincerity of their talk with Levi evaporated into nothingness. They lifted themself upright, gravity pulling ten times harder than usual. "Whenever I'm on the edge of actually figuring myself out or doing something good for somebody, you show up, and everything gets fucked. You always find a way to ruin it for all of us. Congratulations, Waite, now neither of us wants you to be here. If I buy you a drink, will you finish it and fuck off?"

Waite's tongue curled, readying whatever vile comeback Smith imagined. Then, their smirk twitched, vaporized, and sunk into a blank frown. Waite hunched into the same uncomfortable, restless stance that first helped Smith notice them. When Waite finally spoke, even the soft rain nearly drowned them out.

"I changed my mind," they said. "I don't want to die anymore."

Smith wrapped their hands tight around each other, unable to squeeze another word out. Waite wrung out a wet strand of Levi's hair.

"Smith, they kept me up on that thing for a long time. They asked me questions, on and on for so long. Do I feel pain? Am I human? Am I *evil?* It hurts being alone and not knowing. You're right about that. I don't know why I thought I could handle this myself forever. You won't believe me when I say this, but I *wanted* you there. Even though you don't like me, I know you're stuck wondering all the same things about us. If I can't drink my way out of that pain, at least I can share it."

Smith could only guess what Jade did to break Waite. Then again, Smith *let* Ember finish their seltzer. Smith summoned Waite into the trap. Smith *wanted* to punish Waite. For the second time in one night, Levi sat contrite in front of Ellesandra, asking forgiveness.

"I'm sorry," Smith conceded. "You made me angry, but leaving you tied up wasn't fair."

"I'm sorry I haven't listened to you," Waite countered. They extracted the contents of Levi's pockets and set his wallet on the table. "I can't know who I am, but I can learn who *they* are. The people we borrow. I can learn them, the way you do it, if you'll help me."

Smith opened the wallet and tapped Levi's license photo. "We're *lovers*."

"What?"

"Kidding. We're Ellesandra and Levi, and we've been together for years. We're here making amends because you've been hooking up with my brother and lying about it."

"Figures," Waite said.

Smith drew a white plastic card from the wallet's top pocket. Golden script lettering across its center read *Apple Grove Hotel*. "This must where Levi's been sleeping, since she kicked him out," they explained. Smith took Ellesandra's phone from her raincoat pocket, and it welcomed her fingerprint. On a glowing map screen, they typed the address from the card and showed Waite. "See? Three blocks away."

"Sleeping sounds scary," Waite said. "Have you tried it yet?"

Smith hadn't truly considered the option. "Scary or not, Levi should sleep. You can walk him there, drink yourself gone, and he'll be no more of a confused wreck than he was an hour ago."

Waite rotated the phone on the table, aligning the map with the streets around Arcana. They spun it again, then another time, until the screen dimmed into black. Smith tucked the phone inside Ellesandra's back pocket.

Waite rubbed their hands together. "Will you walk with me?"

Smith steeped out from the picnic table, unfurled their purple hood over their head, and extended a reluctant hand to Waite. "I think that's the first time you've asked me to do anything with you."

Waite accepted their hand, skin cold and damp from catching the rain. "Look at us," Waite remarked, "lovers, making amends."

"Easy," Smith warned.

"I'm joking. I *can* joke, Smith."

"You can try."

They led Waite to the misty edge of the sidewalk, across the empty main road, and up a smaller street north. Only a few parked cars lined the curb, water beading and rolling down their glass. A block further, the heartbeat soundtrack of Arcana faded. Counting the blocks, studying the unlit entrances of closed businesses, and tracking the map on Ellesandra's phone, Smith forgot to let go of Waite's hand. They shivered, let go, and stuck their hands in their pockets.

"Here," Smith announced. A yellow *Apple Grove* sign in the same gold script beamed over them from a sleek, white-paneled facade. Smith ducked inside a glass revolving door. Waite shuffled in behind them, pushing Smith into the metal bar as the door swept them inside.

"Sorry," Waite chattered. Their soaked shoes squeaked across the clean marble floor of the lobby. Behind a front desk adorned with huge fake plants, an employee on the phone ignored them. Aside from plastic plants and the low ceiling, the entryway composed every brilliant illusion of excess and extravagance. Smith and Waite slowed to marvel at the soft brightness of it, compared to Arcana. Smith heard their own footsteps echo for the first time.

Waite pressed the tarnished bronze *up* arrow at the elevator. They poked again and again, but nothing happened.

"Oh, the card," Smith realized. "In your wallet."

Waite shook out their pocket. Levi's wet wallet slapped the ground. Smith grabbed it, scanned the keycard, and opened the elevator.

"Too cold," Waite complained as they rose towards the fourth floor. Smith gripped the rail at the back of the elevator to steady themself.

"Yeah. Your clothes are soaked through."

Two doors down the fourth-floor hallway, Smith dipped the card in a slot, and an electronic lock clicked open. The lights in the room were already on. A small suitcase lay open on the carpet, clothes splashed in every direction. A clump of white sheets and pillows piled on one corner of the unmade bed. Two open bottles of whiskey—one empty, another almost—shared the nightstand with a lamp and unplugged alarm clock.

"Oh, wow," Waite exclaimed before reaching the bedroom. They wandered instead into the bathroom and flicked on the light. "I've never seen a shower before."

"Me neither." Smith followed them to see it: frosted glass doors, chrome fixtures, and slate gray tiles. Aromas of sandalwood and vanilla saturated the air. Before Smith could protest, Waite lifted Levi's sodden black T-shirt over their head and threw it onto the floor. They dropped his phone on the quartz countertop, so close to the edge that it nearly fell. Waite reached inside the open shower and cranked the knob to the hottest setting.

"Too cold," Waite hissed. White light reflected off their slickened, tense shoulders. "Fuck, I'm so cold."

"Give it a second," Smith cautioned, and Waite turned the knob partway down. Smith took off their shoes and hung Ellesandra's purple raincoat on the bathroom door. When they reentered the bathroom, the rest of Levi's clothes draped over the corner of the sink. Waite stood behind the hazy glass, head high under a stream of hot water. They laughed and raised a gleeful hand over the top of the sliding door. "Smith, it's like *paradise*. You need to feel this."

Smith caught Ellesandra's blue-gray eyes in the sink mirror. Warm fog from the shower masked her face, and she faded behind its condensation.

Smith took off their clothes—sweater, bra, jeans, everything. Before the air-conditioned cold could wrap itself around them, Smith extended one hand into the shower to test the warm rain. Waite guided Smith's hand into the stream from behind the glass. Smith let Waite pull them further. Steam and the faint scent of metal coated their face. It *was* paradise. They stepped inside, and the glass door rolled shut.

Water flattened their hair and poured down their back. Smith grinned. "It's like a hug."

"Like being kissed by the rain," Waite said.

Smith opened their eyes. "You remember that? When I kissed Ember, you felt that?"

The narrow space from the glass to the tile wall left only inches of shared warmth between their bodies. Waite touched their lips. "I remember the second part, right after. I wasn't there for the first part."

The water split and ran down Waite's reddened cheeks. It clung to their mouth. The wordless hiss of the shower whispered to Smith, urging them to refresh Waite's memory. "The first part was like *this*."

Smith pulled Waite under the showerhead by their waist and kissed them again. Not even the thin veil of water separated their skin. The gentle impact of such complete contact rippled down Smith's body. Waite's hand slid up their back and gripped their neck, holding their lips together. Together, drawing inward under the steaming downpour, Smith resolved not to escape for a breath. They'd see who drowned first.

Smith spun Waite's back to the tile wall and leaned their hips closer. The tip of Waite's tongue slipped into Smith's mouth. Their hands raced over Smith's body, reaching lower, and Smith grabbed back, as if they'd tear apart otherwise. Smith raised one knee up along the tile. Waite's fingers snaked under their thigh, holding their leg right there.

Right there.

The heat and pressure magnified in the air and under their skin. Another gentle pressure touched once between Smith's legs. Waite gasped. Smith trusted the swelling tissues and the will of their body more than they trusted Waite.

"Should we?" Smith whispered into Waite's mouth, hoping for Levi's answer.

Waite's other hand lifted Smith from beneath, angling closer, tighter, harder.

"I want you to fuck me," Waite demanded, "like I deserve it."

Smith slid their hand down Waite's chest, all the way down. They coiled their fingers, guiding Waite. Smith played with them for another moment, stroking and rubbing their body against Waite's, still pinning them to the tile wall.

"And I want you," Smith countered, "to fuck me like whatever creatures you think we are."

An inch, then another, Smith's core muscles tensed. Their nails dug at the skin of Waite's back. Smith smiled, mouth agape, awed by the music of their own heartbeat in their ears. A few measures into that rhythm, Waite lifted Smith's feet off the ground and pressed them against the wall instead. The cool tiles tickled their back. Their legs wrapped around

Waite's hips. Every kiss promised five more. Every thrust lit fires inside Smith's eyelids.

"I'm here," Smith spoke, almost no energy to spare for it. "I'm really, really here."

In the hot mist and sweat, Smith left none of Waite's skin untouched. Here, as close as possible, they pushed closer. Waite's head rolled back, their open mouth filling with water. Drops beaded down their neck, and Smith licked them away. Each movement begged them each to deliver themselves into an inaccessible space at the center of the universe. Its invisible light pulsed louder and brighter between them.

In a final burst of ecstasy, Smith shook and let the power of their body overcome them. They plunged into a flashing muscle memory of sanctuary, desire, and union.

With a fierce moan, Waite pulled away. Smith watched that same explosive delirium twitch across Waite's body and pour itself free onto their own skin. Smith held themself against Waite, trapping heat that threatened to scald them both. They already missed the chill of the rain outside.

Over Waite's shoulder, in the reflective chrome plate of the shower knob, Smith found Ellesandra's face again. No matter how many times the water tried to wash her away, she remained. Even witnessing nothing, her eyes never stayed closed for long.

VII
HOP IN!
THE CHARIOT

VII: THE CHARIOT

When Smith woke up, they believed for as long as possible that they dreamt it. In the dark, seeing nothing, maybe they had—until the soft hotel sheets caressed their skin. The slow rise and fall of Waite's breath, an arm's length away, broke the rest of the illusion. Could Smith even tell Waite's relaxed, motionless body from Levi's? Facing the window, head in a pillow, Waite didn't scare them. Whatever dragged Smith awake from the brief and dreamless quiet, it reheated and swirled inside their blood. Smith ached for another stretch of sleep that wouldn't come. Their body no longer allowed them to pretend.

Smith rose from the mattress too slowly for Waite to hear. They threaded a winding path across the carpet to the bathroom. Smith picked Ellesandra's clothes from the floor and dressed themself in them, assembling her pieces the way they remembered. Her socks fit too tight on their feet. Her bra strangled their chest and hung unevenly from their shoulders. The costume complete, however uncomfortable, Smith hurried into the hallway and let the door click shut behind them.

01:53, read the clock on Ellesandra's phone. Beneath it, an hour-old text from a group message: *I know it's hard but you deserve a clean break. How'd he take it?*

Smith had no time or willingness to reckon with that message, much less reply. Hallway to elevator, elevator to ground floor, they ran from the hotel lobby's stale air into the cold, humid atmosphere outside. Smith started up the street at first, only switching directions at an unfamiliar intersection. Every minute burned. The sidewalk poured them towards the main road with the last of the stormwater. Smith crossed the empty street without looking either way.

"Back for last call?" A-Bomb asked at Arcana's door. "Where's homeboy?"

"Just me," Smith said. In the whole bar, half a dozen people remained. Smith cut straight towards the orange cooler near the quiet room stairs, separated a plastic cup from a stack, and filled it halfway. They sipped, and for the first time, a drink didn't bite or burn them in return. Smith wanted to cry, but they told themself to wait. They picked the same seat outside at the first picnic table, exactly where their night began. Ellesandra might notice the gap in time or the changed drink, Smith hoped to spare her the rest.

They chugged the rest of the water.

The cup landed empty on the table, nothing changed.

"Oh, fuck," Smith's heart skipped a beat. "Not water, then. Water doesn't work."

Smith scrambled back inside. Preparing to close the register, Alea set down her phone. Smith fished around in Ellesandra's pockets.

"Here," they said and flattened a wadded twenty. "A shot of tequila blanco, please. Keep the change."

Alea's eyes widened. "Aye? Alright, hun. Way to close out the night for both of us."

Smith evacuated to the table with their crystalline shot. *2:01*, Ellesandra's phone told them. They unlocked it and typed a careful answer in the group message—enough to build a story, but not too much to confuse Ellesandra.

He never showed up, they wrote. The bubble of words popped into the chain. The die cast, Smith left Ellesandra where they found her: waiting alone in the dark for closure. Maybe she'd never learn what Smith did with her missing hours. Maybe her body would feel the truth anyway. Smith could only protect her so much from themself.

They downed the tequila.

A new night fell. Purple light washed over them.

Purple.

"Her coat," Smith gasped at the empty IPA can in their hand. "I left her purple raincoat hanging on the bathroom door."

"What?" The man next to Smith laughed and signed a receipt on the bar counter. "Dude, you sound like actual *brain* damage right now."

"Sorry, what was I talking about?" Smith hated dropping into conversations.

"The Neon Sphinx, in West Lewesboro. On the list you sent me, that's the spot you wanted next, right?" The man beside Smith wore a blue pastel buttoned shirt, in a striking departure from the standards of Arcana fashion. His all-white tennis shoes flashed a vibrant purple under the blacklight, and a brown leather belt looped through his gray slacks. Smith's new body and two other men loitering at the dance floor dressed in kind. They looked like a matching quartet of accountants in a business casual boyband.

"The next spot?" Smith wondered how many *spots* preceded Arcana.

"I'm ready when you are," the blue shirt encouraged Smith. "This place is freaky as fuck. Hey, Stu? Is Wayne still in the shitter or did he go pull the car up?" The yellow shirt on the dance floor, Stu, ditched his glass on a table and tilted an ear towards Blue. "Christ, my guy, you're fucking deaf. I said, where's Wayne?"

"Car," Stu answered. "We blowing this popsicle stand, or what?"

"Don't ask me." Blue and Stu waited for Smith.

"Yeah," they agreed, fighting down a hiccup. The string lights jittered, and the walls rocked more than usual. "Neon... Neon Sphinx next?"

"Alright, boss. And hey, there's Wayne."

A boxy gray SUV with knobby off-road tires pulled up outside the entryway. Its wide black bumpers blocked most of the corridor between the beige canopy and a row of occupied parking spaces. Smith left their empty can on a bar mat and followed their entourage to the waiting chariot.

"That was some wild shit in there, dog," said a red shirt in the passenger seat. Smith climbed up the towering car into the seat behind the driver, sandwiching Stu between them and Blue. Soiled napkins, ash, and crumpled water bottles littered the rubber floor mats. The gray cloth seats smelled like weed and cheap air freshener.

The driver, Wayne, rolled the rig forward to the sidewalk. "Right here?"

"Left!" Blue and Red shouted together. Red pumped up the volume of a hip-hop track. Each low note in its bassline rattled the speaker in Smith's door rattled.

Stu glanced back at Arcana's nondescript entrance, already shrinking behind them. "Never knew that place was here. What was it even called?"

"Arcana," Smith contributed, unable to say more before blue spoke his mind.

"Ain't for me, that one. I ain't homophobic or nothing, but people in there be *real* gay, you know what I'm saying? Like, why's that bartender gotta be right in our faces?"

Red laughed. "I mean, that's liberal arts Lewesboro, but fuck if this ain't still Marks fucking County. Go five miles any direction, a guy like him better straighten out real fast."

"Ain't gay shit illegal now?" Wayne asked. "What law was them folks protesting back in July or whenever?"

Red slapped Wayne's shoulder. "They can't make a law against being gay, dumbass."

"Not *yet*," Blue said, "but they did pass that law to ban some shit. Drag queens, pronouns, gender, any of that woke communist shit they were pushing before we took back the White House."

Wayne glared at Blue in the rearview. "They did all that already?"

Stu cut in. "It's a mix of executive orders and state laws. So like, half the states, for some of it. One of our state's bans passed in July, but technically it's on hold while the appeal goes to—"

"Stu, shut up!" Red scooted sideways on the passenger seat. "Wayne gets the point, don't you, Wayne? They're all working on it, so we don't gotta worry about those psycho trans freaks anymore."

Blue kicked Red's seat from behind. "I thought you said you ain't homophobic?"

"I'm literally not. You're not listening. Did I say I hate gay people? No, and that's literally what homophobic means, so suck a dick, kindly."

"*Trans*phobic, Bryce," Stu corrected. "That's what you—"

"Stu, quit trying to make this a thing. I ain't phobic of nobody. I just don't fuck with it, alright? And it's a free country, so I can say what the fuck I want. God bless America, assholes."

"Bryce, cool your jets." Blue leaned over the center console, crushing a plastic bottle under his foot. "Stu's just a little sensitive, so we gotta make a safe space. Okay, everybody? Safe space for Stu. Safe space."

Stu growled. "Bro, I will actually fuck you up, talking like I ain't from your same East Hillbrook High School, ready to stab a motherfucker with a mechanical pencil again. You think I give a shit what you say to me? Y'all're being ignorant. I've got a cousin on my mom's side who's transgender, and he ain't even gay, I don't think. He's a real homie, too. Honestly, y'all'd be so cool with him."

"How the fuck does that work?" Wayne let the steering wheel drift until gravel on the street's shoulder sprayed under the car. "Like, is he, or is *she*, like, a dude?"

"*He* is. And he's a much better driver than you, Wayne."

"Isn't it, like, kinda fucking ironic, though?" Bryce, in the red shirt, pointed backwards from the passenger seat at Smith. "Y'all homos talking all this nasty shit, with the man of the hour sitting back here?"

Blue chuckled. "Why's that ironic?"

"He's getting married, jackoff. To a woman."

Blue adjusted his headrest and reclined. "Oh, really? I had *no* idea. I was just buying everyone's drinks for no fucking reason. And for the record, if anyone cares, that's not how irony works."

Wayne initiated a delicate maneuver, parallel parking the oversize SUV in a metered space between two much smaller cars. In the verbal firestorm and the daze from an unknown number of drinks, Smith didn't track which roads carried them to this new area. Relentless thumps from so many stereo speakers only worsened their dizziness. The SUV rocked forward and backward, jolting Smith's seatbelt each time Wayne shifted gears. Bit by bit, the vehicle squeezed into its space. Discordant parking sensor beeps joined the crescendo of Wayne's shouting.

"Am I close? Bryce, can you look out if I'm gonna hit the curb?"

"You're still half in the street. Like two...*four* feet on this side."

"Two or four?"

"Fuck if I know, man. You think I got sonic eyeballs?"

Smith could no longer ignore the sickness of their new body and its companions. They unbuckled their seatbelt and opened their door. A pickup truck swerved to avoid it. Its horn blasted. Stu seized Smith's arm to hold them inside, and Blue yelled:

"Hunter! The fuck?"

Smith vomited out onto the running board. The volume of several mismatched beers and liquors drained itself from Hunter's body.

"Ay, whoa!" Wayne mashed the brakes.

"Did it get on the paint?" Bryce craned his neck over the center console. "Stu, did he get any on the paint? That shit'll corrode."

"Now it's a real bachelor party!" Blue slapped Smith's leg as they spit and wiped their face. "Now he's all clear and ready for more, right Hunt?"

"Yeah. Yeah, man," Smith coughed. An escape drink didn't sound too bad.

Eventually, Wayne wrangled the car into its space at a skewed angle. He spared at least a foot from each tire to the curb, but none of the other guys pointed it out. Wayne and Bryce jaywalked across the road while Blue paid the parking meter. Stu guided Smith to the opposite sidewalk.

"It was the same for mine last year," Stu said. "Went to Nashville with my old crew, Liam and those guys. Pretend to drink if you gotta, but the wolfpack probably won't quit until you're fucking comatose, bud."

Sandstone cladding on the building's outer walls matched the mid-century downtown aesthetics of this cleaner, denser stretch of the city. Tall grasses in giant planter boxes lined the road, each blocking much of the sidewalk's width. Wavy metal benches with arms in the middle graced certain storefronts. The Neon Sphinx presented a towering streetside facade, despite its single floor. Two white decals of Egyptian sphinxes spanned the bar's doors. On the tinted front windows, six copies of the same poster repeated a message in orange and green letters: *Last Call! We are relocating to Virginia in the coming months. Thank you Lewesboro for five great years.*

"They're closing?" Smith read the poster again. Blue caught up to them and Stu.

"Yeah? You literally said so earlier, man. That this place is gonna be wild because they're going out of business or whatever, right?"

"Right, yeah," Smith said. Their legs wobbled across the threshold into the bar. Inside, its ceilings climbed higher, its music rang crisper, and its clean walls sported colorful psychedelic murals, unlike Arcana's grim ornamentations. A few guys in T-shirts shuffled around a pool table in the back corner. A line of college students lounged across the benches that bordered the dance floor, where most patrons spun or sang along to a sugary pop song. Drinks overtopped the cups in their elevated hands.

"Jesus Christ," Blue hissed. "Seven-dollar mixed drinks is a fucking disgrace of a special. You see the size of the cups?"

Bryce shrugged. "Shots, then?"

"Sure. Hunter, shots! What do you want? Yo, Hunter. Hunter?" Blue dragged Smith's arm towards the bar, almost toppling them. He laughed, shook his head, and let Smith fall into a high-top chair. "Fine, get yourself together. Whiskey shots, boys? Stu, Byrce, whiskey? If you want mixed drinks, buy your own. This place is going bankrupt and can't even gimme an actual discount. Hi, yeah. You're so beautiful. Three shots whiskey?"

Smith let a zombielike impulse pull them into the restroom: a double hinged door, two urinals, and a stall. The mirror revealed their new face, Hunter, his skin almost as pale as his half-unbuttoned shirt under white LED bulbs. His hairy chest sweat through the synthetic fabric. Smith leaned on the sink and fiddled with the buttons until they felt less exposed. A new high tide of nausea rose. Smith unbuttoned their shirt the rest of the way and splashed cold water on their face. They slurped a few mouthfuls of water from the sink and spat out the last one.

In the mirror, Smith saw a Hunter drowned by booze, a man alone within his crowd of friends, and an animal in a costume. From deep in their chest, a laugh sprayed water from their lips across the mirror. Minutes after leaving the hotel room, Smith took the form of someone's husband-to-be. Jumping from Ellesandra to Hunter quenched the heat and hid the consequences of last night. Given every opportunity to let loose and enjoy a true party, Smith's body refused.

"Is it my body, or me?" Smith whimpered, grinding their teeth. They slapped more water over their face. Hunter wouldn't cry here, Smith told themself. He wouldn't let his friends see him this way, drunk or not. "This is good. I'm good. I'm good."

The door swung in. Wayne towered over Smith, sober eyes surveilling the scene.

"You hanging in there, boss?"

"Yeah," Smith lied. "Sorry about your car. I can grab some of these paper towels to wipe it down, or—"

"Nah, rain'll come back soon. Hell, this is your party. Ain't no cleanup you gotta worry about."

Smith dried their face and crumpled the wad of brown paper towels. The rest of the roll soaked in a pool of water on the sink counter. "Why do we do all this? Honestly, why?"

"Cause it's fun?" Wayne tried. "I ain't drinking no more, but you know I cut loose back in the day. Making a memory mess, my uncle calls it. He done some bad shit, though. Man robbed a gas station to buy pills and let a buddy cut off his pinky finger for a dare."

Smith banished the image from their head. "It's sick, though. You get the pills, but you get arrested. You win the dare, but you lose the finger. If the only way to win that game is to keep playing, robbing, and drinking, what if winning isn't the point?"

"Man, Hunt..." Wayne whistled and opened the door with his foot. "I'mma pop outside for a smoke."

Smith took their opportunity to poke around Hunter's phone. Its metal bezels glistened like new. Its glass bore no scratches. Hunter's face unlocked the device, and a few group texts hovered at the top of the messaging app: *Where are y'all*, from Bryce, *Down the stairs bitch*, from someone labeled *Deadbeat*—the blue shirt, Smith guessed. In a private thread, a text from three red hearts warned: *Be safe. Have fun. Don't do anything too stupid. I love you.* Smith put the phone away. They left the restroom like a nervous shoplifter, forbidden loot in one narrow pocket. Smith imagined Hunter's nameless fiancé behind those three red hearts.

Stu, Bryce, and Blue stood like stone pillars in the middle of the dance floor. The crowd split and flowed around them while they hunched over their phones.

"I remember that dude from high school," Stu said. "Wasn't he like two years behind us?"

Bryce shook his head. "One year behind. Our senior prom, so his junior prom, he shows up alone in that weird fucking shirt and gets kicked out. You weren't there, that's right."

"Jackasses like him," Blue muttered, "are exactly the ones who don't make it too long after high school. No use to society, so of course he got fucking blown up."

Bryce tapped his phone. "No, cause that was what they *thought*. But this article I'm seeing, now they're saying the cops got it wrong."

Smith eased into their loose assembly between the dancers. "Are you talking about Hayes?"

Stu nodded, reading from his screen. "Yeah, 'Ulysses Thomas Hayes.' I never knew he had such a wild name. Remember that guy, Hunt?"

"No, I just heard about the crash with him and Jul… his girlfriend, right?" Smith guessed that Hunter wouldn't know her name.

Bryce huffed. "Y'all're too drunk for this. I'm trying to say, there's this article from an hour ago—Stu, did you read it yet?"

"I left my fucking glasses in the car. I'm trying, man."

"Fuck it, I'll read: 'Uh-lee-sis Thomas Hayes, aged 23, was declared dead last week after his vehicle was found…' Whatever, y'all heard this bullshit already. Okay, so… 'Hayes is no longer listed as a victim of the crash. On Friday, the Marks County Sheriff's office and Lewesboro Police issued joint statements confirming that one of the two bodies in the vehicle was *misidentified* and belongs to an individual not yet known to the authorities. A representative of the Hayes family says they were notified earlier in the day, and that—'"

Blue shirt laughed. "Oh, fuck! Didn't they have his funeral already?"

"Hell if I know, dude. I'm just reading the article. You think I know more than what's here? But that's only half of it. The police statement says they don't know where Hayes is. He might be dead, maybe not, but he's still missing, and they wanna bring him in for questioning."

"Yup," Blue shirt whistled. "Bet he fucking killed her. Murderer on the run."

"Who's the other body, though?" Smith asked. "In his van, with his girlfriend, who died if it wasn't Hayes?"

Bryce threw his arms up. "Y'all, I'll say it again, I do *not* fucking know."

"Yeah, shithead," Blue said, "so do some speculating. *Conversate* with us."

Stu put his phone away. "Like, sure, *we're* gonna be the ones who solve a murder, *if* that's what it was."

Bryce snaked an arm around Stu's shoulders. "It's a laugh. We're joking around. Loosen up. And hey, what if we *did* do it? Breaking news from the Lewesboro American: 'local heroes catch killer, collect million-dollar reward and unknown amount of pussy.' You're pretty smart. You could solve it, right Stu?"

Stu shrugged off Bryce's arm. "The dead girl is from *Lakeview*. Doubt her folks are putting up a cash reward."

Smith's mind jumped to Colton. The news would find its way to him, if it hadn't already: A misidentified body, a survivor of the crash—not the one he wanted. If anyone stood a chance of finding Hayes faster than the cops, Colton did, and Smith knew where to find *him*. On Thursday night, Colton mentioned his favorite bars. The first name was a bird, and the other started with 'R,' maybe.

"Hey," Smith started to ask Blue, his name still unsaid. "That list, the list of bars I sent you? Can I see it?"

"Sure." Blue opened a screenshot in his camera roll and underhanded his phone to Smith. Arcana made this list, and The Neon Sphinx after it. They zoomed in above those and struck gold: ~~Heron's Landing~~ and ~~The Wreck Club~~. If Hunter's crew hadn't already brushed elbows with Colton at either of his favorite venues, Smith knew where they soon might. They returned the phone to Blue.

"Bryce, you got change for the pool table?" Stu asked.

"You're not playing pool right now, you nerd. Go dance with somebody." Bryce waved Stu in the direction of a group of women, busy posing for photos below a pink neon sign. Blue jabbed Bryce with an elbow.

"Stu's married, sick fuck."

"And what, married guys don't dance? It's just dancing. It's a party. A *bachelor* party, which I guess Stu *ain't* one, but I ain't telling his bitch."

"Dude, chill. He's not like—"

Bryce stepped back, almost knocking a balanced tub of drinkware from a barback's hand. "Why are you speaking for him? Are you his wife now? Let the guy talk."

"Fuck off," Stu tried to laugh, but Bryce wouldn't quit.

"Y'all're so boring, I swear. I need another drink." He waited for Blue.

"Buy your own, man."

"Oh, c'mon. Where were you, three bars ago, swearing up and down you won't let anyone but *you* pay for shit tonight? Don't you wanna feel like a boss, buying the whole party cause you said—What did you say? 'Money comes easy if you're not a dumbfuck,' right? Since you offered *so* nicely, pardon me if I hold you to it."

"Man, relax. You're here for Hunter tonight."

Bryce's goading scored no points, so he pivoted to Smith. "Hunter, buddy, man of the hour. Will you please tell *our* cheapskate friend to buy me a drink?"

Before Smith could hide, play along, or even stutter, Blue dug into a pocket and presented Bryce a quarter. "Flip for it, big guy. Heads or tails?"

"Hey, Stu, guess *he's* got change for the pool table."

"Heads I buy, tails it's on you." Blue flicked the coin off his thumb. It blinked through the air and arced away, inches too far for him to catch. Bryce tried for it, but the coin bounced off the floor and rolled off into a forest of moving feet. Blue and Bryce pushed their way past strangers, chasing it down across the dance floor.

"Are we *all* like them?" Smith asked Stu.

"Like how?"

"Always chasing the next shiny thing?"

Stu ignored them. "Wanna get some air? I think Wayne's still out at the car."

Stu and Smith left the coin-flip duo to settle their beef. As predicted, the giant car waited with lights and engine off in its too-small parking space. Wisps of herbal smoke leaked from the top of Wayne's driver's side window. Stu held the rear passenger door open for Smith.

"Damn, you move like ninjas," Wayne coughed and blew smoke out the window. "I though y'all was cops rolling up. I was ready to show 'em my blue line sticker on the back window, then be all like, 'It's delta, I promise.'"

Wayne's jumble of smelly words sloughed off Smith's brain, unprocessed. Fumes from the wax pen in Wayne's cupholder made them want to vomit all over again. "I don't know if I've ever been this drunk," Smith confessed.

"We should grab food after this place," Stu suggested. "Wayne, you still got that gift card thing from that weird app?"

"That coin app..." Wayne giggled. He leaned back on the headrest and tilted his seat backwards towards Smith. They could smell his hair. "Shit was mad glitchy. My phone got way too hot last time I tried to run that thing. Where'd the boys all go, still inside?"

Smith snapped. "Is this what the rest of my life is gonna be about? Drinking, talking, smoking, getting old, and having sex?"

Wayne sniffed loudly. "Sounds alright. You 'boutta have a hot wife."

"Wayne, don't be a pervert," Stu flicked Wayne's ear. "Hunter, you're gonna be fine. Gonna be a great husband, make a ton of money, have some beautiful kids. You talking like a sad old man just shows you're ready for this."

Living a singular life for one full day—never mind a lifetime, shared with a spouse—terrified Smith at least as much as their broken mosaic of lives. The certainty of every step that Stu narrated, the simple *I love you* text message, and the promise of eternity made Smith's skin ripple with sweat, all at once. Hunter and his fiancé would soon vanish from their docket of concerns. This fear belonged instead to the unspoken vow of whatever cursed fate Smith consummated. The weakest parts of them felt Arcana's magnetism from across town, affording them only one destiny: to cross Waite's path, on endlessly many more nights.

"What happens when we die?" Smith wondered aloud. They meant themself and Waite, but maybe the alcohol meant Hunter or someone else. Stu took his time to consider. Wayne didn't.

"Pearly gates and St. Peter, if you play your cards right."

"Dying won't be something to worry about when you're dead," Stu assumed Smith, "so don't go worrying about it when you're alive."

"Worry about dying a *little*," Wayne countered. "That'll keep you from poking at copperheads. You know how much antivenom costs?"

Outside the left rear window, a pair of silhouettes strode up the opposite sidewalk, hand-in-hand. One wore a fur coat. Smith took it as a sign. However Oren and Twyla found themselves across town, they carried the torch of Arcana's sanctuary. Long-since ready to ditch Hunter's party, Smith fixated on the royal couple and opened the left passenger door. Before they could flee across the street, a speeding flatbed truck clipped the open door. Its two metal hinges popped. Like Jade's hand shearing a page from her sketchbook, the truck cleaved the door off Wayne's SUV.

Only Stu's hand on the back of Hunter's shirt kept Smith inside, clear from the momentary shower of sparks, glass, and metal bits. Across the street, Oren and Twyla gawked at Smith through the empty doorframe. The truck's brakes hissed and shuddered. Bryce and Blue exited The Neon Sphinx across the street, seconds too late to bear witness. For the first time all night, none of the bachelor party's men said a fucking word.

Stu released his grip. Smith slid out of the car, shoes crunching on crumbs of glass. The mangled door spun and skidded until it clipped a curb, fifty feet down the road. The flatbed truck's driver marched around the damaged side of her vehicle, already pressing a phone to one ear. Smith crossed both lanes of the road and waved a friendly hello to Twyla, then Oren.

Neither waved back.

"Do you... need me to call someone?" Twyla opened her bag for a phone.

Oren pointed at the SUV. "That was some metal fucking shit is what that was."

"I just need a drink," Smith told him.

"Hell yeah. You been to Arcana?" Oren retrieved the silver flask from his coat. Smith unscrewed its cap and flipped it open. In case Hunter's bachelor party wasn't already over, Smith drained the flask and sent the aimless, fragile fiasco to its grave.

VIII
STRENGTH

VIII: STRENGTH

The flask became an empty can. It vibrated in Smith's hand, driven by a subwoofer near the garage stage. A sweaty drummer beat their kit, eyes closed. A brittle crack spread between the rings of her rippling brass high hat. A bassist flipped red hair out of their eyes and locked onto some unseen point in the foggy garage air. The band's frontperson shook a lime green guitar, and sticky notes wobbled from wall to wall. The guitarist's vocals buried somewhere in the web of sound, too deep for Smith to decipher any lyrics. The angst and physicality of the band said enough.

A cold hand brushed Smith's hip. "Always better seeing them live," someone with angular neck tattoos told them. The drawstrings of her bright green hoodie swung as she danced.

"Yeah," Smith agreed, still riding the distressing high of dodging the flatbed truck. Speaking felt weird, but they tried to elaborate. "I like the drummer!"

No, it wasn't *speaking* that felt weird. Smith *hadn't* spoken, and neither had the girl in the green hoodie. Her words cycled into Smith's brain, same as ever, but not though their two plugged ears. The conversation occupied an almost telepathic channel, invisible until Smith prepared to speak again. Their hands rose from their sides, almost flinching upwards at attention.

"The fuck?" Smith's mouth spoke for real this time, too soft over the song's chorus. Their new lips and tongue moved fine, but some unusual muscle memory dominated their arms and hands.

"I'll take your can," said the young woman dancing next to Smith. Her fingers formed the words as she mouthed them. Smith read the sentence off her gestures. They relished their new body's awareness of this silent, coded language.

"Thank you," they signed back and handed her the empty can, smiling. "Bathroom," they signed next, one hand twisting in the air. She blazed a trail through the crowd for them both. The song collected itself into one long, fading drone. Applause and shouts at the song's outro rolled like a wind through tall grasses. The door at the back of the room dumped Smith back into the sitting area by the restrooms. Its blue light made a halo over this stranger, an arm's length ahead of them. She pulled down her hood, and Smith recognized her tattoos: the DJ, from their night as Dorian. She continued on to the bar while Smith veered into the first open restroom.

Fuck off, Oren, read the golden marker on the mirror. Behind the messy lettering, Alea's winged eyes reflected at Smith. How did she know the DJ from the other night?

"Hello," Smith began, testing their voice while studying the smooth black gauges in their ears. "I'm Alea. I'm a bartender, and Oren keeps me busy. I run events. You should come to our next Kink Night. Nice to meet you, I'm Alea. People *know* me here. Actually, I'm here with so-and-so, she's my... friend? I don't know."

Smith checked the pockets of Alea's golden-brown trench coat. They collected a bottle opener, a ring of keys on a lanyard, a clip of plastic cards, a rechargeable electric lighter, an unopened pack of cigarettes, three printouts from a photobooth, a safety-locked mini pepper spray, seven one-dollar bills, a small tube of superglue, a kazoo, and finally, a phone—not the easy kind that recognized a face or thumb, but a sturdy retro model with a sliding keyboard.

Smith tried a passcode of straight zeroes, but a vigorous buzz denied the attempt. They pocketed the phone, spun around once, and hoped for a fresh try. If Alea's hands remembered sign language, how hard could a passcode be?

"Oh, did you hear that?" Smith pretended, clearing their thoughts in the mirror. "I got a text. Let's see who it is."

They tried to summon the phone instead of grabbing it, leaving no room to overthink. It worked. Alea's hands mashed the keys so fast that Smith missed the passcode completely. Her unlocked phone *arrived* in their hand. On its compact LCD window, rows of text chains scrolled by the click of an arrow key. Names, unfinished conversations, and half a dozen new messages dangled more threads than Smith could dream of unraveling.

> *stg i never thought shed be the one to call me...*
> *Hey, did Beau leave a pair of shoes at the ho...*
> *Perfect!*
> *Your authentication code is 898011. Do not s...*
> *my bad*
> *i like there music but the vibe is kinda someth...*
> *See a new post from your friend! https://mobi...*
> *what time though?*
> *Grace M. laughed at "one of these guys must...*
> *FedEx: A package from RES LOCAL FREE S...*
> *literally can't*
> *Cool be there in a min*

Like her pockets, Alea's phone carried too much. For the first time, the answers to Smith's universe outnumbered their questions. Smith hated that imbalance as much as its inverse.

"Pockets full, phone full..." Smith signed the words to themself in the mirror and gave up scrolling. For the first time, the tiny bathroom looked like an infinite puzzle box. The entire world shared the space with Smith, stickered and scribbled across four black walls in a thousand shades, shapes, numbers, names, and web addresses.

"It's not noise," Smith assured themself. "It's not torture. It's not random. Why am I back here, every time, at Arcana? I'm being born here, over and over, me and Waite. Is it just us here, surrounded by words that mean nothing to us?"

Smith grabbed the door handle to leave. A fresh line of handwriting in thin blood-red paint glimmered above the door handle. Its wavy, broken lettering stood out too bright to miss:

A thief trumped death. Lesser for it?

Nowhere more so that the bathrooms, Arcana's walls sported an abundance of scripted poetry, lyrics, and quotations. To Smith, none signified anything more important than another, same as Alea's unread texts. One more phrase on that canvas, one more shout in the crowd meant almost nothing.

"*Hayes* trumped death," Smith whispered, wishing they'd read the full article on Stu's phone. At a glance, words were only words, but these letters on the door overtopped the layers of other scribbles and stickers. "Was that there last time?"

Today is Saturday, Alea's phone told Smith. The paint smelled bitter but felt dry. Maybe Colton saw the same article yesterday, or the day before. Maybe his obsession led him back here, painting spiteful messages and wishing Hayes died in Julienne's place.

A hand tapped twice outside the door. Smith plucked the latch and turned the loose handle.

"Hey!" The same woman stood outside, now speaking her words in the glowing blue quiet beyond the garage. "Chris asked if you know where the hurricane glasses are. I told him to ask Oren or Twyla."

"Are they here?" Smith glanced over towards the bar. They owed Oren a whiskey.

"Who knows, girl? This place is owned by its stray cats!"

An auditory jolt from the garage punched the air as the band picked up again. Harsh vocals began the next song's first verse, but a discordant *thump* cut them off, followed by a static buzz of electric noise. A metal *pop* echoed. The woman across from Smith looked confused. All at once, the blue lights, the string lights, the blacklights, and the speakers cut to dark silence.

Gasps, groans, hollers, and shrieks harmonized from every room.

"Fucking circuit breaker?" Someone asked. Others chattered over one another:

"...your phone, the flashlight is..."

"...know who did that?"

"...how you know it's a punk show."

"...just because it's dark in here, you freaks!"

The door from the garage flung open. A louder voice reported from the other side: "The amp's on fire!"

All it took was the word *fire*. Elbows jabbed. Conversations devolved into shouts. The rush almost tilted the sitting room on its axis, dragging furniture. Hands—one the DJ's, reaching for Smith's—hooked their arm until they hit a doorframe and separated from her. "Alea!" Her yell joined a chorus of names and swears in the stampede. Only one person pushed the opposite direction, towards the garage.

"The closet!" Chris yelled into the chaos. Fleeing bodies pressed him back on the other side of the narrow hallway. "Alea, it's in the closet!"

Smith conjured their memory of the unlit area. Where did they lose their companion? Their fingertips inched along the wall, grasping for a corner, any familiar edge. Smith hit the trim of a doorframe. A heavy body slammed their wrist.

"Fuck!" They shook their arm and tried again. Smith found a doorknob below, not loose like the first bathroom's handle. They twisted it and fell inside a narrow room, landing against a huge plastic drum and a shelf of cleaning supplies. "Chris! Where in the closet?"

"Left corner!"

Smith stubbed their toe on a metal cylinder. They clutched the extinguisher's open handle with both hands. Enough people escaped to leave a path back the way they came. The steel canister swung at their side. They pushed towards the garage, where Arcana's last light filled the room. An aberrant bonfire enrobed one of the old square amplifiers near the stage. Its textured panels peeled and bled flames up the cinderblock wall. Smith aimed the nozzle with one hand and squeezed the handle.

Nothing happened.

The fire grew, alone with them in the space, ready to eat Smith and Arcana like Julienne and whoever died with her in the van. Orange tendrils licked the joist above. Did Julienne survive long enough to fight the flames? Did she feel the heat before it took her?

Chris' shouts cut through Smith's stupor: "The pin! Pull the pin!"

Smith did, then tried the handle again. A burst of cloudy gas and mist spewed from the nozzle. Smith centered it, then sprayed again and again until the garage returned to its natural state of darkness. Chris fanned smoke and kicked along the wall. He yanked the plug of the broken amp's power cord. The garage door rattled all the way open. Chris wafted smoke out towards the parking lot with a pair of bar rags. When cool air displaced the smoke and Smith's eyes adjusted, two dozen faces peered in at them. They dropped the fire extinguisher and coughed.

"Sorry, lovely people," Chris cooed. "Some technical difficulties. The show will resume in, uh, whenever we say shit's good to go. Y'all with the band, you still got stuff in here?

Should be fine to grab the rest once we air things out a bit. Okay? Lovely."

Smith dragged the fire extinguisher to the edge of the pavement and emerged from the smoky room. A flash of bright green zipped behind the crowd.

"Alea!" The DJ ran up and hugged Smith before they could lift their arms to match. "That was fucking insane. Are you okay?"

"Yeah!" Smith coughed again. The DJ loosened her embrace. "I tried to grab your hand, but everyone was running."

"Did you put the fire out? Like, *you* just did that?"

Smith checked over their shoulder. "Uh, yeah. Always working overtime, right?"

The DJ tried to laugh, not hiding her shock. "You weren't kidding when you said this place would burn down without you. Hell of a way to impress a gal."

Impress a gal. Was this a date? Or worse, was it a *first* date? The possibility wrenched Smith's mind back to the hotel, and back to the subtle differences between Levi's lips and Waite's. Smith blushed, reading their companion's eyes for another hint. Would she bite her lip, smile, or twitch? No one was that easy to decode. Smith tried to remember the shape of the DJ's name with their idle hands, if only they could hold its letters as easily as she held their waist.

"What was that?" She probed.

Smith reciprocated the hug. "Nothing. I'm still catching my breath."

"We can sit, if you need a minute."

The beams of two car headlights washed over the lot, parting the crowd of evacuees. Smith recognized the glinting bumper of the black luxury sedan they drove with Waite. Twyla parked the car in an open space between a motorcycle and a muddy crossover. She and Oren emerged onto the scene, minutes late for the action.

Oren folded his sunglasses into a pocket. "Alea, where's Chris?"

"He's, uh, at the bar, I think. He was just—"

"Wait a..." Oren looked past her at the smoke, the fire extinguisher, and the band members checking their equipment for damage. To Smith's relief, Oren unfolded his mirrored shades and put them back on. "Whatever. I was gonna tell Chris this crazy shit that happened, but I can tell you. Last night, Twyla and I went out for tapas at that new place in West Lewesboro, Cara-cala-cora-something. I don't remember the name, but it *sucked*. Don't bother. We were leaving, right? And this dipshit opens his car door into traffic. Truck going by *snaps* it right off. And the guy, he's fine, but he comes over—"

"He walks straight up to us!" Twyla interjected. "I thought he was nuts, certified loco-motive, but cool as a cucumber, he comes over to ask Oren for a *drink*. A drink, like he knew! Took a gander at *this one* and said '*there's* a man who carries a flask.'"

"Psh, who doesn't?" Oren clicked his tongue. "But I didn't think he'd drink the whole thing. I'd just refilled that shit. He hands it back, empty, then he's all confused, like he forgot what just happened. Turns out, we were watching the fallout of some sad, white trash bachelor party. These preppy suburban kids, I'll tell you, they had *no* idea how file an insurance claim."

"Mhmm!" Twyla nodded. "That poor truck driver, too."

At the main entrance, A-Bomb corralled people into a reentry line. He threw his hands in the air, apparently struggling to discern who'd already paid to see the show. He redirected that frustration to the co-owners.

"Oren, this is what I was saying! We gotta start doing hand stamps. You said we were gonna get hand stamps."

Oren tapped Twyla's hand. "Did I say that? You remember?"

"I don't know, but hand stamps are a smart idea." Twyla turned back to the entryway. "A-Bomb, sweet, what happened to the marker? The big gold marker?"

Oren tried to interrupt her, but A-Bomb happily explained. "Oh, that one? Your husband *confiscated* the gold marker, pursuant to a... bathroom graffiti investigation." As soon as Twyla looked back to Oren, A-Bomb flipped him off, but Oren's attention already drifted to the DJ's bright green hoodie. Smith bit their tongue to avoid bungling an introduction. Was that too obvious?

Oren spoke first. "Sorry for the yelling. Don't I know you? You played a show here."

"Yeah, last Friday! I'm Logan," the DJ answered, at last. To Smith's horror, Twyla cut straight to the other question of the night.

"Oh, you're too kind. Logan, Alea, this is a date, then?"

Twyla beamed at Smith—so did Logan. Twyla quickly refocused on Oren, who looked at Smith, and Logan at Twyla. Smith's anxiety buzzed around their head like an invisible insect, too fast for them to catch in their hands and answer the damn question.

Again, Oren broke the spell. "Who fucking knows, anyway? I don't know *when* me and Twyla started dating, but one day I find out we're 'married.' Who the fuck needs the labels? Everyone's getting rid of labels, right? I'm old as shit, but I keep with the culture."

Twyla laughed and patted Oren's chest. "Young at heart. Okay, let's go bother Chris. He needs to hear about those boys last night!"

Smith caught their breath once Oren and Twyla headed off. "Sorry, I didn't know what to say. They're my bosses, you know, it's awkward, and if this *was* a date, I feel like I ruined it by almost getting burnt alive."

"Are you kidding me?" Logan's stern disbelief held long enough to frighten Smith, until a smile crept over her lips. "I've always wanted to go on a date with a hot firefighter."

Smith laughed—the uncomfortable second-guessed kind that brought no relief. Maybe Alea and Logan could have shared this unlikely moment together. Smith's feet ached in Alea's shoes.

"You're too nice to me," Smith warned her. Logan only stepped closer.

"I know you spend a lot of time here, putting out fires, pouring drinks, and making people happy. You know who you are here, and so does everyone else. I love it! But I was thinking maybe I could get to know you better, if you'd like, if you *want*, if we..." Logan slowed down, almost begging Smith to end the sentence for her.

"...If we got out of here?"

She blushed. "Is that too much? I misread the tone, maybe too much ASL earlier. Sorry, that's on me."

"No, no, it's okay!" Smith held her hands. Anywhere but Arcana, no one expected Alea to act like a savvy bartender or event organizer. Why should Smith waste their night faking it? In a twisted way, Logan's offer opened a new opportunity. "You're right. There are other places we can go."

"Yay! Where do you have in mind?"

"Have you been to Heron's Landing?"

Logan glanced west. "The pirate-themed bar, by the river? I used to go, but I heard they're closed to have the deck redone."

That explained *Heron's Landing* being crossed off on Hunter's list of bars. "Right, I *forgot* about that. Have you been to The Wreck Club?"

Logan flipped around to the east. "That's only a few blocks up. I'm down if you are, but is that your scene?"

Smith imagine whatever Colton's home turf might be, relative to Arcana and The Neon Sphinx. He moved too slowly for a frequent dancer. He resented the gothic quirks that kept the 'wrong people' out of Arcana, in Georgie's words. Whatever endeared Colton to The Wreck Club, Smith hoped it wouldn't further derail their date with Logan.

"Sure," Smith said. "Might as well see more of the outside world before I'm back here again."

Logan led Smith by the hand up the sidewalk of the main road, the same way they drove in Oren and Twyla's car. Sharp vines knotted the metal fence of the empty lot next door. A red security light blinked behind the glass of Vin's Repair and Tire. Two pickup trucks with squatted rear axles rumbled in the other direction, blaring dissonant rap tracks. Two streetlights further, a block before the downtown park, a green sign marked the intersection with Leader Avenue. Smith figured they'd turn down that way, but Logan waited to cross the street.

"Isn't this the place where the cat guy bit off someone's nose last winter?" Logan started into the crosswalk as a bus pulled away.

"The cat guy?" Smith followed her across the intersection, taking in The Wreck Club's gray metal sign and rusty outdoor seating. A handful of customers, mostly Oren and Twyla's generation, laughed between drags of cigarettes, their beers lining the outside windowsill. "Yeah, this might've been the place."

The bouncer peeked at Smith and Logan's IDs but waved them immediately through, in contrast to A-Bomb's rigid security standards. That explained the bar's odd demographics: wiry bikers, drunken tourists, and some curiously youthful clans occupying two booths in the far corner. Laminated cocktail menus fluttered. Alternating wafts of cleaning fluid and triple sec spun in the air. License plates and hubcaps lined the walls, and the twisted frame of a battered muscle car dangled from steel wires on the ceiling.

Logan shimmied between two seats at the bar and combed through the cocktail menu. She laughed at a hot cinnamon whiskey recipe named *The Hindenburg*. A vanilla rum drink borrowed its name from a long-forgotten racetrack tragedy. A black licorice cocktail referenced a sunken oil tanker.

"Makes you wonder," Logan muttered, "how long until they name one after that crash from the other week?"

Smith wondered if local wrecks were off-limits for drink inspiration.

"Special menu!" Someone suggested. Two seats down the bar, Colton offered up a smaller laminated sheet. "All proceeds from the *Good Samaritan* cocktail go to Julie Chord's family."

Logan took the special menu from him. "I spoke too soon. Wow." Smith read its ingredients.

"Isn't that... kind of fucked up?"

Colton sipped his drink. "Sure, it's all fucked up, but it's for a good cause."

The woman on the nearest barstool winked at Smith and Logan, whispering: "He says he knew her, but he's had like four of those drinks tonight."

Colton pointed two fingers, holding his glass. "What are y'all's names?"

"Logan."

"Sm—*Alea*."

"Nice to meet you," Colton hiccupped and squinted at the woman on the barstool. "And this is, uh, sorry, I know you just said...?"

"Phoebe," she answered after letting him spin his wheels for a few seconds, then whispered back to Smith and Logan: "My name is Annie, but he forgot that, so I gave him 'Maggie' next."

Logan stifled a laugh. "Oh, good luck, babe."

"Love that jacket," Annie told Smith. She angled away from Colton, boxing him out of the conversation so Logan and Smith formed a triangle with her. Smith adjusted their brownish trench coat's collar.

"Thanks. It's got so many pockets; I'll never find them all."

"She has a kazoo in there!" Logan giggled. "Alea, show her. You can serenade us."

"Please, yes, before he starts talking again." Annie uncrossed her arms.

Smith couldn't remember which items made their homes in each pocket. Even worse, they *needed* to talk to Colton. "I shouldn't play the kazoo in here. It'll be too loud."

"Mm!" Colton hummed into his drink, re-announcing himself. "I remembered what it was. It was the lion. The constellation? I was telling Phoebe about this. It's a great story. Guys, it was so good."

"Give me strength," Annie muttered. She rotated her stool back to Colton as slowly as possible, donning her most patronizing visage along the way. Logan signed to Smith that she'd flag down the bartender for drinks. Smith signed back their thanks.

Colton slid his near-empty glass away a few inches. He began in a quieter voice than before, almost too low in the noisy space. "People think I'm crazy when I tell them about this, but it's a good story. Julie, who, you know, she was the one in the accident... We dated for like a year, starting almost two years ago. So, that was late winter, in the really ugly season when all the leaves are down but it's too late for a nice snow layer. I was out past Chesterville, if you follow the road north, where it goes left into that little winding river valley. You know the one? That's fine. It doesn't matter.

"We were up—well, I was working. I'd just started a new job when I quit the dollar store. I said, 'If I'm gonna work like a mule all day, the way these stores do, I'd get paid twice as much in construction.' I didn't know shit about houses, decking, all the renovation and rebuild shit I got into. Turns out, there's folks up on these mountains paying top dollar for whatever contractor is willing to drag their tools up those shoddy driveways. I know, it's whatever. I'll get back to the story. Point is, that's the business I got into with, uh, you know the guy from the commercials, with the jingle? No, I can't sing it. That company.

"Anyway, we're up at this house, probably my third project after I started. Big dark wood lodge of a house, two little barns, wide triangle windows over the valley. We never even saw the homeowners. Imagine that, blowing thirty grand to fix up a house you never visit? These *people*. You know, that time of year, the air gets so clear you could see someone waving from the next ridgeline. Hit a hammer, and it echoes three times. No other sound in the world. Hauling scrap lumber into a roll-off dumpster, I got covered in sweat, but my toes stayed cold in my boots.

"The rest of the crew fucked off by sunset. They left the trailer and took the pickup, and I had my shitty old bike. I wanted to get done loading the scrap for the next day, so I stayed late. Right when I finally wrap up, I hear something coming through the brush down the mountain. I thought it was a bear until I heard metal, like, clinking together. I poke my head around the back of this house, and there's this girl. She's climbing and sliding down these boulders, coming from higher up the mountain. I'm thinking, 'What the hell is up there, and who the hell is on this mountain with me?'

"She sees me, comes down, catches her breath. And get this, she thought *I* lived there! Me, looking like shit, grimy, outside some mountain mansion? I say, 'Hell no, I'm Colton, and I'm building a deck.' She says, 'I'm Julienne, I'm a rock climber, scoping for new, uh, *routes*,' she called 'em.

Apparently, she lost track of time and started bushwacking down towards the road where she parked. She's twice as dirty as me, mud past her ankles, and a big ass backpack. She needs a drink of water, but I'm on my last bottle, so I get the owner's key from the lock box on the work trailer.

"Now, we don't do that usually, and never without our boss onsite, but she *needed* water, so we go in, and this place is fucking huge in there. Big rafters, slate tile, fancy Afghan rugs and shit. I'm as impressed as she is, finally seeing inside the place. We both cool off, drinking water and sitting on the floor. She talked about a cave she found on her way up the mountain. Up here alone, looking in caves! I asked what she's doing alone here. 'Isn't it scary, like, being a girl alone in the woods?' She said she always forgot about that once she's been out there for a while. This girl was a trip, the way she talked like one of the boys from my work crew. I told her I can give her a ride down to the road on my bike, when she's ready, but we're neither in no rush now. You feel?

"I get this other feeling, there, sitting with her, like we're the same almost: Two hard-working lonesome types, up on this rock with our equipment, trespassing in some rich folks' crib. She was the one—I *promise*—she was the one who said, 'Hey, these folks have a hot tub.' And sure, it's cold up there, and dark with no lights on. Who's gonna know, right? Hell yeah. So, we did that. Piled up all our clothes near the door, then got in and warmed up. Like nothing.

"Now, the hot tub was on the last part of the old deck, and with the screen porch torn out, we had this *view*, I'll tell ya. You look up, and it's like you're in outer space. The stars are so close, and she knew 'em. She knew the names of random stars, and also the mountains, the types of rocks and plants and everything. She talked faster than I could listen. She showed me the constellations. I tried to see the animal shapes, but I'm like, 'A lion? I don't see a lion,' but she did. Then, right as I'm looking for it, *boom*: a shooting star!

"I hollered and pointed, but somehow, she missed it. Too quick. She saw the lion, though. So close, but maybe we were looking in different places. I'm gonna keep looking for that one. Her lion, up in the sky."

Colton paused.

"Alea? What's wrong?" Logan's fingers curled between Smith's. They jumped and covered their face with one hand. Where did those tears come from?

"Sorry," Smith choked and pulled free of Logan's touch. "Sorry, I don't know, I'm sorry."

Smith reached in front of Colton, stole his glass, and swallowed the last of his *Good Samaritan* cocktail. It pushed down the lump in their throat. They closed their eyes and saw stars.

IX
THE HERMIT

IX: THE HERMIT

Smith prayed for an intermission. They begged the drink to let them linger in the purgatory of their half-teleported state, somewhere dark and solitary. They imagined a space like Arcana's bathroom, where they would wash their face and forget their blunders as Alea. There, Smith would take the time to forgive themself for not asking Colton any questions and for hijacking Logan's date, but no intermission came. Clutching an empty shot glass, Smith sank onto the fake leather of an Arcana barstool.

"Not yours," Smith whispered to themself. They meant the shot glass. They meant their bodies. They meant the crash, the deaths, and however they felt about anyone else's grief. Maybe danger, loss, intrigue, deception, and love only belonged to the *real* people. Every time Smith absorbed and internalized those second-hand emotions, the end of the night broke their illusion. Dream awakened into dream, always promising truer reality than the last. Smith *could* spare themself these cycles of delusion. They could hide in plain sight as a spectator, an outsider, an eternal barfly, entangled in nothing but their drinks.

They caught themself thinking like Waite again.

"Is Waite here?" Smith asked Chris, as if he would know.

He dumped some empty glasses in the sink and shook his head. "Is *everyone* in on this now?"

Smith tried to hide behind the can in their hand. "In on what?"

"The Smith-Waite tarot thing. Every other night, someone's asking for them, opening tabs as them, or asking to be *called* one of their names. I get it! It's a great bit. You're lovely, but like... I have no *idea* how y'all coordinated this. Is it Oren? Be so for real. I *know* Oren talked to you, right?"

A flutter at the end of the bar distracted Smith. Selene's blonde hair peeked past the quiet room's curtain. Their eyes bounced between Chris and Smith.

"*You*. Did you just finish your drink?" Selene locked onto Smith's can.

"Yeah, I..." Smith reminded themself to begin as a stranger. "Have we met?"

Selene stalked across the room, pushing through the line at the karaoke signup sheet. They bobbed from side to side, studying Smith up close like a clinical researcher. "Feel any different? Like a whole new person? Amnesia, any of that ring a bell?"

Smith couldn't keep their face from reacting. "No, I... *Waite*? Is that you?" If so, Smith couldn't imagine how they gave themself away so quickly.

Selene's jaw dropped. "Holy shit, it worked. Smith? You're Smith, right?"

"You're *not* Waite?"

"No, I'm Selene! Where have you been?"

Smith leaned closer, in case one of the anxious karaoke singers overheard. "I thought you didn't believe any of it. You thought I was making it up. Were you watching just for someone to finish a drink?"

"I *know* what you two are up to," Chris whined before Selene could answer. "Are you starting a tabletop roleplay group without me, Selene? Is that what this is? Stop, that's what it is. Oh my God, you're all *sick* for that. Bye, I'm gonna take my high elf bard somewhere he'll be loved." Chris sulked and shuffled into the alcove near the refrigerator, making himself small in the shadows. Selene rolled their eyes and tugged Smith's arm towards the stairs. Smith resisted, but not enough.

"No, hold on. Be careful. People are gonna find out about me and Waite unless we keep a low profile. Jade must've told you, didn't she? Things could get weird, fast!" At the curtain, Smith broke free of Selene's hand and lingered on the top step.

"Five minutes!" A new hostess of Monday's karaoke announced through the microphone at her table. Rather than the queen from the previous karaoke night, Alea helmed the operation. "Put your name down, put your friends' names down, I don't care. Ember!" Alea switched off the microphone and waved Smith closer. "I'm kinda sorta hungover from last night, and I can't figure out how *June* runs multiple mic channels on this rig. Obviously, it's so valid that she called out for this week, but can you call her in for some tech support?"

"I..." Smith blinked at the box of wires and plugs on the table. Alea summoned them too fast. They tuned out her question while preparing to imitate Ember. How could Smith fake all his confidence? How could they match his monologues?

"C'mon, into the goth room!" Selene hollered from the quiet space down the steps.

"Alea, darling, sorry, I can't right now." Smith opened the curtain and ducked into the dark.

Selene sat at the small table in the corner. "Pull up a chair. Here." A portable LED lamp reflected off the surface, illuminating them—and Jade.

"I'm... Ember?" Smith exclaimed and touched their cheek. "I didn't think that could happen. Wasn't Waite already—?"

"Smith, yes, welcome," Jade interrupted. She flung her sketchbook shut and clicked her pen beside it. "Ember figured it out. After you and him did *that thing*, he tried some other spells. Look at your forearm." Smith rolled up the sleeve of Ember's thin white blazer. Three black stars, each in a circle the size of a large coin, marked the soft skin under their left arm. Jade clicked her pen again. "We tried the ace, then the two, but the three of pentacles did the trick for you."

Smith rubbed the ink, and it smeared. "He drew these on his arm?"

Jade approached Smith and pursed her lips. "I said 'we,' but *I* missed most of the fun." She twisted her own arm towards Smith, revealing an array of five ornately drawn swords. "Jade volunteered to go first. Didn't you recognize me?"

They didn't, then they did.

Before Smith could react, *Waite* hooked one hand over their shoulder and kissed them. Their lips tasted like green tea shots. Smith kissed them back, but only once before the embrace of Waite's arms paralyzed their limbs. Smith expected Jade's touch to feel distinct, but it wasn't hers at all. Waite's kiss zapped Smith's skin like an electric fence.

"Where the fuck have you been?" Waite asked when they released Smith's face. "I haven't seen you since the hotel, two flesh-days ago."

"Two *what*?" Smith stumbled to the drawing table, more than ready to take a seat. Waite slid their chair closer to Smith's, and Selene tuned in. "I was at a bachelor party, then I was on a date. It's Monday now, because of karaoke? How many drinks have I had?"

"Three pentacles, three drinks," Selene said and poked Smith's arm. "Apparently the odd numbers work better."

"Five for me!" Waite chirped.

"Okay, okay." Smith pieced together what they missed. "*That's* why you're in such a good mood. It took Jade five tries to 'summon' you, with those little sword drawings. Five green tea shots?"

"Yeah," Selene confirmed, disgusted. "She wanted cheap and dirty. Didn't know how many it would take. You, I mean, *Ember* got lucky, I guess, after three lemon drops. Not to butt in, but are you two a couple or something?" Neither answered.

Waite grinned. Smith hated it. Selene abandoned their question. "Fine. Keep your secrets, whoever you are."

"We're not anything," Smith insisted, more for Waite to hear. "We don't exist. We just borrow our names and our bodies. We don't have any memories before this. Someone explained it to you, right? You're talking like there's a pattern, numbers, or some science to it, but it's random. Then again, what the fuck do I know? It's been a weird couple of nights for me."

The flatbed truck's tires still screeched in Smith's ears.

"Me too," Waite said. They floated one hand onto Smith's knee. "I figured it out, though. I know who we are." Smith tensed at Waite's touch, not believing them for a second. Waite opened Jade's sketchbook to a blank page. "When you left the hotel, I had dreams while I slept. They were vivid, too, as real as us sitting here right now. I don't remember most of them, but I know how the dreams ended. I had a *vision*."

Waite clicked Jade's pen and scratched a flurry of lines across the paper. They began with a square, then a scene within it, one layer at a time.

"Muscle memory," Smith noticed. "You're drawing in the same style as Jade."

The images of vague, smudged plants and trees expanded outward, or maybe inward. The drawing's foreground transitioned into an enclosed space. A pair of hands materialized, one dripping blood and the other waving a dark object. A second figure flew headfirst across the space, uncontrolled. Waite drew so fast that Smith thought the page might catch fire. The pen's ink scattered stray flecks across the scene, each becoming intentional details of airborne debris in a blur of motion. Waite turn the scene into a perspective from inside an overturning vehicle, its hood erupting in flames on impact with the trunk of a tree. The drawing *did* catch fire.

"I remember dying," Waite declared. "I remember dying next to you in a van, Smith. But same as my name's not Waite, Smith's not really your name, is it?"

"It makes sense," Selene agreed. "Tell Smith the rest."

Smith grabbed the sketchbook and searched for themself in the frantic mess. "No, no. That's not right," they insisted. "It's not your story. It's not mine. Waite, you already knew how those people died, so you can imagine the crash as easily as anyone else. Why should your dreams mean anything?"

Waite sighed. "You taught me to pay attention, and I have. I spent the last two days putting the clues together. I pulled the leaked photos of the crash from an anonymous social media page. I counted the days I remember, and I aligned them with the calendar days of the past month. Today is my tenth day, and the seventeenth real day from my first. It's the same for you, isn't it? Even if we have *some* different days, I know we started at the same time. Selene, I started as you, and Smith, you were that Andy guy. Can you guess what else happened that same night, according to Lewesboro Police reports?" Waite tapped the back of Jade's pen on their sketch. "I was able to prove that *this* was less than an hour before. The fire was still cooking our corpses when we took our first drinks! It was something you said as a joke, Smith, but you and I *were* lovers."

"We can't say that." Smith fought the temptation to believe. "That doesn't work, and there are too many problems. Ghosts? You're seriously saying that we're *ghosts*?"

"Damn right," Selene affirmed. "We went through the notes together. Me, Ember, and, uh, Waite? What do I call you now?"

"Call me Hayes," Waite suggested, as if choosing their breakfast from a diner menu. "I *was* Hayes, wasn't I?"

Smith shook their head. "I'm not calling you that. First of all, you're speculating, and second, it's disrespectful. Third, you don't even have your facts right. One of the bodies was misidentified. Hayes didn't die in the crash. He's *missing*, and someone else died in the van with Julienne."

Waite huffed. "What the fuck are you talking about? Have you spent your past two nights researching, too?"

Smith's fingernails scraped the sides of their seat. "I almost died, Waite! I almost got hit by a truck. I got trampled in a fucking stampede, I put out an electrical fire, and I ruined Alea's date. I've been a little busy with real-life problems that don't happen to *ghosts*. But I *did* see an article where the police said—"

"Whoa, whoa," Selene interrupted. "Hit by a truck?"

"*Almost.*" Smith carried on. "Point is, ghosts don't die, and I'm pretty sure *I* almost did. Give me a minute, and I can find this article about the crash." Smith palmed Ember's bedazzled red smartphone and picked through its customized menu layouts, chasing after a web browser.

Waite folded Jade's sketchbook closed. "Call it whatever you want. Two people died, and a few minutes later, the two of us started wearing the flesh of people in this bar."

"Whatever. Sure." Smith waved Ember's phone over their head. "*This* bar? Explain that part. Why here?"

Selene laughed through their nose and pushed back their hair. "Look around, Sherlock. I mean, this place was already creepy. When some people drink, they're basically haunted anyway, so it's not too huge of a leap."

Smith grumbled. Custom red icons disguised the apps on Ember's phone, and they couldn't focus long enough to let his thumbs guide them to the browser. Convincing Waite might take forever. Even if Jade and Smith didn't see eye-to-eye at Kink Night, Smith wished she could kick Waite out of her body and talk some sense into Selene.

"Fine," Smith caved. "Let's assume we're the ghosts of these two people we never met, one of whom we don't know anything about. We still can't remember shit, so how do we know who's who?"

"I *know* I wasn't Julienne," Waite said.

"You 'know?' How?"

"I'm way too masculine." Waite leaned closer to Smith. "You remember *that*, don't you?"

Smith stopped themself from smacking Waite's stupid face—Jade's face.

"Whatever," Smith shook it off. "Excuse me for thinking your gender might be more complicated than *Levi's* body, which wasn't even yours. Did you ever think about using his body like that, when you have no idea if *he* would've consented?"

"For real?" Selene recoiled at the implication, and Smith's reddened cheeks betrayed them. "So, y'all *actually* fucked. Yeah, I've got questions."

Waite reclined against the wall, barely balanced on their stool. "Is that what you're so worried about, Smith? What *Ellesandra* wanted?" They pronounced her name with manufactured poise. "Because you were very clear about what *you* wanted."

Smith wanted to knock them to the floor. They still saw El's face, reflected in the flat chrome shower fixture. Every few minutes, even three bodies later, Smith failed to reconcile their own selfishness.

"*We* were never lovers," Smith hissed at Waite, "and what we did with their bodies, pretending they weren't part of it, was a mistake. In her texts, Elle wanted to break up with him. I think we hurt her. *I* hurt her, and you're talking this ghost romance bullshit like that would make it better."

Waite stuck out their tongue. "Then what are we? Fuck buddies?"

Smith lunged for Waite's face.

Selene seized each of their hands. "Hey, hey! I'm not just gonna sit here and watch my two best friends squabble like an old married couple. Am I gonna have to call a priest in here to sort you two out? You know, the worst part is that Jade and Ember would know *exactly* what to say here. They *get* this witchy shit, meanwhile I'm the fucking mechanic who grew up *without* religious trauma. It was them two who summoned you here, and now you're literally arguing about your ghost genders and the consent of the possessed. You make me miss alcohol, and getting possessed by Waite was what made me *quit* drinking! Sorry. I'll chill. I'm chill, just a little more freaked out than I thought. I'm talking to dead people, alright? I'm sober, and I'm talking to dead people. This is great. I have to go to *work* tomorrow."

If Selene had more to say, they lost their chance when a karaoke singer began screaming death metal vocals from the next room. Smith reopened Jade's sketchbook. They leafed through it backwards, beginning from Waite's sketch of the crash, then a few recent doodles, and then the ominous ball of darkness from the night of the hot dog.

"I don't understand the spells," Smith confessed. "If they do work, I don't know why."

Selene fixed the collar of Ember's blazer. "*You* knew. Not you, Smith, I mean him. He explained it, but I could never. Waite, you paid attention, didn't you? How does the summoning work?"

"Fine. Give me a second." Waite stretched their arms behind their head. "Ember said there are four symbolic objects we need: Swords, cups, wands, and coins. The right number of objects grants us our flesh."

"Right, sure..." Smith thumbed further back into Jade's collection. "What numbers? Why certain numbers?"

"He talked fast, Smith. You met him. You know what he's like. I remember *some* of it. He said the first test used wands, the other night." Waite cleared their throat and wrung their wrists. "When I was tied to that crucifix thing, in *your* flesh. His flesh, Ember's. You remember."

"'Ace of wands,'" Smith whispered. Where did that phrase come from?

"What of wands?" Waite asked, over the loud karaoke singer.

Smith glowered at them. "*You* said it! Jade did, not you. Jade said 'ace of wands,' right when Ember put the riding crop against the wall. *That* was the wand. One wand, the riding crop, the ace. Three stars in circles, like coins on my arm. Five little swords on yours. And cups, so many cups, every time we drink, we have cups. But unless Jade and Ember are actual fucking wizards, how did they come up with this?"

"Ugh!" Selene rubbed their eyes. "It's tarot. It's all just tarot. They didn't come up with any of it. *ARCANA*, the whole ass bar, is full of tarot stuff. You two named yourselves Smith and Waite! It doesn't take a coven of witches to guess that maybe your *situation* has got to do with tarot." Smith waited for Selene to continue. Waite did the same. Selene stewed, glaring at each of them. "You two know how to walk, drink, fuck, and speak English. Don't you know anything useful?"

"Sign language," Smith offered. "My last, um, *host* knew sign language. Alea."

"Fun. Okay, well, Ember would bitch-slap me for saying this, but tarot is like astrology, plus some even more hokey bullshit. It's fortune-telling for lazy fortune tellers. There are a bunch of cards, all the swords and cups and shit, with a bunch more random ones, and they each mean whatever you want. You can flip them upside down, too, and they mean the exact opposite. People use tarot to whine and speculate about their problems without actually facing them."

Waite raised one hand. "I thought tarot was a religion. A type of sorcery, right?"

"It's just a deck of cards. You don't worship a deck of cards. And no 'sorcery' either, except... now there *is* sorcery, I guess. Hate that."

"It's not a bad thing," Smith assured themself as much as Selene. "We can learn. We can figure out how to control this."

Waite nodded. "Yeah, we can use it. We can harness the power. This could be the start of something incredible for us!"

"Good for you! *Great* for you." Selene clapped their hands slowly. "Sorry, but this has me fucked up. It's exciting, I'm with you there, but I don't know how to deal with a world that operates like this. You spend enough time down inside engine bays, and everything looks like a machine. History, relationships, capitalism, it's all a bunch of parts that push and pull on each other. I can see the parts, take things apart in my head, and put them back together... but not this. I don't *believe* the things I'm seeing. The parts that are pushing and pulling are invisible, not mechanical. It's messy, it's strange, and I'm not ready for it. I'm like that stone-age cave hermit, whatever they say, stepping out and seeing the hands that cast the shadows. Big, clawed, monster hands full of tarot cards. How do I see that, then keep on living in my cave?"

Smith agreed but said nothing that might feed Selene's dread.

"Even without my own memory," Waite spoke with renewed vigor, "I see the artifacts of spirituality everywhere. The figurative cornerstones of language are theological hierarchies, mythological and legendary heroes, prophets, villains, gods, and commandments. Believers or not, you all say 'oh my god,' and 'what the hell.' Those are colloquial glimpses of prayer. What if they stand for a deeper memory? Not of the crash, not any one mythos, but something shared across time. Language itself recalls humanity's millennia spent seeking absolution, immortality, and communion with the divine. Holy wars rained fire over long-forgotten faiths that never validated themselves, but now, Selene, *you* hear the first true calls from the beyond. Here we are, two pilgrims from the afterlife, nameless and atheistic, staking our claim in a deck of cards— a novelty, an oddity, a commercial tool of divination. We've sprung the ironclad lock of mortality. Here we are, Smith and I, these living answers to death, known only by a chance few young people in a bar called Arcana. You believe it, don't you, Selene?" Waite clicked Jade's pen. Smith stole it from their hand. "What, you don't want to be worshiped as a god of a new religion?"

"You're hilarious." Smith tucked the pen in the spiral binding of the sketchbook and fanned through its pages again. They stopped at a full-page rectangular frame, surrounding a short stone bridge between two wooded hills. A jagged bolt of lightning split the page and struck a figure at the bridge's center. Loose rocks burst from the impact and tumbled into the valley below. A Roman numeral *XVI* topped the ornamented frame, and capital letters spelled *THE TOWER* at the bottom.

"Tarot, again," Selene flicked the page. "That's one of those special random cards, whatever they're called. I told you; it's a big thing here."

Smith pushed the sketchbook to the middle of the table. "If you hate tarot so much, why do you come here?"

"Friends, music, and cheap drinks. Not so much the last part anymore, so call it my habit. Maybe this place is something deeper, now that y'all are here, but my queer ass just needs a foxhole until this country finishes collapsing."

Out in the main room, another singer snagged the mic for a drunken rendition of an old country song. Half a dozen others lent backup vocals. Alea swayed her arms in time with the slow tune. Three people weaved through the crowd past the signup table and carried their drinks into the quiet room—the *goth* room, as Selene called it. The trio failed to lower their voices, so Smith heard everything.

"...Using the default filters? I hadn't seen that since middle school!" Georgie's voice registered like an alarm over Smith's shoulder.

Saint feigned a gag. "What even is social media, you guys? How do you spend your time on that?"

Oz hummed loud enough to silence them. "Mm, yeah, you're too busy for social media, working double shifts because you hate yourself and don't want to see your friends."

Saint pretended to have a heart attack. "Um, fuck you, I *love* you, and I missed exactly *one*—"

"Oh, fuck," Georgie steered Saint to face the church pew. "That's him. That's him. That's him."

Smith felt three pairs of eyes darting up and down their body from behind. Hand next to their head, Selene pointed at each of them, especially at Smith. "You know them, the ones who just walked in? What am I missing, here?"

A smile snuck over Waite's lips.

"Shh," Smith warned. "Don't you *dare* invite them over here."

Selene laughed. "Chill out. That's Oz, I've met her."

"Oh, no you haven't," Smith realized. "You met *me* when I was in Oz's body. And she met *you* when Waite was in *your* body. You two haven't actually met, but you both *think* you did, on completely different nights."

Selene's jaw clenched.

"Yeah," Waite added, "and Smith has also been that taller one. Named what? 'Saint,' sure. Smith was *Saint* when they kissed Ember to summon me with the ace of wands. Ozzy and the short one watched it happen. See, Smith? I pay attention, now."

Smith waited for any indication from Selene. "Are they coming over here? Are they gonna—?"

Two fingers tapped Smith's shoulder. Saint hovered half a step away, sporting a cropped white anime T-shirt and baggy gray jeans.

"Saint!" Smith stood and channeled their best impression of Ember's bravado. "Oh, uh, *darling*, I almost didn't recognize you without the corset. The sequins! What a miracle of the universe to cross your... lifepath, again."

"Wow, we're matching again, too!" Saint traced the collar of Ember's white blazer. "Reds last time, and whites tonight. Right?"

Smith shifted an inch closer, narrowing the space enough for a semi-private conversation. "You don't remember us kissing, do you?"

Saint's eyes widened, flitting to Oz and Georgie, then back. "Ha. Um, no. I'm sorry. I get nervous around... pretty boys. Boy? Sorry, I assumed. I'm sorry about the other night if it was weird for you. I must've spaced out, but my friends filled me in."

Oz and Georgie silently cheered Saint from across the room, no idea the game they'd sent them to play.

"It's okay," Smith said. After all, Ember encouraged *them* to participate in the kissing ritual. "I'm sorry if *I* was a bit... intense. I'm sorry you don't remember, though."

Saint shrugged and bit their lip. "I *would* remember. I will remember, I mean, if you want to kiss me again."

The walls closed in around Smith. The lights seemed to dim. Smith's first instinct told them to continue the show, do as Ember would, and make out with Saint in front of everybody. A second, persistent impulse held them back. The distorted reflection of Ellesandra's face broke through the fog, eyes open. Ember would pounce at another opportunity to show affection, especially with an audience, but Smith couldn't be him for this. They refused to cross that line again.

"I can't," Smith told Saint. "Well, I can, but I shouldn't."

"Oh." Saint tucked their hands in their cargo pockets and hugged their elbows at their sides.

"It's not you! It's..." Smith shed their nerves and let loose a full-throttle Ember impression as damage control. "You're sweet and hot and a *damn* good kisser, but a little birdie tells me you've got your eyes on a certain someone else. A certain... *bartender*." Smith mouthed the word. "You see, I *can* play with you. And I'll play to win, but I play the short game. It's no less romantic, but you strike me as a player of the *long* game. For that, I'm too distractible. Easily bored. You want something gentler, don't you? Then keep your eye on the ball. Keep dazzling him with those androgynous eyes. Then, down the line, if you find out that he's the sharing type... we'll see about that kiss. *Darling*."

"You... *You*." Saint giggled and turned in a circle, bouncing on their toes. "I like your words, funny magic man. Who told you about him? Was it...? Oh, it *must've* been. Georgie!"

Saint targeted Georgie like a laser, and he threw his innocent hands up. "Me? What? Why me? No, don't come over here. I'm too young to die!"

Saint gave chase.

"That was impressive," Selene told Smith as they sat back down. "Do you two want some drinks, or are you sticking around tonight?"

Waite spun Jade's pen in their hand. "I've got nowhere to be."

Selene nodded towards the main room. "No, actually you *do* have somewhere to be."

"Jade and Ember! Jade and Ember, where'd you go?" Alea called into the microphone.

Smith hunched. "No way. I'm not singing again."

"Too late." Selene towed Smith and Waite across the room, up the steps, and towards the microphone. "Jade signed y'all up for a duet. How's that for unfinished business?"

WHEEL OF FORTUNE

X: WHEEL OF FORTUNE

"How about you follow my lead for a change?" Waite yanked the microphone from its stand. "You sing the parts you know, and I'll sing what I know."

"I'm the one who's done this before," Smith reminded Waite through gritted teeth. Selene abandoned them, already vanished back down the steps. "Unless you were here last Monday, when I wasn't."

"I *was*, actually." Waite tapped the mic. "Do you believe me?"

"I don't believe you *sang*."

Waite leveled their eyes with Smith's. "I guess you'll never know."

Stomping bass guitar notes introduced the song and cut off their sparring. Alea, at the table, howled an encouraging *woo* into her mic. Waite focused on the projector screen, readying for lyrics to scroll. Smith waved at the crowd, performing Ember's dramatics until Waite stepped on their foot. The song's title appeared first: *Psycho Killer, as made famous by The Talking Heads.* Its instrumental buildup lasted longer than Smith expected, freeing them to agonize over its unfamiliarity. They glanced at Alea to make sure the equipment was working.

Waite stole the first monotone lyrics off the screen. Embarrassed by their distraction, Smith rushed to catch up. Waite sang something about tension and nervousness, sounding more relaxed than Smith felt. Maybe Jade knew the song better than Ember. Waite hogged the mic and continued their solo into the first chorus. They wandered closer to the projector screen, the words *psycho killer* illuminated in white across Jade's body as Waite sang them. Smith melded into the audience, until—

French? The lyrics shifted to French.

Waite stopped mid-line. They straightened one arm, pawning the mic to Smith. The screen changed too fast, and Smith only managed a few *fa-fa-fa*'s. Waite took over again. The crowd *loved* that. Waite nailed the timing. Smith wondered how much Waite owed to Jade's muscle memory and how much they siphoned from blind, nihilistic confidence.

The bridge snuck up on both Smith and Waite. The microphone landed in Smith's hands again, and they guessed their way through a staccato stanza of French words. Waite wrapped one hand around Smith's on the mic, not taking it back, but joining them for the *yeah-yeah-yeah* at the end of the bridge. Smith focused on the beat rather than Waite's eager face.

One lyric at a time, Smith survived to reach the outro, clinging to the empty mic stand and pronouncing French lyrics for Waite. The last line faded from the screen. When a few people cheered, they aimed it all at Waite, who dumped the mic on the signup table for the next singer.

Smith stepped towards the goth room, but Waite cornered them into a hug. "See? You just need to trust me more."

Smith kept their arms down, letting jealousy and adrenaline overpower the shame of something worse: *attraction*. Even through walls of guilt, Waite's touch steered Smith like a magnet hijacking a compass.

"We're going to be okay," Waite whispered in their ear.

Smith shut their eyes and let themself believe it—only until Waite kissed them again. Smith opened their eyes and pushed them away fast enough to avoid making a scene, but not fast enough to dodge their lips.

"Seriously?" Smith wiped their mouth and slipped away through a gap in the crowd. They took a few hits from elbows and shoved their way to the bar counter.

"Another lemon drop?" Chris balanced four tall beer glasses between his hands and fired the quick ask to Smith as he passed.

"No, I..." Smith waited for him to circle back around. Smith weighed which bottle of bottom-shelf liquor might best disinfect their tongue.

"Hey!" Waite caught up to Smith, who ignored them. "You can't just push me away like that."

"Yes, I can, and you're drunk."

"So are *you*. Neither of us even knows what 'sober' feels like. What, suddenly you hate me again, cause Jade took two more shots than Ember? Cause you're too—"

"Waite, quiet down. It's not about the alcohol, and it's not about karaoke. It's what we *do* with their bodies."

"We didn't choose to take their flesh." Waite rubbed their eye, smudging Jade's smoky liner. "They bring us here by drinking. They invite chaos, surrendering their control to us. This time, Jade and Ember *asked* for it."

Chris passed Smith again, who held up one finger and mouthed, "*vodka*." Selene's blonde hair bobbed through the crowd, and they landed in the seat between Waite and Smith. Selene's phone screen lit their face from below.

"Okay, Smith, you were right. This is from the Lewesboro American, today: 'Business Owner Dead in Crash.' It's super confusing. Like, why would this random guy be dead instead of Hayes, in *his* van? Waite, all your research, how did you miss this?"

"Doesn't change anything," Waite insisted. "Two people died, and we can't remember who we were. Maybe *I'm* Julienne, and *Smith* is the random dead guy."

Smith imagined Waite as Julienne, the rock-climbing wanderer from Colton's story. Did she stand on the chair at her own family's funeral fundraiser, mocking her own death? Did she forget the face of her own mother? Worse still, Smith considered the opposite possibility of being Julienne themself. Her story moved Smith more than Andy's, Ember's, or even Jade's. Against the seductive option of claiming Julienne's life as their own, Smith clung to the freedom of their voided memory. Why claim ownership of another life, and especially of such a tragic one? Smith hated the defeat, absurdity, and limitations of calling themself a ghost, never mind *Julienne's* ghost. Chris couldn't pour Smith's shot fast enough, but once he delivered it to their hand, they understood it could only delay these worries.

"We don't know!" Smith reminded Waite and Selene. "You're answering a question that's too big for us. We don't have any proof of *why* or *how* we're here. It's nice to make up theories, but in the meantime, we're just guests. We need to know what's at stake before we start making waves. I don't wanna do or say shit that'll alienate me forever. Isn't that important to you?"

"Sure..." Waite scrolled Selene's phone, browsing the article. "So, you still don't believe me? These people *conjured* us with tarot sigils on their skin, and you're doubting what we are?"

A pair of college girls next to Waite started listening. Selene scowled and waved them away. "Ignore them. I mean, her. She's crazy."

"Whatever we are," Smith spoke to Waite, quieter now, "let's not fuck up anyone else's lives by thinking we're *better*."

Selene laughed. "Good rule for non-ghosts, too."

Smith took their vodka shot, but not fast enough to miss Waite's closing jab: "So *dramatic*."

Bright lights—even harsher than those in the hotel lobby—filled Smith's field of view. Arcana's eerie deep reds and warm yellows washed away under white daylight bulbs, tucked above the rafters. The karaoke singers disappeared. The folding signup table stowed against a wall behind a red couch. The barren dance floor resembled a movie set, an hour after wrapping the day's shoot. The clean LEDs highlighted cracks in the chessboard floor tiles, faded grime in the stitching of corner seats, and the spiderwebs of every sloppy extension cord or power strip that pumped energy into the space. Most unsettling of all, Smith held their empty beer can at the bar alone. Not even Chris or Alea escaped this apparent purge of all life inside Arcana.

"Hello?" Smith called out, as if into the eye of a hurricane. The stench of bleach diffused from the sink. The murmurs of a lo-fi playlist descended from the speakers. Smith had hoped for a night without Waite, but they never envisioned a night without anyone. After closing time at the Arcana, life's waterfall slowed to a drip. Smith could sit at any barstool, talk to themself in the bathroom all night, or hunt down the nearest hot dog stand. This night offered Smith a moment to breathe, and they spent it sitting still.

Down the hallway, at the end of the blue room, the door to the garage squeaked open. On the other side, a heavy weight thumped. Four rusty castor wheels screamed. A wooden dolly jolted over the threshold, bounced off the hallway walls, spun across the room towards Smith, and bucked its cargo onto the floor. The burnt-out amplifier from Saturday night's concert thudded to a stop at Smith's feet.

"Fucking piece of shit!" Oren hollered after the amp. He stomped into the main room and kicked it one more time. Smith waited, stunned. Oren remained dead serious until a giddy smile overcame him. He rested one heel on the amp.

"This is me as a mob boss, taking care of a rat motherfucker. Was that cool, or what?"

"Yeah!" Smith played along, acclimating to their gruff new voice. Metal piercings clicked against their teeth. A discreet brush of one hand over their buzzed haircut found a tall mohawk at its center. Of *course* A-Bomb drank after hours; when else could he? "You scared me, you know, kicking that thing through the door back there."

Oren hung his fur coat on a hook beside the bolted double doors. His ripped white tank revealed two arms wrapped in tattoos, some cleaner and newer than others. Smith could almost count the years of Oren's life in his ink, like tree rings. Oren stooped and placed one knee on the wooden furniture dolly. He tested its sturdiness, grunted, then shifted the rest of his weight onto it. He raised a hand towards Smith.

"Gimme a boost, A."

"You want me to... Is that safe?" Smith rolled his empty can across the bar top, where it fell into a trash can.

"Fuck no. I'm gonna scare Twyla."

"She's back there?" Smith got behind Oren and centered their hands on his back.

"Yeah. Chris and Alea are explaining a meme to her."

Smith pushed Oren up to speed while he pumped his hands along the ground to roll faster. They released him. He threaded the needle through the hallway, but the dolly rotated half a turn, sending him back-first through the door to the garage. The castor wheels caught the threshold, and Oren tumbled off the dolly onto the ground.

"Oren!" Twyla shouted from inside the garage. "You two see what I have to deal with every day?"

Smith caught up to Oren and lent him a hand to stand back up. Alea stood on a metal stool, fishing through boxes on a high shelf.

"Should've gone for the extended warranty on the amp, I guess," Chris teased Oren while coiling up some cables alongside the stage.

"Pretty sure I stole that one from our shitty landlord back in Arkansas," Oren admitted, "or I snagged it from an estate sale. Dead people always have the good shit. You see an estate sale sign, you *run*, don't walk. There's a reason tools and electronics are gone in the first hour."

Twyla laughed. "Chris, I bet that amp was older than you. You're what, 27?"

Chris gagged, as if stabbed in the chest. "Do I look like Nosferatu? Alea, do I look *ancient* to you?" Alea ignored him. "I am a *spry* 24."

"Yeah, yeah," Oren muttered and kicked around the furniture dolly. "At least a few more years until *you* burst into flames, then."

"Between that and twink death, honey, light me up."

"Tell you what!" Oren planted himself in the old amp's space at the side of the stage. "I could trick out the whole fuckin' audio setup here with some of that reward money."

"Reward money?" Smith asked, unsure what they missed.

"Oh, it's *terrible*." Twyla sighed. "That poor family."

Oren laughed. "No, no, that *rich* family. Alea, Chris, y'all didn't hear about that shit either? The guy who died in the interstate crash was a fuckin' millionaire. Like, a good couple of millions, helping all the other rich folks building up houses on the hills. You see those ads for them on channel eight? 'P.K. Mullard, built for your yard?' He made big bucks off those shitty patios."

"Wait, what?" Chris' thumbs hammered at his phone screen. "I thought the dead guy was, like, my age?"

Twyla tutted. "Nope, it got mixed up. *That* young man is still missing. Cops had it all wrong."

"Per fucking usual," Oren quipped. "Now, Mullard's family put up forty grand to find the missing dude who owned the van. If he split from the crash and ran, I bet they'll take him dead or alive, gunslinger style. What's the kid's name? Yeah, *Hayes*. Scum of the earth, leaving two people to die like that. Including his girlfriend!"

"I don't understand it," Twyla mused, "how one family collects for a funeral, while another throws a fortune at revenge. Even if that Hayes boy was responsible, what good is siccing a mob on him?"

Oren paced the barren stage side. "Gonna nab his ass and buy me a proper sound system."

Chris stifled a laugh. Alea tossed a stack of party hats to the ground. "Found them!" The hats slid apart and rolled in opposite directions. "They're all for St. Patty's Day, though."

"Oh, *those* party hats." Twyla scooped one off the floor and fitted it over her head. "They were half-off after the holiday a few years ago." Twyla grinned at Oren. "I told you we'd use these."

Oren offered a hat to Smith.

"Better not," they declined, not wanting to flatten A-Bomb's tall, sculpted hair. Oren wore the hat instead.

"Now it's a fucking party. The real one is still Friday, sure, but today is the *actual* day. Seven years ago today, Twyla poured the first cocktail at the bar out there. Seven years of this place, and we're going strong. Chris, do you know the story?"

Alea donned her party hat and sat on the metal stool. "Chris, you'll want a chair for Oren's story hour."

He perched on a low cinderblock windowsill instead. "At some point, I *do* plan to go home. Am I being paid for this?"

Smith, meanwhile, settled at the edge of the stage and stretched their legs. A-Bomb's heavy boots hurt their feet.

"Wait, wait," Twyla stopped Oren. "I thought it was Wednesday. The seven-year anniversary? I put it in my phone for Wednesday."

"Yes!" Oren agreed. "Yes, Wednesday. No, you got it. Right now, it's fuckin'... quarter to three. We're Wednesday-ing. That counts. Aw, y'all see that? She loves me. I know, look at us, the gross old straight people. Ew! Anyways, I was gonna tell the story on Friday, but no way folks are gonna simmer down and listen up when this place gets jumping. Somebody's gotta hear the whole legend, you know, to carry on the Arcana legacy.

"So, open scene, I'm 20 years old, just got kicked out of Oxford for being too cool. I'm kidding, it was a community college in Arkansas, and I wasn't cool, but I *was* fucking hot back then. I got busted selling acid to a bunch of whiny nerds on the intramural volleyball team, so I rented a room over this old guy's oil painting gallery. He gave me a deal, you know, bartering like the olden days. He was a real one.

"Problem was, sleeping above the fucking oils and tinctures and powdered pigment shit he had in his workshop, I got all sorts of fucked in the head for a while. It didn't last, not mostly, but I had crazy fuckin' dreams when I moved into that spot. I remember spinning, everything spinning at night, like I was strapped down to a giant wheel of fortune that never landed on anything. I was in the middle of a Roman amphitheater, thousands of people yelling down at me. Sometimes, I saw some Caesar guy in the crowd, who built the whole coliseum, looking down at me like I'm nothing. It was fuckin' weird. What the fuck am I gonna do about a dream like that?"

Twyla lifted one hand and wagged her fingers. "Oh, I know."

"Booya. Babe, you tell the next part."

"He went to the *bar* about it! I was working the early shift, when no one's around, and in comes this guy. You can imagine how he talked my ear off about the symbology of these dreams, all evening long. Religious parents have a way of raising blasphemers like me, who've got a high tolerance for strangeness. And lucky for Oren, I had with me a deck of vintage Smith-Waite tarot cards, which I bought at—" She and Oren joined in unison: "—*an estate sale*." Twyla unbuttoned a pocket on the back of her purse and extracted a delicate, leatherbound deck of cards.

Oren continued the story. "Of course, she wanted to interpret my wacked-out dreams, so she asked to give me a tarot reading. Me, I didn't know shit about shit back then. I didn't wanna touch those cards, thinking they'd be too holy to somebody's religion, what with the biblical shit all over 'em. And yeah, tarot is based on a lot of ancient shit, but, you know, it *psychoanalyzes* that. Twyla taught me, that night, how it's not quite Christian, it's not quite Pagan, it's separate from 'em all. You get it?" Chris and Alea nodded unconvincingly. "Psh. A-Bomb, you follow?"

Smith cleared their throat. "Yeah, man. It's... the real shit."

"It's like astrology, right?" Chris tried. "I see people get tattoos of the cards. They're cute."

"Tarot is descriptive, not prescriptive." Twyla explained. "The cards are the patterns of human life. They're the people you meet, the ways you feel, and the challenges you face. Religious scriptures view the universe deterministically, so most theologies suggest a master plan, which aligns to a set of master rules. I prefer to see tarot as a reframing of the world with chaos as its only master. Change and randomness are represented by the shuffling of a card deck. Religion is built and tuned to feed you a holy, scriptural, pre-interpreted answer when you're lost. Modern tarot is, by its own terminology, *arcane*, built on the secrets of the Victorian nerds who dreamed it up. The cards give us no answers, no line in the sand to discern good from evil, but they beg you to ask questions. Who are you, and what are you going to do about that?"

"But there *is* good and evil," Alea interrupted. "I mean, c'mon. Murder, abuse, landlords?"

"Yes! Yes." Twyla agreed. "Morality exists at the scale of a human lifetime, as it should. At the scale of centuries, though, good and evil mean different things. Four hundred years ago, there were a dozen *moral* reasons to chop off each of our heads. Tarot endures by allowing the change that each century brings. I've carried these cards long enough to guess that if there is a true, *eternal* evil, it's the denial of change itself. If your values never change, if you don't entertain the curiosity it takes to learn and evolve, you're gonna chop off everyone's heads forever."

"In other words," Oren tapped his temple, "open your fucking mind, bro. Sorry, where was I? I had the thing. The story."

Twyla tilted the box of cards over her open palm. She coaxed the cards out like baby birds from a nest. Smith stepped closer. The cards were a fraction larger and longer than those of a poker deck.

"My dreams!" Oren remembered. "She asked me about my dreams, then she gave me a tarot reading. You know the wildest part? I don't remember what fucking cards she pulled. But hell, we talked on and on that night, hours and hours. At some point, I said, 'why can't I go to the bar and have it be this good, every time?' Cause in fuckin' Arkansas, like, this time stood out. I mean, I was in *love* or whatever, obviously, but there was more. Suddenly, I wasn't the only heathen chasing down the meaning of life. I said, 'I need to find the place where people like us are at.' I was gonna skip town. I was done there, but Twyla saved me the trouble."

Twyla fanned the deck of cards across a tabletop. "I just told him what *I* saw in his reading. I said, 'you might be a prisoner in your dreams, spinning the wheel of death forever, but you can live your real life as the Caesar. The Caesar builds the dream, the wheel, and the coliseum that suits him.'"

"That's it?" Chris asked when Oren stopped interjecting. "Okay, yes, I love it, duh. It's sweet. You inspired each other. But it was that fast?"

"Eh..." Oren trailed off and crossed his arms. "Took us another fourteen years to get married, then eight years before we moved out here. Odd jobs, bullshit, bad luck, and some tornado damage. When Twyla says chaos rules the world, that's the fuckin' truth, but we got here anyhow: Arcana, the coliseum, or whatever. Seven years ago, this was an old bicycle repair shop full of junk, but we filled it up with *new* junk. Better junk. It's the dream: a place for all the freaks and weirdos who need it. And you guys, all of you, are the ones keeping the dream alive. So, uh, yeah. Thank you, seriously."

Alea clapped her hands softly. Chris yawned and snapped his fingers. Smith saluted Oren and Twyla, thinking A-Bomb might do that sort of thing, at least in the ironic, punk way. Twyla split the tarot deck and began an overhand shuffle. Chris pouted.

"I still don't understand the dreams. How does that connect to any—?" He tried to sidebar with Alea, but she shook one hand in his face.

"Don't think too hard about it."

Twyla beckoned Smith and the others towards her table and the shuffled deck. "Now, who wants a reading first?"

Chris and Alea looked at each other. They appeared to form an alliance, diverting their stares to Smith.

"A-Bomb?" Chris encouraged. "Seems like your vibe."

"What, uh..." Smith sharpened their tone. "What the hell's that mean?"

Oren sauntered over and put a hand on Smith's back, guiding them closer to the table. "Yeah, brother. It's been a minute since you got one, too. Fuck, a couple years! Where've you been hiding?"

"Missed the last anniversary," Twyla called A-Bomb out.

Oren grumbled. "Oh, shit, that's right. I remember. That Eraserhead guy worked a few of your shifts."

"Henry?" Alea suggested.

"No, that wasn't his name. Something else."

Alea hid her face. "Not the... I meant Eraserhead. The main character in the movie is named Henry, played by Jack Nance."

Chris' head spun. "What are *any* of you talking about?"

"Hey, knock it off!" Oren snapped. "You're making me feel old again. At least Alea knows her David Lynch. Better than me, apparently."

"Oh, *David*," Twyla muttered as she cut the deck again. "That was his name, the other bouncer we had. Never mind that. A-Bomb, what spread are you thinking?"

She switched topics too fast. Smith stalled. They forgot how to break the paralysis. "I... Sorry, you're asking me...?"

Twyla laughed. "You can take your time, hon. For the reading, you remember?"

"Right, the reading. I know this, but it's been a minute." Smith coasted through most of the night without a stressful turn like this. Whatever Twyla needed from them, A-Bomb could deliver in an instant. Smith bristled, not ready to confess and reveal themself to four more people. Maybe they could plead for a small shot of liquor before the reading.

"I don't get it," Chris complained and spared Smith. "So, like, what's he doing now? Also, are we still gonna be here when the sun comes up?"

"Okay, okay," Twyla relented. "We'll do a quick three-card spread. A-Bomb, what question do you have for the cards?"

Smith tossed aside their laundry list of questions about themself, this world, and everyone else in it. What would A-

Bomb want to know? They settled for a question that could come from anyone: "What's, uh... What does the future hold?"

Alea snorted.

"No, no, that's good!" Twyla ran with it. "I'll break it down. First card is the past, then the present, then the future." She flipped the top card from the deck. On its face, a red winged lion hovered over two figures, who held cups towards one another. "The two of cups."

This time, Chris laughed. "Sorry. Ignore me. I'm dumb. I thought they'd be, like, fortunes? And it's just, *boom*, two cups. I can't. I'm too unserious."

Twyla traced the figures on the card. "This is a relationship in your past, a close one. It may be romantic, or it may be familial, like a sibling, or any other sort of union. There is a test taking place, or an exchange, represented by the Caduceus. That's... not worth explaining. This card would mean harmony, or peacemaking, but it's inverted. See, towards you, it's upside-down. This partnership may have been too powerful, or it may have brought danger into your life. Does that sound relevant to you?"

Smith drew a blank, trying to imagine A-Bomb's private life. "Maybe. A little."

Twyla positioned a second card next to the first. A red-cloaked monarch sat on a throne, with a scepter and two worshippers at his feet. "The Hierophant is the sixth of the major arcana."

"Sixth?" Chris raised an eyebrow at the Roman numeral *V* on the card.

"Starts at zero," Alea explained.

Oren humphed. "I was gonna say that."

"The Hierophant is the connection," Twyla stated, "between the living and the dead. He embodies a sacred system or order, which could be as simple as your daily routine or as vast as a literal ecclesiastical hierarchy. The card encourages you to acknowledge your alliance with that system—utilize it, question it, strengthen it, or whatever suits you. This is the card of your present. How do you feel about it?"

"Good," Smith said. They didn't want to shoot down her energy.

She gave them a second. "That's all? That's okay. We can go on to the next one. You asked for the future, so here it is."

Twyla flipped the last card. When it landed, Alea sucked her teeth.

"Damn," Oren whispered.

"What is *that*?" Chris stooped lower over the table. On the card, two characters fell headfirst from a burning tower in the night.

"The Tower," Twyla told him, "is the seventeenth major arcanum, and in my opinion, the most *dramatic* card in the deck. There may be violence, great challenges, or a crisis in your future. Those may already crop up at work, but I hope The Tower means more for you. The omen of this card is one I view more seriously than the arcanum of Death."

"That's so... *bad*." Smith expected a more ambiguous explanation, like the first two. "The Tower sounds like the worst one. And that's my future?"

"Maybe." Twyla shut her eyes, then reopened them. "The Tower may be your opportunity to rebuild from its ruins, after it crumbles."

"Yeah, that's true," Oren agreed, "or it means you're gonna die soon."

XI
POLICE
JUSTICE

XI: JUSTICE

The air on Smith's face jumped, same as when the flatbed truck ripped the door off Wayne's SUV. Death crossed their mind again, now closer than the swirling gossip about the van crash. Every hint of danger set their nerves on edge. No matter how many times Smith reminded themself about the whole *ghost* thing, dying in any body scared them. Maybe they'd come back, same as always, drinking another cheap beer at Arcana. Maybe they'd die for good, dragging their imprisoned host to the same grave. They imagined death's sensation similarly to their life's beginning, as Andy: sudden, confusing, and solitary.

"You're wrong," Smith declared and stepped back from the card table. "I'm not gonna die."

Oren chuckled. "Shit, man, I'm just fucking with you. You're spooked that easy?"

"Spooked? *I'm* spooked?" Smith let Alea, Chris, Twyla, and Oren soak in nervous silence. "It's hilarious that you think I'm scared. You'd be laughing, and you should be, but I don't think you're paying attention. You don't get it. Alea, do you remember putting out the fire the night of that punk show, on your date with Logan? Twyla, do you remember how you cut your hands? How about Chris, you and Oren don't remember going to the funeral fundraiser, do you?"

Chris stammered. "I... I mean, I was drunk, it's not like—"

"Aha!" Smith grabbed Alea's half-empty seltzer can off a tool shelf. "Your memories are like Swiss cheese, and you all accept it. You fill in the blanks with the stories you hear about your missing hours, and you tell yourself you didn't *really* black out, don't you?"

"A-Bomb..." Twyla gathered up her cards.

Oren wiggled his fingers at Smith. "My guy, you drink too. Glass houses, motherfucker."

"This!" Smith hoisted the seltzer can over their head. "This isn't *just* a drink. There's more going on in this bar than any of you are ready to accept, but fuck it. I'm not A-Bomb! In a few seconds, he won't remember any of this. My name is Smith, and I'm one of the motherfuckers who's haunting your asses. Yeah, you get it now? Don't tell me I'm gonna die, cause apparently it's too late for that. You can go ahead and deny it or forget about it, same as I keep trying to do. It doesn't make a difference. I'm gonna find whoever did this to me, and you can all keep pretending I wasn't here."

All four half-listened, joking along until Smith stopped. Whether by tone, context, or the element of surprise, they quit fooling around. A-Bomb wouldn't pull a prank like this. Someone else stood in his shoes, and one by one, they seemed to notice.

"Smith?" Twyla asked. She poured such concern into their name. "Whatever's in your cards, I hope you find peace."

"Cheers to that," Smith muttered. They gulped the flat contents of the stolen seltzer.

A flurry of new voices chattered around Smith. The music kicked back into gear. Smith sat on a red couch in the corner of the main barroom. The last sip of a red wine dissolved on their tongue. They lowered its lightweight glass onto a low table near the arm of the couch. The fragile glass stem refracted the beam of A-Bomb's flashlight as he checked a newcomer's ID.

"Apparently, he can't remember shit," a man on the couch next to Smith carried on, "but I saw it happen. Out of nowhere, he's just looking out the car window, and he grabs the door handle. I reach to keep him in the car, but—"

"I know." Smith locked eyes with Stu and finished his story for him. "Then, Hunter opened the door, and a flatbed truck ripped it off. Right?"

Stu coughed out a short laugh, matching it with a face of mixed fear and confusion. "You're... right. Sorry, did I already text you this story? That's on me, I—"

"No, stop." Smith crossed their legs and examined their yellow acrylic nails. "I don't want to interrupt your date, if that's what this is, but I have to get going."

"*My* date?" Stu bit his lip and leaned closer, whispering. "You don't gotta be nervous. I've used the same site once or twice before, and it's really fine. You don't tell your husband, I don't tell my wife, and no one in this shitty bar knows either of us."

Upon remembering that Stu was married, Smith would've assumed themself to be his wife, but he gave up the game. To their disappointment, Stu's relatively upstanding behavior among his friends didn't correlate to a faithful marriage. The tarot reading lit a fire under Smith's ass to go handle their own shit tonight, but Stu's veiled threat held two marriages hostage. Smith couldn't ditch this one.

"Stu, it's..." Smith recoiled at the chore of explaining themself again. "What did I tell you my name was?"

"Katie. Is that not...?" Stu scratched his head. "I mean, it's fine if you use a fake name on the site. They allow it."

Ulysses Thomas Hayes. Hearing Stu's voice, Smith recalled the full name he read from the news article at The Neon Sphinx. Lucid fragments of the bachelor party preserved just enough traces of Stu to recover some details about his life. Above all else, he and Hayes attended the same high school. A more sober Stu could shed new light on the missing van owner. Maybe puppeteering the rest of their adulterous date night could benefit Smith as much as Stu.

"Call me Smith. *Katie* Smith, if that helps." Smith found a new rhythm, a new tactic, at the cost of a couple lies. "If you promise me not to blow my cover, I promise not to blow yours. Deal?"

"I mean, yeah." Stu tapped his foot. "When you say it like that, you almost sound like a cop."

Smith only needed to twist the truth halfway. "I'm not a cop. I'm a private investigator."

"Oh, okay. Wow." Stu ran a hand through his hair. "You told me that whole story about meeting your best friend, working at the credit union. If that's a cover story, like, holy shit. You could have a career in Hollywood. Was that all fake, seriously?"

"The bank is my day job," Smith decided. "I'm a bank teller by day, P.I. by night."

"Wait, you're a *teller*? I thought you were an internal auditor?"

Smith wondered what other traps Katie set for them to dodge. "Tellers and auditors, same thing. It's whatever. The point is, I'm working for an anonymous client, and I need to find someone who's missing. Have you heard of Ulysses Thomas Hayes?"

Stu set down his beer can. "Whoa. You're chasing that reward money, then."

"No, no." Smith liked the idea, but it wouldn't mesh with their 'anonymous client' lie. "You know him, though, don't you? Hayes?"

"I mean, I haven't seen him in years. We had, like, pre-calculus together, but he was younger and kinda sketchy. I once saw him take a stapler, open it up, like, to stick something up on a wall, and he just *whacked* it down on his left arm." Stu reenacted the motion with his phone, pressing its edge into his skin. "He put a staple in, right in front of everybody. I don't know what the hell he expected. He pulled it out and got blood on his desk. Teacher sent him out, I think. That's the way he was, though: not a mean guy, but definitely not *right*. That's how I knew him. Now he's caught up in this whole horrible thing. Kid like that grows up in South Hillbrook, he wasn't never quite destined for great things. You hate to say it."

"South Hillbrook?" Smith pretended to take notes on the locked screen of Katie's phone. "That's... south of here?"

"Southeast, yeah." Stu waited for Smith to stop typing. "I mean, that's bad of me to judge. I know some great guys who came outta there, and it's no one's fault what their family's got, or not got. Now I look back, and I think of what I coulda done or said to him, right? Any of us, maybe we coulda made this not happen. So, you're investigating the van crash?"

Smith put the phone away. "Yes, the crash. What do you think happened?"

Stu took a breath and sipped his beer. "I wasn't there. I haven't seen the guy in ages. What's it matter what I think?"

"If it helps me find Hayes, it matters."

Stu reclined into the couch cushion and rested his ankle on his knee. "I think his girl borrowed the van. The one who died. Maybe she and that old rich dude, the other one who died, linked up over a website. There are worse sites out there, you know. If his wife never knew, she might blame some fuckup whose beater van fell apart and killed him. She'd be the one to hire somebody like you, wouldn't she?"

"No. Well, I can't say." Smith stood up and looked past Stu at the parking lot.

"You leaving? I thought you said—"

"It's only nine thirty now. I've gotta go down to South Hillbrook and look for Hayes, then I'll come back here to finish our date. Sound good?"

"Now, hang on." Stu picked up his unfinished drink but stopped short of taking another sip. "You had that whole glass of wine. My car's a mess, but I'll do you a solid and drive you there and back, so we can keep talking in the meantime." He left his beer on the table next to Smith's dry wine glass. "I'll close my tab and meet you out there."

It didn't sound like a question.

Smith used a few seconds alone in the parking lot to open the camera app on Katie's phone. Her thin gold necklace and clean white teeth shined. Around her eyes, delicate touches of makeup stole back a couple years. Judging by her satin yellow dress, the credit union paid her well. On a hunch, Smith searched Katie's buttoned yellow purse that slung over their shoulder.

Stu emerged from Arcana. "I doubt he'd run back to his family, and that's gotta be the first place anyone looks around. You sure about this?"

"You can drive my car," Smith offered, finding a key fob in Katie's purse, "if that sweetens the deal for you." They squeezed the 'unlock' button on the fob. A sporty yellow hatchback blinked its ambers at the back of the overflow parking lot. Stu pulled his hands out of his pockets and accepted the key.

In the car, he and Smith buckled their seatbelts. Smith waited for him to start the engine, but he held the key an inch away from the ignition.

"I feel outmatched," Stu said.

Smith tried to finish his thoughts for him. "Outmatched because you've never been on a date with someone who can afford her own drinks?"

Stu dropped the key in the cupholder. "Because I wanted this to be simple, you know? Marriage gets complicated real quick. Once in a while, I need one night away from that to feel like a real man again. Now, here I am feeling like tonight is gonna get complicated even faster."

"You *are* a real man," Smith assured him, wishing they'd gotten Hayes' address and ditched Stu already. After stringing Logan along, Smith knew how this could end. The odds of any positive outcome drew slimmer by the minute. "What's so complicated about driving a pretty woman in her car?"

"You're not just using me for this, are you?" Stu squeezed the key fob. "You actually *want* me, like you texted before?"

"After you help me with this job?" Smith swallowed their pride and rested their left hand on Stu's leg, praying that the pain of their next words would buy them his trust. "I'll want you even more."

"Yeah. Yeah, alright." Stu inserted the keys and started the car's engine. The dashboard screen and buttons poured dim orange over them.

Katie's phone automatically connected to her car's Bluetooth. A ferocious, bass-boosted Latin pop track shook the car. Smith jabbed the dashboard to shut it off. Stu found the steering wheel's volume control before they did. Smith pushed their hair back over their shoulders and tried to disappear into their bucket seat. Stu reversed the car and aimed for the lot's back exit. He said nothing until they hit a red light heading south.

"Have you done this before?"

Smith juggled a few assumptions. "You mean...?"

"Well, finding people. For your job, tracking people down who might not wanna be found."

"Sure, I have." Smith dug Katie deeper into their tunnel of lies. "People hire me to follow people. Spouses, enemies, or, uh, whoever they want, really."

"Uh-huh." The light changed, and Stu hit the gas a little too hard. He quickly eased back. "Sorry. Powerful engine. So, like, what's your plan with his family?"

"See how it goes," Smith figured.

Stu checked the time on the dashboard clock. "You ever roll up to South Hillbrook this late at night before?"

"No. Maybe, once or twice. Why?"

"Hang on." Stu slowed the car and signaled a turn into a grocery store parking lot. "Hayes' folks ain't gonna talk to you for nothing. No offense, but you kinda look like you're from the bank. I mean, you sorta are, but not like that. I mean, if you show up late, you gotta show up with good news, not bad news, and definitely not asking a whole boatload of questions. You know what I mean?"

"Okay, sure." Smith marveled at the 24-hour supermarket's huge, illuminated sign.

"You gotta bring them food." Stu parked in the sparse lot under a tall, flickering lamppost. "One of my homies used this same trick after his girlfriend tried to dump him."

"It worked?"

"For a few days. A day or two, then she broke it off for good. He had it coming; he got mean after a few beers, and he for sure talked shit behind her back. Never mind. Point is, you need them to like you in the first few minutes, so you give 'em food. You coming inside with me?"

"Yes. Yeah, I will."

If only for curiosity, Smith followed Stu into the vastness of Kabe's Neighborhood Market. Fluorescent white illuminated the grocery store like the hotel, but the store's ceiling rose three times higher. Mellow, wordless Muzak tweeted from invisible corners in the distance. Wooden produce crates and misted shelves of organic vegetables tempted Smith's attention like carnival games. Forgotten hunger stirred in their gut. Smith read the signs at the ends of the aisles, seeking the words *hot dog*. Stu bypassed each corridor until he reached the curved glass displays of the deli counter.

"Sheet cake," Stu pointed. "That's your golden ticket."

"Sheet cake?"

"No one says no to a sheet cake. Question is, what should it say?"

From the deli kitchen, a lethargic employee emerged and donned an apron. "No customs," she droned. A sign above the cake counter advised that custom cake icing required two hours' notice.

"Shit," Stu whispered and checked his watch, "we don't have that kinda time. Do you see a Halloween one?"

Smith checked the cake options. "When's Halloween?"

"When's...? Uh, couple weeks, so maybe too early. What about—?"

"The birthday one. I have an idea for the birthday one."

"Okay, sure. The white and blue?"

Before Smith could explain to Stu, the employee slid the cake from the back of its display case and rang it up at the counter. Smith reached for Katie's purse, only then discovering no weight from its strap on their shoulder.

"Shit," Smith muttered. "I left her—uh, my purse in the car. Sorry."

"No, no, it's all good," Stu assured them, his voice a rigid monotone. He tapped his phone against the checkout console, not bothering to read the price. The deli employee stuck the receipt onto the cake's clear plastic lid and handed it over to Stu.

"Have a nice night," she said, compressing all four words into a portmanteau. She took off her apron and retreated to the kitchen.

Stu passed the cake to Smith. The chilled plastic container sweat condensation onto their hands. Wavy blue icing on top wished Smith a happy birthday. "Thanks. Sorry."

Stu started back towards the car. "What's your plan?"

Smith walked Stu through their basic strategy during the fifteen-minute drive from the supermarket. They tried to sound professional, like a hardened investigator who'd executed many undercover stings. The lying and improvising came easier than the technical language and attitude. Stu listened with his eyes on the road and only interrupted to ask key questions.

"Are you sure you want me to walk up with you?"

"Would that make you uncomfortable?"

Stu scrunched his nose. "There's always a chance they might recognize me. Even if they don't, a man's got worse odds knocking their door this late. They see me, they know I ain't selling bibles, know what I mean?" Smith didn't. Stu took one hand off the wheel to mimic a handgun firing. "My folks don't never answer the door unarmed. Middle of the night, I don't reckon the Hayes clan are much different. When his dad or uncle comes up to the door, that cute yellow dress might be the only way he lets his guard down."

Smith squeezed the smooth fabric of their dress between two fingers. They were simultaneously the P.I. in the dress, Katie as the P.I., Smith in Katie's skin, all carrying the real cake. They felt like so many trojan horses, nested within one another, rolling blindly towards the enemy gates. "You can wait in the car, then."

"How long do you think you'll need?"

Smith couldn't know. "Until just before they shoot me, I guess."

Stu slowed the car and turned off the two-lane street onto an unlined road. The beam of the headlights revealed a patchwork of old asphalt, loose gravel, and soggy pits in the ground. Stu weaved between the gaps and eased the tires over muddy bumps. The road forked, looping in opposite directions. At the fork, wooden posts held a sheet metal sign for South Hillbrook Estates. Telephone poles slung thin black wires over three long rows of single- and double-wide homes. In the dark of the forest surrounding the neighborhood, only a few purple streetlights and motion-sensing outdoor lamps lit the area. Pulses from television screens escaped the thin white curtains of a few houses. Rugged old coupes, battered pickups, and plain minivans occupied grassy parking gaps between each plot of land.

"You've been here before?" Smith questioned Stu.

"Old lacrosse buddy lived down here. Hayes family was a few houses over. Down here, on the third row." Stu switched off the car's headlights and backed into an empty lot at the corner of the gravel loop. "Is this close enough?"

"Yeah."

Stu killed the engine. The milky cabin lights waited for a door to open. "So, you're really doing this. And I'm really help-ing you do it."

Smith unlocked their door. "Problem?"

"No, it ain't. Just not the night I expected us to have."

"The night's not over," Smith reminded, but he ignored that.

"When you get out, go right. It'll be the fifth or sixth one on your right. Oh, and lemme see the cake." Stu peeled the receipt off its plastic lid, crumpled it, and dropped it in the driver's door pocket.

"Right. I'll be back soon." Smith pushed the door open. They imagined Stu taking off, stealing Katie's car, and leaving them alone in South Hillbrook. Did they deserve that for lying to him? Did Katie deserve that for cheating on her husband? Everything rested in Stu's hands. This night needed Smith's full focus.

Cake in hand, Smith walked themself through their cover story one last time.

A tiny dog barked at them from a window. The engine brakes of a large truck growled beyond the trees. A few houses further, a thin metal pole in the dirt hung a carved sign from its hook: *Hayes*. Smith stepped up to the single-wide's porch side door, opened the screen, and knocked below the peep-hole.

They waited. Maybe no one would come. This late, they'd be asleep. If no one answered the door, at least Smith wouldn't face the barrel of a gun. They'd settle for that small victory, at the cost of another wasted night. They could—

The deadbolt clunked. The knob rolled. The door opened.

"Hello?" A girl, maybe five years old, stared up at Smith from the short foyer. Smith planned for several possibilities, but not for her.

"Hi! Um..." Smith peered over her into an open kitchen and living room. "Is there a... Are your parents—?"

"Maycee!" A woman's harsh whisper sent the girl scurrying back from the entryway. "You call *me* over to answer the door. You know that." A woman wearing a silky pink hair cap and an oversized gray T-shirt took the girl's place. Like the double barrels of a shotgun, her dark brown eyes aimed at all of Smith's vulnerable spots. "So sorry for my daughter. Can I help you, ma'am?"

Smith began their script. "Hi! I'm sorry, I know it's late. I was at your neighbor's house for my godson's birthday party. We had this cake I bought, and I, well... He's got an allergy, a gluten thing, and I don't want it to go to waste."

"Aw, the poor baby! None of y'all wanted the rest of it?"

"No, yeah, we..." Only now considering the question, Smith *did* want a slice of cake. "We can't go eating it in front of him, not on his birthday."

The woman exited onto the porch. Smith backed against the wood railing. She pointed to the house next door. "This is over at the Calverhil's place?"

"No, uh, the other direction."

"The McCool's?"

She knew a lot of neighbors.

"It's one further down," Smith tried.

"Oh, the Angelinos! Sad to say I don't see them too often. Here, you come on inside before I let all the bugs in the house." She ushered Smith into the living room and let the screen door close behind them. She cleared a space on the countertop and took the cake from Smith. "I'm Evelyn, and this is Maycee. Say hi, May."

Maycee pouted and waved from the couch.

"I'm Katie. Smith." They forgot to invent a new first name.

Evelyn popped the lid from the cake and knocked on the counter with her knuckles. "You had me *worried* for a second there. We've had some terrible business with my brother-in-law's kid, all sorts of strangers showing up and asking around for him." She picked a long chef's knife from a kitchen drawer and waved it at Smith. "I've about *had* it."

"Cake!" Maycee rushed from the couch, but Evelyn blocked her with a dish towel.

"Shh!" Evelyn pressed a finger to her lips. "You'll wake your father. Go sit. I'll bring you a plate, May."

"Business with your nephew?" Smith asked as quietly and casually as they could.

"Tommy," Evelyn muttered, cutting a corner off the cake. "My nephew, little Tommy, all grown up, still a wild child. First they say he's dead, then he's alive and might've m-u-r-d-e-r'ed his girlfriend and a rich fella. Then, the rich guy's widow starts making statements through her lawyer, putting up a *bounty* to find Tommy. You believe that, in this day and age?" Evelyn slid the blade under the cake slice and flipped it onto a paper plate. She handed the plate to Smith with a plastic fork from a box on the counter.

"Thanks. Wow, I'm so sorry." Smith pinched the strap of Katie's dress.

"It ain't on you, it's just a whole *thing*." Evelyn prepped another slice. "Now, I'm in a big fight with my brother-in-law over this. I'm about darn sure Tommy's the one who stole his bicycle last week, and he ain't even interested to get some justice for *that*. Tommy ain't a kid no more, and I say he oughta learn about consequences."

The first bite of cake sent Smith's mind to another plane. The overpowering sweetness of cool vanilla and corn syrup coated every inch of their mouth. By the time they swallowed the first bite, Smith forgot their whole cover story.

"Tommy," they realized aloud. "I didn't know he went by that. 'Ulysses Thomas Hayes.' It's a..." Smith caught themself too late. The ruse collapsed. A car rumbled up the gravel outside. Its headlights pierced the screen door and glinted off Evelyn's knife. She stopped cutting the cake.

"Ma'am, now, I don't know what you're here about, but I need you to leave. Right now." Evelyn shoved the cake off the counter and into an open trash can. She aimed the knife past Smith at the idling pickup truck outside. Blue frosting dripped on the carpet. "That'll be my brother-in-law, Walter, and if you don't make him eat your dust in seven split seconds, this knife's gonna be the least of your troubles, you hear? Now get on!"

"The cake!" Maycee whined and started to cry.

Smith rushed out through the screen door and nearly fell down the porch steps. They wanted to apologize somehow, but a voice from the idling pickup truck stole their chance.

"Who the *fuck* are you?" Walt Hayes gripped the open door of his truck, half invisible behind its blinding high beams.

"Who do you *think*?" Evelyn answered before Smith could. "She's another one here about Tommy!"

"You think you know my boy, do you?" Walt slammed the truck door and planted himself, blocking Smith's path. He towered one head over Katie's modest frame. "I'll teach you vultures to show up to my house, acting like we don't know what you're..." Walt growled like a bull about to charge. "You ain't just another vulture. I know exactly who you are."

Smith avoided his eyes. He wore a plastic boot cast on his left leg. Stuck between Walt and the side of the house, Smith gambled on a quick jump towards the street. Walt lunged after them but slipped and toppled down in the dirt. He cried out in pain. Evelyn and Maycee ran to the porch. Smith hurried away towards the corner of the gravel loop.

"Walt!" Evelyn called over the railing.

"I'm fine. This damn leg, I gotta... Hey! Don't you walk away from me!"

Even in Katie's tall yellow shoes, Smith could outpace him in a straight line. Maybe Walt made the same calculation. The truck door squeaked open and slammed once more. Its throaty diesel motor raised its voice.

"Stu!" Smith shouted towards the yellow hatchback. Only Stu's phone screen underlit his bored visage in the dark cabin. "Stu, start the car! Start the car!"

Smith wrenched the door open. Stu jumped and dropped his phone.

"Jesus! What happened?"

"We have to go. Let's go! The keys. You have the keys?"

"Yeah, right here. Okay, alright! I'm going. Did they know where Hayes was?" Stu put the car in gear and turned right. Walt's truck rumbled and bounced closer down the gravel.

"Other way!" Smith grabbed the steering wheel and sent the car fishtailing. Pebbles and dirt spattered the back window.

"Holy *shit*!" Stu gunned the engine. Tires ripped into the uneven ground. Both their bodies flung back into their seats. "What the hell happened over there?"

"We're not the first ones here looking for Hayes. They're sick of it. His dad came home, and I might've re-broken his leg."

"You did *what?*"

The car rounded the corner at the front of the neighborhood. Stu's side mirror missed a mailbox by an arm's length. The truck's high beams chased them like the spotlight of a helicopter. Its dual rear wheels tackled every bump straight-on.

"He's gonna hit us," Stu fretted. "I don't wanna wreck your car!"

"We'll lose him at the exit. Go!" Smith directed Stu around the sheet metal neighborhood sign. Smooth asphalt returned up beneath them. Stu signaled rightward without slowing. The pep of the hatchback shot them forward. No traffic in sight ahead, Smith caught their breath. In a few heartbeats, they cleared the first hill northbound.

"They don't know where Hayes is," Smith reported. "If they did, his aunt would've turned him in already. Bounty money or not, she thinks he's a nuisance. She thinks he stole a bike from his dad, who was the one driving the—"

"Oh, you gotta be kidding me."

Stu checked the mirrors. So did Smith. An angry diesel engine crested the hill behind them, still locked like a missile on their tiny yellow lifeboat. Stu notched the automatic transmission into sport mode. He looked to Smith for approval.

"Yeah. We gotta lose this guy." Smith clung to the handle over the passenger door.

"I actually miss my wife, now, dammit." Stu steadied his hands on the wheel. "If this isn't the *last* thing I ever do, it better be the coolest."

THE HANGED MAN

XII: THE HANGED MAN

Racing through the night landscape in Oren and Twyla's car liberated Smith from the only space they'd ever known. Tonight, the confined interior of Katie's speeding vehicle imprisoned them. Every twisty backroad intersection tied their stomach in knots. No matter how fast Stu executed his turns, each random detour added slim margins to the gap between their car and Walt's pickup.

"I can't do this forever," Stu warned. Smith heard the exhaustion in his breath.

"Neither can he."

"You got any ideas?"

Smith monitored the lights behind them. "If he's trying to scare us, he's done that. If he's trying to run us off the road, he could've done it a few turns ago. I don't know what he wants. Something doesn't fit."

Stu hit the brakes. Smith braced an arm against the dashboard as he swung a hairpin turn onto a one-lane road. "Whoa! What are you—?"

"You're right," Stu said. "Something doesn't *fit*."

Signs at the pull-off forbade through traffic. Ahead, a reflective yellow diamond cautioned: *NARROW TUNNEL.* The gray stone arch of an old railway underpass hung over the pavement. Stu maintained their speed. The short tunnel swallowed them. Dead vines on its jagged, crumbling wall streaked past Smith's door at arm's length. On the other side, the detour road curved and widened past the locked fence entrance of a scrapyard.

"Can't put a dually through there," Stu smiled. Sure enough, the fiery brights of the truck stopped shy of the tunnel. Stu eased off the accelerator and coasted down to the local road's speed limit. Smith released the handle above the window and flexed their tense knuckles. Time slowed back down. Stu took the car out of sport mode. Smith shut their eyes.

A heavy rumbling shook the car through the ground. Smith open their eyes. The red and white striped gates of a level railroad crossing blocked their path. The diesel locomotive of a freight train blasted its horn twice before cutting across the road and stranding them on the junkyard side of the tracks.

"Shit," Stu huffed and stopped the car.

"I'm sorry," Smith said. "You were right. That was a bad idea."

Stu gave up his chance to gloat. "Katie, was Hayes your secret boyfriend?"

"What?"

"It would explain a lot." Stu spoke slower than before. "I ain't no investigative professional myself, but I know the Internet. While you were out there, I did some research on my phone. I found your picture on the credit union website. Finding out about what's going on with you, I think I see why you told me your last name was 'Smith.' I saw your bio said you're into younger guys like me, and your profile has been up for two years. That's plenty time to meet other guys like Hayes before me. Dumbass I am, I've got a photo on my page wearing an East Hillbrook lacrosse shirt, so you knew I went there around the same time he did. You knew you could use me to find him if he's hiding from you. I wasn't gonna say all this, thinking we've each got equal shots at blowing up the other's life, but that don't seem quite true anymore. I know you're not really a P.I., Katie, and I hate to ask, but you don't exactly *have* a husband, do you?"

"*What?*" Smith's reaction burst from their lungs. "No, I've never met Hayes before. I didn't..." Without time to conduct their own research on Katie, Smith couldn't whip up a fresh alternative to their P.I. cover story. They had no choice but to double down on it. "Anything you read about me on the Internet is there because I want it to be. You really think everything you read online is true?"

"I know it ain't," Stu told them. "But I know I do not trust you, Katie *Smith*."

Smith accepted that. "We don't have to finish our date. If you just want to get back to your car, that's fine."

The last few cars of the train rolled through the crossing. "Yeah," Stu considered. "I think this was a mistake. I need to—" He sprung back in his seat. "Oh, fuck. What the fuck?"

With the train gone, the gates rose. On the other side of the rails, Walt Hayes' truck blocked the whole road. He leaned on its front fender, a high-caliber pistol tucked in the waist of his jeans.

"Y'all get on out," Walt ordered, as if inviting them to an ice cream shop. "Let's have a talk."

Stu grasped the shifter, ready to reverse towards the tunnel. Smith pushed his hand forward and parked the car. "Stay here. I'll go."

"Stay here, my ass," Stu scoffed. "Man with the firearm said 'y'all.'"

Stu and Smith opened their doors and kept their hands out, palms visible. They inched away from the hatchback and walked onto the train tracks. Walt stayed at his truck, letting them approach.

"My name is Walter Hayes," he told them. "Driver, who're you?"

"Stewart Emmells, sir."

Walt nodded and kept one hand on the gun's grip. "Stewart, you know my son?"

"In school," Stu told him. "We played lacrosse, sir."

Walt clicked his tongue. "Don't remember you. Guess you remember my son being a fuck-up who couldn't shoot a ball worth shit?"

Stu waited as long as possible to answer. "No, sir."

"Well, he was, and he is a fuckup. That shithead's caused me more trouble than he's worth, and I reckon I've done about the same to him by now. Bet I was younger than you the day he was born. That was a hard thing for both of us, my bringing Tommy into a world neither of us was ready for. He'd tell you the same. Stewart, you have kids yet? No, I thought not.

"When you do have a child, I want you to promise me something. Promise me that you'll do better than I did. Listen to 'em if they tell you something difficult. Give 'em everything you can when they're little, and give 'em nothing but love when they grow up to challenge you. Cause if, God forbid, you get that call one day, that call, the... 'there's been a terrible accident' call..." Walt's voice cracked. He rubbed his eyes. "I hurt like I never thought I could when they told me I lost Tommy. Next day, I hurt ten times more because I knew I could've saved him. So many years, I could've done more, cause I thought I had more time to.

"Now, I *do* have more time. I got my Tommy back, wherever he is, and I got a chance to be something right for him this time. Katie, I dunno what he's done, but I do know the price on his head, so I'm begging you." Walt carefully lowered his good knee to the pavement. One hand flat on the ground, he bent his injured leg to match. "Both of you, I'm begging you. The only man who can't change is the hanged man. I don't have the stacks of cash to buy you off this thing, but please let Tommy go while he's still got time to change. I wanna be a *father* again."

Walt froze on the ground at that, wilted over, holding still enough to almost hide his sobbing gasps. A mile north, another pair of horn blasts wailed from the train. Smith wished to be anywhere else in the world. They didn't fear Walt's gun, his truck, or the rest of him anymore. The possibility of finding Hayes put a bigger weapon in Smith's hands, its bullet angled down at the bald spot on Walt's head.

"Get in the car," Smith mouthed to Stu. He climbed back in and shut the door as quietly as possible. If Walt heard, he didn't react. Smith approached Walt, scuffing the soles of Katie's shoes on the asphalt. Stu waved them to come back and ditch the man, but Smith walked closer.

"I'm not the person you think I am," Smith confided. "I don't want to hurt anyone."

"Then leave him be," Walt choked and sat upright again. "Don't hurt him. He's not who you think he is, either."

Smith reached one hand down to help Walt to his feet. "All I need is to talk to your son. If I can settle my unfinished business with him, he's all yours. You really don't know where he'd be?"

Walt batted their hand aside. "Enough with this bounty madness, then, okay?" He braced his other arm on the bumper of the truck and stood himself up with a grunt. He checked the empty road for other witnesses before wiping the tears off his cheeks. "Tommy hasn't wanted nothing to do with me for months, but I reckon you can find him yourself. And if you do see him, you tell him..." Walt met Smith's eyes for the first time. "Tell him his old man said, 'I love you.'"

Smith left Walt by his truck. The night marched on.

Back inside the car, Stu asked Smith what they said to Walt. Smith told Stu it didn't matter, and Stu drove them back the way they came. He stopped trying to start new conversations. Smith tried to absorb the late-night scenery or think about anything other than Walt. No one else talked about

Hayes the way his father did. Colton, Stu, and even Evelyn pronounced his name like a curse. They assigned 'Hayes' all the evils of the world, and only Walt saw him differently. Did that change anything?

At Arcana once again, Smith made Stu park Katie's car in the same spot as before. He returned Katie's keys to Smith, who stowed them in Katie's purse. Streaks of gray mud and dirt coated the yellow hatchback's wheel wells and side panels. Smith wondered how Katie might explain that to herself.

"Still need another drink?" Smith caught Stu staring at the bar entrance.

"I'll buy my own, Katie *Smith*."

Smith ordered one vodka shot on Katie's open tab. They brought it to the table from earlier and sat in the same spot on the couch, as similar as possible. Stu ordered himself a second beer, same as the one he never finished.

"Thank you," Smith told Stu and raised their glass to him. "For what it's worth, thank you."

Stu didn't raise his glass. "I think you're the scariest person I've ever met."

Smith crossed their legs. "Forget my whole P.I. thing, South Hillbrook, all of it. Tuck it away. I'll pretend it never happened, after this drink. Seriously, I'll act like I don't remember, and you can start the whole date fresh from the beginning."

"You know what?" Stu stood up and set his untouched beer on the nearest table. "I'm just gonna go. You're a twisted, sick woman, and believe it or not, I *do* love my wife."

Stu strode out the door without looking back.

Smith knocked back their vodka.

Another night swallowed them and spat them out thirty feet away, in the goth room. The smooth dark wood of the old church pew pressed up under their new legs. Two white sneakers on their feet barely scraped the floor. The bitter rush of gin and tonic tickled their mouth, so Smith tongued an ice cube from their highball to dilute the flavor. Even from across the room, the crisp fade of Georgie's hair stood out in the goth room's framed mirror.

Only a foot away from Smith, Saint perched backwards on the pew. They parted the blackout curtains to snoop at the street.

Smith scooted further. "What are you doing?"

"It's so—" A flash of lightning washed over Saint's face. Near-immediate thunder rattled the glass panes and interrupted their giddy storm watching. The steady static clatter of heavy rain muffled the chorus of a glam rock ballad from the next room. "The storm's right over us, now. We should sit outside! Georgie, we gotta."

Smith balked. "Out in that? We'll get soaked."

The thought of water on their face reminded smith of the shower. They ate another chip of ice and tried to erase that memory. It made them sweat.

"What am I, your butler?" Oz carried two tall beer cans down the steps towards the pew. "Alea's the one working tonight, but here I am ordering for you anyway."

Saint accepted the drink. "Thanks, *Mom*."

Oz recoiled. "Ew. Georgie, bully Saint for me."

"Bitch," Smith attempted. Oz thumbs-upped and sipped her beer.

Saint flicked the curtain at Smith. "Wow, the Napoleon complex really popped out."

Oz gestured to the main room. "Georgie, did Saint ask to sit outside yet?"

Smith nodded. "They just did."

"Yeah. Big gay nerd. Future meteorologist, Saint Perez."

Saint pulled their face back from the window. "It's not *my* fault thunderstorms are sexy. Have any of you seen *Twister*? No, that's right. You just saw the sequel, like a couple of beta losers. Go back and watch the original, wherever it's streaming. The storms are treated like characters! They bring drama. They flaunt their funnel clouds, strutting up and down the farms. Flipping cows."

Saint shimmied like a tornado, and Oz almost spat her drink. "You're so weird! I love you."

"Do we ever get tornadoes here?" Smith couldn't place Lewesboro in relation to tornado alley. Come to think of it, they couldn't place tornado alley, either. Saint rubbed their palms together, relishing the question.

"Okay, so basically, we can't. The mountains block supercells from rotating, except in wide enough valleys, in rare cases when—" Another thunderclap steamrolled their explanation.

"Hm." Oz licked her teeth. "Okay, this could be something. How about we sit outside and tell ghost stories?"

Saint let the curtain drop and climbed down from the pew. They stood and sipped their fresh beer at Oz. "Okay, yes! You're on. Let's get spooky." Another barrage of thunder roared. "Georgie, you in?"

"Yeah!" Smith pretended. Of course, it had to be ghost stories. "Gonna grab another drink first. I'll meet you out there." They swirled their melting ice.

"Bet," Oz chirped. She and Saint paraded up the steps. Smith took a breath, fixed the curtain shut, and dragged themself away towards the bar.

An average medley of patrons milled up and down the checkerboard linoleum. A few danced loosely to the thrum of a funky prog-rock track. Behind the bar, Alea twisted the cap off a cheap vodka bottle, pried the spout from its empty twin, and swapped it onto the new bottle. As Smith waited for her to notice them, Twyla shuffled on her barstool and fluttered a thick sheet of paper. She held it up to the chandelier light, then set it back down. On her left, Jade set up her tabletop drawing light.

"My eyes ain't what they were," Twyla said.

Jade sighed. "It was gonna be more."

"Oh, isn't that wonderful! You drew all this?"

Smith snooped over Twyla's shoulder. On the tall white sheet, the detailed sketch evoked none of Jade trademark violence and menace. Her ink formed the irregular stems and fine-ridged petals of various flowers in a bouquet. A shaded bow died them together, and along each loop of its ribbon, the ink stitched Oren and Twyla's names. Below, Jade's handwriting proclaimed: *Seven years of Arcana.*

"I made more!" Jade insisted. "For the anniversary, I wanted to illustrate a full tarot deck for you, based on this place. It was gonna be the 'New American Arcana,' full of local legends and cryptids and all that. I sketched it all out—all twenty-two trumps and fifty-six lessers. I finished making trumps, too, but someone stole them from the last Night Market."

Twyla gasped. "Darling, I'm so sorry. Do you know who? Tell me who, and I'll rough 'em up."

Jade shook her head. "I didn't see."

"You could've told me, hon."

"I know, but it was a big surprise. It's okay. I pivoted, see? Roses and lilies?"

Twyla grinned. "Like Smith's original card backs from 1909. You're such a smarty-pants. I can keep this? Are you sure?"

"You and Oren. For making Arcana an institution."

Twyla walked around the pink pole to hug Jade. She resisted at first, then relented and hugged her back.

"Georgie?" Alea locked onto Smith. "What're you having?"

Their mind blanked—stuffed full of flower petals and missing tarot cards, no room for a drink order. They skimmed a white board marked *Specials* and told Alea: "I'll have that one."

"The Arcanniversary special?"

Smith accepted. Alea assembled an intricately layered cocktail in a glass banquet goblet. Blue tendrils of fruity liqueur spread across ice shards. Alea topped the punchy potion with toothpick skewering a pineapple cube and a maraschino cherry. She plunged a straw into the mixture and turned it over to Smith, then charged it to Georgie's tab.

"Do *I* get a drawing?" Alea asked Jade.

"What's next, my truck?" Avoiding Alea's eyes, Jade ogled Smith's drink. "Do I get one of *those*?"

Alea turned away. "Twyla? May I trade one drink for one sketch?" She pressed her palms together in prayer. "When the revolution comes, we'll all depend on the barter economy."

As Twyla considered that, Smith ferried their gaudy cocktail outside to meet Saint and Oz. They sampled two big gulps from its straw to keep it from spilling. A rich burst of sugary, cold alcohols electrified their brain. In their first ever flash of brain freeze, Georgie's body seemed to reject Smith's presence from within. They winced and stopped in the doorway to the parking lot. Lightning fluttered, or maybe Smith imagined it behind Georgie's eyelids.

"Wow!" Saint cackled at them. "Tropical party boy, reporting for duty."

"Am I dying?" Smith asked. The new and unwelcome chill in their soft palate ebbed.

"Ooh," Oz said, "you got the anniversary thing. Nice."

Smith braved the splattering rain and ducked under the canopy. They settled onto the bench beside Oz. The toothpick of fruit sank into their glass. "I don't know if I can think of any ghost stories, since I just froze my brain."

Saint drummed their fingers on the picnic table. "Oz, since it was your idea, wanna go first?"

Oz shrugged. "Okay, fair. Lemme think. I know a few good ones, but I gotta get the vibe right. Do I need to shine my phone flashlight under my chin or something?"

A burst of wind sent the canopy's edge flapping. A pocket of water sloshed and dumped a few feet away, splashing Smith's ankles. The sky grumbled again.

"It's *already* a dark and stormy night," Smith reminded Oz. "What more can you ask for?"

Oz shut her eyes and tilted her head. She scrunched her nose. "I was gonna tell the one about Bayonet Bridge, but y'all already know that one."

Saint plucked the metal tab off their beer. "That's not even a *real* ghost story."

"I don't know that one," Smith said. "What's Bayonet Bridge?"

"It's *totally* real, first of all." Oz circled a point in the low southeast sky with her index finger. "Big old stone arch bridge, where that super curvy road goes into East Lewesboro."

"More like over *there*." Saint held their beer due east.

"No, cause it's up Holowell Mountain," Oz countered. "I grew up here, genius!"

"It's at the north end, though! You cross downtown, turn right before the tunnel—"

"Okay, whichever it is," Smith stopped them, "what's the story about it?"

Oz buttoned her denim jacket against the wind. "There are a few versions, and I'm sure Saint knows a *better* one, but it's so old that no one really knows, so, whatever. Holowell Mountain has this long ridgeline, and the north end is cut off like a... mini mountain, where there used to be a huge mansion, like a hundred years ago." Oz hopped two fingers across the gap between her end of picnic table and the next. "Two sisters lived in the mansion. They probably had more family, but no one tells that part of the story... One of the sisters was blind, so the other one read and wrote for her, kept her safe, and cared—"

"Important detail!" Saint interrupted. "Oz forgot that the sisters are, like, supermodel-beautiful. Sorry. Go on."

Oz blew a raspberry at them. "The sisters are already rich; I'm not giving them pretty privilege in my version of the story. Anyway, the road to the mansion was shitty, so the sisters paid a young stonemason to build a bridge from the south ridgeline. *He* was hot as fuck. Like, *shredded* for the early twentieth century. The sighted sister fell in love with him immediately, but she was too scared to make a move. She hid up in the mansion, but as the stonemason built the bridge, the *blind* sister sat by a tree and talked to him about, I dunno, European literature? Suffrage? Point is, *she* wasn't scared of him, and *he* liked her back. The sighted sister was pissed because she lost her shot to shoot her shot, but you snooze, you lose, I guess.

"So then, the bridge is done, and hunky rock boy is gonna propose to the blind sister, but oh no! World War I goes off. Saint, don't test me; I *know* they didn't call it 'World War I.' But yeah, the stonemason guy goes on his trench warfare vacay. Without him, it's real sad girl hours for the blind sister, so the sighted sister reluctantly dictates her letters to him while he's away witnessing *the horrors* and getting shot at. The blind sister waits at the bridge every day, listening for his voice when he comes home."

"Let me guess," Smith predicted: "He never came home?"

Saint muffled a grim laugh. "You ain't ready for the fucked-uppedness of true Appalachian folklore."

"Wait!" Oz hushed them. "Okay, meanwhile, the sighted sister gets *so* jealous that she does the *worst* possible thing. She never sends the blind sister's letters, and when the stonemason writes back, she burns his letters after reading them herself. When he finally writes that—surprise, surprise—he *is* coming home, the sighted sister panics because she's gonna get busted, right? He's gonna know she burned the letters, and then her blind sister is gonna know, and she'll lose both of them. So, she does the *even worse* thing and writes a letter to soldier boy *as* her blind sister. She lies and goes like, 'I've fallen in love with someone else, I never loved you,' whatever, and finally sends *that* letter. Mad evil shit.

"Cut to the blind sister, waiting at the bridge all night for this man. He marches up the mountain, pissed as fuck, and probably, like, *also* traumatized from the war. He sees the blind sister, and before she can hear him coming, he takes his rifle and stabs her through the heart with the metal... pointy thing."

"The bayonet!" Saint whined. "It's called *Bayonet* Bridge!"

Oz folded her arms. "I was getting there! I would've gotten it."

"That's a horrible story." Smith cleansed their mouth with a sip of their bright blue cocktail. It didn't help. "How tall is this bridge, if one guy built it?"

Oz continued: "After killing her, the guy shot himself on the bridge."

Smith shivered. "Aha. So *that's* the end."

"No. The sighted sister found them both in the morning, and she jumped off the bridge and died too. So now, if you ask any parent in Marks County, they'll say all three ghosts haunt Bayonet Bridge and chase away dumb teenagers who park underneath it to make out."

Smith took a larger gulp of their cocktail. They needed another round of brain freeze to wipe those grisly visuals from their mind. Were ghost stories allowed to have happy endings for the ghosts?

"Like I said," Saint gloated, "not a *real* ghost story."

Oz threw up her hands. "Hey, I don't believe in ghosts anyway, but this was your idea."

"You've never seen a ghost?"

"Fuck no," Oz retorted with as much surprise as concern. "Georgie, what about you?"

"No, I don't believe in ghosts." Smith moved with the herd.

"Georgie!" Saint whined at Smith. "You were literally *there* with me at Reina's. I know we never talk about old shit, especially that, but you remember, right?"

What did Georgie know? Alarms sounded in Smith's ears, louder than the thunder or the rain. They cooled their clammy hands on the goblet glass and bit its straw to stall for time. They needed to be Georgie. What would Georgie remember? Who was Reina?

"Oh, shit," Saint whispered. "You're still freaked out about it. You never told Oz?"

Oz leaned all the way over the middle of the picnic table. "Tell me what? Georgie! Tell me what?"

Smith shook their head. "Brain freeze. Sorry. Saint, you tell her."

"Ugh! Typical. Oz, I never told you either?"

"I don't know what you're talking about, and you're raising my blood pressure." She drummed the table. "Speak, child!"

"Fine!" Saint slurped their beer. "In high school, like, sophomore year, me and Georgie went to his friend's place like an hour away. It was a weekend, so we—"

Oz halted them. "This is during the *time*? The time we don't speak of?"

"Yes, I was dating Georgie, and no, we never got past hand stuff. Shut up. So, he drove us to his friend's house that's on a fucking farm. A farmhouse. Think Shyamalan, cause it was literally Pennsyl-fucking-vania. This place was built in the *sixteen hundreds*. His friend, Reina, grew up there as, like, the seventh generation in that house. Big ass log walls, *nary* an eco-friendly lightbulb, and some elite grandma furniture."

Oz swooned. "Aw, look at you picking up 'nary,' like you ain't from fucking Philadelphia."

"Oz, shh! So, at this house, we baked cookies. Reina used her family's recipe, and we baked chocolate chip cookies when it got dark. Then, I see a mouse run under the cabinets, and I almost screamed. Out the corner of my eye I see another, then another one a minute later, and another. I keep seeing their little shadows. Reina notices me tweaking, looking all over, and she says to me in the *coldest* fucking way, 'don't look straight at them.'

"So, I'm like, 'babygirl, you gotta get these mice outta your house.' She says, 'no, they're not mice, and don't look at them.' Like, she really said that. 'Not mice.' In her old ass house, we're just putting cookie dough on a tray, trying to ignore these *things* running down every nook and cranny. The quieter we get, the more we start to hear them moving in the walls. It made the floorboards squeak. It tapped across the ceiling. It wasn't one thing, it was *everything*. I felt... You know, I felt like an *animal* for the first time. Like my own body got more scared than I did. My instincts just *begged* me to run, run, get away.

"No one said 'ghost' until we went into the living room. Big broken brass naval clock on the mantle, cookies in the oven, and the fucking place is coming alive in every corner. Reina tries to talk about whatever bullshit I'm using to distract us. Her voice is normal, but her face? She starts crying. Georgie tries to help her, and it's like she didn't even notice. Reina says, 'oh, sorry, these aren't *my* tears.' Then, this girl tells us she's been through this whole kind of thing before, but never so bad. See, apparently she's a *medium*. Like, whatever's trapped in this house is trying to escape *through* her.

"And realistically, I don't believe in that shit. I do not believe in ghosts. Whatever some people believe in, no. I still don't buy it. What I saw, what we saw, this was something different. This was *way* more than it looks like in movies. You can't film the way it makes your skin tingle. You can't *believe* in ghosts like that. It's so unbelievable that sometimes I'll text Georgie and ask, 'Did we really do that? Like, that actually happened?'

"When the shadows got taller than us, Reina asked it to leave us alone. I could see it twisting her like a knife in her chest. She let loose and screamed at it to go away, so loud that she scared me. I guess she scared *it*, too, cause the shadows and the noises stopped. That's how I knew it was real, right? The silence after it left.

"Then, only one sound... a metal *ting*! The broken clock over the fireplace started ticking. Eight o'clock, right then, it hit the mark. And it was *exactly* eight, right then. That broken clock kept perfect time while we ate the cookies, all the way until we went home. So, yeah, that's the kind of ghost stories I thought we were telling."

Saint finished their beer.

XIII
DEATH

XIII: DEATH

Smith let out their breath. The storm quieted. The rain gave up.

Saint crushed their beer can against the edge of the table. They straightened their back and almost frowned. Reticence didn't belong on Saint's face. Even without it, the unsubtle can crush signaled an overdue crossing of paths. Smith couldn't decide whether Waite did it on impulse or as a calling card.

"Why'd you just crush that?" Smith asked.

"Because I can," Waite said, no introductions needed. "It's weak enough to bend, so I make it mine. It'll never be the same again, this little can. That's how powerful we are." They flicked the flattened aluminum up the table into an ashtray.

Oz rubbed her eyes. "What the fuck did I miss here? Are you two having a moment?"

The act didn't matter now. Waite wouldn't spare the decency or discretion to let Smith hide any longer.

"Oz, it's *me*," Smith told her. "I'm sorry I didn't tell you earlier. I was trying to let you and Saint have a good night. I'm Smith, since Georgie's last drink. I sang *The Who* for you at karaoke. I tried to introduce myself when I was Saint at Kink Night."

Oz fidgeted with her nose ring. She shook her head in a steady rhythm. "What is this? Is this part of y'all's ghost story?"

"Bold," Waite complimented Smith. "I like seeing you come out of your shell."

"No, no," Smith sighed. "Oz, this is Waite. We're... the people you *become* between drinks. Not every time, and not just you, but lots of people here at Arcana. It's what I was trying to tell you after you tied me up, but too much got lost in translation."

Waite turned out Saint's pockets. "Where's this one's phone?"

"'This one?'" Oz repeated. She shifted her voice to imitate Saint. "Oh, look at *me*, I don't remember who I *am*! I'm not *Saint*! If you're making fun of me, that's not fucking cool. I told you about my shit because I trusted you. I thought you'd understand, not act so ignorant and throw it back in my face for no reason. What the fuck, Saint?"

Waite opened their mouth, but Smith intervened.

"Me!" They shouted. "Oz, you told *me*, not them. You told me, Smith, when *I* was in Saint's body. Saint and Georgie don't know, and they'd never make fun of you like that. This is all Waite, not Saint. Seriously, *this* is real. I mean, it's *all* real. What happens to you is real, but this is different. I don't know how to explain it, prove it, or—"

"Georgie, I..." Oz fumbled her words. "Did Saint tell you I'm plural?"

Smith had to explain. They needed another angle. How could they forgive themself for breaking the trust between Oz and her friends? Smith clawed at the table and bit their tongue, waiting for perfect line, metaphor, phrasing, or promise would bring Oz to their side. It had to. Before Smith found it, Waite found the opposite:

"What sort of pretentious religious nutcase names their child *Saint*?"

Coming from Saint's own mouth, the earnest, broken question did the trick.

"You...?" Oz started, then corrected herself. "Saint chose their name themself. The fuck? Oh, fuck. You're *really* not Saint. So, *you*, you're not Georgie. Motherfuckers. Who the fuck? I was about to fight a bitch. I need another drink. I need smelling salts. Beer, *beer*." Oz slurped her beer, launched herself up from the table, and shuffled away towards the overflow parking lot. "If I'm gonna tolerate some spooky psychic body-snatcher business, I need some good fucking weed in my hand right now."

Smith watched her go. Waite didn't seem to care, glaring at Smith.

"I haven't run into you since karaoke. Where the hell have you been?"

"I was busy trying to figure out—" Smith cut themself short. Waite stole their cocktail and sampled it, then smacked their lips and gave it back.

"Figuring out that I'm rich?"

Smith coughed. "What?"

"Paul Karl Mullard, who died in the crash. After you left, Ember helped me dig up all sorts of dirt on the guy. Fifty-six-year-old father of two sons, divorced, married to a woman twenty years younger than him, lived in mansion half an hour west. He owned a contracting company that builds outdoor spaces, and they're *buried* in debt. Word on the street is he paid himself first, then started taking bigger contracts to pay for the smaller ones. The week before he died, half a dozen clients opened a class action lawsuit against his company for unfinished work. You get it now, don't you?"

"No." Smith bounced their leg under the table.

"The clients can't sue a dead man. His mansion, sports cars, boat, everything is mine if I can convince his wife who I am, that I really *am* Paul Mullard. I'll live like a king, and if you're done pretending to be mad at me, I *could* be convinced to share the wealth. How's that sound?"

"Waite..." Smith shook their head. "At karaoke, you said *you* were Julienne, and I was the 'random dead guy.' You can't just slip that in there, like I won't notice you flipped it around. As if you have any way of knowing which of us was who, and as if it matters, without their memories!"

Waite cracked their knuckles against the bench. "If you're still waiting around for answers, good luck to you. You're not intuitive like I am. I can *feel* it." Waite unclenched their hands and traced the lines of Saint's palm prints.

"Oh, you *feel* it?" Smith laughed. "Sounds to me like you're changing the story to whatever's best for you. You're Hayes when Julienne's family bothers you, you're Julienne when Hayes is still alive, you're this fucking *Mullard* guy when you want to steal his money. You don't even care what's true, do you?"

Waite rolled their eyes. The pinkish disco light under the canopy made the fog of their breath glow. "The truth is what people believe, people believe what I tell them. With one exception." Waite aimed their middle finger at Smith.

"You act like this world is yours to win. We're not playing a game. We can't control what other people do or think."

Waite grabbed Smith's hand from across the table. "Controlling other people is the *only* thing we can do. We're dead, but the clock keeps on ticking. If this isn't a game, why does it feel like we're in overtime?"

Smith jerked their hand free of Waite's. They didn't bother answering.

"Fine," Waite conceded. "I brought it up as an olive branch, but I don't need to share the money with you."

"You don't *have* the money," Smith reminded them. "I can barely convince Oz that I'm not Georgie and that you're not Saint. How are you gonna convince some rich widow that *you're* her late husband, temporarily reincarnated in the body of a non-binary film nerd from Pennsyl-fucking-vania?"

"Stay tuned," Waite assured them. Before Oz could finish her smoke break, Smith stood to leave the picnic table. The dormant thunderclouds grumbled. Waite pointed at Smith's glass. "Hang on. What is that thing?"

"Arcana's seventh anniversary special."

Waite clicked their tongue. "So, it's *Friday*. Two days early."

"What, you have appointments, now?"

"Yeah. I tell my people when to summon me."

Of course, Waite's 'people.' Already doubting Jade and Ember's tarot rituals, Smith seized the chance to get under Waite's skin. "By 'summon,' you mean doodle on their arms and order shots until they get lucky?"

Waite took Smith's drink again. "See, that's how I know *I'm* Paul and *you're* Julienne. Only a girl could get in bitchy moods like you do." Waite threw back the fruity remnants of the cocktail. Saint returned to consciousness, not missing a beat from the end of their ghost story:

"I guess the movie *Poltergeist* was onto something, cause that's the best comparison I can ma..." Saint twisted the empty goblet in their grip. Bewildered, they traced their crushed beer can to the ashtray. Oz returned to the table's bench seat, trailing an invisible herbal cloud. "Where'd you go?" Saint asked.

Oz brushed a few thin raindrops from her hair with one hand. She angled for them like a crouching carnivore ready to pounce. Saint leaned away, growing tense from their shoulders to their brow. "What? What's that? What are you doing?"

Oz gripped Saint's head from both sides. "Now who are you? *What* are you?"

"I'm... an idiot sandwich?"

Oz released them. "Okay, you're back to normal. Are *you*?" She zeroed in on Smith.

"Still Smith," they confessed. "Sorry you had to deal with Waite."

"Wait for what?" Oz sniffled and laughed at nothing.

Saint yawned and attempted to talk through the tail end of it. "Oz, you are so *elsewhere* right now. Georgie, I know I used our ghost story, but do you have one to share?"

"I'm gonna use the restroom first," Smith lied and excused themself. "Ask me when I come back."

"Don't fall in!" Oz cautioned.

Smith stepped back inside the bar. At one end, Twyla helped Alea pack a few loose cans into the fridge. Jade remained with her open sketchbook near the furry pink pole. A patchwork of bold ink icons smeared down her arms—wands, swords, cups, and pentacles, some more faded than others. Smith claimed the stool to her left.

"It's me," Smith told her.

"George, right?" She shut her sketchbook.

Smith prepared to regret this later. "No, Georgie, but no. I'm Waite."

Jade reopened her sketchbook. "I didn't summon you. It's only Friday, so no Selene or Ember tonight."

"Yeah, I'm two nights early, right?"

Jade nodded and turned her sketchbook around on the bar top. Smith expected another gothic scene, abstract ghoul, or even one of Jade's custom tarot designs, but the page bore only a bulleted list of handwritten notes. Jade tucked her pen inside the spiral binding.

"In case you're me on Sunday, I listed some questions to ask him."

Smith speculated. "To ask Ember?"

"No. *Him*. Our pen pal."

Smith read Jade's questions:

> *Why did you take them?*
> *How did you get past A-Bomb?*
> *Why risk meeting me for this?*
> *What happened the night of the crash?*
> *Why hide if you've done nothing wrong?*

"By 'pen pal,' you mean Hayes," Smith realized. Their face reddened, imagining Waite contacting Hayes faster than they could. "These are your questions for Tommy Hayes?"

Jade pressed a finger to her lips and closed the sketchbook again. "Careful. Anyone overhears that name, we lose our shot at getting him alone. Fuck knows why he's asking for *me*, but I won't make him ask twice. And don't call him 'Tommy' like you know him."

Smith cleared their throat and swallowed the agitation in their voice. "You talked to him, then?"

"No, he's way too smart to leave any more of a trail than he did. He picked exact, weird, careful messages that no one else would understand. It wasn't subtle, but how many people pay attention to some red nail polish on a door that's covered in so much other crap?"

A thief trumped death. Lesser for it?

Smith commended themself for memorizing the red painted letters inside the bathroom door, last Saturday. "'A thief,'" they whispered. "You're sure the thief is him?"

Jade looked askance at Smith. "*You* fucking said so. Don't tell me you're getting cold feet. What is this?"

Smith steadied their shaking hands, mimicking Waite's abrasiveness. "Smith is the coward, not me. The only weak thing about me is the flesh I wear. They'd lose their fucking mind if they knew we planned this without them. They're too... *soft* for it."

"Right, right," Jade droned. "Is that why you're still so horny for them?"

What did Waite tell her? Smith debated whether to face down the allegation or to embrace it, but Jade cut them off the hook.

"Relax. If I was one of two immortals in the universe, I'd fall for some soulmate bullshit in a second." Jade slid her empty highball glass forward for Alea to collect. "Are you waiting for me to buy your escape drink?"

Smith welcomed the idea. "Since you offered *so* nicely."

Jade and Alea exchanged a few words at a distance, in sign. To Smith's dismay, they no longer understood the gestures. Alea translated Jade's order into a golden orange shot of liquor, which she handed to Smith. They flinched when its bitter vapors hit their nose.

"What's this one?"

"Try it," Jade said. "Show me how fearless you are."

"What's in it?"

"Death." Jade cracked a smile. "Kidding. Drink up. Happy Arcanniversary."

Smith held their breath and poured the liquid between their lips. The vile burn of high-proof booze stung their throat like a swarm of bees. Georgie would take the brunt of it, as the baton passed back to him. Poor guy.

On the other side of the fragile darkness between Smith's nights, the death-shot transmuted into a milder cocktail of vodka and an energy drink. Thrashing, aggressive, amplified metal instruments assaulted their new ears. The ruckus seared a squealing, ringing, fuzzy sound under its cacophony. In the garage, silhouettes bashed into one another. A flinging wrist clipped Smith in the ribs.

They doubled over and spat on the concrete floor. They spun out of the mosh circle towards a chair in the back corner. Still fresh in their mind's eye, Jade's signed request to Alea translated itself into English: "What's the grossest thing you have?" To Smith's surprise, their new body understood sign language again.

"Logan!" Alea's voice caught Smith's ear, inches away. Her hand hovered on Smith's shoulder. She continued in sign: "Need a water break?"

"Bathroom," Smith signed back. Alea kissed Smith's cheek and dove back into the crowd. Whatever transpired after Smith's time as Alea, it didn't stop her and Logan from attending another show together. For once, Smith's nightly rampage healed its scorched earth in the daylight world. Rather than accept the unexpected win, Smith lamented tonight's fresh chance to ruin a happy couple's lives, this time as Logan.

They fled the garage into the blue of the sitting room, where shadows under both restroom doors marked them occupied. Smith pulled two neon orange earplugs from Logan's ears and tuned out the searing metal noise as much as possible. It almost buried the unmistakable brightness of Ember's voice behind them.

"Mankind, *humankind* bites at the chains that confer... no, that *condemn* us to morality. *Mortality*." His rambles slurred and wavered in intensity, lacking their usual punch. A leaning tower of four drained shot glasses piled up from the table by his knees. "If that's not what this bullshit is all about, then what is it, even? What if, I mean, even drunk off the fountain of youth, we're limited, you know? There's always fine print. These cosmic twists that tempt us, they're... the strings on them, right?"

Next to him on the black couch in the corner, Jade thumbed her phone's keyboard with both hands. She only acknowledged him once he stopped talking. "I can do it myself," she sighed. "I didn't want to, but we're running out of time."

"Selene, our divine lunar ferryperson has abandoned us on the..." Ember broke their lament to hiccup, "...on the near bank of the River Styx."

"Their dad's awake and talking now, but he's not getting out of the hospital tonight. The doctors have him under observation. Either I take us in the Frog Truck, or it's off."

Ember picked at a hole in a couch cushion. "Why do they call it that? *River Styx*. It oughta be Styx River, like every other damn river."

"Nile," Jade parried. She produced a black marker from her bag, uncapped it, and pressed it to her forearm, tracing over a faded collage of swords, pentacles, and the like. "Fucking clusterfuck of a night. There's no point doing this without Waite. I'm getting another shot from Chris."

One bathroom door opened, but not the one with the red paint. Smith waited for the other restroom, praying a drunk Ember would spill more details about Waite's appointment with Hayes.

"Jade!" Ember snagged the marker from Jade's hand. "And then what? Who's gonna drive?"

"Waite can use my muscle memory. They've driven before. Give me the—"

"Shh!" Ember dropped the marker down his shirt. "Your big, beautiful brain is missing the pattern. Speculate with me, doll. I don't think we can double-dip. You've been haunted by each of them once, and so have I. Summoning hasn't worked all week. What if Waite and Smith can't possess the same body twice?"

The marker tumbled out the bottom of Ember's shirt. Jade caught it. "We can't just twiddle our thumbs until Waite takes the form of somebody else. Are we gonna grab a stranger, buy them a drink, and draw pentagrams on their fucking face?"

"Ah, time. The essence of it..." Ember mumbled while still searching his shirt for the marker. "Let's go without Waite. We don't need our unfor... unfriendly spectral crusader. Hayes asked for *you*."

"Don't say his name so loud." Jade jammed the marker down into its cap on the table. "It's almost eleven forty. I'll close my tab." She collected her bag and brushed past Smith into the hallway. She jumped, noticing their attention, but she hurried away without making eye contact.

The second bathroom door squeaked open. Smith froze, face to face with a man unseen since their night in his body. "Do I know you?" Dorian asked, locking eyes, maybe for too long. He stepped towards the garage.

"No," Smith told Dorian. "Sorry, you look like someone I met once."

Smith closed and latched the bathroom door behind them. They winced at themself in the mirror. Logan's cheeks reddened under sparse gold glitter. Safely alone and too energetic to think straight, Smith talked to themself. "It's Sunday. Today's Sunday. Dorian's here. Waite isn't. Selene isn't. Jade and Ember are meeting Hayes. He left a message for Jade. For Jade, how?"

A thief trumped death. Lesser for it?

Smith reviewed the chipped red nail polish on the door. They glided their fingers over the letters. Nothing about the message addressed it to Jade, no matter how many times Smith reread it. It still sounded more like Colton than something Hayes would write about himself. Why would he be 'lesser' for not dying the crash? Did stealing his dad's bicycle make him a thief?

Smith zoned out on the lower half of the door. When their eyes refocused, their heart lurched. They almost fell backwards. Another smattering of red nail polish—smaller, shorter, and fresher—blazed across the door below the first: *THE TOWER. Sunday. Midnight.*

"*The Tower*," Smith remembered aloud. Jade sketched a tarot card with that name. "Hayes collects guns. He played lacrosse. He's not the type to know tarot, not unless he..." Smith remembered the flower drawing that Jade gave Twyla. That wasn't the gift she planned to give. Somebody at the Night Market stole Jade's tarot deck. Shit, not a whole deck. She only drew the important cards. The *big* ones. What the fuck did she call them?

A thief trumped death...

Trumps, she called the major cards. Hayes hid the language of tarot in his first message to catch Jade's attention. He was the thief who took the twenty-two trump cards before Jade could finish the fifty-six lessers.

"*Lesser* for it," Smith reiterated. "He wants the *lessers*, the other cards, to complete the deck he stole. He wants Jade to bring the lessers and meet him at *The Tower*."

Only Jade and Hayes ever saw the stolen trumps. Smith stood no chance of speaking their shared tongue. They only saw Jade's sketches, and only one showing a tarot card. They squeezed their eyes shut, revisiting their best memory of that sketchbook page. It wasn't just *any* card. Blurred and dulled by alcohol, it struck them nonetheless.

"Lightning," Smith said to themself. The card had lightning striking a person, falling off a bridge. Not just a bridge, a *stone* bridge. Jade based the cards off local legends. "It's Oz's ghost story, with the two sisters and the stonemason. *The Tower* is Bayonet Bridge!"

Smith yanked the bathroom door open, alarming Ember, who remained on the black couch.

"So *aggressive*." He hiccupped again. "You look like you've seen a ghost. Did you know I kissed a ghost? I shouldn't be talking to you."

Smith ignored him and probed Logan's pockets for a car key. She carried none. Smith rushed back into the garage. A stream of staticky guitar distortions roiled their brain. Alea raised her arms and swayed her hips at the center of the dance floor, back towards Smith. They rushed up to grab her, tell her, ask her... ask her what? For a ride to the haunted bridge, right now? Smith stopped themself. They backed away before Alea noticed. Smith escaped under the half-open garage door.

"Super curvy road," Smith muttered fragments of the directions from Oz's ghost story. "East Lewesboro. West? That way. '*That* way,' Saint said. Hollow Mountain, across downtown, turn at the tunnel. No, *after* the tunnel. How the fuck am I gonna do this?"

Cars packed every space in the main lot, each useless to Smith without keys or a driver. They rounded the metal gate into the overflow parking. At its far end, one gray minivan idled near the side street. Its red taillights beckoned Smith. What would they tell the driver? How could they make someone new understand fast enough? Halfway there, the fence rattled behind Smith.

Ember rubbed his shoulder where it clipped the edge of the gate.

"Careful!" Jade chastised him. She raised one hand and clicked a key fob. Smith hid between two SUVs. Ten feet away, an old light-duty pickup truck blinked its lights, illuminating a huge green decal of a jumping cartoon frog on the tailgate. The top of the lily-pad-shaped sticker read: *HOP IN!*

Running out of sane ideas, they ran towards the Frog Truck, cursing at themself. "Fuck it. Sure, why not?"

Before Jade and Ember reached the next row of cars, Smith scaled the Frog Truck's rear bumper. They grabbed its locked tailgate and pulled themself into the dusty steel bed. Smith laid flat on their back and shimmied as deep as possible into the bed's shadows. As Jade and Ember opened the cab's two doors, Smith prayed they wouldn't check their mirrors or look out the back window.

The doors shut. Ember's window rolled down.

"If you're gonna puke, let me know so I can pull over," Jade told him.

Ember spit out the window. "I'll have you know, I'm a *bastard* of physical fortitude. Bastion!"

The truck's engine spun up. Its bed rocked Smith backwards, then forwards. They kept their head low and shifted closer to the back window. Smith clung to the ridges of any surface their hands found in the dark, but each unexpected turn threw them off balance. The downtown streetlights and moderate skyline appeared over the bed walls at the first few intersections but thinned fast.

Buildings gave way to rows of sidewalk trees, then denser, natural foliage with older growth. The air wash over the pickup sucked some falling leaves into the bed. Smith plucked one that caught under a bolted washer near their face. They felt its fragile bronze arteries and pointed symmetrical edges. Smith let their heartbeat slow, focused only on the tiny world of this leaf, their fellow stowaway. The wind intensified as the truck accelerated from a red light. The leaf's thin membrane cracked between Smith's fingertips. Its remnants whirled off into the sky.

The next road weaved side to side as it climbed upwards. Sharp hairpin switchbacks tested the strength of Logan's arms and balance. The repeated and unpredictable oscillations nauseated Smith. Clear of the city's light pollution, only the stars and a waxing moon illuminated Smith's surroundings. Each row of tree trunks encroached inward, closing the canopy's gap over the narrowing road. The Frog Truck coasted and slowed. The parking brake squealed. The engine silenced. A wide shadow blanketed Smith from above and blocked the stars like a sheet across the sky. A heavy drop of cold water tapped the back of Smith's neck.

"You awake?" Jade prodded Ember. Smith heard no response, and only one door opened. "'Bastion of physical fortitude,'" she teased.

Jade's bootsteps trailed forward from the truck. Smith waited for their eyes to adjust. Another water droplet hit their cheek when they turned their head. The overbuilt gray span of Bayonet Bridge curled over them. Damp, ropelike rags of vegetation hung from gaps between stones, thirty feet above. Pockets of grass and weeds anchored in veins of dirt along the arch walls. Before the bridge could drip on them again, Smith crouched and scouted over one side of the pickup's bed. Jade turned to march up the hill behind the bridge and disappeared around its corner.

Smith watched Ember's chest rise and fall. His head slumped on the inside of the passenger door. Smith rolled over the bed's side wall and followed the unpaved shoulder by the base of the arch. A few beer bottles, spray paint cans, and a deflated volleyball piled in the gap of a missing stone. An abandoned bicycle leaned against one corner.

Smith followed Jade's boot prints in the leaves, not seeing another route to the top of the bridge. The thin and weathered path up the back hill bristled with exposed roots and nettle tendrils. Earthen scents of mud, wet leaves, and tree bark folded onto one another. Smith grabbed the base of a scraggly plant to steady themself. Its thorns pinched back, and their foot slipped. They ducked behind a rotten tree stump and waited a few seconds in case Jade heard.

The scrapes on their palm burned. Each step took longer. They listened to their own blood pumping in their ears. It beat and rang like the echoes of the metal show. The top of the path leveled off, meeting the far corner of the bridge deck's wall. Smith backed against the low wall's corner, inches out of sight from the overgrown clearing atop the bridge. They imagined the blind sister waiting for the vengeful stonemason, unaware of the threat sneaking closer.

"Hayes?" Jade's voice split the chilly air.

"Jade?" A man's voice asked. "Nice to see you again."

"Again?" Jade questioned. Smith spied over the wall. A lanky young guy in track pants and a thin jacket sat against the wall at the center of the bridge. Jade kept her distance, hands on her hips. "I've never met you before."

"Right, sorry. You only met Julie," Hayes amended. "The night she talked to you changed her whole life, and so did the sketch you gave her. Changed my life, too, but she wanted so much more. That's why I need the lesser arcana."

"So you can steal them, too?" Jade kicked a rock towards him. "Pardon me if I wasn't too motivated to finish making the lessers."

"You *need* to make the rest," he commanded.

"Not even gonna deny taking them, are you?" Jade forced a laugh. "Pretty sure you have bigger shit to deal with than card collecting."

"I wish I—" Hayes tried, stopped, then started over. "We figured it out, me and Julie. It was a miracle. Something went right for once. We had a way out of this: a plan for our whole lives. I'd give it back to die instead of her."

Jade eased closer to him. "What happened the night of the crash?"

His legs stiffened, and he grabbed something near his feet. "I don't know, and it doesn't matter. Only the cards matter now. I have to do this for her."

Jade closed in on him, step by step. "I don't believe you, and you stole the trumps *before* the crash, while Julie was alive. Now she's gone, and you've got a price on your head. What's so important about meeting me for some stupid cards?"

Hayes leaned forward. He gripped his knees. "You got my messages. You came all the way here. I figured *you* understood better than anyone. You made these cards, but you don't even know what they are?"

Before Jade could answer, Logan's phone rang like a siren in Smith's pocket.

XIV
TEMPERANCE

XIV: TEMPERANCE

Smith shrank behind the wall and wrestled their pocket for the phone. It blasted a cheery percussive melody three times before they poked its red icon and interrupted the fourth ring. *Incoming Call: Alea* darkened from the screen. The forest stilled. Smith let themself believe no one heard it until Jade put their hope to bed.

"Hello?" She sounded as scared as Smith felt. Clutching Logan's phone to their chest, they inched out onto the bridge and offered a meek wave.

"Sorry."

"What are you doing over...?" Jade's question faltered. "Logan?"

Fuck.

Smith brushed dirt off their hands. If Jade recognized Logan, they couldn't pretend to be any random stranger in the woods. They couldn't play it off. Leaving wouldn't help, and when would they have another chance to meet Hayes? Smith couldn't take their eyes off him: his unkempt sandy stubble, nylon tool belt, and that metal object hidden in his lap.

Hayes returned the favor, studying Smith. "I was wondering when you'd join us," he said.

Jade's head spun between them both. "You *know* her?"

Hayes tilted his head. "Isn't she with you?"

"No! She's my ex-girlfriend." Jade glowered at Smith. "*You* know *him*?"

Oh, no.

"Well, I was looking for—" Smith thought the better of it. "No. No, I don't."

Jade shook both hands at each of them. "What the hell is happening here?"

Hayes pointed down at the road. "When your truck came up, I saw her laying in the bed."

Jade narrowed her eyes and started towards Smith. "What the *fuck*, Logan?"

Smith gulped. "Jade, I'm sorry, I fell asleep. Before, in the parking lot, in the truck, and when you... I woke up, and the truck..." Smith stretched the lie to its breaking point. Jade unzipped her bag. She unfolded a pocketknife and aimed it in their direction. Every word Smith spoke, she came closer. "Okay, no, I can explain. Please don't—"

"Don't hurt her!" Hayes shouted but kept his place along the bridge wall.

Jade stopped two paces away from Smith. She seemed to run into an invisible wall. Unfreezing one limb at a time, Jade chewed her lower lip and wagged the knife at Smith. "You're playing with fire, tonight."

"I'm sorry," Smith repeated. "I'll just go."

"Don't play dumb," Jade scolded. "Where've you been since you were me, *Smith*?"

The veil lifted. Smith's knees wobbled.

"Hey!" Hayes interjected. "Are you and her cool?"

"*Them*," Jade corrected.

"Them?" Hayes challenged. "You're the one who said 'girlfriend.'"

Jade ignored him and shook the tip of the knife at Smith. "Tell me what's going on, chop-chop, or you're getting *chop-chopped*."

"Okay, I lied," Smith confessed. "When you talked to Waite on Friday, that was me, not them. Tonight, I overheard you and Ember. I figured out the message in the bathroom. I needed to meet him, in case he knows what happened to me. What if he can fix this?"

"As you fucking wish!" Jade closed her pocketknife. She grabbed Smith's arm and wrangled them out onto the grassy bridge span. "Hayes, are you *sure* you don't know Smith?"

"Yeah," he reaffirmed, but walked it back. "I dunno, maybe."

"There's something you need to know," Smith raced to explain. Jade pinched their arm, but they kept going. "Don't ask me how, but I don't think Julie's actually gone."

After a mournful pause, Hayes spoke rigidly: "I promise you, she is completely, definitely, absolutely dead."

Jade pushed Smith back and reopened her knife at Hayes. "What about the messages? You snuck past A-Bomb just to leave a message for me. You're hiding from something, and it's not the cops. What do you know that I don't?"

"Yeah, I was trying to tell you! Wait. Hey, put that phone away," Hayes told Smith. "The fuck? Are you recording this?"

Smith wrapped their hand over Logan's phone's camera. "No! What?"

Hayes stood and revealed the metal linkage in his lap. It belonged not to a tool belt, but to a harness around his waist. A ring of red nail polish adorned the linkage's gray finish. A sturdy, lightweight rope looped down through it into a coil at Hayes' feet. "Jade, you need to make the rest of the cards."

"What are you doing?" Jade gestured at the rope.

Smith pointed at Hayes' harness. "That's rock-climbing gear, isn't it?"

Hayes kept the pressure on Jade. "I'm begging you; I need the lesser cards."

"You might not be afraid of this knife, but you've got nowhere to go," Jade warned him. She dropped her knife into her bag and zipped it shut. "Tell me why you need the cards, or Smith will call 9-1-1."

Smith raised their hands. "No! No, I won't. Hayes, I was supposed to tell you, your dad told me to say—"

"I don't have a father." Hayes lifted the rope coil under one arm and hurled it over the edge of the bridge. He stepped backwards onto the wall. A double-segment of ropes pulled taut between the metal device on his harness and the stone wall on the opposite side of the bridge. There, it looped into the wall itself. The two loose ends of the rope hung between his legs, uncoiling into the void below. Hayes gripped the downward ropes close to his waist with both hands.

"Stop!" Jade yelled, but Hayes leaned backwards over the wall. The rope held him, sliding faster as he angled his grip. He dropped over the edge. The rope sang, flowing through the metal linkage. Jade and Smith peered over the wall. Hayes rappelled all the way down and landed on his feet, dead center along the road's yellow line. He unclipped himself from the rope and retrieved the bicycle from the front of the bridge. Hayes pedaled away down the road without looking back.

"You've got to be fucking kidding me," Jade seethed.

"His dad's bike," Smith realized. "He must've stashed it there when he arrived, before us."

"In my *truck*. You hid in my truck, you sneaky fucking bitch!" Jade slapped Smith's face and stalked away towards the dirt path. She raised and lowered her shaking fists as if lifting barbells.

Smith held the stinging warm spot on their face. "Was that for me, or for Logan?"

"I don't care! You're *both* fucking liars."

"You lied to *me* first. You knew Julie well enough to 'change her life,' apparently. You never told me about the tarot deck, the Night Market, or the writing on the bathroom door. You cut me out of everything that matters!"

Jade faced the path and talked over her shoulder. "Some things need to stay private. You're too good at making yourself the center of the universe, needing to know everyone's business. You're almost as bad as Waite."

Smith cackled. "That's rich, coming from the one who believes whatever bullshit Waite tells them!"

Jade tapped her temple. "At least Waite has original thoughts! All you do is drag us down with your woe-is-me whining and half-assed people pleasing. You don't know who you are? Great, welcome to life. No one knows who they are. If you waste all your time thinking about your place in the world, you'll never get anything done. Oh, except for stowing away in my truck and making me accidentally kidnap my *ex*!"

"At least I'm not pulling *knives* on people!" Smith fired back. "I'm not violent. I'm not constantly broadcasting to everybody how dangerous I am. I'm not a venom-spitting *frilled lizard*, like you!"

Jade grinned. She stretched her fingers. Her cheek twitched. "It's a rubber knife," she whispered.

"What?"

Jade retrieved the knife from her bag, opened it, and stabbed the limp blade at her palm. It bent harmlessly. "Frilled lizards, that's their secret. They aren't venomous. People *think* they are because of the way they look, but they're not. They almost never even bite, only as a last resort. In an environment surrounded by predators, looking scary isn't a reflection of who you are; it's a plea to be left alone. I don't *want* to bite back. It's not who I am, Smith. The knife is made of *rubber*. It's an act. The drawings, the goth shit, that's not me. My favorite color is peach, like a warm sunrise. I used to draw cartoon characters, flowers, little animals. I want you to imagine the vile shit they said to me in school. Then, after I dropped out, when people saw a gentle, easygoing, baby-trans girl who needed a place to sleep after her grandfather walked her out of the house at gunpoint, you don't think they took fucking advantage? This place wanted to eat me, and it still does, more than ever, and it always will. I adapted to survive, and it worked. I *did* scare you, didn't I?"

Smith pretended to be distracted by Logan's phone, the trees, or the abandoned climbing rope—anything to avoid Jade's piercing glare.

"You're standing on a haunted bridge, talking to a ghost," Smith reminded her. "Who should be afraid of who?"

"Ghosts don't scare me," she said. "I'm scared of *real* people. And now that we both know you're not one, I'm almost sad for you." Jade removed the tie from her hair and departed down the dirt path. Her uneven steps echoed through the woods, under the bridge, and back to her truck until its door slammed shut.

Smith lingered at the top of the bridge where Hayes made his descent, too defeated to even watch Jade and Ember drive away. They plucked at Hayes' slackened rope. The air grew colder. Smith encountered none of Bayonet Bridge's three resident spirits. Maybe they heard everything from their hiding places in the stones.

"Why come back to this?" Smith asked the ghosts. "We can't put our lives back together. Why come back from being dead just to be miserable in new ways? You can't even hear me, I bet, without bodies. I'm talking to a pile of rocks."

A silver station wagon rolled up the nearest switchback at half the speed limit. It halted on the shoulder below the bridge, short of where Jade parked. Its engine idled, and its headlights glowed through the empty archway. Alea emerged from the station wagon alone, phone flashlight in hand, ready to search the steep woodland.

"Logan!" She called.

"Up here!" Smith yelled back. Their voice bounced between the trees. Alea turned off her car, dragged a shopping bag out through the passenger window, and vanished under the bridge towards the trail. Smith waited at the top of the hill while she ascended.

Alea gawked at Smith from the steep path below. "Baby, what the *what* is this all for?"

"I'm so sorry," Smith said. What else could they tell her? "I'm glad you're here."

"That. *That* is why we always share locations. And yes, I know I'm *never* beating the maternal instinct allegations." For all her remarkable strength, Alea grew winded by the time she summited the bridge. There, Smith identified the sharp corners and blue-gray logo of a box of six beer cans in the thin shopping bag.

"You brought drinks?" Smith peeked inside the bag when Alea set it down in the grass. They tried not to think about chugging a beer.

She wiped her brow, sighed, and nodded. "How'd you get here so fast?"

"Magic powers? No, kidding. I got a ride."

Alea nodded. "From?"

Not from Jade. Anyone but Logan's ex-girlfriend. The last thing Smith needed was another love triangle to annihilate. Who else could have driven them to Bayonet Bridge? Their brain spun through every name but landed nowhere.

"Some metalheads," Smith tried, "in a minivan. I didn't get their names."

"Baby..." Alea sat on the wall next to Smith, but a few inches too far. "Why not ask me to drive, if you wanted to get away so bad?"

"I don't know," Smith admitted.

"Is it me? If I said something, or if you need me to—"

"No! I promise, no. I just needed air, and probably a beer, then I'll be back to normal."

"If it was something I did to make you decline my call, you'd tell me, right?" Alea didn't leave space before her next question. "Do you *want* me here?"

"Yes, I do," Smith assured her, saying anything for a drink.

Alea rolled the plastic bag down around the six-pack of cans. She popped the cardboard flaps open. "Oren had me buy these for stock, but Twyla said they're too strong for cans, and people will get messy. She vetoed eight-percenters on the basis of temperance." Alea placed a warm can in Smith's hand. Its label boasted of its high alcohol content. She cracked open her can and folded the box closed. "Brought them up here in case, like, that was your *plan*."

"My plan?"

Alea blushed. "Late night, making me chase you up to the kissing bridge? Well, okay, I guess saying it now makes it *my* plan."

Smith opened their can, too. Bitter-sour vapors of carbonation invaded their nose. "Do people really kiss up here?"

"Not even once," Alea joked, or maybe it wasn't one. She tapped her can to Smith's. They took one huge sip, then another. The putrid, saturated, sour beer tasted like rotten soda, but every drop in Smith's throat brought them closer to tomorrow. They almost reached the bottom of the can, but the need for a breath cut them off.

Alea whistled. "Slow down, Speed Racer. These were a good pick, huh?"

"Yup," Smith burped. Their stomach tightened.

"Sorry," Alea flinched. She set her can down on the wall. "I'm trying to be, like, flirty, but I've got this *thing*. This feeling, and I don't want to sit with it." Smith waited for her while their body protested the influx of beer. Alea talked at her shoes. "You said you bummed a ride from some metalheads, and I believe you. I do. It's just, also, you know, a really weird coincidence that I saw the Frog Truck coming back down Holowell Road on my way up here."

Of *course* she saw. Smith swallowed their next burp.

Alea cleared her throat. "Logan, you know I don't wanna have to ask, but it feels like I shouldn't let this linger. Did you come up here with Jade?"

Smith answered by vomiting the contents of Logan's stomach over the edge of Bayonet Bridge. The liquid splattered the pavement and returned a sickening echo. Neither Smith nor Alea dared speak after it. In one trembling hand, Smith lifted the last of their can, swung it back, and forced the last sip down Logan's burning esophagus.

"Can you hear me now?" Oren's voice, louder than life, crackled through a sturdy wireframe pair of headphones that cradled Smith's new ears. An empty beer bottle left their lips. Smith set it on the bar top while reorienting themself in their new body, now standing upright near Arcana's pink pillar. Smith's left hand held an expensive tablet in a rubberized case. On its screen, green waveforms twitched whenever Oren shuffled his fur coat or mumbled to himself. "Am I coming through, Major Tom?"

"Yeah!" Smith confirmed. Hearing *Major Tom*, they believed they'd taken the form of a soldier, but their khaki pants and blue fishing jacket suggested otherwise. Another voice through the headphones cast a wave of green across the tablet.

"I *love* that song." The woman next to Smith swooned. Her long gold earrings shimmered. "Did you grow up listening to Bowie?"

"Mm-hm," Oren reminisced. "I recorded his second self-titled album on tape, with my old man's radio cassette player. Had to call the station a million times before they played *Janine*. I hit record on the deck, then prayed the antenna wouldn't fuck up. That tape sounded like shit even before I played it to shreds. Course, your generation had it easy. Spotif-iTunes, boom, any song's yours. Do you even know what a cassette is?"

Further down behind the bar, Twyla laughed and delivered a couple their cocktails. "Of *course* she does!" Her microphone's waveforms joined the other two on Smith's tablet.

"I've seen a few of our mom's old cassettes," the woman with the gold earrings smiled at Smith. "Rachel, how are the levels?" She angled the question at the tablet.

"Looks good," Smith told her and hoped Rachel handled her 'levels' before they arrived. Smith pulled one side of their headphones off their ear. Except for Smith, Twyla, Oren, and the woman with the earrings, everyone sat far along the perimeter of the room. Whatever caused this interruption in Arcana's service, it had the dozen regulars hushing their conversations and sipping slow enough to make their drinks last. Even Chris staked his claim on the edge of the crowded red couch, his phone inches from his eyes.

"I'm gonna do a little intro first, then we'll get started," the woman with the gold earrings told Oren. She took a swig of her beer bottle and dabbed around her pink gloss lips with a square cocktail napkin. "Okay, Rachel, here we go."

"Got it. Yup." Smith stared at the buttons on the screen.

She cleared her throat and took one full breath. "Good evening, and thank you for tuning in to episode fourteen of *Haunted America Today*, the podcast that brings you real stories of our supernatural land of liberty, straight from the source. I'm your host, Radhika Umar-Levine. Tonight, we travel to the deep Appalachian city of Lewesboro for a story that's guaranteed to leave your spine tingling." Radhika read the remainder of her introduction off her phone's screen. "Lewesboro is a small, artful city nestled in the ancient bosom of the Blue Ridge Mountains. It's known for mighty waterfalls, temperate year-round weather, and a robust craft brewing industry that's earned Lewesboro the unfortunate distinction as Restauranteur Magazine's 'Alcoholism Capital of America.'"

Twyla hid her face in her hands. "I'd just forgot that hullabaloo," she muttered.

"Fucking rag, that online-only tabloid shit," Oren added. "Nobody reads that crap. Am I allowed to curse on here?"

"We'll bleep those," Radhika assured him. "I'm speaking to Oren and Twyla Sciavila. They co-own one of the bars in Lewesboro, where we're recording tonight."

"Lovely to have you here," Twyla beamed.

Oren seemed less sure. "The *best* fucking bar in in Lewesboro."

Radhika ignored him. "Twyla, how do you introduce your establishment, for people who don't know it?"

"Hm," she thought aloud. "Well, it's called *Arcana*. Some people put a 'The' before it, but it's one word. When we started up here, we wanted someplace different than all the other new bars that keep springing up. We're off the beaten path in darn near every way. Where they go mellow, we go loud. Where they go light, we go dark. We're not for your coworkers, but we're for you."

"Is it true what this building used to be?" Radhika asked. Near the door, A-Bomb hopped and tapped two fingers on an old bicycle sprocket nailed to a ceiling joist.

"Bicycle repair shop," Oren confirmed. "You shoulda seen this place on day zero. Tools, metal, junk, and grease running down the walls. Looked like the set of an alien arthouse splatter flick."

"And now, look at it," Twyla gestured to the jeweled fake skull on the shelf, "even *scarier*."

Radhika laughed. "I'll try to paint the picture for everyone at home. Arcana is a gothic dive bar with an occult theme. Tarot cards and similar art dominate the walls, tacked up in corners, framed, or printed as posters. The walls are black. The bar table is black. It's black almost everywhere, but with cute lights from a bunch of odd lamps, a chandelier, and tiny string bulbs in every color. We asked Oren and Twyla to pause their speakers for our microphones, but there was screamo music playing when we arrived."

"Thrash metal, technically," Oren murmured.

"No, *black* metal!" A-Bomb corrected in a harsh whisper. Oren shushed him.

"We like our music how we like our drinks," Twyla told audience, letting them think for a moment, "*heavy*."

Radhika scrolled down on her phone. "Now, recently, something unusual has been happening here at your bar. I've done some research that I'll share with you two later in the show, but Twyla, can you describe the first supernatural phenomenon you observed here?"

Oren leaned over the deep metal sink and gritted his teeth.

"It's complicated," Twyla warned, "but let me try. A few weeks ago, I was grilling up some hot dogs and finishing my drink. Then, lickedy-split, I'm all the way across the parking lot with a ripped-up beer can and cuts on both hands."

Radhika waited. "Is that... what do you mean? Is there more?"

Twyla folded her arms. "I don't quite remember. That's exactly the thing. The next night, Oren and one of our bartenders go off into downtown and get into some trouble, but neither of them remembers, either."

"Trouble? Like, what kind?" Radhika finally tried Oren. "What happened when you went downtown?"

"No idea." Oren thumped one palm on the sink. "Mad shit, like it wasn't even me. Then our other bartender, she saves the damn garage from an electrical fire, but she can't remember it the next day. Next, it was A-Bomb, going *off* on us over something weird. What was that about, my guy?"

At the entrance, A-Bomb threw his hands in the air. "When?"

"Anniversary party. This was, I dunno, last week sometime?"

"Wednesday," Twyla reminded Oren.

"Bingo. Yeah, our crew was celebrating Arcana's seventh anniversary, and Twyla did a reading for A-Bomb. Tarot reading, yeah. He freaks out, saying 'my name is Smith,' and waving his beer around, like 'this isn't just a drink, I'm a ghost, coming to get my revenge' or whatever."

"Bullshit," A-Bomb scoffed.

"No, it was *exactly* like that. Twyla?"

She squeezed her purse. "It was about tarot. Somehow, the drinks and the cards are a part of it."

Radhika typed something into her phone. "Wait a minute. So, did the rest of you also think you were ghosts? I want to make sure I understand where the supernatural aspect connects to each of you blacking out."

"Us?" Oren sounded offended. "No, not *just* us. C'mon, y'all in the back. Anyone, any of y'all, raise your hand if you've had something similar happen here, in the past month or two. Who else lost their memory, but *only* between two drinks? And maybe some other folks said you acted funny, but you don't remember?"

Along the walls, patient spectators surveilled one another. Selene raised their hand, but so did a few new strangers. Smith wondered whether Waite took over their bodies, or whether they drank themselves into normal, old-fashioned blackouts.

Radhika counted the hands. "For everyone listening, four other people in the bar just raised their hands. My question to them is... well, okay, we need to rule out the obvious. Keep your hand up if you *don't* drink alcohol." Three hands lowered. Only Selene's remained. "You. This blackout happened to you when you were sober?"

"No," Selene admitted, "but it's why I *got* sober. I can handle blackouts, and I have, but this wasn't that. I was the first person to get possessed by a ghost we call Waite, the ghost of P.K. Mullard, on the night he died in a car crash."

Radhika glanced at Oren and Twyla, who eyed Selene like they'd just spoken in tongues. The others along the wall began chattering.

"What?" Selene laughed it off. "Loads of you know me. Yeah, I *look* crazy, but I'm not. I tried to ignore this shit when it started, but I can't deny it anymore. I've talked to both ghosts, Smith and Waite. They're legit. Arcana's haunted."

Murmurs about 'both' and 'Smith' and 'haunted' slithered along the back wall. Radhika waved Smith closer to speak in private. "Rachel, we're gonna need a room mic for the hillbilly peanut gallery. You know how hard it is to make *me* a skeptic? This isn't a haunting; it's an alcoholic circus. Are you still recording?" She drank the last of her beer, her initial confidence running dry.

"Yeah. Recording, yeah." Smith wasn't. They swiped through menus on Rachel's tablet. "We need a... room mic? That's, um, that's gonna be in a bag, or something, probably. Need a toolbox, maybe. Could I use a phone?"

"What the fuck are you doing?" Radhika snapped her fingers in front of Smith's face. She looked suspicious. The chatter died down. Smith gulped, lowered the tablet, and sat backwards on a barstool.

Smith sighed. "Sorry. I'm not Rachel. I'm not your tech person, sister, or whoever she is. I'm who Selene was telling you about. I'm Smith."

No one responded. No one even moved until Radhika laughed, forcing all the air from her lungs. She lowered herself onto the stool beside Smith and tousled their hair. She patted their shoulder and cooed: "Aw, Smith. How do we *always* find each other?"

Smith stopped Radhika's empty bottle from rolling off the counter. "Waite?"

Waite winked and pulled Smith closer by the zipper of Rachel's fishing jacket. "Fill me in. I'm what, a journalist? I'm in this fucking pantsuit, so where are the cameras? Don't tell me it's audio-only. Hey, you go get yourself a drink if you can't handle our captive audience, but you already started telling them the truth. I think this is our big moment." Waite stood and clapped their hands. "People of Arcana, thank you for your attention!"

"The hell?" A-Bomb glowered at them.

Waite paced the checkerboard floor. "I don't know who's heard the news, but let me put your doubts to rest: I am Paul Karl Mullard, and *this* is Julienne Chord. Call us Waite and Smith, if that's too hard to remember. Some of you know me. I've haunted some of you personally, so don't be shy. Tell everyone the good news! Spread the word, because death is not the end for all of us. By all accounts, I spent my mortal life cheating customers, abandoning my family, and getting filthy rich, but here I am, *immortal*. Take it from me: Don't waste your life chasing absolution. Your religions have lied to you, but did you really think all your good deeds would earn you eternal peace? They don't know what I do. Help me find the man who killed me and Smith. Join me, and once I settle the score with Ulysses Thomas Hayes, I'll reclaim my inheritance in this afterlife. Then, I can free you all from death, same as us. Lend *me* your faith, and I will make you in our image. Me and Smith will—"

"I'm not *with* you!" Smith leapt from the barstool and swung Rachel's tablet with both hands. The screen cracked across Waite's face and sent them to the floor. A mix of gasps and screams ricocheted across the room.

"Holy *fuck*!" A-Bomb rushed to check on Radhika's unconscious body.

"Please, just stay calm," Smith told everyone. "Don't trust anything Waite says. They don't know why this happened to us, to Arcana, or to all of you. I want to know the truth, same as you, but all *they* want is Mullard's money, and they'll say anything to get it. They'll *hurt* anyone to get it."

"*You* just hurt *them*!" A-Bomb shouted up at Smith, two fingers checking Radhika's pulse. "And how about that anniversary night? It wasn't them who took over my body. It was *you* who made me freak out and yell at the people who I'm in charge of keeping safe. Why should I trust you any more than Waite, if I don't know either of you fucking ghouls?"

Smith rode the wave of adrenaline and pointed Rachel's tablet at Oren and Twyla. "I need a drink, and another for Waite when they wake up. Don't let them hang around."

"Why not?" Selene challenged Smith, from across the room. They crossed the floor and joined A-Bomb to help Waite sit up. Blood dripped from a gash on their cheekbone. "They're the only one who appreciates what a real, active haunting could mean. We might have chance to beat death while the door's still open, and you're recommending some quiet time to sit around and think about it?" Selene scanned the faces of onlookers for support.

Oren fished around the shelves for some shot glasses. He barely finished pouring two sloppy shots of rum before Smith collected them. They placed one on the floor next to Waite and held onto the second. They walked as close to Selene as they dared. "You think Waite and I have it good, don't you?"

Selene shrugged. "What beats living forever?"

"*That* does!" Smith shook their open hand at Selene. "Having your own body, that's the price I paid. Having your memory, all yours, not borrowed or stolen from anyone else. I'd die again for that. I'd die to even remember what it felt like."

Smith drank their rum.

XV
THE DEVIL

XV: THE DEVIL

The many lights darkened. The liquid in Smith's throat transmuted into mezcal—a smoother and smokier bite the blunt assault of house tequila. Smith's widening pupils beheld a dim, small room. The musk of metal and brick dust placed them somewhere in Arcana's garage. Windowless cinderblock walls enclosed them on three sides. A pilling black wool curtain crossed the fourth, hanging from a steel cable along the rafters. Loops of twine knotted to the curtain fed plastic pulleys near the side walls. In this cramped backstage zone, only the triangular roof joists leaked light over the curtain.

Smith parked their shot glass in the nearest corner, in lieu of a chair or table. The backstage area only provided square footage for a wheeled clothing rack and two barstools—both occupied.

"Scandalous!" Ember exclaimed and swung his feet, sitting still on one stool. Natalia sat opposite, adjusting the knot of his red and white bowtie.

"He should have brought it up with her, right?" She asked him, equally focused on his tie.

"Oh, immediately. Does he think this is the big city, where he can strut about in his pleated slacks like Patrick Bateman, immune to consequences? I assume he's not a serial killer, nor a snob about analog audio, but 'adulterer' is as severe a brand around here. You know, these hypocrite hipsters play progressive and open-minded, but Lewesboro lifers still clutch their southern pearls when it serves their fragile cultural dignity."

"Easy, now. You're talking to one of them forward-thinking southern belles." Natalia kissed Ember's forehead and readied her own bowtie.

"You know I adore duality. I embrace contradictions. I *lust* for them, in your case, but even if this weasel of a man is playing at polyamory, he's contravened the requisite balance of communication. Indria brings her complete and honest self to the date, and he arrives pretending *not* to be a married? Pretends not to have a *child*?"

"She didn't ask, though."

Ember huffed. "If you didn't recognize his picture, someone would have. He's a fool if he thinks he can hide it. He's untrusting, therefore untrustworthy. Suppose he retroactively claims some mutual arrangement with his wife. Why should Indria believe him now? He's played his hand, and it's a full house of shame."

Natalia dragged a thin brush over her eyebrows, then checked its effect in the preview of her front-facing camera. "Indria's gonna be alright. To be honest, Em, I was less worried about him than about his wife and daughter."

"Hm," Ember reconsidered. He held his tongue for longer than Smith imagined him capable, but not forever. "The male psyche is a vicious snare. Probing its depths, I forget the overarching background of—"

"Mm. I'll probe your depths, tonight, how's that?" She swung an underhand slap at Ember's ass, but he tipped his barstool far enough to dodge her. "I'll have you arching *your* background."

"Ha!" Ember cackled. "I'm writing that one down. Chris, did you hear what Natalia just said?"

Maybe Smith misheard over the chatter of people beyond the curtain. They peeked over their shoulder and behind the clothing rack for Chris. There was no one else. "What?" Chris' voice came from Smith's mouth. "Oh, *me*."

Ember flailed his hands in defeat. "Never mind! Never mind. Is that our cue? Nat, was that it?"

Natalia tuned him out, listening. "Almost."

Ember snapped his fingers. "Chris! Ready with the curtain?"

The audience quelled. An unseen microphone spit feedback, then thumped. Smith reached for the pulleys and frayed twine at the edge of the stage. In another body, on another night, they may have asked for better instructions from Ember, but this called for improvisation. Smith needed Chris' intuition, assuming he rehearsed these stage cues. Anyone with so many hours behind the bar depended on strong muscle memory. Chris would grab the right rope. He'd time it right. He'd—

"Guys, gals, non-binary pals!" Twyla's cheery introduction filled the air. "Welcome back to the second half of our show. And now, please welcome to the stage, the drivers of an ice cream truck!"

The numberless audience hollered, though tinged with confusion. Smith's right hand yanked the twine through the pulleys before they knew they'd done it. The curtain split, and the front lights illuminated Natalia and Ember's costumes: matching bowties, blue blazers, and papery white hats. The duo waltzed through the break in the curtain, and Smith shut it behind them. The imbalanced garage speakers cut from Twyla's microphone to Vanilla Ice's *Ice Ice Baby*.

Smith's eyes adjusted back to the dark, forced to imagine the performance based on reactions from the audience. It sounded like a popular event. The crowd shouted, *woo*-ed, and laughed with each musical turn of the song. Their cheers stacked, each more vigorous than the last. The buzz from the mezcal clouded Smith's focus.

The end of the song played out, replaced by applause. Smith reopened the curtain. Ember and Natalia stepped backstage, their costumes reduced to white garters, underwear, and fishnet stockings. Natalia's transformed ensemble featured a bra with waffle-cone-shaped breasts, and Ember's showcased a matching conic jockstrap. From the outfits at the start of the song, only their two paper hats remained, which they each threw towards the audience as Smith shut the curtain.

"How did you...?" Smith tried to ask Ember, who squeezed behind them to pull new garments from the clothing rack. The cone over his crotch wobbled. "Where did *that* thing come from?"

"Call it magic," Ember quipped. "No one needs to know about a coiled metal spring that's forever broadened the definition of *chafing*." He donned a silk robe over his scant costume and relieved Smith of their post along the curtain. "You ready to bring it home, darling?"

Smith couldn't tell why Ember spoke to them, not Natalia. "Ready to...? Yeah, yeah." They pretended to understand. "Wait, *me?*"

Twyla's mic reverberated through the speakers. "Now, I have some sad news to report. We only have one more act in tonight's character burlesque showcase. I know! I know. However, we have a very special performance for our grand finale. Please help me welcome to the stage... the devil himself!"

Ember tugged a twine pulley. Stage light streamed through the breach in the curtain, illuminating Smith. They wore heeled golden boots, a black buttoned shirt, and swirled deep crimson pants that matched a two-tailed coat jacket. Only now, they noticed fang-like tooth caps poking against their tongue. Smith lifted their eyes to the modest but energized audience, and the weight of two tall horns shifted on their head.

Saint sat in the front row, rapt with delight. Smith inched forward. The curtain locked them out at center-stage. Sweat beaded on their forehead. Whatever Chris planned, Smith needed to execute. Time accelerated back to its brisk natural pace. Somewhere, Twyla pressed a button and cued the opening melody of All-American Rejects' *Gives You Hell.*

Smith relaxed their muscles. The music shepherded them across the stage. Their movements settled into a clear rhythm. Each step, hand motion, and unexpected song lyrics crystallized in the instant after it: obvious, certain, and connected. At the edge of the first chorus, Smith caught the tail of their coat with one boot heel and flung it off with a kick. Whether the move belonged to Chris' body or Smith's intuition, a few in the crowd howled.

The song's chorus became a verse, then the chorus again. Somewhere in a series of controlled kicks, spins, and hip thrusts, Smith noticed the hidden snaps along the back of their shirt and pants. When instinct told them to take the leap, they tore both garments away. Each landed at the foot of the stage, revealing Smith's metallic Speedo and ornate gold-painted pentagram on their chest to match their boots. By the time the song's bridge arrived, the sequence of Chris' choreography brought Smith down to their knees at the edge of the stage.

Seated so close, Saint blushed and bowed their head, almost cowering. Smith met their timid glance between beats, and their tempo slipped. Inside the imagined space where Smith hid themself to let Chris' body dance, the walls fractured.

A few more fist pumps and boot stomps led Smith back onto their feet for the last chorus. The front rows of chairs clapped along to the beat. Smith measured the approaching end of the routine. Saint blew them an unexpected kiss. Would Chris blow a kiss back, if he saw? Smith decided to add it, in the last steps of the dance. The curtain opened behind them. Near the finish line, Smith wrested back control of

Chris' body again. They lost their rhythm. Smith tripped backwards on a heel and toppled backstage too fast for Ember or Natalia to catch them.

The song played out. Onlookers gasped, murmured, or laughed. The curtain snapped shut. Out in the dark, cautious cheers and claps followed.

"Stuck the landing!" Natalia joked and helped Smith off the ground.

Ember held Smith's other arm. "A greater poet than myself would say something about the devil falling back down into hell, or about the folly of man for mocking the powers of the underworld. Otherwise, how'd it feel?"

"Fine." Smith unzipped their gold boot, perched on a barstool, and squeezed their throbbing ankle. "I kinda became someone else out there."

"Your leg okay?" Natalia buttoned the ice cream truck driver shirts and folded them into a bag. Smith stopped touching their ankle and let their legs hang from the stool. The pain dulled. Compared to a punch in the face, this fell on the milder side of Smith's encounters with pain.

"Ankle. It's fine, I think."

After re-dressing in regular clothes, Ember and Natalia left their bagged costumes in one corner and dipped through the curtain. The garage speakers switched sources, and one of Arcana's staple rock tracks masked the din of dispersing guests. Smith limped to the clothing rack and flicked through the hangers, unsure what belonged to Chris.

"Chris?" Saint probed from the other side of the curtain. "Are you okay?"

"Saint?" Smith snagged a pair of sweatpants and shoved their bare legs into them.

"Yeah. Sorry, I just saw you fall. Making sure, you know?"

"You can come back here," Smith invited, not sure they'd accept. The curtain fluttered twice before Saint found the gap in the middle and slid one foot into the dark.

"Me? You want me to...?" Saint choked on their words until Smith finished putting on a shirt. "Easier to talk when I couldn't see you. Now, like, I don't know *what* I'm doing. I can go. It's—"

Smith yanked Saint's hand and sat them on a barstool. "It's not me. It's *me.*"

"Wh—hold on, what?" Saint wrung their hands close to their chest.

"Chris won't remember any of this, so you don't have anything to be nervous about. Is Oz here? Or Georgie?"

"No, just me. What's wrong?"

Smith rewound their conversations with Saint over so many incomplete nights.

"Oh, fuck. Sorry," they sighed. "We've met a few times, actually, but I never introduced myself to you. I'm Smith. I was Oz when she sang The Who, then I was you at Kink Night, and I was Ember when he sang a duet with Jade, but technically *she* was Waite, and then I was Georgie the night of the thunderstorm, but *you* missed part of that. Point is, I'm one of the ghosts everyone's been talking about." Smith waited. "You get what I'm saying?"

Saint zoned into Smith's shirtless, painted chest. "A ghost?" Saint averted their eyes. "Oz told me a bit, but she was high and I was drunk, so it's wishy-washy. You said Kink Night? Hang on, did I kiss *you* when you were Ember?"

"No, no, I was *you* that night, which is why you don't remember. Ember was Waite. Waite's the *other* ghost. They're out of their fucking mind. Maybe I am, too, but that's not my problem tonight! Anyway, nice to meet you for real this time."

Saint crossed their legs. "It's the drinks, isn't it?"

"What?"

"That's what Oz said. It's coming back to me. She said you can switch bodies when you drink."

Smith borrowed an oversize T-shirt from the rack and fitted it over their head. "Well, yeah, close enough. You've seen a ghost before, so you kinda get it, even if that was a different situation. *Poltergeist*, or whatever. Most people either get freaked out and need me to explain over and over." Smith hunted along the back wall for a Chris' phone.

"Huh," Saint said, still not looking towards Smith. "I don't think anything scares me as much as talking to you. Not *you*, but Chris, I mean. How wild is that? You could be the freaking Zodiac Killer, and I'd be less afraid than of you than I am asking him to pour me a drink. Like, there's ghost-scary, and there's Chris-scary." Saint held one hand close to the floor, and one high in the air for contrast.

Smith looked down at Chris' body. "Doesn't that make me *both* levels of scary for you?"

"No. You look like him, but *he's* not here. It's..." Saint frowned at Smith's wrinkled shirt. "Now that I say it, it's weirdly affirming, right? Like, I thought I was only into Chris physically, and I *can* be a fiend like that, but if I feel nothing for someone who has his exact body, then clearly he's stirred up *something* in this gay little heart. Don't get me wrong, I'd totally *have* you right now in this cozy little backstage zone, but I wouldn't *feel* any kind of way about it."

Smith's mind nagged at the thought. "I don't have time for... Was that a serious suggestion, or...?"

Saint blushed. "It wouldn't be the first time you've been in my body, would it?"

"Uh, yeah. No, it's not like that." Smith reminded themself to breathe. "I've been down this road when it comes to sex. Between us, I do hope you and Chris get together, but I can't consent for him. At the end of the night, that's still your body, and *this* is still his."

"Yes! Oh, yeah. Sorry. I'm a fiend, like I said, and I know how delusional I get. I'm not the first person to fall in love with their bartender, right? His job is to be personable, and I'm way too receptive to it. It's my problem. I won't make it his. Yours, whichever. And I'll try to stop picturing your gold speedo under those pants, or I'm gonna..." Saint twisted their feet around the legs of the stool. "Was that *you* dancing, or Chris?"

"Not now. Remember how there's another ghost, Waite? They're trying to start a new religion and frame someone for two deaths. I need to get back in touch with that *someone* before Waite can get to him. Is Jade here tonight?"

Saint sucked their teeth. "Who?"

"You don't know her?"

"Maybe?" Saint shrugged. "Everyone sticks to their cliques, and people change their names a lot. That's Arcana, baby."

"Okay, I'll look around." Smith adjusted the waistband of their sweatpants and peeked through the sliver of light between the closed curtains. "Are you gonna help?"

"Me?" Saint laughed. "I gotta take a minute to come to terms with being catfished by a ghost."

Smith walked downstage and into the center aisle that divided two clusters of abandoned chairs. Twyla folded two and stowed them along a wall.

"There you are!" She beckoned Smith close enough to kiss Chris' cheeks. "You were *magnificent* up there. Damn those uneven floors; I'll get Oren to level them out. Are you okay?"

Smith returned her smile. "Ankle hurts, but yeah. I'll be fine. It's... *me*, actually."

Twyla cocked her head and lowered her voice. She whispered under the music: "Smith or Waite?"

"Smith. Waite's not here, are they?"

"Don't think so, least not yet. Lucky you."

"How about Jade? I'm not in a great place with her, either."

"Not tonight." Twyla held Smith's arm when they started towards the door. "Sorry. I don't want to keep you from anything, but I've never had the opportunity to ask: What's it really like for you, on the other side?"

Smith considered faking an answer for her. They could cobble together a platitude to slake her spiritual thirst. They could use a framework she'd understand, using the imagery or symbols of tarot to the best of their knowledge. Smith could borrow Ember's tricks and regurgitate a knot of words for Twyla to untie all night, but what use would it be to lie to her about something as trivial as the afterlife?

"I wish I knew what it was like," Smith told her. "If I'm right here with you, maybe this is the only side there is."

She nodded and released Smith's arm. They continued into the sitting room. A pile of cards on a coffee table drew Smith's eye, but they were ordinary cards, surrounded by a quartet of euchre players. One player waved away a cloud from her vape. As her teammate dealt hands of five cards around the table, she waved the illuminated device at Smith."

"The devil himself! You were *so* good. Like, so good. I have the video if you want me to tag you. I'll cut out the end, don't worry."

Smith spoke for Chris. "Sure, go for it. And thank you!"

They snuck down the short hallway to the main room. Before Smith could borrow a phone, rally a friend, or bum a ride, a middle-aged woman in the center of the room scowled at them. She wore a long floral skirt and a gray sweater with white buttons. She stood out, even from the odd circles of tourists. She fixed her ire on the space above Smith's eyes. Without a mirror, Smith forgot about their horned headdress and forehead pentacle.

"Sign of Satan," the woman complained in a raspy tone to a younger woman at the bar, who ignored her. "*I'm* not having this. Suit yourself, but I'll be outside."

Smith rubbed their forehead. Black ink smeared and transferred to their fingerprints. As the annoyed woman stalked towards the parking lot, Smith remembered her. Even here, even while irritated, she kept her stoic poise from the funeral fundraiser.

"Julienne's *mom*," Smith realized. "What the fuck?"

Maybe Waite spoke to her, with so much religiosity between them both. Maybe she heard rumors about the ghosts, similarly to Saint. One way or another, someone dragged Mrs. Chord to Arcana, however briefly. Smith walked closer to the younger woman at the bar, to whom Mrs. Chord vented her frustration. Under a shawl of canary yellow, she signed a receipt and sipped a glass of white wine.

Smith couldn't ignore her resemblance to Stu's illicit date. "Katie?"

She turned, and there she was. Of all people, Katie from the credit union knew Julienne's mom. Even stranger, she came back to Arcana after a date Smith assumed was a one-off. Whatever colorful world Katie hailed from, its perfumed aura clashed against the bar like a stormfront. Every inch of her hair, skin, and clothes boasted a cleanliness foreign to the space. Now free to observe Katie in her own skin, Smith beheld her true affect. It made them dizzy.

"Do I know you?" She curled the tail of her question like a scimitar. Smith balanced on their heels.

"No. Sorry, I didn't—"

"Buddy, whatever some clickbait headline told you, I've heard worse. I've had five flavors of feds sniff up my ass in the past two months. I'm not scared to tell the truth, whether guys like you believe it or not. You wanna know why Paul was shot and ejected from a van full of guns, flying down the highway in the middle of the night? So do I." Katie sipped her wine.

"Wait, wait, he wasn't shot," Smith insisted. Bewilderingly, the real Katie sounded as preoccupied with the crash as they did. Their hasty P.I. ruse wasn't too bad a fit for her. "He and Julienne burned in the fire. No one was shot."

"Go refresh your gossip websites," Katie told them. "Marks County coroner revised their reports. That girl took a bullet through her hand. Paul was bleeding out from an eight-millimeter shot to the chest when the van rolled. He was dead before he went through the windshield."

Smith raised their hands. "Okay, okay, you know more than me. Sorry, I'm just surprised."

Katie laughed. "Buddy, I was the last one to see his work truck leave the driveway. If that ain't enough for you, go lawyer up and sue me once the estate settles out. There's already a Mullard lawsuit Facebook group for people like you to jerk each other off. Meanwhile, I'm the one putting up a forty-thousand-dollar reward for the Hayes boy. That's my *own* forty grand."

"What?" Smith thought they misheard her. A horrible revelation overcame them. "If *you* put up the reward money, then you're..."

Katie Mullard, P.K. Mullard's widow.

In jarring flashes, Smith reviewed their night as Katie. Even if Evelyn knew Katie's name, she never recognized her face. At the train tracks, Walt only asked for Stu's name. When Walt told Smith he knew *exactly* who they were, he meant it. He didn't think Katie was another bounty hunter. He knew she put up the reward. Even before Walt chased her down, Stu looked up Katie on his phone. He confronted her to say she didn't *have* a husband because she'd just *lost* one. Smith spent their night threading a sharp needle between Katie—the widow on a date with a married young stranger—and themself, delivering the Mullard heiress straight to the Hayes family's doorstep.

"A cheater was your safest shot at romance," Smith whispered as their head spun. "Even if Stu found you out, telling anyone would blow up his marriage."

Katie spat wine back into her glass. "Excuse me?"

"Never mind. Your husband, Paul Mullard, is *alive*."

Katie grimaced like Smith had cursed at her. "No. The cops made me 'identify' what was left of him. You're not with another podcast, are you?"

"Right, yeah, you saw his body. There's more, though." Smith danced around the truth, gauging how much she could handle. Behind the bar, Alea collected Katie's receipt. Every night, there were so many receipts. "Oh! There's a receipt in the driver's side door pocket of your car. It's for a sheet cake, and it has last Thursday's date on it. Do you know how it got there?"

Katie stared past Smith, seeming enthralled by the furry pink pole and the rafters above. Smith settled into the seat next to her.

"They say the devil is in the details," Katie warned. "I audited Paul's accounts for the credit union. That's how I met him, years ago. I flagged the first warning signs of... *alleged* violations. This was long before any client's complained, but I knew exactly who I married. See, I organize my papers, my home, my car, and my life so I can notice the details. Everyday fools like Mrs. Chord beg people like me to see through the noise and solve their problems. I'm her best shot at noticing details that'll explain why her daughter's dead. I notice things like dust, mud, and *gravel* coating my car, or some weird grocery receipt, or a fucking *hour* that's somehow missing from my life. Don't think I didn't notice the way you interrupted me after I asked who you are." She brushed her finger up one of Smith's plastic horns. "Seems to me that the *details* are in the *devil*."

Smith took off their headdress and placed it on the bar next to the wine glass. If Katie made it this far, they figured she could handle the truth.

"Ask anyone here," they told her, "and they'll say I'm Chris, the bartender. This *is* his body, but tonight, *I'm* not Chris. I call myself 'Smith' because I can't remember who I was before I haunted this bar. Yes, *haunted*, even though I hate that word. Since the night of the crash, there are two ghosts here at Arcana: me and one other. Do you see what I'm telling you? On Thursday, you missed an hour because I haunted *you*." Smith waited while Katie swirled her wine, then did it in the other direction, and again. Smith pointed at the liquid in her glass. "I don't think the other ghost has haunted you yet, but that's how it can happen. I haunted you because you finished a drink at this bar."

Katie tipped the last of her wine towards her lips. "I knew it."

Smith puzzled over her claim. "That's not possible."

Katie faltered. She lowered her glass and released a deep breath. "In banking, every transaction resonates. I apply that principle to my life. Even after losing Paul, even with the lawsuits, my life is a symphony of resonating tones. I hear all their sources, or I *did*, until something on Thursday made an *impossible* noise." Katie dipped her middle finger in the wine. She held down the base of the glass and dragged her wet fingertip around the rim. It hummed an eerie monotone. "What you're telling me, Smith, is what I expected: *impossible*."

Smith didn't need to fill in the blanks for her. Katie reached even the most difficult conclusions on her own, in seconds, without complaint. In fact, she seemed a few steps ahead.

"So which ghost are you?" Katie sized up Smith. She gestured between herself and Mrs. Chord, still pacing the parking lot.

Smith shrugged. "The other one, Waite, *thinks* they're Paul, but they also think we're immortal, so who knows. They're looking for you because they think they can marry you, take Paul's estate as theirs, and maybe start a new religion. I'm guessing they'd claim someone's body long-term, then act as your... spouse."

"Oh, is that *all?*" Katie snickered. "It's not like a ghost could seriously challenge my right to Paul's estate. How did you come back, though? How did you both survive?"

Smith shook their head. "That's what Waite and I are trying to figure out."

Katie shifted her yellow snakeskin purse from her side to her lap. "Smith, you seem sweet, but it sounds like you're holding the key to limitless life. I hope you realize what that means."

"If ghosts could live forever, wouldn't this world be full of them?" Smith couldn't shake the dread of their tarot reading. "I don't know. What does it mean?"

"The only thing more valuable than money is time. Death is the last barrier to building infinite wealth, and *you* can teach me to overcome it. You're coming home with me tonight, and you're going to help me find the other one, too, before this gets out." Katie unclasped the purse in her lap and opened it towards Smith. The hilt of a small silver pistol glistened. "I'd threaten to kill you, but you're already dead. Do you feel pain?"

As Katie closed her purse, Smith seized her wine glass and drank what remained.

XVI
THE TOWER

XVI: THE TOWER

An empty plastic rum shooter bottle quivered in Smith's hands, and they let it tumble into their lap. Smith shuddered as if Katie's gun still angled for them, through the handbag, through the cinderblock wall, across time and space. They couldn't breathe anymore, at least not until its image faded from their head: steel, shine, and packaged death. *Gun* was the word that drew closer by the hour. It was something Hayes collected. It was the way Stu's family answered the door. It was Walt's sidearm. Now, it was a threat from Katie Mullard. The clear, simple promise of a gun agonized Smith at least as much as their tarot reading.

Across from Smith, Colton folded his arms on the grimy picnic table and rested his chin on them.

"Phoebe, I don't know why you're still listening to me," he told Smith, using Annie's fake name from the Wreck Club. He drank and talked too much to pay attention. "You're so pretty. If I looked half as pretty, you wouldn't catch me wasting time on some unemployed, broke loser. I mean it, how pretty you are. I think more people should say what they feel about each other, especially the good stuff. After Julie and I split, I waited to talk to her because I thought we'd reconnect, right? There's a thing Julie said after I wrecked my bike, that we're the type who never break out of the Lewesboro vortex. It's that thing, you know, where even the folks who leave this city come back, over and over, no matter how it breaks us: our minds, hearts, even my fucked-up shoulder. I figured she meant to say it romantically, like we'd stay close here forever, but maybe all she meant was that we're all dying here."

Colton snuck a fresh whiskey shooter bottle from his bomber jacket. He twisted its tiny cap, hid his face from A-Bomb's lookout, and sent half the liquid bubbling into his open mouth.

"My name is Annie," Smith corrected him.

"What?"

"You called me Phoebe. I'm Annie." Smith spared him the full story. They'd let him think *he* made up the name.

"Fuck." Colton smacked his forehead. "I'm a fucking dumbass." He choked down the second half of the whiskey shooter. Like him, Smith couldn't imagine why Annie kept devoting her attention to his nightly rambling. How many more times did they go out together? Who sought the other's company? Smith wished they could inject themself into Colton's body and hear the truth from Annie.

"You're not a dumbass," Smith told him. "You're just scared." They traced one fingernail along the gap of the table's planks, dreaming of ripping it apart along the grain. "You're scared that somehow, this was your fault, like you could've protected her. You're scared that her dying had nothing to do with you. You're scared that she wouldn't have mourned you like this. Mostly, you're scared to die, like the rest of us, and have it mean nothing. You're—"

Colton grabbed Smith's finger and yanked their hand across the table. His empty shooter bottle clattered onto the bench. "Do I *look* scared?" His eyes refocused, lucid and boiling.

"Hey, let me go!" Smith twisted their arm, but Colton's stronger hand held firm.

"Do I look scared? Answer me."

Smith watched the tiny plastic bottle roll away towards a storm drain. "You look too drunk for me to sit here forever, listening to you without saying anything back."

"You're slower than I thought." Colton jabbed with unexpected cruelty. "Give me one reason not to take your finger and scoop your eyeballs out of your fucking skull, *Smith*."

Smith flinched. Before they could clock Waite, Waite already clocked them. "Waite, stop. This isn't *my* body. You'd hurt me now, but you'd hurt *her* more."

"Rich, coming from you!" Waite licked their teeth. "When you swung that tablet, Radhika's face was as good as mine for you, wasn't it?"

"You're right, okay? Is that what you needed to hear?" Smith tried to yank themself free or pry open Waite's grip, but Waite wrangled their other hand, too. Smith prayed for A-Bomb to peer out the entryway and intervene. Waite's fingers tightened.

"I spent four hours in a hospital getting stitches before I could drink a paper cup full of rubbing alcohol. I had four hours to think about every way I'd return the favor when I found you again. If you want us to spend forever inflicting maximum pain on one another—"

"There *is* no forever!" Smith lowered their voice. "If we can hurt, we can die. We're not immortal, no matter how badly you want to be."

"Great theory. Mind if I test it on you?" Waite rose halfway from the table. Smith kicked at their legs. Waite buckled and fell back down onto the bench.

"Truce!" Smith yelled. "We need to call a truce, starting tonight."

"Convenient to plead for peace while you're waving a white flag."

Smith rushed to offer an olive branch. "And a few nights back, I had Katie Mullard's body, but I didn't *know* I was her. Last night, I met her here. She had a gun in her purse, and now she's after both of us. She thinks we can help her live forever."

Waite rolled their eyes. "I don't care that you ran your mouth and ruined my shot at Mullard's fortune. The missing cards are more important. Hayes is the one I need, but Jade said you *impersonated* me and scared him off!"

Smith couldn't deny that one. "You're making a scene. Someone is gonna come over here."

"Oh, a *scene*: some everyday alcoholics squabbling in a parking lot. Even if they hadn't seen it all before, half these people know what we are, and A-Bomb's never gonna come rescue the *ghoul* that possessed his body. For a creature who talks a big game about consequences, you never seem to face the music, do you?"

"It wasn't like that," Smith tried to convince themself, but doubt festered. Selene felt violated enough by Waite's possession to quit drinking. How did A-Bomb feel? He staked his reputation as a bouncer on vigilance. What did it mean if his defenses fell to Smith, threatening the bar from within his own body?

Waite tightened their grip again. "We are standing on the brink of the greatest revolution in human history. If these tarot cards are the key to our immortality, we can't let Hayes, the Mullard widow, or any other *mortal* control them. You're too worried about being *harmless* when you'll have eternity to forgive yourself. You can be 'good' later. We are the stewards of a new world order, and revolutions are measured in blood."

"Fuck you." Smith hated themself for every kindness they ever showed Waite.

A white coupe backed into a parking space behind Waite. Its milky headlights cast Waite's shadow over the table. For the first time, Smith saw Waite as they imagined them: a faceless silhouette with an iron grip.

"I'm going to change the world," Waite promised Smith. "If you want to live in this delusion, cosplaying as one of the weak people, then stay out of my way, and I might let you. How's *that* for a truce?"

The driver of the coupe locked his car, and its lights died. The driver walked around the picnic table, sneaking towards the open garage door while A-Bomb remained inside. As the driver passed, Smith recognized his gait, or maybe his neat beard.

"Dorian?" Smith called.

Dorian slowed and paused. "Do I know...?" Dorian abandoned his question. Waite still pressed Smith's hands down on the table. Dorian narrowed his eyes. "Y'all good, here?"

"Fuck off," Waite grumbled, not even looking.

Dorian's shoulders lifted. His fists curled. He positioned himself over the end of the table, then cracked his knuckles on its edge. On the night of the hot dog stand, Smith never met the real man under Dorian's orange sweater. Tonight, the cutoff sleeves of his thin green T-shirt exposed his thick arm muscles as they flexed. "I don't know about you, buddy, but where I come from, we don't touch a female like that."

"Sure." Finally, Waite released Smith and leaned away, slowly. "But *that's* not exactly a female."

Too fast for Waite to anticipate, Dorian's open palm struck their temple. It knocked them flat sideways across the bench. Dorian readied another blow. Smith lunged over the table and blocked Dorian's hand. The pink disco light glinted off his thumb.

"Are you sure?" Dorian asked. "Are you *sure* your boy's had enough?"

Smith took a closer look at one of Dorian's meaty fingers. Each of his nails sparkled with glittery red polish. "What is this?"

He relaxed his arms. "Ma'am, I... What's is *what*?"

"I need to know where you got this color for your nails."

Dorian slid his hand free from Smith's. Waite groaned and propped themself upright, clutching their head as they shook themself off. "That's not the color," Waite coughed and pointed at Dorian's fingernails. "The message in the bathroom? It's not the same red."

"You don't know that." Smith retorted. "The lights look weird out here, and you just got whacked on the head."

Dorian flattened his palms on the table, showing off his nails. "Ma'am, the shade is called *Explosive Watermelon*. You spotted it so quick, I guess my work in the bathroom made a hell of an impression."

"Wait, *you*?" Smith wrestled against Dorian's assertion. "No, Hayes wrote that message. How...?"

"I don't know a Hayes," Dorian insisted, equaling Smith's confusion. From his back pocket, he retrieved a stout glass vial with a tall silver top. More *Explosive Watermelon* nail polish swirled inside it. "The guy who paid me said not to tell anyone, but it seems like you already know more than I do."

Waite weighed in, cautiously. "You talked to Hayes?"

"I just said I don't know who that is, dude. All I know is some chickenshit guy on a forum who posted that he'd pay a local to do some writing here. *Writing*, you know? 'Graffiti.' Guy said it had to be this crazy color, but whatever. He transferred extra Ether for me to buy it. I had plenty left over, and it looks kinda sick on me, yeah?" Dorian showed off his nails under his phone's flashlight. "I didn't paint 'em too neat, but whatever. Who are y'all, anyway?"

Waite shook their head. "Let's not get into that."

"I'm Smith," Smith told him. "You were here on Sunday, right?" Smith didn't need to ask. They ran straight into him when he left the bathroom. Seconds afterward, they found the smaller painted message under the first: *The Tower. Sunday. Midnight.*

Dorian checked his phone. "Yeah, Sunday was wack, cause last Friday, the forum guy paid me double to come back and write a second line under the first. He got pissed cause I didn't send him a picture for proof, so I came back Sunday after I got off work."

Waite tapped the table. "Could we take a look at the posts from this 'forum guy?'"

Dorian crossed his hefty arms. "For a fair price, maybe."

Waite turned out Colton's barren pockets.

"Here." Smith dissected Annie's fanny pack and unfolded a fifty-dollar bill from a narrow zippered pocket. They hoped Annie wouldn't miss it.

"Paper money is gonna be worthless in a few years, you know." Dorian took the bill anyway and shoved it into his back pocket. He set his phone flat on the table and tapped until a white page of indented black text filled the screen:

> *Burner782256414: Any Lewesboro writers taking commissions? Small, easy, and low risk, but specific. Need to send a message rq. I'll pay half in advance, half after photos. Dm.*
> *DorManGainz1000 (you): @Burner782256414 bet. i dmed u*

Dorian shook his head at the screen. "That was a while ago. I've got a whole lot more direct messages with the guy." Dorian tried to take his phone back, but Smith's and Waite's heads followed it, still reading. "Do y'all... want to see those too?"

> *Sunday*
> *Burner782256414: Got photos of the second one?*

> *DorManGainz1000 (you): bro chill i jus forgot*
> *DorManGainz1000 (you): gimme like an hour*
> *DorManGainz1000 (you): okay yeah is right here. wtf is the tower.? <image deleted>*
> *Burner782256414: Just transferred the rest. Thx.*
> *DorManGainz1000 (you): word up*

Smith hatched an idea. "Dorian, could you—?"

"Can you send him another message?" Waite interrupted to suggest the same thing. "Ask him if he can meet up tonight."

Dorian began typing. "I can ask, but he's not gonna bite. Dude's mad skittish or whatever."

"Say it's Jade," Smith suggested. "Tell him this is Jade, using your phone. Tell him I have all the lessers, this time, and he can meet me in the same place."

Dorian nodded along, mouthing the words while writing. Waite kept tapping the table but didn't object.

"Thought your name was Smith, but alright, *Jade*," Dorian clarified. "You said tell him you got the letters?"

"*Lessers*," Waite corrected. Dorian bristled at them, and Waite calmed their tone. "Sorry. It is 'lessers,' though."

"I sent it," Dorian said and tucked his phone away. "That one's on the house, cause this guy doesn't text worth shit. Guess y'all know what this guy is like, then. He always so hard to reach?"

Smith looked away. "You could say that."

Dorian's phone buzzed. Waite and Smith sat upright.

"Y'all, chill. That's just my boy with the…" Dorian checked the message. "Shit. Nope, you're right. He wrote back. He'll be there in twenty minutes."

"Shit," Smith murmured and glared at Waite. "You're not good to drive, and I'm *not* driving again. We can't walk there in twenty minutes."

"Walk where?" Dorian probed. Smith wanted to leave him out of this, but maybe Dorian's dusty white coupe could beat Hayes' bicycle up the mountain.

"Bayonet Bridge," Waite told Dorian, but they stood up to leave alone. "I'll get my own ride. Someone will do me the favor now that people know who I am." Waite wobbled on his feet and clung to a pole of the canopy. Too many shooters and a blow to the head took their toll on Colton's body's balance.

Dorian rubbed his palms together. "If y'all got another fifty bucks, I'll get you to Bayonet Bridge and back."

Smith unzipped the same pocket of Annie's fanny pack, but only twenty-eight dollars remained. They paid Dorian the twenty and the five. "We'll find our own way back."

"Dope."

Dorian readied the coupe. He shoveled dirty paper towels and fountain drink cups into the void behind the driver's seat. Crumbs hid in the folds of the gray cloth seats, too many to bother sweeping from the narrow stitches. Air from the plastic vents smelled like cheese and dead insects. Dorian slid the passenger seat forward.

"After you," Waite tried, but Smith maintained their distance.

"Let your girl ride up front, guy." From Dorian to Waite, the suggestion was a command. Waite squeezed through the low doorframe. After them, Smith repositioned the passenger seat in the farthest forward notch to avoid provoking Waite. Dorian wouldn't be around to protect them forever. As they left Arcana's parking lot, Smith felt Waite's eyes boring into the back of their skull through the headrest.

Dorian turned up the volume on his rap music. He drove at least as well as Stu. The jaunt across town and up the bends of Holowell Road took no more than ten minutes, or two and a half songs from Dorian's playlist. At the mouth of the bridge arch, Dorian stopped the car along the shoulder and paused his music.

"I ain't waiting up for the guy," Dorian announced, "and I don't fuck with whatever voodoo they got up in this place." He swiped away his playlist from his phone's screen and charted his quickest route home.

Smith exited, tilted the passenger seat forward, then let Waite escape onto the leafy shoulder with them. One of Colton's unopened shooter bottles tumbled loose from his bomber jacket. Smith shut the coupe's door and handed back the bottle.

Waite rejected it. "I'm not leaving."

"It came from your jacket. That's all."

"Whatever." Waite took it. Dorian swept a wide turn across the middle of the road, backed up, and let the coupe's squeaky engine coast onward down the hill. Waite tracked the vehicle's vanishing path like they could make it drive faster. "I hope he crashes and burns like we did."

Smith ventured further off the road through the tall, dry grass and rediscovered the narrow path up the bridge's far side. They let Waite follow but didn't bother instructing them. Maybe Jade already brought them here. Close behind Smith, Waite swatted and tore at wild plants that bobbed in their way. They lost a brief battle with a nettle vine. Waite kicked it aside and sucked blood from their palm.

"Hayes is expecting Jade." They reminded Smith. "He won't know either of us. We don't have the lesser cards, if Jade has even finished them yet. What's stopping him from bailing straight away?"

"Jade is drawing the lessers?" Smith relished Waite's rare slip-up. Waite ripped up a bare tree sapling and tossed it down the hill behind them. They offered no more useful information, so Smith continued. "Hayes *will* know you. You're

Colton, Julienne's ex-boyfriend. He's still obsessed with her. Hayes won't know me, but I think I can make him listen."

Waite grunted and hurdled a fallen tree trunk. Colton's lethargic limbs threatened to slip and send them tumbling. Waite massaged their shoulder, the one Colton complained never healed right. "You can say whatever keeps Hayes here long enough."

"Long enough for what?" Smith whirled and faced backwards at the top of the path, blocking Waite. Walt's plea still rang in Smith's ears, begging for his son Tommy to have a second chance. Smith kept that from Waite. They could take it as a challenge or an opportunity to twist a knife. "We're not turning him in. Not to the cops, and not to Katie."

Waite flexed their hand, staunching and releasing drips of blood where nettles pricked their skin. "I think I told you not to stand in my way," they chided, "but here you are, violating the truce."

"I have to tell Hayes who we are. He's the only person who might know why we're here. If he's no help after that... then sure, he's all yours." Smith instantly regretted their words but couldn't afford another physical fight in the isolated woods. No matter how drunk, Colton's body had an advantage over Annie's.

Waite threw a fistful of dirt at Smith. "Let's go. Why are you *still* in my way?"

Smith crested the top of the path. They sifted through the grass near the middle of the bridge deck and found no trace of the coiled rope from last time. Hayes would need a new trick to escape Waite, if they tried anything.

Under the papery chatter of wind over the leaves, a distant mechanical click rose in volume. Its rhythm steadied. Smith hunkered along the bridge deck's wall and snooped over it. As promised, Hayes' bike rounded the bending incline of

Holowell Road. He pedaled in a low gear, and the chain skipped a metal spur tooth once per cycle.

"Waite, you should hide. If he—" Smith lost sight of Waite, then spotted them halfway behind a large tree on the ruined mansion's side of the bridge. Waite straddled its knotted roots and concealed themself further on the far side. Sitting under the cover of the bridge wall, Smith pictured the two ill-fated sisters awaiting the stonemason's return. Who was blind, them or Waite?

Smith listened for the bike clicks to stop, then for Hayes' scraping and crunching steps up the path. Annie's heart beat their chest from the inside, longing to escape. Smith couldn't think about her now—their passenger, their prisoner, no idea that a rum shooter could lead her to *this*. Smith diverted all their attention to Hayes. He emerged at the top of the path, noiseless and slow like a cat on a hunt.

"Jade?" He called into the wind. Smith rose to their feet. Hayes backpedaled and checked all around. "Where's Jade?"

"It's me, Smith. I was here with Jade last time. You thought I was filming, remember?"

"Bullshit," Hayes rebutted. "She was with..." He strided closer, fast enough that Smith retreated a few steps. Hayes stopped so close that Smith smelled his unbrushed teeth. Recognition flashed across his stubbled cheeks. "Annie?"

"No, I'm not—"

"From Sunday school. Annie, it's *me*." Hayes trembled, then almost laughed. A wave of apparent nausea rippled down his body. Hayes scratched his beard. "Sorry. Forget I said that. You don't know me."

"I'm *not* Annie. I'm Smith, from last time, and I'm in her body! Do you believe me now?" Smith opened their arms widely towards him. "It doesn't matter. Katie Mullard has already been to Arcana. Waite and I are the talk of the town, so now Katie knows that we survived. You've heard, right, about the two ghosts with no memories? About the people who drink at Arcana getting possessed, since the night of the crash? The ghosts of Paul Mullard and of... Julie?"

Hayes' legs bent. He wilted down into the grass and wrapped his arms around his knees. He rubbed his hands together. "I'm thinking. Hang on." Hayes shut his eyes and held his breath. Smith stooped down against the wall again. They waited until he gasped and opened his eyes, gripping wild grass in both hands. "Oh, fuck. That's where the trumps went."

"What, the major arcana? What do you know about them?"

Hayes' rapid gasps dissolved into delirious laughter. "You're alive. You're alive, but you forgot. You're not who you think you are. The cards saved you *twice*. The fire, of course it was the fire!"

Smith picked apart with Hayes' conclusions. "You're saying I'm Mullard? What am I missing?"

"No, you're not *Mullard*!" If Hayes registered Smith's second question, he only answered it with another. "What happens if you set fire to a stack of twenty-two stolen, hand-drawn tarot cards?"

Smith kicked the wall. "I don't know, what?"

"No one knows. Tarot cards don't come with instructions, but no one in the world is dumb enough to *burn* them!" Hayes rushed forward and grabbed Smith's face. He held them tight, just soft enough to quell their fear. "This isn't what I had in mind when I said we'd be each other's living memory." Before Smith could protest, before they could ask what he meant, Hayes kissed them. The tender bizarreness of his embrace disarmed Smith so completely, they never saw Waite emerge from behind the tree.

"Time's up!" Waite's drawling command split Hayes and Smith apart from one another. Hayes' legs twitched, ready to flee if not for Smith, who planted their feet in front of him.

Waite's fury still filled every inch of their drunken, bleeding, and dirt-spattered frame.

"Colton?" Hayes said the name like the title of a sticky chemical in a vial marked *X*.

"No, that's—" Smith started, but Hayes understood.

"Waite, or Mullard, the other one. I see it, now." He started away towards the far side of the bridge, faster and faster, building the distance between himself and this new threat.

Waite clapped their hands at Smith, who now stood alone. "Congratulations, you had your moment. You got your answers. Now, it's my turn to meet the man who killed us."

Smith stepped left and right, blocking Waite from crossing further along the bridge. "He didn't do this. He can help us!"

"Us?" Waite shoved Smith back with their forearm. "You broke 'us' when you tied me to the wall. When you fucked me and ran off. When you *impersonated* me, hospitalized me, and stood in *my fucking way*." Waite grabbed Smith's arms again, steering them sideways and dragging their feet over the grass. Smith mistook the maneuver for a miscalculated tackle. Then, Waite clasped their hand over Smith's face. They bent Annie's body back, forcing Smith down, leaning over the edge of the craggy stone wall.

"Waite! *Stop!*" Smith's words muffled under Waite's bloodied, firm hand.

"I say it's about time we put our immortality to the test. Think the reward for Hayes goes up if his online messages lead to a third body?"

Waite grinned in serene satisfaction. Flailing against Waite atop the towering omen of destruction itself, the iron cradle of Twyla's prophecy gripped them with panic. "Waite, wait! What if you're right? If you live forever, you'll have to live with this!"

"And if I'm wrong," Waite snarled, "you'll never get in my way again."

A fierce impact pummeled Waite's side. Their grip peeled away. Smith clung halfway over the stone edge, lightheaded. In a blur of bodies in the dark, Hayes brought the fight back to Waite. Arms swung. Shoes scraped over the dirt. Hayes tripped Waite and shoved with both hands. Waite slipped and braced one arm to catch themself on the wall, but Colton's shoulder popped loudly. Waite screamed. Their arm buckled. Feet away from Smith, Waite's whole body crossed the precipice of the bridge wall.

Inverted, they fell. *Waite* fell from *The Tower*. Colton's living body fell, and it made no sound until the pavement. Forty feet of gravity dealt one massive blow. The gaping mouth of Bayonet Bridge magnified the wretched noise of a wordless impact below.

The rest of their night existed only in toxic flashes of horror. Their legs poured them down the path like stormwater. Hayes cried through closed teeth. Smith reached inside Colton's jacket to seek a heartbeat. In its place, they found an unopened whiskey shooter bottle. It had no blood on it. Hayes begged Smith to close Colton's red-mottled eyes. Smith crammed onto the bicycle behind Hayes, whose feet rattled the pedals even while coasting down the mountain. The wind cooled none of the heat on Smith's face. They licked their bone-dry lips and tasted the blood Waite's hand left behind. They clung to Hayes' slender body, close enough to pretend his comfort meant anything. Hayes talked to the air until his voice turned raspy. He begged for sleep to relieve him from this impossible dream.

Hayes left Smith at a church. He said it was Annie's. He tried to embrace them but recoiled from the blood. When his bike wheels disappeared into the opposite side of town, Smith collapsed on the concrete church steps and laughed. As wrong as it felt, they laughed. It hurt too much to stop. Smith read and reread the church's notice board: *And each person was judged according to what they had done.*

After so many readings stripped every morsel of meaning from the sign, Smith cracked open the shooter bottle. They drank alone.

XVII
THE STAR

XVII: THE STAR

The whiskey transmuted into a flat, watery beer. Smith dropped its aluminum shell. It bounced across the picnic table, rolled off one corner, and skittered along the asphalt. Beer couldn't wash down the rock in Smith's throat. They sat in the same seat as last time, at the far end of the beige canopy. No one joined them. In the fresh uncertainty of Waite's absence, Smith weighed the threats of two possibilities: either they would someday die like Waite, or Waite would return and enact their revenge.

Whichever proved true, *someone* would find Colton's body under Bayonet Bridge. Annie would wash the blood from her skin, then maybe atone for however she imagined it got there. If Colton had friends or relatives, no one would answer their questions. Would Dorian confess to driving Colton and Annie to the bridge? Would Katie or the cops tie Colton's death to Annie or Hayes? No matter how Lewesboro rationalized this fresh tragedy, Colton and Waite's demise struck a fragile system at its weakest point. Someone would hold an innocent person's feet to the fire for this. Smith's ears pulsed. Their eyelids squeezed for tears, but none flowed. This new body refused to cry.

Smith lifted a smartphone from their jacket pocket. They'd seen it before, and soon they knew where. The locked wallpaper flashed an image of Ellesandra, in a silver cocktail dress, smiling next to a Christmas tree. Smith mashed the phone's side button. The screen blanked, and they flinched at Levi's reflection. Waite spoke through those lips in the shower; their voice cut like razors through the veil of steam:

"I want you to fuck me like I deserve it."

Smith threw the phone onto the tabletop, same as Waite discarded it across the hotel bathroom counter. It flipped and teetered on the edge, screen down. No matter where they looked, Smith's mistakes surrounded them.

Nearby the entrance, A-Bomb snapped his fingers. "I asked you a question, jackass." His commanding inflection made Smith hold their breath. A-Bomb approached a man at the middle picnic table. "What's your badge number?"

The man at the table wore a dark red flannel shirt and navy baseball cap. He tilted his chin up at A-Bomb. He didn't move a single muscle below his meaty neck. "Hey, man, I'm just having a conversation with these young ladies here."

Selene and Jade exchanged glances on the opposite side of his table.

"First off, you injected yourself into *our* conversation," Selene scolded him, "and second, *I* ain't a lady."

The man in the cap eyed up Selene, forfeiting his chance to respond. A-Bomb rested his knuckles on the table until the man looked back at him. "This ain't your place tonight, sports fan."

"I don't understand," he tried, "what gives you the right to deny me service?"

Jade laughed and barked back: "And what gives you the right to come asking *us* about some dead guy up Holowell Mountain, pig?"

The whites of his eyes widened under his hat brim, enough for Smith to see from the farthest table. "Whoa, whoa. I don't see no farm animals here, and I back our boys in blue. Lewesboro is a safer city for the hard work we—*they* do."

Selene chuckled. A-Bomb crossed his arms. The plain-clothes officer excused himself and marched out the far end of the canopy. He shimmied behind Smith, fleeing to the overflow parking lot. At its back corner, his unmarked cruiser straddled three spaces.

"Aw!" A-Bomb twisted his fists in front of his cheeks. "Did we hurt the little piggy's feelings?"

Selene shrugged. "They train to suppress emotions."

Jade pried back the tab of her seltzer can. "You like playing with fire, don't you, A-Bomb?"

He folded up the collar of his leather jacket and tapped a flowery pink *ACAB* patch. It filled the gap above a Palestinian flag and a big, round antiswas. "If I didn't have a job to do, y'all... It's funny watching how they play civilian but squeal after you call them out for being dickheads. Some nerve to show up asking about Colton, like it's some casual business, like I'm not fucking devastated, like I didn't talk to him just last night. Prick can come back with a warrant."

Smith started sliding down the bench towards Jade and Selene, but a nervous paralysis stopped them. Everyone saw Smith hit Waite. No one had a reason to trust them anymore. They could hide behind Levi's face, but asking too many questions would blow their cover. They might even get Levi banned a second time. Besides, what would make *them* any better than the undercover cop? The more Smith considered, the more they saw open doors slamming shut. They'd face the music soon, if not tonight. The curse of the drinks doomed them to meet the consequences of every night before.

"Jade?" Smith dropped Levi's phone into a pocket and slid further down the bench. Selene and Jade quieted. "Jade, I'm sorry. I met him at The Tower without you. Waite came with me. They were Colton. Colton was Waite. They're both dead, and it was my fault. It was..." Smith's throat contracted. Levi's watery eyes blurred Jade's stunned expression, but Smith continued. "Selene, I know I scare you the same as Waite scared me, but I swear I never meant to hurt them. And A-Bomb, I'm sorry for how I acted when I was you. I knew from the start there was something broken in this world, and it turns out, it's *me*. Every way you've suffered for these past few weeks is on me. Colton is *dead* because of me. I don't even know if Waite deserved to die, but maybe *I* do. How am I supposed to live when all I'll ever be is a blackout that wrecks your lives? Fuck, I can't breathe. I can't..."

The toxins and grime of Arcana permeated Smith's skin, tissues, and bones. A sob rolled through their body hard enough that they wretched. Smith collapsed onto the bench, spitting beer and bile across the pavement. Their arms refused to lift them back up. Their head refused to face anyone. Each heartbeat of Smith's willpower pushed them further away, over the bench's edge, down onto the cold ground, and into the puddle they created for themself. They clambered along the edge of the canopy, clutching its plasticky fabric until they could stand without it. Smith forced Levi's legs to carry them faster, as fast as possible, until they managed to run.

Smith cut across the overflow parking lot. The nearest sidewalk funneled them past a desolate strip mall and a half-constructed restaurant. A panel van cruised in the same direction, and Smith raced it to a red light. Around one more corner, Arcana disappeared behind so many meaningless buildings. They lunged up a grassy hillside walking path, imagining a universe without a dive bar at its center. Here in the real universe, distance meant nothing to the gravity of another drink, but even this false escape let Smith breathe again. They pretended they'd never go back.

At the top of the hill, dry mulch surrounded a peeling wooden sign marked *Lewescroft Park*. A meandering path encircled a patchy grassland space, a rusting playground, and a tennis court with no net. The basin of the land hid the city, save for a few rows of older homes and a red-blinking cell tower at the far end of the park. Its warm glow filled the low clouds that shrouded Lewesboro.

Smith trudged down the hill and planted themself at the center of the cold concrete court to catch their breath. They borrowed Levi's face to unlock his phone. By its light, the middle of the tennis court became the brightest spot in the park. Smith sought Levi's chain of text messages to Ellesandra:

> *You literally said so, tho*
> *Haven't been able to sleep without you here*
> *Do you want your purple raincoat back?*
> *I don't understand what changed. I thought we were good*
> *You seriously don't remember either?*

She answered none of his messages. Smith closed the application and opened a web browser. In its search bar, they typed *Colton* but couldn't recall his last name. *Julienne Chord*, Smith searched instead. The *Lewesboro American* hosted a local obituary on its website, plus an article about Mrs. Chord's fundraiser for funeral expenses. A larger regional paper reported on the identification of Paul Mullard's remains, not mentioning Julienne in its headline. Smith clicked the link, scrolled, and landed somewhere in the body text:

> *embroiled in civil proceedings. A representative of the claimants alleged that Mullard delayed projects, embezzled contract payments, and stole clients' property from project sites. At the time of the crash, no charges had been filed, but a fraud investigation by the state has now been suspended following Mullard's death. Last month, a request to the court by claimants to search the Mullard residence for stolen property was denied.*

The female victim of the single-vehicle crash, identified as 23-year-old Julienne Olivia Chord, was not a person known to Mullard, according to a statement released by his widow, Katelyn, via a lawyer. Her lawyer did not respond to our questions about why her husband was aboard the van at the time of the crash. Authorities have not explained when or how Paul Mullard sustained his fatal gunshot wound beforehand, nor how Julienne Chord came to drive the van with a gunshot wound to her hand. Sources close to the Chord family attested that the vehicle was registered to Walter Hayes—the father of Julienne's boyfriend, Ulysses Thomas Hayes, who is wanted for questioning by the Lewesboro Police Department. Katelyn Mullard has independently raised a $40,000 reward for information leading to Hayes' location, although LPD has not alleged any direct connection between him and the crash. Walter Hayes could not be reached for comment, but LPD has not cited his name in relation to the ongoing incident investigation.

In a tragic turn, LPD also reported this morning that Colton Isaac Schern, former boyfriend of Julienne Chord, was found dead overnight along Holowell Road. He was 28. Foul play is not suspected, and a representative of the Schern family has asked for privacy at this time.

Smith returned to the page of search results. They shut their eyes before tapping the link to Julienne's obituary. When they let themself look, Julie's stern and focused face spanned the top of the page. She wore a bright blue helmet and held the narrow ledge of a granite rock face with both hands as she stared up at the camera.

Julienne Olivia Chord went to be with the Lord last week, the obituary began. Smith stopped reading. They zoomed into the image above it. In the shadow of the cliff, a rope tied through the double loops of Julienne's climbing harness. The pixels of the photo blurred its details, but her helmet shone clearly under the sunlight. A wavy red line zig-zagged over its crest.

Explosive Watermelon, Smith suspected. Hayes escaped Bayonet Bridge using equipment marked with the same glitter paint. In Colton's story of meeting Julienne, she rappelled like him, descending down the mountain behind that fancy house. He didn't mention her equipment, just that she ran out of water. That was why he stole the spare house key from the work trailer, under his boss' nose.

"His *boss*," Smith repeated to themself.

They thumbed the search bar and typed *P K MULLARD*. The results directed Smith to the construction company's website. A bold header proclaimed: *P.K. Mullard, Built for your yard!*

On the night of the anniversary, Oren mentioned that slogan from ads on Channel Eight. At the Wreck Club, Colton said he worked for a company that aired popular commercials, with a jingle he refused to sing.

"P.K. Mullard," Smith chanted, making up the tune, "built for your yard."

The rest of the website loaded. Beneath the header, a squadron of men in orange vests and hardhats crammed behind a fabric banner bearing the company logo. Far to the left, Colton's gloved hand held its corner.

"What the fuck?" Smith's head hurt, weaving together the threads of so many people's lives. Colton's story backed up the accusations of Mullard stealing from clients' homes. If an employee could access the keys to a property under construction, why couldn't the company's owner? Even deeper, Julienne knew all about Colton's work. They broke up, then Julienne met Hayes, and she died in the crash with Mullard. Despite so many gaps in the timeline, Smith accomplished something the newspapers hadn't: connecting Julienne to Paul.

Maybe Mullard had another affair. Maybe he and Julienne robbed houses together, in secret. Maybe Hayes was in on it, too, somehow.

Whatever the truth, its closeness prickled like a foreign substance in Smith's body. It begged them to stand up from the tennis court. Smith shut off Levi's phone and searched the midnight clouds for inspiration. The artificial glow atop the cellular tower flared in *Explosive Watermelon* red.

Out on the road bordering the park, an engine downshifted. A small black truck stopped alongside a *NO PARKING* sign at the curb closest to the tennis court. A big green cartoon frog adorned its rear.

Smith sighed. Jade exited the Frog Truck. She walked straight towards them, ignoring the park path and cutting across the grass. When she reached the edge of the concrete, Smith asked: "What's your knife made of tonight?"

Jade produced her knife from her bag and jabbed its rubber blade all over her torso. "The last thing this city needs is more corpses. You think I'd track you down just to stab you?"

"I'm not the harmless kind of lizard," Smith warned her. Jade sat at the edge of the court and leaned on the bare metal net post.

"That's okay."

"It's *not* okay, how I keep messing up everyone's lives. Don't just forgive me for—"

"Forgive you?" Jade knocked a pebble across the court. "I'm not a church. Forgiveness is their thing. Just get better, or don't."

Smith hugged their arms around their chest. "I can't live like this, Jade. I'm missing parts of myself, and what's here shouldn't be. I was *supposed* to die in the crash. You get that, right?"

"Fate is bullshit. And for what it's worth, you obviously *are* some kind of miracle, if you wanna smell the roses for a change."

Smith tightened the laces of Levi's sneakers. "What do you want from me, Jade?"

She slid down and sat against the metal post. "I came back because you want to know about Julienne, and I want to know about Hayes. If we each know a *little* more than each other, why not trade?"

Smith sighed. "Fine."

"Good." Jade looked east, towards Holowell Mountain. "So, how'd you get Hayes to come back?"

"We got lucky," they admitted, "me and Waite. Remember Dorian, who Selene thought drugged you? He was the one painting messages from Hayes. Anonymous website, digital money. Dorian came back to take a picture of the second message so Hayes would pay him. I noticed he had the same nail polish. It's this special color. Anyway, I paid him Annie's money to send Hayes a message online."

Jade pondered. "Okay. That's a lot. What message did you send?"

"I, uh, said I had the lesser cards. I said I was you. Sorry."

Jade waved her hand. "Yeah, fine. It worked. What next?"

"After that, I paid Dorian to drop us off at the bridge. Hayes came on his bike, and I kept Waite out of it for as long as I could. I told Hayes everything, but he said I'm not who I think I am. He seemed so *sure*, like he already knew more than me, and he said the cards 'saved' Julienne. What does that mean?"

Jade cleared her throat. "Right. It's about the Night Market, at Arcana, when I met her. She came alone, already drunk. For whatever reason, drunk people love to talk at me, so she unloaded. Like, she *really* went for it. She got into some serious personal stuff that's not my place to share. She said she wanted to move north, get away from family. She mentioned her partner, who I guess was Hayes, saying how he wouldn't understand. She had a bad fight with her mom, kinda related to the whole souped-up Christian thing. That's why she showed up to the one place her mom would never come looking: the 'demonic' bar. But that's what people get wrong about Arcana. The people who go there are sweetie pies, usually. They've got nowhere else to go. A lot of them are queer, or POC, especially indigenous folks. Lewesboro pretends to be *so* diverse and accepting, but it's a white southern Christian ethno-city underneath. I think Julienne felt comfortable at Arcana because she understood that it's our shield.

"I showed her the tarot sketch I'd just finished, The Star. I drew Pleiades for it, the Seven Sisters. She knew the constellation, which was cool, so I let her keep it. Buying tarot cards is bad luck, anyway.

"I guess she really loved it, too, cause she had Hayes steal the rest of the cards from my display at the next Night Market. Now he's obsessed with collecting the rest, which I never even finished."

Smith took account of her story. "What's the part you skipped?"

"What?"

"The personal stuff about Julienne. I know it's private, but Hayes said that talking to you changed Julienne's whole life, and so did your sketch. So, what did you tell her?"

Jade stretched her legs out on the flat concrete. "We talked about the stars, and what they mean."

"Okay," Smith allowed, not pushing their luck any further. "You remember how Hayes told you that the cards are more than just cards? Well, he said something even weirder to me. 'Fire burns,' he said that twice. He said tarot cards don't come with instructions, but no one in the world is dumb enough to burn them. If Hayes gave Julienne the stolen cards, they might've burned with her and Mullard."

Jade clapped her hands together. The stunning *bang* reverberated across the court. "Oh! Okay, yes. That's *something*. I mean, he's right that destroying tarot cards is sketchy business, but yeah, a rulebook would narrow the interpretations that make tarot valuable. The cards themselves aren't even supposed to hold any power. He didn't say what it was? What he thinks the cards do?"

Smith flashed back to the last moments of their conversation with Hayes, right before Waite interrupted them. "No. He, uh, he kissed me."

"He... Interesting."

"He didn't *say* I was Julienne, but he sure acted like it. And he talked about being a 'living memory.'"

"Now that is weird." Jade gritted her teeth. "He told me, 'she is completely, definitely, absolutely dead.' You overheard him say that, when you were Logan?"

Smith nodded. "It was like he had this epiphany, right before Waite... right before, you know." Smith cut themself off, but not fast enough to block the resurgent memory of Colton's body striking the pavement, over and over, loud as a thunderclap in their ears.

Jade tapped her foot. "Smith?"

"Yeah. Yeah, I'm fine." Smith rubbed their eyes. "With Colton, though, there's more. He worked for Mullard, which is kind of how he met Julienne. After they broke up, I think

Julienne and Hayes somehow worked *with* Mullard. Why else were they in the same car? It doesn't—"

"Enough." Jade stood and swung her arms at her sides. "That's enough, for now."

Smith couldn't stand up yet. A rolodex of ideas spun inside their head. Jade started towards the Frog Truck.

"There's another Night Market tomorrow night," she told Smith. "If Hayes is still active online, he can see Arcana's event calendar. He might come back to steal the lesser cards."

Smith lifted themself off the concrete. Levi's half-numb legs protested. "You finished the rest of the cards?"

"Almost," Jade said, but her voice wavered. "I will, tomorrow. I made *most* of them. It's fifty-six fucking cards. They're the boring ones, so it's not my best work, but I'll have them at my table tomorrow. I'll post a picture, he'll see it, and when he turns up, I'll get some real answers out of him."

"He's snuck past you before," Smith reminded her, "and you should be careful. Colton said Hayes is a gun collector."

Jade idly flicked the rubber blade of her knife open, then closed. "You were the one who said he's harmless. And since when do you care so much about my safety?"

"I just can't let anyone else get hurt," Smith explained, but Hayes seemed less of a threat than before. He favored flight over fight. He only attacked Waite in Smith's defense. Stu, Katie, and so many others billed Hayes as some dangerous outcast, but Smith never met that version of him. Only Waite ever scared them like that.

Jade waited for Smith to follow her off the tennis court. She unlocked the Frog Truck and spun one finger at the sky. "You headed back to Arcana?"

"I'd rather go home, but my, uh..." Smith tapped their chest. "This guy's girlfriend kicked him out."

"No wonder. I watched you roll through your own puke earlier." Jade taunted and spread a blanket across the passenger seat. "How about I buy you another shot of something awful, and you can let that be his problem?"

Smith circled the front of the truck and rested one hand on its tarnished passenger door handle. "Why are you being nice to me again?"

Jade shook her head and hooked her fingers under the steering wheel. "You still think I'm that dark and stormy bitch. I *am* pissed at you, but hey, that means you're a real person. You're one of us. You're not worth scaring off." She cranked the engine and levered the gearshift into reverse. "You coming, or are you sleeping on a park bench?"

Smith spotted one bench, back up the hill, under a leafless tree. Another attempt at sleep beckoned them. Maybe they'd dream, like Waite did at the hotel. They could live a new fantasy of normalcy, simplicity, and peace. In the morning, of course, they'd return to this bizarre life, remanded to Levi's body until their next drink. For his sake, Smith resolved to drink it at the bar where they found him. Dreams or not, a night shivering in the park would leave Smith and Levi worse off.

They opened the Frog Truck's door and took their seat beside Jade. "Thanks for the blanket," Smith said, but she heard nothing over the engine.

The short drive revealed that Smith ran no more than a few blocks. The Frog Truck crossed the same distance in maybe two minutes. Jade claimed her space in the overflow lot, where Smith first jumped aboard the truck. They opened their door, careful not to hit the yellow hatchback in the adjacent spot. Smith hesitated. They eased their door shut and leaned close to the small car's window. They scanned its pristine interior. A faulty streetlamp flickered to life, and the car's freshly polished fenders glistened.

"She's here," Smith warned.

"Who?" Jade walked towards the canopy, undeterred. Smith raced after her.

"Katie. You're parked next to Katie Mullard's car."

"Seriously?" Jade kept walking.

"Slow down. I forgot to tell you, I met her! I told her too much, and she thinks I can teach her how to live forever."

"Her, over at the middle table? She's kinda cute." Jade pointed. Smith batted her hand down.

"Don't let her see you! She's... perceptive. She found me on her own, just noticing the littlest details I left behind."

At a picnic table, Katie traced one finger along the rim of her wine glass. She tipped the last sip into her mouth, then spotted the two of them approaching. Smith's heart skipped a beat. Jade led them closer.

"She doesn't know us," she assured them, "so be cool, and we're fine."

"She has a gun in her bag," Smith cautioned.

"What's she gonna do, shoot you *before* you lead her to the fountain of youth?" Jade poked Smith's side. "At least I brought a knife to a gunfight, huh?"

Katie flagged Smith down as they passed her table. "Excuse me? You two? Yes, sorry. I just got here, and I'm looking for someone. Do you know a ghost named Smith?"

The confrontation happened too fast for Smith to lie. Jade took their hand in hers and tried to laugh it off. "I'm sorry, ma'am, but I don't believe in ghosts."

Katie rose from the bench and approached them. Her yellow heels crunched on the lot's broken pavement. "What about you, quiet guy?" Katie unclasped her bag. She withdrew her pistol and aimed it at Smith with both hands. "Seen any ghosts?"

Air left Smith's lungs as a hushed: "Oh, *fuck*."

Jade pulled them a few feet away. "Whoa, Katie. Katie!" Jade tried to distract her. At the entrance, A-Bomb's head swiveled.

Katie smiled at Smith. "It's *you* tonight, isn't it?" She chambered a round in the gun and fiddled with the safety, flipping it on and off twice. "Funny how I can always tell. I think there's something broken in our eyes when we don't know our own flesh."

"Jade," Smith choked, "that's not Katie Mullard."

Of all the things they wished to go back and change, Smith wanted nothing more than to fall asleep on that cold park bench.

"Hey!" A-Bomb barked, already sprinting to intervene. Waite glanced back. The gun angled lower for a second. Jade leapt forward and tried to grab it.

Smith tripped her. "No!"

Waite squeezed the trigger.

The shockwave of a gunshot jolted Smith backwards. A-Bomb bodied Waite. He took them down. The pistol tumbled away. Patrons flooded from the bar's doors. Drinks clattered. Frightened shouts and fast footsteps spiraled around Smith in a whirlwind of distress. Smith lay back on the asphalt and tried to breathe a sigh of relief.

Instead, they coughed blood all over themself.

"Smith, hold still." Jade's face blocked their view of the stars above. "Your neck, Smith. It's—" Jade pressed her palm above Smith's collarbone. Pain rocketed through their head and chest. She released them, and blood dripped from her arm. Smith tried to ask where it came from, but more blood filled their throat.

A-Bomb forced Jade aside. "Ambulance! Jade, now! You call 'em. And you, get inside. Alea has the first aid kit behind the bar. You two, don't let her drink that! Shit, who's got the..."

In their struggle to breathe, Smith stopped hearing voices. The starry sky darkened. New points of light sparkled, falling from far above. As Levi's body died, Smith oscillated between pangs of overwhelming despair and lengthening bouts of complete resignation.

Waite is back, Smith reminded themself. *We're immortal. Oh, fuck, we're immortal.* How many torments and deaths would follow this one, each meaning nothing to the next? Life, death, and resurrection shrank in the face of that future. The star at the center of the night sky, last to fall, enveloped Smith and drowned them in a bath of red.

THE MOON

XVIII: THE MOON

What followed was not quite a dream.

The bedsheets had the soft metallic texture of slippery satin, or a commendable imitation with sufficient stretch and breathable coldness. On the windowsill across the room, a boxy air conditioner finished sucking away the heat. Its motor idled. Outside, drips of condensation ticked on the rusty iron fire escape. The stable air of home soothed Smith's lungs. They didn't need to open their eyes to know this place. Each familiar sound massaged their mind. Smith awoke complete, knowing their total self for the first time.

Dangling next to the air conditioner, an exposed green circuit board chittered. A square electric motor and its plastic gearbox whirred. A blackout shade spooled upwards, unveiling the bedroom window inch by inch. Brilliant forks of orange skewed through the glass and illuminated the fronds of a spider plant on the dresser. Smith's eyelids rose with the shade, too accustomed to marvel at another Saturday sunrise.

The undersized motor strained when the shade reached the top of the window. The shoddy gearbox ground its teeth. The end of the roller jumped free from its plastic bracket and crashed the whole assembly onto the floor.

Smith—if they were, anymore—sat up from the bed and tossed the covers off their legs. They scrambled to the window and plucked a tiny red wire from the circuit board. The motor stilled, but the damage was done.

"Lifestyles of the rich and the famous," a groggy voice commented from the opposite side of the bed, still in shadow.

Smith propped the fallen shade against the air conditioner panel. Sunlight warmed their bare chest.

"Once I dial it in, the automatic shade will be the touch of luxury this place needs."

The man on the bed propped himself up against the headboard. He unplugged his phone from the frayed cord on the nightstand.

"So early," he yawned. "Are you giving the neighborhood a show?"

Outside, several feet above the window, strangers strolled along an elevated city subway platform. Two stories below, a cement truck thudded across a sewer grate. The owner of a cell phone repair shop unlocked its roller doors. Two parents guided a double stroller around a table of incense and baseball caps. No one on the subway platform looked up from their phone long enough to notice Smith's exposed breasts, but they darted back from the window anyway.

"It's called body positivity, *officer*."

The man in bed giggled. "Well, I'm up now, so I think this'll be a gym day." Smith pouted. "You should come. They reset a few routes, and there's a new five-point-eight you'd like."

Smith opened a dresser drawer to select a shirt. They extracted a purple tee from a folded row. "I'll belay you, happily, with my feet on solid ground."

"If I make you breakfast, will you try it? One more time?"

Smith pulled their head through the T-shirt and smiled at him. "I'd do *most* things in exchange for you making breakfast."

He slid off the bed and tied the drawstrings of his basketball shorts. He stretched both arms, tossed his phone onto the unmade sheets, and crossed the room to shut the dresser drawer for Smith. "Your body, your choice, but you're still *built* for climbing."

"I'll climb *you*, how's that?"

"Yeah, you will." He pinched Smith's chin and kissed their ear. "What's your plan for the day?"

"Print new gears for the window shade," Smith said, "take my book to Prospect Park before it gets too hot, then answer an email."

"Working on the weekend?"

"Not work, thank fuck." Smith unfolded a laptop on the nightstand. "It's in *our* inbox. I could use your help with this one."

"Oh, for sure," the man called back to the room, already out the door and halfway down the narrow stairs. "I'm gotta crack some eggs and burn some toast. Can you bring your computer down?"

Smith tidied the bedspread and raised the temperature setting on the window unit. They gathered the man's phone with their laptop, then tucked their feet into a pair of pink and blue slippers.

The wood floorboards creaked, and so did the shaky railing along the stairs. They positioned the phone on the kitchen counter, reopened their computer, and clicked a flagged email from a generic dot-com address. Smith read it aloud.

Dear Cartomancers,

My name is Luna, and I live in Eagle Moor, South Dakota. The people at the center told me not to share my name, but I want the people who saved my life to know it. I get why you kept yourselves anonymous, but I wish I could find you just to give you both a hug. There's no way to tell you how much better I am since you shared your cards with the center. I still have one more year of school, so even though the change has been crazy, I followed all your advice. I already made the varsity softball team. It's a small school, so we suck ass against the girls from Doverby, but I never thought I'd get the chance to play on any team. It's amazing. Even in a town of 2000 people, I have new friends, and there's even a guy who asked me to prom this past spring. I said no because I know him too well, but I still have one more year.

I wanted to ask how you two keep the secret. That's the hardest part for me, even though I know why it's so important. I feel like a superhero, like the luckiest girl in the world, but I can't tell anybody why, or they'll think I'm crazy. I especially want to talk to the other kids at the center. You gave two of us the easiest way through it all, but how do we connect with the ones who have to take the hard way? My card partner told me he's frustrated about it too. It's such a privilege that I can pretend my whole life has been like this, but should I? How do I be a silent ally from the other side of the fence, when our team is down so many points?

Sincerely, Luna

P.S. Someday when it's safe, I'll bring you flowers from my new family's garden.

Smith took a long breath. The man at the stove shimmied a spatula under a fried egg and flipped it in the pan. Butter simmered. He twisted a pepper grinder over the pan, set it back in a wooden rack, and rubbed his teary eyes.

"Fucking, what the shit? I wasn't ready to cry today! Not yet at least."

Smith closed the email window. "Sorry. I didn't want you sleeping with all that, last night."

"No wonder you were tossing and turning." He plucked two slices of browned bread from the toaster and cut them diagonally. "We can't reply to her, can we?"

"Probably not," Smith agreed. "We're in it with her. It's always gonna be the weirdest shit that's ever happened to a person, and it's not like we're experts."

The man spread homemade watermelon jelly across the toast slices, shaking his head. "She's onto something, too. Even if Jade could make enough cards for everyone out there... Do you ever wonder if we did the right thing, Julie?"

Smith didn't bat an eye at that name. "I wonder a lot of things. I can't imagine being the only ones, but yeah, Jade handed us Pandora's box, and we tore that shit open. We pushed the button, and we don't have to fight for survival anymore. I hate to think there's some merit in suffering the 'hard way,' but we *did* give up community for this."

"We didn't give up *everything*," he clarified, pointing at Smith's slippers. "And if we ever want a do-over, you know where I hid The Moon."

Smith shook their head and held out a plate of toast to receive an egg from the pan. "I love you too much for that, Tom."

"You love me making you *breakfast*, is what you love." The spatula scraped the pan. "And yeah. I love you t—"

Hot blood funneled down Smith's throat and disappeared, like a drain unclogging. The vicious gunshot wound in their neck stitched itself closed. The apartment kitchen collapsed into itself, dragging its nonexistent world into oblivion. Smith lost every memory of their unreal minutes in that space between death and life. Their Saturday morning in a faraway city dissolved like a beautiful face in a midsummer cloud, forever lost to the sky.

The iron flavor of blood washed into a burn of oversweet cinnamon whiskey. Smith lowered a shot glass from their lips and opened their eyes in a desolate Arcana. Fresh black marker formed a pentagram on their palm. Alea and A-Bomb occupied barstools on either side of Smith. Chris leaned back against the register. All three surrounded Smith, motionless, empty-handed, and attentive.

"Well?" Alea urged them, but to what end?

"I..." Smith licked the cinnamon flavoring off their lips. Inside each of their cheeks, a smooth steel ball knocked the enamel of their teeth. They had encountered enough regulars to recognize unique facial piercings, and these two stood out. Just to be sure, Smith pinched the top of their ear and found a straight industrial rod.

"Dammit, I can't tell." A-Bomb frowned at them.

"See, Chris?" Alea wagged a finger at Chris. "It's one of them."

Chris spun his hands at Smith. "Selene, stop it. Say the password."

Smith tried to laugh it off, but they fooled no one. To be dead on the pavement one second, then alive at Arcana the next—Smith couldn't find the levity. Levity... *Levi.*

"Are you the chill one?" A-Bomb punched the pink furry post next to Smith's head. "Or are you the fucker who wasted that kid last night?"

"I'm Smith," they whispered. Six shoulders untensed. A-Bomb flexed his fingers. Smith touched their fingertips to the clean skin of Selene's neck. "I died with Levi, but I didn't. *He* just died. It's hard to... talk."

"Jade told us it was you," Alea said. "She explained what she could last night. Waite stole someone's beer and got away, but the cops arrested Katie. She kicked one of them. Things happened fast."

"Enough for Selene to drink again." Smith flicked their empty shot glass. It wobbled.

"It's *really* not you, Selene?" Chris hovered their hands in Smith's direction. "Like, yeah, I've seen this thing a couple times, but it doesn't get less freaky. What the fuck is this world, right?"

A-Bomb sighed. "Right in front of everybody, man. If I'd been *that* much faster, lemme tell you... This place ain't gonna be right, now folks know this went down. On my fucking watch, too. I tried to resign, but Twyla wouldn't hear it."

Smith gazed at the main doors, no longer propped open. "What happens now?" They didn't mean the question so much for anyone in the room as for the doors themselves, the absent music, and the barren red couch. The space mourned its own vitality, like an overdecorated funeral parlor wrapped inside a haunted house. On other nights, Smith wished for this silence. Now, they craved the warmth of a crowd.

Alea brushed Smith's shot glass into the sink. "It sucks to say, but I never really knew Levi."

Smith shared what they could. "My first night, I was his friend, Andy. I thought I *was* Andy, before I understood how this all works. Levi was my life preserver. He was tough, but so sensitive behind it. He knew Andy, so I felt like he knew me. I liked that, being known by Levi. He was my first friend when I didn't even know him. He was my first kiss. My first..." Not everything needed to be shared. "I was his ex-girlfriend, too, another night. He tried so hard to care for her. I don't know why he came back here last night."

A-Bomb dismounted his barstool and crossed the room to answer a knock at the door. He jostled the push bar and eased the door open a crack. "Private event," he told the stranger outside, which might have convinced anyone who'd never experienced the racket of an Arcana event. "Yeah, I know. We'll be fine." He shut the door. "You'd think the current *situation* might stop folks coming back, but ain't that the thing they say about Lewesboro? It's the vortex that keeps sucking you back in, no matter how many times you try to leave."

Smith watched the light of the stranger's car drift away. "Did the cops shut down Arcana?"

"No, they got what they were looking for," A-Bomb told them. "Even Katie 'Moneybags' Mullard can't lawyer her way out of two dozen witnesses. Only *we* know she's not the real problem. Reopening is too big a risk."

"*Ceci n'est pas une* light beer." Chris rolled an unopened beer can back and forth on the bar top. It left streaks of condensation on the black wood. "That sounded better in my head. I can't speak French. Alea, you get what I mean?"

"Yeah," she said. "The other one, Waite. You can't catch a murderer who has no body. What happens next time some random townie drinks a beer and turns into them?"

"Arcana's fucked, ladies and gentlemen," A-Bomb announced, "...and, uh, non-binary... ghost." He kicked a zebra-print chair shaped like a stiletto but caught it as it fell.

"*Finishes* a beer," Smith corrected. "You can drink as much as you want as long as you leave a sip." Smith read the dangling black noticeboard near the entrance. Handwritten days of the month enumerated June's karaoke nights, punk band sets, themed events, and a bold green *Halloween* at the bottom. On the last Sunday before it, orange script advertised *Night Market*. "Jade was supposed to bring her cards tonight. Is she here?"

"Whoa," Chris murmured. "Sorry, it's weird, cause like, you *just* came out of the goth room, so you know Jade is... no!

Not you, *Selene* knows she's back there. Am I the only one who still can't handle this?"

"That's your hangup?" Alea spun her phone between two fingers. "Smith *and* Waite came back from the dead!"

Smith left their barstool and headed for the closed curtain above the goth room steps. "Who else is here? Oren or Twyla?"

A-Bomb counted on his fingers. "Us three, you, Jade, and Ember, so far. We're open for friends, and we gotta stand guard on whoever takes a drink. Strict orders from Oren and Twyla until they come back from Oklahoma."

Smith grabbed the folds of the curtain. "What's in Oklahoma?"

"Cherokee Nation. Long story." Alea dismissed them with one waving hand. "Go meet your people."

Smith never thought of anyone as their *people*, especially not Jade's crew, who showed such affinity for Waite's restlessness. However, the dual losses of Colton and Levi marked a shift in the tide for everyone. Selene broke several weeks of sobriety when they summoned Smith here tonight. Even last night, Jade traded information and offered them a ride. Ember slouched on the goth room's windowsill, doing the most unusual thing of all: keeping his mouth shut.

Next to him, Jade perched on a tall chair behind the corner table. Her portable lamp illuminated her face and the room's back wall. Instead of her regular collage of sketches and larger inkworks, a neat array of rectangular sheets covered the painted cinderblocks—twelve across, seven down. Tiny plastic clips hung them like crisp linens on a clothesline.

"Selene?" Jade studied Smith. She flicked the switch to darken her lamp, then ran from her chair to Smith and hugged them. "I'm not a hugger, but I'm sorry. I'm so sorry." Jade spoke in their ear so softly, Smith worried they had read her thoughts.

"You finished the cards." Smith counted up the collection of seventy-eight complete tarot cards on the wall. The scale and detail of the inkwork gave them chills. "Even the trumps, you remade them?"

"I couldn't sleep after last night." Jade let Smith go and hugged herself instead. She faced the wall. "I camped out in bathroom until the cops left. I couldn't wash all the blood from under my nails, so I covered it up." Jade showed Smith her ink-smeared fingers. She wagged them behind her neck, like a frilled lizard. "Selene offered to bring you here so I could forgive you. It's not every day you can say that to someone *after* they've died. But seriously, for all the shit you did while you were drunk—which is all of it—I do forgive you, Smith."

"Smith?" Ember raised his head off his knees but remained on the windowsill. "You and Waite are... It's true, then?"

"That we're immortal?" Smith sat on the end of the church pew and squeezed their wrists. "That's what *they* called it."

Ember slid one curtain to the end of its rail, revealing the long bay window over the front sidewalk. Even at night, between streetlights, and without cars on the road, more outside light spilled into the goth room than its reddish bulbs produced. Ember picked at the black paint between the window-panes.

"I used to sleep in a chicken coop," he said. Neither Jade nor Smith questioned him, so he continued. "In Rangerville, my parents kept thirty-odd chickens, which is to say, *I* was deputized to keep thirty-odd chickens while my parents chased dragons and fought windmills. I preferred my bed most nights, but one winter, our heat broke down, and I didn't know the number to call the repairman. What I *did* know by then was that chicken's bodies are warmer than humans' by several degrees. So, I unlocked their little wooden door and squeezed on in."

"Ember...?" Jade guided him back to Earth, or as close to it as he orbited.

"Yes! I'm getting somewhere, trust me that. One night, maybe my third or fourth in a row with the hens, I woke up to this pitiful knocking outside the door, and I couldn't see. The door kept popping open a bit, then bouncing shut. I figured one of the chickens got stuck outside at sunset, which happened periodically. I kicked the door open for her, and I..." Ember rubbed his eyes. "I never saw any of it. No light inside, just snarling and screaming. Beaks, teeth, and little clawed toes, in this bedlam of animal war. I made myself small. I covered my face. I crammed into a corner of the roost, and I hid. All I got were some thin scars on the back of my hands and forearms. When my parents found me, hours later, they said it was a fox, but we'll never know.

"I dug holes under a spruce tree and buried the hens. My parents sprayed me with cold water from the hose by the shed, and I shivered all morning. We lost all but five chickens, and they shivered for the rest of their lives. *That's* the part of death no one needs to mythologize. It's the endless counterpart that the living know. We see it; we share it. Witness death once, and every day you see the marks of its talons on your skin is a day you survive again, until you don't anymore. Then, someone else becomes your witness, like a bird with a lifelong tremor. Who was it who said that no one dies until their ripples are gone? I'm not so delusional to think I'm treading new ground, waxing poetic about scars."

"Terry Pratchett," Jade whispered, "but you paraphrased him."

Ember dropped down from the windowsill and brushed the dust off the back of his magenta jeans. He walked a wide circle around Smith, stroking the organ console keyboard along the way. "When you choreograph your life along the blurred lines of love and lust, fantasy and reality, you can learn to tune out those ever-churning ripples of death. I've been ungrounded, one foot skating along the astral plane, tickling invisible fires like a slutty modern Prometheus. Although it pains me to rebuild any barriers in the boundless realm of the psychic, you were right to show caution for these new forces, the ones bending our lives." Ember too embraced Smith, who again accepted the gesture. "Truly, I am sorry." He straightened his arms, held Smith's shoulders, and widened his eyes at them. "Stand clear of the fire, my darling Smith. We all burn, even the deathless."

A shadow crossed the window behind Ember. Jade jumped up from her stool and knocked it over. "I was right!"

Ember whirled in place, clueless, while Jade rushed to the window.

"What did you see?" Smith slid down the church pew to look with her.

Jade whipped the curtain closed and slid past them towards the steps. "That was Hayes' bike."

Ember caught her arm. "Honey, you're not leaving me asleep in the Frog Truck this time. I'm getting an eyeful of this missing man of mystery."

Smith hurried to the back wall, plucking Jade's cards from their clips two at a time. They stacked as many as possible in one hand.

"Hey!" Jade shook free of Ember and snatched the partial deck from Smith's grasp. "I worked too hard on these to hand them over to this man."

"I know." Smith kept unclipping the rest of the cards. "If we want answers, we should at least show him a bargaining chip."

"Fine. Hurry up, then!" Jade joined them, unclipping cards from the wall. Ember headed up the steps first, and they followed him to the shuttered entrance.

Behind the bar, Chris assembled a small pyramid of shooter glasses. "It's aesthetically *and* geometrically efficient."

Alea shook her head and returned the top glass to its shelf.

A-Bomb lounged on the red couch, scrolling his phone when Jade, Smith, and Ember made for the door. "You three ain't leaving, are you?"

Ember kicked the door open. Outside, its stickered metal heft knocked a man and his bicycle to the ground. A few dozen envelopes flung loose across the pavement.

"Fuck!" Hayes scrambled on his knees, recollecting the envelopes. Jade emerged from inside, and he stopped. "I was trying to knock."

"Sorry," Ember stepped over the envelopes and shrank against the nearest canopy post. Jade fanned her handful of tarot cards.

"Is that all of them?" Still winded, Hayes sprang to his feet and counted the partial deck. "All fifty-six lesser arcana?"

"No," Jade said, "all seventy-eight, major and minor. Smith has the rest of them."

Hayes observed Selene with perplexed relief. "I can't finish this myself," he announced. "Took me long enough to find enough envelopes for the lessers. Jade, take these. I addressed them, but they need postage. It's too risky for me to buy stamps. Cameras everywhere in post offices. Just put one card in each envelope and send them as soon as possible. It's what Julie wanted, more than anything."

"Okay, slow down." Jade held the door. "You coming inside, or what?"

Hayes picked up his bike. "I'm too visible. Someone will rat me out."

"Didn't you hear?" Jade squinted at Hayes. He shrugged at her. "The heat's off. No more bounty. No more investigation."

Hayes swung a leg over his bike. "What do you mean?"

Ember spun an ashtray on the picnic table. "I suppose news doesn't travel so fast when you're on the lam," he mused. "Katie Mullard was arrested for a murder here, last night."

"Murder?" Hayes squeezed the bike's handbrake. "Whose murder?"

"Mine," Smith breathed, "and Levi's. Katie was Waite, and they shot me."

Hayes dismounted and dropped his bike again. "That's impossible. I saw... No, *we* saw what happened to them. They came back? *Both* of you came back?"

Ember nodded. "Farewell to the quaint old era of life and death. Whatever Jade's cards are, they've ushered in the age of the undying. Is that what your dearest Julie wanted? To spread the curse of these cards, whatever it is?"

Around the corner, two car doors slammed.

"Careful," Hayes warned, stuffing the enveloped into his open gray backpack. "When the major arcana burned in the crash, that wasn't part of our plan. If there *are* rules to this game, the crash broke them, but the game isn't over. Right now, the deck is stacked in our favor. These cards *are* tickets to a new world, if we exchange them delicately. I meant to ask, Smith, you've never had the same body twice, have you? And Waite hasn't either, I bet?"

Smith considered their nights, one by one. "I don't know. And I don't know about Waite. We don't always cross paths. Jade, didn't you and Ember talk about this? The night I hid in the truck, Ember, you asked the same thing."

Ember pondered, lounging on the picnic table.

"Really think about it, Smith," Hayes insisted. "This is important. How many bodies have you had?" Smith shook their head, unable to account for so many disparate nights. The unshaven corners of Hayes' mouth twisted downward. "You're not gonna beat the dealer unless you can count cards."

Andy, Oz, Jade, Dorian, Oren, Saint...

While Smith tallied up their sequence of nights, Ember laughed. "Hayes, I'm pleased to meet a man of *substance* like yourself. Save some riddles for me, won't you?"

"Ember, chill!" Jade retrieved one of Hayes' stolen envelopes from under the first picnic table and read its handwritten address. "Why did Julie want to send my cards to Eagle Moor, South Dakota?"

A vibrant ray of digital white light swept across the parking lot. It approached from the overflow lot, brighter and brighter, accompanied by two sets of footsteps. A woman's harsh whisper set everyone on edge.

"Rachel, are you getting this? I am *not* re-recording another episode."

"Yeah, yeah, I'm always recording," Rachel insisted from behind the light of her cracked tablet's back camera. Radhika stepped forward next to her, a large white bandage stretching from the top of her cheek to the edge of her jaw. Rachel held a tiny microphone towards Hayes. "Sir, can you confirm your name for the camera?"

Hayes wheeled his bike towards the street and hid his face with one hand. "Sorry, I have to go."

Ember snapped his fingers at Radhika. "Excuse me, Miss Unsure-lock? You're *intruding* on a private conversation, and frankly, your wrinkled-ass pantsuit is intruding on my field of view."

Radhika motioned for Rachel to hold the mic closer to Ember. "What can *you* tell us about the events that transpired here last night?"

Ember gasped dramatically, hands on his chest. "He *told* you? Last night was supposed to be a beautiful, *private* evening of passion between myself and your father!"

While Ember distracted Radhika and Rachel, Hayes raised the bike's kickstand and coasted further from the camera's beam. Jade elbowed Smith, pulled them aside, and cupped their ear: "Go tell A-Bomb the podcasters are back."

"What about Hayes?" Smith watched the bike slip away again, westward down the main road.

Jade didn't even look. "If we go after him, these jackasses will follow us. Go drink, and we'll bring you back tomorrow to figure it out." Jade collected Smith's stack of cards and combined it into the full deck. She stowed it in the South Dakota envelope and pushed Smith through the door.

They returned to the bar, where Alea poured a shot of berry-flavored liqueur, unprompted. "Time for Selene to come back?" She offered Smith the shot. They wafted its fruity aroma.

"Those podcasters showed up again."

"Fuck, of course. A-Bomb!"

On the red couch, A-Bomb dropped his phone on his face. "Shit. Whaddup?"

"Podcasters out front need to be taken off-air."

A-Bomb cursed and collected himself to confront the situation. Smith took the shot.

XIX
THE SUN

XIX: THE SUN

Another spin of the wheel ejected Smith into a room too bright for Arcana, seated on a closed plastic cooler. The last crumbs of a sandwich scattered over a crinkled sheet of aluminum foil on a tiny table. Only the fire extinguisher in the corner marked the location of the cramped space within the bar: the utility closet. Across the narrow table, Oren sat on the floor and bit into another sandwich.

"You still drink those?" He asked through a mouthful of bread, lettuce, tomato, and cheese. He pointed his sandwich at Smith's right hand, which held an empty can. *Mango Hibiscus Kombucha*, its label read. Twyla's bracelets dangled from Smith's wrist. Who else would share a meal with Oren in the utility closet?

"Yeah, I do." Smith mimicked the careful steadiness of Twyla's tone.

"Fucking nasty slime at the bottom of the can, all that probionic symbiotic alien bacteria," Oren squirmed. "Never again, baby. That's all you."

Smith refused to believe Twyla would take the risk of finishing a drink here—not after she and Oren took such militant precautions for everyone else. Twyla knew the danger of inviting Waite back into Arcana. Smith examined the rainbow-patterned can and found a clue in tiny white print at the bottom: *Contains less than 0.5% alcohol.*

"Shit," they winced.

"What?" Oren wrapped up the remainder of his sandwich. "Gonna finish mine later. You mind chucking this in the cooler?"

Smith stood, took Oren's wrapped sandwich, and stowed it in the plastic cooler. "This drink had less than 0.5% alcohol," they told him.

Oren chuckled. "Yeah, you'd have to chug a dozen of those to get a buzz. If that counted as a 'drink,' you wouldn't still be the one talking to me, would you?" Oren wiped a crumb off Smith's lower lip.

"I'm *not*," Smith said, blushing. "It's me, Smith. I think half a percent still counts."

"Oh, fucking *what* now?" Oren rubbed his eyes. "Baby, you've got the whole cleansing thing to do tonight. I can't take the lead on that!"

"I won't stay all night," Smith promised. "I just need to find Jade. Twyla will be back later to do whatever she needs to do."

"*Fuck*, okay. I know it's you, Smith, but this shit's tripping me out." Oren dug a lighter out of his pocket. "I'm gonna go smoke out behind the garage. You keep Twyla safe, okay?"

"Absolutely. Thank you."

Oren eased the door open. Smith let him go. Two guys in the hallway dodged him, almost spilling their beers. "Slow down, Speed Racer," he tutted. Oren buttoned the top of his fur coat and snuck away towards the garage. The cacophony of more voices matched the volume of the classic rock from the speakers. Smith entered the hallway and shut the bright utility closet behind them. Their eyes readjusted to Arcana's standard murkiness, swimming with strands of colorful bulbs.

The usual suspects populated the barroom: two couples crammed onto the red couch, a guy taking a picture of his friend on the stiletto-shaped chair, a bachelorette party congregating in the farthest corner, two greasy metalheads colonizing the dance floor, and A-Bomb scrutinizing at an out-of-state driver's license at the entrance. At the bar, college kids and townies outnumbered the regular punks and scared tourists. Alea and Chris tag-teamed the excess demand for cocktails and shots, even resorting to plastic cups while the dishwasher steamed through a load of dirty glassware.

Alea stepped onto a short plastic stool, towering over the sea of heads. She clapped her hands twice and smacked the specials menu. The crowd quieted long enough for her to shout:

"Once again, by ordering a drink, you are agreeing to the two rules of the limited-time special! Rule number one: return your unfinished drink and get two dollars off. Rule number two: return a *finished* drink, and it costs two dollars extra. Okay? Okay. No cheating."

"Is that legal?" One of the bachelorettes called back to Alea, but a rush of hollers and cheers drowned her out. Smith forced their way through the eager swarm, desperate for the safety of the goth room. There, seventy-eight empty plastic clips still dotted the back wall, but boisterous strangers colonized the high top, low top, church pew, and couch. If Jade, Selene, and Ember gave up this sacred territory, then Smith already missed their chance tonight to reconnect.

"It's not like I *don't* like her music," Oz's voice rose over the noise. She shared the bench of the broken organ keyboard with Georgie and Saint. "I just don't wanna talk about a billionaire like she's still some new indie artist. Am I crazy for that?"

Georgie played with the switches next to the keyboard. "Not crazy! It sounded like a good date until that part."

"Exactly!" Oz frowned and squeezed her phone. "She was *so* cute until she had basic taste in music."

"It sounds like an excuse for you being nervous," Saint prodded. They sipped the last of their draft beer, then spat it back into the cup. "Fuck, my two dollars! Almost forgot the special."

Oz stepped on Saint's foot. "You're one to talk about *nerves*, bud."

"I have faith," Georgie began, pressing his palms together, "that Oz will have her first girl kiss before New Year's."

"Shh, shut up!" Oz scrunched her nose. "As a bisexual woman, don't come at me. I'm the 'B' in our big 'ol acronym. I *am* that 'B.'"

"Yeah, 'B' for b—" Saint tried, but Oz stomped their foot again, and Saint pretended not to feel it. "Does that feel nice, stomping on my foot with your federally recognized gender?"

"Okay, okay, children!" Georgie tapped his beer can with his phone, but it didn't make a noise. "You two need to stop talking like you're in a comments section. Yes, Saint, I know the feds want to eradicate trans people, but do you think they'd stop there? No, but we all lose rights *faster* if we're too busy fighting each other!"

Oz and Saint shouting over each other, slowly redirecting their ire onto Georgie. One accused him of sounding even *more* like a comments section, while the other recounted his habitual taunts of Saint. Outnumbered, Georgie toppled off the organ bench and barely kept his beer can upright.

"Whoa! Good catch." Oz helped him up, just as he noticed Smith watching the tumult.

"Oh, is it starting?" Georgie asked, waiting to sit back down. "Oren told us about your cleansing ritual, to get rid of Waite. Did you find what you needed in Oklahoma?"

"The cleansing ritual..." Smith fished through the layered pockets of Twyla's large purse. Instead of talismans or potions, they found Twyla's leatherbound tarot cards, breath mints, a phone charger, house keys, and a second, larger stack of cards. Smith flicked through the deck. *THE SUN*, bold handwriting clawed across the bottom of one card. Sometime during Smith's latest absence, Jade's seventy-eight arcana finally reached Twyla's safekeeping.

"The drink special is *sweet*," Saint said, "but we mostly came out here to see you do your thing."

Oz bowed her head. "After Levi, this has to end. And last night, too, we got *so* lucky that Waite's only weapon was a matchbook. If they come back again, I'll bet they'll destroy more than just the canopy out front."

"What?" Smith shut Twyla's purse. "Waite destroyed the canopy?"

Georgie's brows shuffled. "Weren't you *there*?"

Smith raised their hands and cleared their throat. "Sorry, no. It's me. It's Smith."

"Oh!" Saint and Georgie exclaimed at the same time.

Oz bit her lip. "Wait, why'd Twyla finish a drink? No offense, but she, like, knows better. Her whole game plan is stopping Waite from coming back."

"It was, uh... kombulia?" Smith forgot the name. "Some health drink, with a tiny bit of alcohol in it."

"Kombucha!" Saint laughed. "Damn, that's wild. It has trace amounts of alcohol from fermentation. That actually works? Like, that was enough?"

"There's no rulebook," Smith reminded themself. "What day is it?"

"Wednesday," Georgie said.

"Fuck, I just got here from Sunday. Did Waite hurt anyone?"

Oz shook her head. "Nah. Alea texted me the whole thing. Apparently, Oren drank from his flask, sitting out in their car. He probably thought that wouldn't count, but Waite got ahold of him, set the canopy on fire, then tried to fight A-Bomb, who won, obviously, and got them to swallow a shot of schnapps. Couple of guys knocked over the canopy and stomped it out before the firetruck arrived."

Oz's voice competed with a dozen others, each drunker and louder than usual. Smith rubbed their temples. "Sorry. It's so much."

"Yeah, this drink special's got folks acting up." Oz stood and pulled a set of keys from her pocket. "Georgie, Saint, I know I *could* just make this call as DD, but are y'all about ready get out of here?"

"My tab's closed," Georgie said. "Saint?"

"Sure." They smiled. "Can we hit up a drive thru? Maybe go smoke by the river?"

Oz nodded vigorously. "Smith, you in?"

"That sounds nice." Smith wondered if the drive thru had hot dogs. "I promised Oren I'd take care of Twyla, though. I should finish a drink and let her do her thing."

Oz and Saint started towards the steps, but Georgie took Smith's hand. "Smith, if Twyla's really about to cast some spell that banishes you forever, don't you think you deserve to make your last night count?"

"What?" The word *last* made Smith's mouth dry. Maybe Twyla couldn't exorcise just one ghost. Smith arrived at Arcana with Waite, so what if they needed to leave together, too? No one asked their permission to sacrifice themself. "I already died twice. I can't do it again."

"We all die. Some of us more than others." Georgie tightened his grip on their hand. "But first, we live." Georgie guided Smith up through the barroom, then out the exit where he could make himself heard again. "If you don't let yourself live, what are you gonna do? Drink about it?"

Smith settled into the left rear seat of Oz's hybrid crossover. She rolled down everyone's windows. Arcana shrank in the side mirror. Saint recounted a confusing scene from an obscure movie while Georgie prodded them with useless questions. Oz sang along to an indie folk song from her playlist, almost too quiet to hear in the wind. Smith stopped paying attention to the turns of the dark roads. Grassy fields lined one side of the street. At their farthest edge, a glasslike river flowed behind a veil of old-growth trees.

"Tacos or burgers?" Oz asked.

Saint groaned. "Do I need to pick?"

Georgie leaned across the rear middle seat and pointed out Smith's window. "Still there, still closed! Heron's Landing."

Tall wooden posts supported a long, blue-gray building. Hefty marine netting draped from its corners, and a disproportionate statue of a pirate guarded the entrance to its gravel driveway. Oz kept her eyes on the road but slowed the car. "Damn, I miss that place."

Saint twisted backwards in the front passenger seat. "You know Captain Heron was a real pirate, right?"

"Really? You've only told us that every time we've *ever* been there," Georgie groaned.

"When are they gonna finish their new deck?" Oz slapped the steering wheel. Logan also mentioned the bar's renovations, which explained the unlit windows.

"Colton used to go to that place," Smith remembered.

Georgie leaned closer. "What?"

A heavy-duty pickup truck parked in the bar's gravel lot. A white-paneled work trailer hitched to its bumper, and blue letters on its side advertised: *P.K. Mullard*. Now, Smith understood.

"Oz, stop!"

She braked. A car behind them honked and swerved across the double yellow line to pass them. Oz gripped both hands on the steering wheel. "Shit! What's wrong?"

"Turn in here!" Smith begged her, their palm pressed to the window. "Heron's Landing. Yeah, this driveway, left here. Sorry. I know it's closed, but I need to check something I just saw."

Oz parked her crossover near the pirate statue. Smith bailed from the backseat and ran straight to the Mullard trailer. As Colton described, they found a black metal box above one of its fenders. They tore open its unlatched door.

"What's going on?" Oz caught up to Smith.

"The keys aren't in here," they showed her, scratching around each corner of the cold steel box. "Colton said Mullard's crews keep an emergency key for each work site right here, on the work trailers. So where is it?"

Oz stooped to examine the box. "Why does that matter?"

"Okay, okay…" Smith gathered their thoughts. "Colton met Julie while he was working on a deck rebuild for Mullard. He used the keys on a work trailer to let her into the house on site. If *she* knew about the keys on the Mullard trailers, who might she have told?"

Oz gasped, covering her mouth. "Her new boyfriend?"

Smith ducked under the wooden steps that led to the front entrance. From underneath, they wrangled the handlebars of a bicycle and dragged it into the open. "And when he needed a place to hide, all he had to do was find a P.K. Mullard work trailer. With Paul gone, the construction crew wouldn't come back to find him."

Petrified, Oz stared at the elevated entrance to Heron's Landing. "Do you think he's still…?"

"I'm going up there," Smith told her. "Wait here a minute. I don't want to scare him away again."

"This is too much. Too fucking much." Oz fumbled for her weed pen.

Smith started up the stairs.

The unfinished wood creaked under their delicate footsteps, all the way to the upper landing. They twisted the door's brass handle and pulled. A dangling chime clattered. Smith's eyes adjusted in the dead space. Plastic sheets covered the pool tables. Nails and ropes held maritime memorabilia and artifacts to the walls. With no warning, the lights came on and almost blinded Smith. They shaded their face with a hand until they could see the man standing behind the uncovered bar.

"I can tell it's you." Hayes took his hand off the light switch. "Did you remember yet?"

Smith shook their head. "You said I'm not who I think I am. What if I'm not who *you* think I am?"

Hayes smiled and sipped his glass of water, leaning over the bar sink. "You still found your way back here."

"I've never *been* here. Julie wasn't here, was she?" Smith searched the walls as if they'd find her there.

Hayes poured another glass of water from the soda hose. "So you *really* don't remember."

"Just talk to me!" Smith barked. "No one suspects you of anything anymore. Not the crash, not Colton, nothing. You're free. You don't have to keep hiding here. If you want your stupid tarot cards, tell me what happened the night of the crash. Tell me why Julie and Paul were in your van. Tell me who the fuck I am, so I can try to live my own life for once!"

Oz bounded up the steps and appeared in the entryway, crouching alongside the coat check table. Further back, Saint and Georgie peeked in over the outside landing. All three kept their eyes on Hayes. He unstacked three more glasses and stretched the hose of the soda gun to fill each with water. He craned his neck over the bar top. "Are these your friends?"

"Yeah." Smith waved them closer. All three filed inside, sidestepping piles of trash and construction debris. Georgie inspected a pair of muddy hiking boots.

Hayes greeted everyone and slid their glasses forward. "I'm Tom. Pardon the mess."

"This is Saint, Oz, and Georgie," Smith spoke for them. "You go by Tom?"

"These days, yes." Tom grinned. "C'mon. Grab some chairs. You'll want to be sitting for this."

Smith and the others obeyed. "Nice to meet you," Georgie muttered to Tom and accepted his glass of water. Tom hoisted himself up to sit on the service side of the bar top.

"The night of the crash," he began, "Julie was driving us into town when I first spotted that Mullard truck, the one parked out front with the trailer. I'd been on the lookout for one here, cause the crew hadn't been here for months. Finally, there it was, in the middle of the night. Julie and I were celebrating, and we'd come across the mother of all liquor cabinets to raid. She parked the van; I popped the box on the trailer. We snuck up those steps and poured ourselves some glasses, right here. She left the van unlocked because we thought we were alone until..." Tom combed his fingers through his hair. "I guess he was asleep, laying in the backseat. I never checked the backseat. The man in the truck was here before us, probably for the same reason. He'd already drank enough that he couldn't drive himself home. When he came through that door, Paul was just a drunk with a gun—Julie's shotgun, from the van. He screamed at us that we'd cost him his reputation, ruined his company, everything. He was slurring his words. There was nothing we could say, and then, *bang*. He fired, missed, and sprayed the ceiling over there, but that shotgun kicked him back *hard*. He fell out the door and halfway down the steps. He was knocked out but still breathing when Julie took the gun. She begged me to just get in the van, leave him, and go. We were ready. That could've been it, but I said no. I made her help me lay him in the back of the van. I told her to get him to the hospital while I covered our tracks. The last thing she said was she'd be right back. An hour later, I took Paul's work truck out looking for her, but I was too late. I ditched that truck up north, and I ran."

Smith studied their glass. Its simple shape and perfect clarity held water, but no color. The cylindrical glass lacked stems, flat faces, ridges, or waviness. Even filled to its brim, it appeared empty. "That *can't* be everything," Smith insisted. "Why were you trying to mail Jade's cards?"

Tom's breath shook when he exhaled. "Julie and I had more in common than anyone knew. Sometimes, I felt like we were the same person, like ninety percent: Ignorant parents trying to make us turn out different than we were, both working service jobs, stuck in the Lewesboro vortex forever with nothing to do but climb rocks and collect guns. We were at least as good at hating ourselves as loving each other. We couldn't afford shit, living out of the van, so we took what came to us. The Mullard trailers, she told me, they kept keys for the—"

Oz took her water glass first. "Emergency ones, on every site?"

Tom scratched his chin. "Yeah. We scored booze, food, whatever the rich fuckers with big houses wouldn't miss."

"No one noticed?" Georgie eyed a couple security cameras in the corners.

Tom wiped one finger along the dusty countertop, leaving one polished streak on the finished wood. "A little dirt or sawdust on a camera lens does the trick. We showed up after dark and kept the lights off."

Saint scooted their chair back a few inches. "Okay, sorry, but what about the important stuff? The ghost shit?"

Georgie hushed them. Tom smiled.

"It started with the first tarot card," he explained, "the sketch that Julie got from the Night Market. She had a serious fight with her mom that night, so she needed a place to escape."

"Jade told me Julie wanted to move, get away from everyone," Smith interrupted. "Why didn't she talk to you about this, if you trusted each other so much?"

Tom finished his water. "She did, after I picked her up from Arcana. I drove the van to her favorite spot by the river.

We sat in the back. She had the card on the floor between us, face down. I have to show you. Smith, do you have the cards this time?"

Smith opened Twyla's purse, drew *XIX: THE SUN* from the deck, and held it between two fingers. "Why do you need it?"

"I *could* explain," Tom said, jumping back off the counter, "but you won't believe me unless I demonstrate."

Smith gave him the card. He flipped it in his hand, passed it from one to the other, and laid it face down on the dusty surface. "Julie told me what she told her mom, the same thing she told Jade. She told me what I already knew, in the same way I knew myself. There *was* something distinct that brought us together. It's a unique fear that we hid from, that we armed ourselves against." Tom slid the card down the counter, placing it between him and Saint. "I wonder if you've felt it too. Do I have to say the word, to any of you, or do you *know* like Julie and I did?"

Saint squinted at Tom's hand on the blank side of the card. "Are you saying what I think you are?"

"Saint..." Georgie muttered. "It feels like Reina's house in here."

From no single place, a delicate hum spread through the space. A darting shadow behind the liquor shelf distracted Smith. Another one danced over a doorframe. A flurry of ticking and creaking sounds snaked beneath the floor. The air steadied like an animal sensing a predator in the underbrush. Tom gripped the edge of the card with his thumb.

"Julie came out as transgender," Tom said, "and so did I."

"Wait, *no*." Oz rejected her glass and pushed it towards him. "You still say 'she' and 'her' when you talk about Julie. So either you're lying, or you're just being cruel!"

"Neither," Tom whispered, "because Julie showed me what Jade gave her. Right in front of me, she flipped the card, and *this* happened."

Tom turned the card over on the bar top, forward towards Saint. The lights flickered. The creaking ceased under the floorboards. The tiny shadows stilled in the corners of the room. The upturned face of Jade's card simmered under a heat haze. White paper fibers and thin channels of black ink peeled and curled themselves off the page. Each bit of the card unraveled itself upward into the air. Smith knocked their barstool backward, and it clattered across the floor. On the bar top, the card ripped itself inside out until none of it remained but dust in the air.

Oz shrieked.

"What the *fuck*?" Tom spun in circles, rubbing his hands together and shaking his head at Saint. "This isn't happening. This isn't real. Oz, did you see that?"

"Tom?" Oz shot Smith a nervous glance.

"No!" Tom shook both fists in the air. "It's me. Oz, it's me, *Saint*. I'm in *Tom's fucking body*!"

"You mean *that's* Tom?" Georgie pointed at Saint, seated calmly on the barstool.

"Yeah." Saint's mouth spoke Tom's words. "I hope you can forgive me, Saint, if I scared you. Smith, would you mind sacrificing another card to flip us back?"

"This is... this..." Oz scrambled to hit her weed pen.

Smith rummaged in Twyla's bag for a second card. They didn't even check which one they pulled. They smacked it on the table. Tom positioned it between himself and Saint once more.

"Fuck this shit," Saint hissed and stood as close to the card as possible. Tom placed his hand on the second card. All the bizarre noises, electrical interference, and peripheral shadows briefly returned, only to dissipate when Tom flipped the second card. Smith recognized a numeral *IX* in the ink, accompanying a collection of swords. Same as the first card, the ink untwined from the paper, which in turn disintegrated into a vapor once more. The second card disappeared like the first.

Tom and Saint returned to their bodies. Saint heaved as if they'd run a marathon.

Smith wrestled with Tom's explanation. "You told us everything backwards. You told us the opposite side. You're Tom, but before you flipped bodies with Julie, you were—"

"Yes," Tom affirmed. "You heard me say that Julienne Chord is completely, definitely, absolutely dead, and I meant that in two ways. Her name died to me when I exchanged it for mine. The woman I loved, who took that name, died in the body I gave her."

"So, if Julie died in the crash..." Smith let themself think aloud, one step at a time, reversing their understanding of everything, "...then Walt Hayes was *her* father. She drove the van that night because she *always* drove the van. *Her* van. Meanwhile, you stole Jade's major arcana because you knew she wouldn't recognize you anymore. And you knew Annie from the Sunday school your mom sent you to, right? All that climbing gear was *yours*. That's why you know how to use it. 'Explosive Watermelon' nail polish isn't a tribute to her; it's *your* color. Colton was *your* ex-boyfriend. All this time, Tom, you were... *you*."

He blushed. "After my mom, Jade was the first person I came out to. That's why she gave me the card sketch, even if she had no idea what she actually gave me. After the flip, how could I tell her, or anyone?"

A new agony twisted Smith's insides. All this time, Jade protected a man she believed dead. She attended his funeral fundraiser and listened to Mrs. Chord misgendering her own son. Jade never outed him, even in death, even when it could have spared everyone so much confusion. Jade carried his pain, she kept his confidence, and she honored him in silence. When Jade met Tom on the bridge, how could she have known the reunion for what it was?

"I need a drink," Smith decided.

"Now?" Oz protested. "You're leaving, now, in the middle of this?"

"I have to find Jade. Tom, she needs to know that you're alive. She needs to know what her cards can do. I've been calling myself the ghost of 'Julie' for weeks, and Jade bit her tongue about what she knew. Please, she deserves to know!"

Tom pulled a shot glass from a stack and uncapped the spout of a vodka bottle. "You know, I have questions for *you*, too."

"Save them," Smith told him, then pointed at themself. "Twyla needs to know about the cards. Let me go, so you can tell her all of this. She'll be more useful to you than I'll be."

Tom poured Smith's shot. He held it away from their reach. "Here's my theory: If the van flipped all the cards at once, or if the fire activated them, but there were no bodies left to swap, maybe Julie and Paul landed in *other* bodies, straight from the source, where the cards were drawn. Twenty-two drunk bodies for each of them, to match the bodies they lost in the fire. Did you count your bodies, Smith, like I told you to?"

"Yeah," Smith lied.

"Well, if I'm right, how many bodies do you have left?"

Georgie, Oz, Saint, and Tom waited, but Smith couldn't answer. Tom gave them the shot, and they drank it.

XX
JUDGEMENT

XX: JUDGEMENT

A splash of hoppy ale washed down the vodka. The un-heated air of Heron's Landing transformed in Smith's lungs, now an atmosphere tinged with burnt sage. A new line of Arcana patrons jammed themselves along the bar, exploiting the unfinished-drink special. An empty can between their fingers, Smith emerged in the thick of it.

"Dammit, Wayne, you dumbass!" A man with brown eyes and a stubbled chin laughed close to Smith's face. He swiped at their can but missed. Having Wayne's body gave Smith the context to recall the man from Hunter's bachelor party. He never had a name, just that buttoned blue shirt, and the contact name *Deadbeat*. Tonight, Blue chose a *gray* shirt.

"It's two fucking dollars, bro," Bryce piped up behind him. "Wayne, what did that beer cost? Ten bucks?"

"I dunno." Smith tossed the can towards an overfull recycling bin at the end of the bar. Their arm skewed left, and they missed by a mile. The whole room swayed like an ocean liner. Smith widened their stance and braced for a night of stormy seas.

Blue cackled at Smith's botched throw. Chris collected the can from the floor and judged Smith behind hollow eyes.

Bryce patted Smith's shoulder and reassured Chris. "This man's a tank. He'll work on that aim."

Smith nodded, deep enough in Wayne's intoxication that their head lolled. A-Bomb weaved from the door towards the group of young men. He aimed his flashlight at the floor. Other people parted around him.

"He okay?" A-Bomb asked Bryce and Blue. "I saw him finish what, his fifth, sixth beer?"

"Yeah, Wayne's fine. What's the problem?" Bryce sneered at A-Bomb's patchwork jacket and towering mohawk.

Blue dangled a key fob at A-Bomb. "Don't worry, killer. Got these off him, so he ain't driving anytime soon."

A-Bomb didn't appear to care, so Blue put the keys away.

"Is Twyla here?" Smith asked A-Bomb.

He clicked his flashlight off and threw an arm around their shoulders. "Fuck yeah, Smith. I knew I recognized you!"

"Uh, what?" Bryce tried to laugh.

A-Bomb ushered Smith down the short hallway. "It's all good," he called back, "we know each other!"

In the blue sitting area outside the restrooms, Twyla waved a bundle of burning white sage. Oren clambered up one of the couches and swatted smoke away from his nose. High on the wall, he unlatched a painted-over window and propped it open. "Lord, that's strong shit," he coughed and lowered himself onto the couch. "I don't know if the smoke alarms work anymore, but we ain't finding out tonight."

"Twyla!" Smith interrupted her trancelike procession.

"Oh?" She beheld Smith's sweaty, graceless body.

A-Bomb patted Smith's back. "This dude finished a beer. They're the good one." He winked at Smith and marched back in the direction of the entrance. Twyla took Smith's hand and steered them towards a set of large chalk characters on the door to the garage:

ᏦᏍᏗᏓᏔᏫ ᏤᏍᏗ ᏱᏍᏚᎩᏍᎨᏍᏗ

"*Tsosdidanuwi tsesdi yisdugisgesdi*," Twyla read. "An old friend suggested that we mount our defense of this land in its original tongue."

Smith studied the door, no clue what she or the chalk lettering meant. "Did Tom tell you about Jade's cards?"

"Don't be scared, dear," Twyla soothed. "Her new arcana are powerful, but we have the power to withhold them from our enemies."

Smith touched the cold handle of the door, ready for some spell or spirit to shake the walls or flicker the lights. The door pushed into the dark, but no trap sprung.

"Go on. I'll be out here," Twyla promised. She resumed her ritual.

Smith entered the garage. Oz crouched on the stage, laying five rows of cards across it: the trumps, the swords, the wands, the cups, and the pentacles. Two blank spaces broke the first and second rows—the cards lost to Saint and Tom's double-flip. In the middle of the room, Tom paced the concrete, scratching his beard.

"Saint doesn't understand," he fumed. "Julie said these are the ultimate tools of our liberation. You know I'm right, don't you?"

Oz picked up a card and turned it under the stage light. "They're Jade's cards, in the end. Besides, as a cis woman, it's not my place to decide for *either* of you, is it?"

"Silence *is* a decision!" Tom kicked a chair. "We've tried legal reform, and they outvoted us. We've tried cultural reform, and they banned the *mention* of us. This country is ready to eradicate us, along with every trans kid born after us. Why do you think Julie bought body armor? Why she learned how to make thermite? She blew half her savings on rifles, ammo, and high-capacity magazines. These cards were her last alternative to armed resistance. I don't care how it *feels*, if our only other choices are violence or surrender. If we weren't supposed to resort to witchcraft, this country shouldn't have prosecuted its doctors and scientists."

Smith shut the door. Oz and Tom froze.

"I'm Smith," they assured them. Both released a breath. Smith stepped closer but struggled to follow a straight line. "What were you saying about Saint?"

"Doesn't matter." Oz walked between the cards and retrieved the chair that Tom knocked over. She stationed it in the center of the room for Smith. "Jade will be here soon, and we can get this done."

Smith took the chair. Their legs relaxed, and they burped.

"That's the other thing," Tom started again, circling Smith. "If there's any way to get your memories back, or your body, somehow, it's gotta be through the cards."

Smith imagined starting over as Julie, as her own ideal self, free to live the life she wanted with Tom. No matter how badly they wanted to share her dream, they couldn't. They didn't want Tom to call them Julie. Somewhere in these nights at Arcana, Smith stopped wanting to be someone who already existed. They stopped wanting to steal their missing years of memory from someone else—not if it would cost them all their *own* memories as Smith. They wanted to tell Tom all of this, but they refused to snuff the gleam from his eyes.

Oz checked her phone. "Ember just DM-ed me. Frog Truck's almost here. Selene's staying with their dad at the hospital. It doesn't sound good."

The door to the blue room creaked open. Twyla leaned inside the garage, the clamor of music and voices leaking around her.

"I was wrong!" She cried, one hand on her cheek. "I'm so sorry. I think I got it wrong."

The door opened wider, and Blue squeezed past her into the garage. "I'll handle this," he told Twyla. "Keep everyone out there." He shut the door and stalked towards Smith. As he surveyed the scene, a faint smirk leaked from behind his mask—*their* mask.

"If *I'm* Smith," Waite accused, pointing a finger at Smith, "then *that's* Waite."

Oz and Tom backed away from Smith's chair.

"No. No!" Smith shook off the daze of alcohol. "Shit, *that's* Waite! Can't you tell?"

"I'll hold them!" Waite shouted. They rushed Smith and locked one arm around their neck. Pinned to the chair, Smith kicked their legs but couldn't twist loose. Waite's free hand suffocated Smith's mouth and nose. "Don't let them drink, and don't let them near those cards!"

Oz blocked the stage and swept the cards into a pile. Smith clawed at Waite's hands, desperate to uncover their mouth. In one breath, they could spill any secret about Oz or Tom that only they knew. Waite tightened their arm around Smith's neck, maybe thinking the same. Smith pried Waite's fingers off their nose, but only long enough to save themself from passing out.

Oz snapped her fingers at Tom. "Hey! You got your climbing stuff with you?"

Tom lifted his bag off the floor and dumped its contents. "Just what's here. Why?"

"This is nylon, right?" Oz scooped Tom's coil of rope off the floor. "If Waite wasn't a literal murderer, I'd ask their consent for this." She unraveled the rope, looped it, and threaded it under the legs of Smith's chair. She ducked behind Waite, snaking the rope faster than Smith could follow. Soon, Waite released Smith's neck and face, but the tension of Tom's climbing rope restrained their arms firmly behind the chair. Smith couldn't move their legs, either, but savored an overdue breath.

"Oz... stop! I'm not..." Smith tried, but Waite took off their gray shirt and twisted it into a ball. They grabbed Smith's jaw and forced their mouth open.

"Nicely done, Oz." Waite stuffed the shirt between Smith's teeth, pushing their tongue back until they gagged. Their eyes welled. Smith tried to scream, but it came out as a watery groan. Waite whispered in their ear: "I won't repeat the mistake of killing you too quickly."

"Smith, how *do* we know it's you?" Tom asked Waite, already too late.

"You *can't* know," Waite rebutted, brushing themself off. "You have to trust me. I promise you; I *am* the same person who drank the shot Oz bought me on that first night. Even before *I* knew who I was, she knew me like she knows me now. Am I lying, Oz?"

Smith writhed. Oddly enough, Waite *did* drink that buttery nipple, as Selene.

Oz finished arranging the pile of cards into a stack, which she held to her chest. "No," she decided, "you're telling the truth."

Tom slumped onto the stage. "That was close. That was way too close."

A heavy shoe kicked outside the garage door, in seven rhythmic knocks. Oz jogged across the room and tugged the latch on the door's vertical rail. She set the deck of cards at her feet and waited for Tom's approval.

"Who's that?" Waite bristled.

Tom nodded. "Oz, let 'em in."

She unbolted the door and heaved it upwards. The steel rails creaked. One wooden panel at a time, the door rose, pouring moonbeams over the concrete. Jade ducked inside, holding a stack of envelopes and a roll of stamps. Ember entered next and lowered the garage door behind him. Jade cocked her head at Smith and Waite, setting her pink bag on the floor. "What are these two chuds doing here?"

"I'm Smith," Waite told Jade. Smith tried and failed to spit the shirt from their mouth. Waite scowled at them. "I caught *Waite* impersonating me, trying to steal the cards."

Ember bit his lip and shamelessly ogled Waite's bare upper body. "Smith, darling, we have serious work to do tonight, and I, for one, look forward to seeing those lean muscles break a sweat."

Oz bumped Jade's fist. "I'm Oz. Seen you around."

"Jade. Funny how you can see someone sing The Who a hundred times and never actually talk."

Oz smiled. "Arcana cliques, right? Nice to meet you, officially."

Jade counted heads. "Speaking of cliques, where's yours?"

"Saint and Georgie?" Oz shook her head. "I think they saw enough at Heron's Landing. I dunno. It's something about giving up control of the cards. They think Julie's plan could backfire."

"Oh, yeah?" Jade unzipped her bag and collected five identical black pens. "Well, what do you think?"

Oz leaned against the shelf of equipment boxes. "I think it's not my place to say."

Tom took one pen and a handful of envelopes from Jade. He reached inside the first one and removed a slip of paper. "Read this. Julie wrote instructions to make sure no card gets wasted or misused."

Oz took the paper, and Ember read over her shoulder. "Oh, lovely. 'Dear Card Holders, You have received the enclosed tarot card in support of your clinic's provision of gender affirming care. Handle the card with caution because it only works once. This card is capable of permanently flipping two people between one another's bodies, as an ungovernable alternative to medical transition. Designate one transmasculine patient and one transfeminine patient as Card Partners. Instruct Card Partners to prepare to live out one another's lives after the flip. When ready, place the enclosed card face down between Card Partners and instruct one partner to flip the card towards the other. Maintain the secret of the flip at all costs. Sincerely, The Cartomancers.'" Ember whistled. "And the people call *me* dramatic."

"Gender-affirming care?" Waite snagged the paper from Oz's hand. "That can't be it. Seriously?"

Jade crossed her arms. "Why not?"

"You ignorant *insects*!" Waite snarled. They bolted towards the garage door and grabbed the stack of cards, hoisting it like a trophy. "These give you the power to swap bodies at will, and you're *wasting* them on a meaningless fight about 'gender?' Get a grip!"

Ember knelt in front of Smith's chair and whispered: "Fox in the henhouse?"

Smith nodded. At last, Ember pulled the T-shirt from Smith's mouth and began untying Oz's elaborate Shibari knots. "Careful," Smith croaked. "They'll kill again for those cards."

"A thousand times over!" Waite roared. "Jade, your art is the foundation of our future. What if everyone could choose their perfect body? Buy, sell, and trade their own flesh using your technology? These cards will build a fortune to rival gods. Who needs medicine, cosmetics, or hormones when you can *reflesh* yourself on demand? Gender itself will be a detached relic of these dark ages. Jade, you can draw as many cards as you want, sell them forever, buy younger flesh, and join me in *true* immortality. You are the high priestess of a new world order. Fuck anyone who stands in our way!"

Ember helped Smith up from the chair. Tom handed Oz a sharp steel climbing tool from his pile of equipment. Jade cracked her knuckles. She reached back into her bag, dug out her knife, and opened its false blade. She pushed back her hair. "The only person standing in *my* way is you."

Jade lunged at Waite first. For the first time since picking a fight with Dorian, Waite crumbled like a pillar of sand. They raced out the door to the blue room.

"Go, go!" Jade lunged for the open doorway after Waite. The others charged behind her.

Only Tom remained in the garage. "I can't go out there. Just get the cards!"

From one of the couches along the wall of the blue sitting area, Oren lectured a captive audience of four strangers waiting for the restrooms:

"...back when people had the *brains* to interpret art on their own. Now, writers have gotta tell the audience *exactly* what to think, and it's—" Waite cut through the restroom line. Jade tailed them. Oren sprang up from the couch. "Whoa, easy!"

"It's Waite!" Smith warned Oren through the jeers of hassled bystanders.

Ember hurried after Oz through the hallway. "Stop that hunk!"

In the main room, Bryce laughed at Waite's bare torso. "Dude, what're you even—?"

Waite knocked him over on their way to the exit. Some guy one-handing two frothy beer glasses caught Bryce with his free arm. The beers spilled between two women at the bar, who screamed. A third woman reached for napkins but knocked over a tray of sliced lime wedges. Waite slipped in the spilled beer. Ember grabbed them, but they spun free. One domino or another lit A-Bomb's fuse, and he halted traffic at the entry.

"Chill, people! *Easy!*"

Waite shoved A-Bomb against the doorframe and bolted into the parking lot.

"Don't let them leave!" Jade shouted.

Only a few steps from the threshold, Waite slipped a second time. They fell face-first on the asphalt, catching themself with both hands. The stolen cards fluttered and scattered across the ground. Twyla stood over them, almost done pouring a line of rock salt around the building's perimeter. The salt scattered where Waite slipped, breaking the line.

"Oh, careful!" Twyla reached to help Waite stand, but Smith raised their hands to stop her. She gasped. "No! They lied, didn't they?" Twyla buried her face in her hands. "And I let them in! I *knew* I drew the chalk wrong, and this is the wrong type of salt!"

"It did the trick, darling," Ember reassured her.

Scraped, beer-stained, disoriented, and topless, Waite rolled over on the dirty lot and groaned. Pebbles of gravel stuck to their skin. Oz straddled them and held the hooked metal climbing tool across their neck. Jade wasted no time gathering the cards.

"You got them all?" Smith scanned the area. Jade counted up her deck. Ember hugged Twyla. Oz stepped off Waite's body and tucked Tom's tool into her belt loop.

"I'll handle it from here!" A-Bomb called from his station. He halted the line at the door and stomped towards Waite. However delirious, Waite crawled away, dragging themself closer to the street. A-Bomb gave them a head start. "You four, get back inside and finish your witchy business. I'll make sure this jackass doesn't wander back here tonight."

No one questioned an order from him. While Chris and Alea cleaned up the mess at the bar, Twyla and Oren calmed the drunker factions of irritated customers. However incidental, the wake of Waite's stampede left enough cover for Smith and the others to sneak back through to the garage. Only a few of the folks in the restroom line glared at them. Jade held the door for Ember, Selene, Oz, and—

"Wayne?" Bryce, busy dabbing beer off his shirt with paper towels, stopped Smith. "The fuck are you doing, hanging out with those fags?"

Smith though about kicking his ass or maybe letting Ember care of him. Instead, already halfway into the garage, they shut the door in his face.

"We're sucking your dad's dick!" Ember answered, then latched the door.

Tom rose from his seat at the edge of the stage. "You got the cards? Thank fuck."

"No thanks to you," Jade muttered.

Tom bowed his head. "I'm not ready to be out there. I thought I was ready."

She put the cards near the envelopes in the middle of the room. Ember knelt on the concrete and returned the loose instruction slip to its empty envelope. Oz began sorting the deck of cards into the envelopes, one by one. "Looks like the trumps have addresses already. Do we have a list of clinics for the rest of them?"

Smith wandered onto the stage, still dizzy from Wayne's beers. "Tom, there's something Waite said, about people buying and selling their bodies with the cards. A world of people living forever, paying their way to the perfect body sounds ridiculous, obviously, but Katie Mullard said the exact same thing. She wanted the ability to buy younger bodies forever, just to make more money. Now, I'm thinking about the opposite side of that world. What if someone's deaf, or blind, or lives with any disability? What about mental illnesses? And what if someone can't afford the cards? If Julie's plan goes wrong, if the cards get out somehow, what's gonna stop every other Waite and Katie from turning all our bodies into *currency*?"

Fiddling with the loops of climbing rope on the floor, Tom didn't answer. While Oz and Ember sat among the envelopes,

Jade planted herself on the chair. She tapped her foot, opening and closing her knife. After a long enough silence, Oz capped her pen. Ember placed a hand on Jade's knee. "You're freaking me out. Speak, girl."

Jade unzipped a smaller pocket on her bag and withdrew a small, taped bundle of bubble wrap. She peeled the tape, unrolled the packaging, and pinched a tiny glass vial between her fingers. "When I was twelve, I didn't wish for this. I didn't wish to inject myself with a dark web drug, risking deportation to a foreign torture camp. I wished to wake up in a girl's body. *That* was gonna save my life. Even if these cards *can* grant that wish, it'll be like hormone replacement therapy. Maybe you *do* get to wake up in your 'perfect' body, but in this country, that body isn't yours anymore. You can defend it however you want—collect guns, hide out, dox Nazis—but you're defending your body from people who already think they own it. And don't they control it, a little? Those people are the ones who made it so important to be skinny, to be pretty, and to *pass*. Estrogen makes peace in my body, but the war isn't inside me." Jade rolled the vial back into its wrapping and hid it in her bag again. "Even if you 'pass,' even if you flip your card and land in your 'perfect body,' this country will force you to hide who you are, forever. *That's* what you're scared of, isn't it, Tom?"

Tom sniffed. He squeezed the rope in his hands. "I don't regret it. I don't, but I'm not ready to disappear inside this body. Not if that leaves fewer of us in the fight."

Jade leaned forward and slid from the chair to the floor. "I'm changing my wish, and I'm taking back my cards." She shook an envelope, and the *PAGE OF CUPS* fell out. She turned another one over, letting the *NINE OF PENTACLES* land on top of it. In a frenzy, Jade dumped the rest of the envelopes. Instruction sheets and tarot cards accumulated in a messy pile before her. "Here's my real wish, for however long I make it: I want to be able to look in everyone's eyes and say,

'I am transgender, you will know that forever, and you will respect me because I am a human who did not choose my body, and neither did you.' That's my wish. I might suffer, bleed, or die bending my body to my will, but it's the only thing they can't take away from me yet. It's my deadliest weapon, and I'd never trade it for some fucking cards."

Tom shut his eyes. "I don't know if Julie was right, but I know you are. *No one* in America should have these cards."

Oz scooted backwards on the floor. "Whoa, whoa, you mean *destroy* them?"

Jade emptied the last set of envelopes and tidied the stack of cards. Ember flicked the wheel of his lighter.

"No!" Smith seized Ember's wrist. "Don't burn them. That's how Waite and I ended up here."

Ember pocketed his lighter. "Smith, I suppose you're keen to reveal your secret ghost powers that'll destroy the cards for us?"

"Not exactly 'destroy,'" Jade corrected him. "Think about it. 76 is an even number. Ember... let me give you a reading."

Ember grinned. He moved himself across from Jade and sat cross-legged, with the restacked cards between them. "Jade, my dear friend, your divine genius continues to seduce me. I know I've asked before, but will you marry me?"

Jade flipped the top card from the deck towards Ember. The disorganized shelves trembled. The stage lights shimmered. A faint static fizzled. The *TWO OF WANDS* disintegrated in the air. Only traces of its ink and paper fibers lingered between Jade and Ember.

"Fuck off," said Jade, now in Ember's body. She flipped the next card. Another wave of pressure rattled the room. Another card incinerated itself.

"That was *transcendent*!" Ember exclaimed, back in his own body. "Faster, let's go!"

One card at a time, Ember and Jade flipped back and forth. The tremors in the floor grew in frequency, soon almost constant. Oz, Smith, and Tom stood transfixed around the puddle of envelopes that danced in the vibrating air. Jade flipped a card, then Ember, until the deck thinned to a fraction of its initial height. If not for Ember's unmistakable word choice, Smith couldn't distinguish who was who. Ever more bits of evaporated paper formed an eerie dry fog in the center of the garage. The curtain pulleys bounced. The garage door clattered.

"Do you hear that?" Smith asked.

"Yeah!" Oz marveled at the trembling stage lights.

"No, like a truck or something?"

Tom jumped forward. "Jade, Ember, stop!"

They both stood.

Like an eldritch beast, a large engine roared. The entire garage door splintered. Shards of wood and rusty hinges exploded inward. Fragments spun in the brilliant headlights of a muscular vehicle. The bulbous tires of Wayne's gray SUV squealed across the floor. As it tore through the room, Tom grabbed Smith and dove towards the shelves. The SUV plowed onto the stage but high-centered on the metal chair. Wheels spun, useless. The engine whined.

Smith sprinted and leapt into the doorless passenger seat. They ripped the keys from the ignition. Still shirtless and concussed by the airbag, Waite flashed a bloody smile from the drivers' seat.

"You fucking psychopath!" Smith screamed and tackled them over the center console. They both toppled out Waite's side onto the stage. Smith's ears rang. Their hands strangled Waite's neck.

"Billions remain..." Waite hissed. "Billions, *billions*."

"What is *wrong* with you?" Smith cried, unable to hold their hands tight.

"Twenty-two..." Waite coughed and tried to swat them away. "I've had twenty-two bodies, billions to come. Don't need your useless cards. I'm immortal, same as you!"

"Think again." Smith placed their hand back on Waite's throat. "Twenty-two cards burned in the crash, one for each of our bodies. Your next death is your last, and *we* just used up the rest of the cards." Smith choked Waite until they stopped trying to talk, but no longer. Even now, it hurt Smith to hurt them—and to hurt their nameless body, Blue.

"Is everyone okay?" Oz shouted from the back of the room.

"Smith and I are fine!" Tom returned. He put his head under Smith's arm and ushered them off the stage. "Waite's out cold."

Smith whimpered. "The fucking keys. I *knew* they had the keys, and I didn't... I was too drunk."

"Oz, we're over here!" Jade dragged a piece of shredded curtain off the front of the monstrous car. As the curtain fell, she ran forward and released a wail of terror.

One voice still said nothing.

Tom and Smith climbed the fallen curtain and costume rack to reach the steaming hood of the SUV. There, they found Ember. The black bars of an aftermarket grill guard pinned him against the cinderblock wall. Below, the bumper wedged deep into his lower body. Both his hands on the hood of the vehicle, he spat blood.

"No, no!" Jade shrieked. "Smith, help me. We need to extricate, delicately, to avert further injury."

"Ember?" Oz checked his wrist for a pulse.

"I'm right here!" Jade cried—or, not Jade. Ember's voice grew hoarse. "We had one more card to flip."

Smith's stomach dropped. Jade lay dying in Ember's body, pinned to the back wall behind Arcana's stage. The lights beamed down on her through a thick cloud of exhaust. Oz squeezed her hand.

"Hey! Okay, say something. Jade?"

"Yeah," she whispered. Blood spilled from her mouth. "I'm not okay, am I?"

Ember fell to his knees on the ruined stage. He screamed and forced his trembling hands up beneath the bumper, but the giant vehicle hardly shifted. Even so, Jade yelped and shut her eyes in pain. Ember let it go, muttering apologies over the crumpled hood.

"We have to call someone," Tom told him.

"There's no time. I need to..." Ember stumbled back into the field of debris behind the SUV. He flipped a spilled cardboard box and kicked away bits of the broken garage door. "Get down here and help me find the last card!"

Oz and Smith left the stage and scoured the floor. Smith coughed through the dust and scent of burnt rubber. Oz crawled under the wedged rear of the SUV. Tom stared at Ember, as if paralyzed. "With the last card? Are you sure?"

Ember tucked Jade's auburn curls behind his ears. "Darling, I'd sooner wear *basketball* shorts than let my friend die in my place. That's my body, and this is my—"

"Judgement!" Smith shouted. They rolled Tom's bag aside and uncovered *XX: JUDGEMENT*, the final card, wedged underneath it. In the foreground of the card's face, a tall tornado siren wailed. Behind it, a funnel cloud ripped apart the earth of a cemetery. Ember swept the card from Smith's palm.

"A fitting coincidence," he said, quickly returning to the stage, "but that's tarot. That's life: one string of oddities and fortunes, to the very end." Ember held Jade's hand and placed the card face down on the hood between them. Jade tried to knock it away, but Ember held it down. One more unnatural shudder and a small storm of shadows rocked the garage. "Jade, I need you to tell Natalia how grateful I am that we saw the best of one another. And to you, my dearest friend, don't you *dare* hide yourself forever. There are people nearly as fine as me out there, just waiting to love you." Ember squeezed Jade's hand as he turned to face the others. "The rest of you, all you bright and dangerous sparks in this bitter winter, please..." Ember smirked one last time at everyone, everything, and whatever spirits he envisioned in between, "...fuck yourselves. Fuck each other. Do what it takes to keep warm."

Ember flipped the card towards Jade. The last of her arcana eviscerated itself into silky fibers.

Jade returned to her own body and doubled over, clutching a phantom pain in her chest. Smith and Oz embraced her as she sobbed. Restored to his own body, Ember died as he demanded: center stage, in a gruesome spectacle, witnessed by an adoring audience, who he left inconsolable.

A-Bomb probed his flashlight into the chaos. He guided a brave few through the jagged hole of the garage door. A pair of off-duty firefighters transferred Waite's unconscious body to a picnic table. Oz collected Tom's bag and ushered him out into the dark. When A-Bomb found Ember at the far end of the room, he ordered the others to clear out. Oren and Twyla began sending everyone home. Alea dialed 9-1-1.

Smith unlatched the door to the blue room. Every zombielike step towards the bar drained them like a parasitic siphon, drinking their own guts from within. In the deserted barroom, a sloppy mosaic of unfinished drinks covered the bar top—hundreds, in every flavor, color, glass, and can.

Smith chose one at random.

XXI
THE WORLD

XXI: THE WORLD

Sirens, shouts, and the ringing of Wayne's ears cut to muffled music. Four black walls of stickers enclosed Smith when they opened their eyes. A sip of vodka and cranberry juice trickled down their throat. Rather than a glass, a can, or a bottle, their new hands held only the rim of a white ceramic bathroom sink. Above it, a line of gold marker on the mirror read: *Fuck yeah, Oren!* Through the tangled layers of more multicolor graffiti, Smith saw the reflected visage of a ghoulish, open-mouthed phantom.

"Shit!" Smith jumped and pulled the rubbery white mask off their face, revealing Tom's face underneath. Between Smith and their reflection, a fresh new message in *Explosive Watermelon* red bled down the glass: *Back pocket.*

As instructed, Smith reached inside their black costume cloak and checked both back pockets of their jeans. In one, they found the closed bottle of nail polish. From the other, they pulled a sheet of white paper. Smith unfolded it and read:

Dear Smith,

Been a few days. Worried your time ran out. If you're reading this, I'm glad you've got cards left to burn. Take as much time as you like to live with this body. I trust you'll utilize it as responsibly as I have. Maybe more. If you were Julie, this was <u>your</u> body for 23 years.

> *At first, I wrote this letter to her, but I know it's a futile exercise proving to you that you're her. Our lives are defined by the memories that change us. You and Waite have your own memories, now. I don't think that's a curse. I don't think it's a punishment. Julie died trying to save a stranger, so maybe that's why she came back as one.*
>
> *Thank you for watching out for me. I hope we can catch up again somehow. And I hope I was right about holding the last sip of my drink in my mouth all the way to the bathroom, otherwise I'm gonna feel like a real dumbass in this corny outfit I picked out for you.*
>
> *Happy Halloween,*
>
> *Tom*

Smith read the letter twice, but its finality only deepened the heartbreak of several minutes ago. They could still hear Ember's voice. Life moved too fast in those unseen days between Smith's bodies. They re-folded the letter and put it back in Tom's pocket. Smith bunched a handful of paper towels and dried their eyes. They ran another few paper towels under the faucet, then wiped the wet nail polish off the mirror. Its bloody sparkles thinned in the water and washed down the sink. Smith trashed the wads of paper towels, fixed the ghost mask over their face, and opened the bathroom door.

In the deep blue glow of the sitting room, an angel posed on a couch while a vampire took her picture. Dozens of painted eyes spanned from the angel's forehead to her arms. The vampire showed her photo to a 1920s gangster, who helped toggle the camera's night mode. In the hallway, Smith passed a pair of green-eyed insects—maybe aliens—as one explained their online feud with a local bookstore. At the near end of the bar, a cat and a rabbit clinked their rocks glasses and sampled their crimson cocktails. A zombie bride pointed to the new special drink on the board behind Chris, and he began mixing the same recipe for her. *Fool's Blood*, the board read.

Most people congregated at the end of the bar near the dance floor. Natalia sang in the purple LED wash of the projector, lyrics illuminating her closed eyes. She found the words without opening them or turning to see. She left the microphone in its stand but gripped it with both hands like she meant to suspend all her body's weight from its narrow pole. The nineties pop-rock ballad itself meant nothing to Smith, but Natalia's voice meant everything. If she could find the strength to sing karaoke after losing Ember, his absence couldn't overwhelm Smith.

Natalia breezed through the chorus, striking high notes about fearlessness and love. Her vibrato prompted a few cheers. Smith found a free space for their feet on the checkerboard floor and shut their eyes behind the ghost mask. They tried to hum a quiet harmony, visualizing the rises and falls of the song's last chorus. Did Natalia see Ember's mischievous grin too, when she closed her eyes? His dancelike gait, his unyielding insults, and his final wishes lingered, still minutes fresh in Smith's mind. The drinks robbed them of time to mourn, to rest, and to inhabit this new realm of loss. Natalia's voice sewed the first stitch through the unhealed wound, deepened by so many troubled nights at Arcana.

Andy, Oz, Jade, Dorian, Oren, Saint, Ellesandra...

Smith stopped counting when the song ended. During the gust of applause, Twyla stood from her seat by the window and whispered into Natalia's ear. She hugged her. Behind

Natalia's back, Twyla snapped her fingers at Oren, who waded onto the dance floor and hugged them both from one side. His rings glittered under the swirls of the projector lamp. From the table with the signup sheet and laptop, Alea blew a kiss to the three of them.

"Okay, I see what you mean," said a Viking warrior in front of Smith. They nudged the green velvet dragon by their side. "Halloween is too big here to cancel, but after these past few weeks... karaoke?"

The dragon shrugged. "June would be pissed if we let the tradition die, after fuck-knows-how-many Mondays."

"Yeah, yeah, true." The Viking watched Alea queue the next track. "Alea's doing great, of course, but no one'll ever host like June."

"Where is June?" Smith interjected. "You're talking about the drag queen, right?"

The dragon bit his lip and waited for the Viking, who took a deep breath. Smith backed away, embarrassed at interrupting them, but the Viking leaned closer. "No, sorry, it's okay. Um, so, you know about Ember? *Ember* was short for December, his full name. *June* is the opposite month in the year from December. That's why he chose it, like, as his drag name."

Smith's hands shook. The room rocked. Last time Alea led karaoke, she asked Smith for help from June. She said June took the night off from hosting, and she had. *Ember* took that night off to summon *Smith*. They assumed he knew June, but they never imagined that Arcana's two loudest personalities were *one*.

"Sorry. I'm new here." Mortified, Smith waited for a break in the crowd to escape the Viking and dragon. Their own hot breath inside the ghost mask became suffocating, so they lifted it above their face again.

The dragon pushed his glasses up the bridge of his nose and squinted at Smith. "Do I know you? Have we met?"

"I don't think so." Smith couldn't handle matching faces to names, not with an invisible vice crushing their chest. What if the dragon or the Viking knew Julie, before she left Tom's body behind?

"You're famous, or something." The Viking spun one finger in a tight circle, aimed between Smith's eyes. Before they could connect Tom's face to a headline, Smith let their ghost mask slip back down.

"No, just one of those faces. I'm gonna go get some air."

Smith sidestepped a pair of plague doctors and a pin-striped magician. Through the double doors, a brisk autumn draft ballooned under their black cloak, which they drew tighter around their waist. Smoke weaved around Smith's hooded head, pouring from the cigarettes of a leopard, a swordfighter, and a basketball player.

"I can't believe this shit!" Oz laughed. Smith followed her voice to the middle picnic table, where she wore an orange astronaut jumpsuit. She, Georgie, and Saint huddled over a smartphone. Smith circled around the opposite side of the table for a closer look.

Saint shook their head so fast that they seemed to shiver. Their silver-white dress left their shoulders bare, so maybe the shiver was real. "It's not just bad audio production anymore; it's bad narrative. She's setting up all these plot holes and conflicts for us to wonder about, then covering them up with new ones."

"Tom!" Georgie beckoned them. The fringes of his cowboy jacket danced. "Get back over here and stay warm. We can rewind the thing; it's almost over."

Smith climbed onto the bench next to Georgie but left some space. "It's *me*, actually. Smith."

"Oh, shit!" Oz gasped. "I was worried! You were gone all weekend. There were *so* many cops, and the news was here.

You know that guy from the morning show with the blue coffee mugs?"

"They... don't," Georgie reminded Oz.

"Right, sorry. Oh my God, so Arcana made it onto *national* networks on Saturday morning. It's not just about Ember, but *Levi*, too. Typical that no one hears about Levi getting shot until a pop gossip account *outs* him. It's a huge deal, you know? Now, both murders are part of the pattern of, like, hate-fueled violence. That's what's all coming out. *Not* the cards, not Waite, not anything like that, but Katie getting denied bail, and Waite sobering up in county jail and getting a psych eval, then the leaked photos of the smashed-up car, and the garage. Ember is everywhere! You wouldn't believe it. Total strangers from all over are posting the most *beautiful* artwork of June, and of Levi, too. Surreal, right? Might even jump-start a new wave of antifascist protests. Plus, there's a viral news clip with Oren in the background, telling a cop to kiss his ass, so instead of 'fuck off, Oren,' everyone's been saying 'fuck *yeah*, Oren.' It's wild. Cultural moment, et cetera."

Oz sipped her beer. Wind flapped a sealed blue tarp covering the garage doorway.

"I feel like I should've been there," Georgie whispered.

Smith coughed cold air from their lungs. "Don't say that. Ember could have been any of us. You and Saint were right to stay home."

"Rewind the thing!" Saint rolled their long white glove off their right hand and dragged a finger over Oz's phone's screen. "I want Smith to hear this garbage. We're roasting *Haunted America Today*, the podcast that recorded an episode here. It's gonna be a two-parter now, but the first one came out today."

Oz tapped the *play* button, and Radhika's voice droned from her phone's tiny speakers: "...an unspeakable tragedy, so as always, our first thoughts must be for Colton's family.

However, a shocking death at the infamously haunted Bayonet Bridge was not *all* that happened on Friday night. We spoke to an anonymous Lewesboro resident and fan of the podcast, who witnessed a full-body apparition outside her window. We've disguised her voice for her safety."

A low, distorted monotone replaced the show's host: "I got up to let my dog outside, and she started barking at the window. Of course, I go look, and over on the steps of my church across the street, there's this woman! She looked young, and so pale. She starts shrieking, and she's *covered* in blood. I see her run from the church, down the sidewalk, and when I finally opened the door for my dog, she's completely *gone*. I believe her spirit was a..."

Saint groaned and talked over the podcast. "This is the problem with spooky comfort media. You get one side that's sad voyeurism about random people's lives, and it's surgically grafted onto this other half: lonely people, making up *generic* ghost stories for attention and ad revenue. It's *worse* than disrespectful. It's lazy!"

"Yeah, it's weird." Smith tried not to fear for Annie. They left her confused and alone on those church steps. "It's hard to keep track of what's real. Sorry, I'm still... It just happened, for me. Colton, Levi, and Ember were alive, minutes ago. Hours, days, however long it's really been."

...Hunter, Alea, Ember, A-Bomb, Katie, Georgie, Logan, Rachel...

"Hey, let me help you out of this one." Oz produced a slender black object from her jumpsuit pocket. She waggled it between two fingers. A clear chamber glimmered inside one of its ends. "Come hit this with me?"

"Is that a question?" Smith couldn't tell, but they stood from the table after her.

Saint pouted. "What am I, chopped liver?"

Georgie rolled his eyes. "Saint, your job tests your piss like every other month!"

"We'll be right back," Oz promised. "Smith, c'mon."

She led them to the black fence gate between the main lot and the overflow parking. Smith inspected the weathered leather of an old bucket seat on the ground. Oz warmed one hand in her jumpsuit and took a long drag from her pen. "A-Bomb notices the smell if we do it any closer." Her words filled the air with pungent fog. "You do know what weed is, right?"

Smith took the pen. "I remember everything except me. So, yeah, weirdly enough, I do." They sucked a puff from the device and let it half-fill their lungs.

Oz fiddled with the headrest of the junk seat. "If you asked my psychiatrist, she'd probably say you're missing your 'autobiographical memory' or your 'ego state' or something. Funny how you've got no ego state, while I've got several. Ain't that a bitch?"

Smith returned Oz's pen. A rush of manic mellowness warmed their veins. "I wish I knew how to talk about it like you do. You've seen me try, and I sound crazy."

"Don't use that word," Oz scolded, and Smith blushed. "You gotta accept that you're allowed to feel how you do, otherwise you're joining the fight against you."

Smith's head buzzed. "What?"

From the picnic tables, a chorus of voices called out: "Tom!"

Smith worried they imagined the sound, but Oz shoved them forward. "Go! You're up. Karaoke, go!"

Smith jogged back to the door, cursing Tom for adding his name to the signup sheet. His elaborate letter to Smith neglected to warn them, teach them lyrics, or designate a duet partner. Back inside Arcana, costumed bystanders made way for the unmasked ghost in their midst. Smith twisted the microphone from its stand. Alea hit the track: *All my Friends, as made famous by LCD Soundsystem*. Jumpy, asynchronous piano keys set Smith further on edge. Oz's weed infiltrated their head and limbs faster than booze, but without the boost to their courage. Worse still, the progress bar on the projector screen warned them to wait out an eighty-second instrumental intro.

"Yeah, Tom!" A-Bomb clapped his hands. The repetitive piano bored most strangers enough to resume their own conversations. Oz, Saint, and Georgie cut a path to the nearest corner of the bar. Only their attention and Georgie's phone camera persisted, but Smith's uneasy high wouldn't let them relax. Gentle drums joined the piano prelude, or was that Smith's heart beating in their ears?

Oz and Saint flailed their frantic hands at the screed. Smith turned. Lyrics began. They missed the whole countdown. Smith rushed into the next line, then overlooked the following one altogether. Any hint of muscle memory collapsed under discordant tones and off-beat breaths. Smith realized, too late, that even Tom may not have practiced singing his chosen track—not in *this* body, at least.

A few more lines into the verse, Oz took mercy on Smith and joined them in the middle of the dance floor. She dragged Saint with her, and the two of them lent backup vocals that soon overshadowed Smith. Neither Oz nor Saint seemed to mind them mouthing the lyrics, all the way to the next long instrumental break.

"Here," Smith said and handed Saint the mic.

"No, don't stop now!" Saint resisted, but Smith slunk away to the corner where Georgie kept filming. He too directed Smith back towards the stage.

"Don't quit. It's your song!"

Smith held out one palm, offering to hold Georgie's phone. "They're *your* friends."

Georgie watched Saint and Oz through his phone screen. The next verse neared, and seconds ticked down the last of the interlude. Georgie passed his phone to Smith. He fixed their arm's angle to record, then rushed to the mic. Smith held the camera steady and let the trio steal Tom's song. They found an eagerness and excitement in the lyrics that eluded Smith. As their laughter and listless dancing became pixels on the phone's screen, Smith appreciated why Georgie took these videos. The three singers became the cast of a movie, like one of Saint's favorite classics, with vague morals and a musical montage. That movie, the song, and the video ended on a repeating question. Alea, Natalia, and anyone else who didn't mind the seven-minute karaoke number offered some applause to the singers.

"Thanks," Georgie told Smith when he took his phone back. "I owe you one."

"Good work, team," Saint exhaled. "I haven't heard that one in forever, but—" A tap on Saint's shoulder interrupted them. A sharply-dressed man at the bar smiled.

"So sorry to interrupt," he said, "but I love your costume, Chi-Chi."

Saint gasped. "Oh my God, thank you! I feel like no one knows *To Wong Foo* anymore. Would you believe I had to make the whole damn necklace and earrings myself, cause there are only like three frames of her finale look to reference?"

Smith gasped too, for another reason. They knew the gray-blue irises of the young man who complimented Saint. Even in his formal black suit, he looked the same as he did on their first night. Oz squeezed Smith's arm.

"Is that...?" She didn't need to say.

"Andy?" Smith craned over Saint's shoulder. "What are you doing here?"

Saint glared at Smith. Andy forced a smile. "I'm bad at names, sorry. Were you at the funeral?"

"Funeral?" Saint reeled. "I thought your suit was a costume! I'm so—"

Levi's funeral. Smith retreated. "Sorry! I'm sorry. We met here, a while back, but don't worry about it. My condolences."

Andy looked down at his fresh, neat black jacket. "I know, pretty wild for me to go out on Halloween looking like this, but Arcana is the last place I saw my best friend. It's fucked up, but like... he *died* here, too, so it felt like the right place to say goodbye." Andy quieted and hid his hands in his pockets. "Anyway, I love your whole look. I'll leave y'all alone, soon as I can get this bartender's attention."

"Chris!" Saint hollered on Andy's behalf, louder than Smith had ever heard them speak. Chris almost fell over himself, running to fulfill Saint's first-ever drink order.

"You called?"

Saint let two of their fingers fall over Andy's hand. "Tequila okay for you?"

Andy nodded. "Thank you."

"Tequila reposado, please. One shot for him, one for me, and who else?" Saint surveyed Oz, Smith, and Georgie. All three declined with sour faces or shaking heads. "Weaklings. Just the two shots."

Chris fetched the glasses. Andy watched him go. "Lord, that's a fine man."

Saint lifted one hand to straighten Andy's tie. "I've seen finer."

Oz and Georgie took that cue to take a restroom break. If Andy took issue with Saint coming onto him so shortly after Levi's funeral, he didn't show it. Instead, he raised his tequila shot alongside Saint's, and they drank like the terrors of the past few weeks never happened. For all the grimness and horror of the holiday, they checked grief at the door. How did Arcana do that to people?

Nothing left to say to Andy, Smith breezed past the curtain of the goth room. Inside, they bathed in the characteristic emptiness and dull red glow of the space. However many regulars even noticed the room, fewer still *needed* it the way some did. The peaceful antechamber balanced Smith's unsteady high. They closed their eyes, found their place, and returned to counting their nights.

...Chris, Annie, Levi, Selene, Twyla, Wayne, and—

"Tom," Smith murmured to themself. Their ghost mask slipped back into place.

At the back of the goth room, the rearranged church pew faced the wall. The plastic clips that had displayed Jade's cards now hung a collection of posters, ribbons, photos, drawings, and flowers. Handwritten notes stuck to the bare wall between pictures of Ember and June, lush with joyful memories and inside jokes. As ever, Ember's presence dominated the space, but on closer inspection, some messages and images belonged to Levi, Colton, and even Julie.

Smith stood behind the pew, not noticing Selene or Jade on the bench until Selene lifted their head off Jade's shoulder. "Fuck, Tom, you're hovering like an actual ghost. No offense."

"Shit, sorry." Smith removed their mask and stuffed it into the pew's prayerbook pocket. "Selene, are you... I heard you were at the hospital. Is your dad alright?"

They rolled their eyes. "The needy bastard's taking his time, for now. Wait, I told you already, didn't I?"

Jade spun around on the bench seat. "Smith?"

Smith nodded. "Tom left me a note." They passed Jade the folded sheet from their pocket and hurdled the pew. Smith took a much-needed seat on its hard wood, still absorbing the immense memorial wall. Selene laid their head back on Jade's shoulder. After reading Tom's note, Jade held her sketchbook on her lap and rendered sections of the wall in ink.

"Does it make things worse," Smith wondered aloud, "if nobody knows what they all died for?"

Jade capped her blue pen and shook it. "I don't think they died for the cards."

"They didn't," Selene agreed. "They died trying to do right by someone they loved."

Smith still tasted the dust of evaporated paper. They sank lower onto the pew. "If people need martyrs to challenge the hate in this country, that's one thing. But do we have to pretend that the cards never happened?"

Jade shut her sketchbook and snapped a rubber band around her assorted pens. She pinched the bridge of her nose. "I've got the rest of my life to wonder why my art resurrected two dead people and killed three more, including my oldest friend. I've got time to drink alone and figure out this body-tarot-spirit magic shit for myself. So please, Smith, I don't want to talk about the cards tonight."

Smith's face burned. "I'm sorry. You're right. I just..." They waited for a round of applause to simmer while they gathered their courage. "I think I'm gonna die next."

"What?" Selene perked up again. Jade scooped up her pens. She dumped them into the open pocket of her bag. The sketchbook came next. She dragged the zipper closed, slung the bag over one shoulder, and stood from the pew.

"Tom makes twenty-two, then?" Selene whispered as if someone in the next room could overhear. "All your bodies, you counted?"

Smith bit their lip, re-counted one more time in their head, and nodded at them. "If Tom's right, and this is my last body, then at least Waite's in their last one too. Next drink each of us takes, we're gone for good."

"You're still here, tonight," Jade reminded them. "You gonna make it count?"

Smith hunched their shoulders. "Well, I tried hitting Oz's pen. Bad idea."

"I have a better one." Jade yanked Smith up off the church pew. "Selene, you're coming too."

Selene dragged themself down to the end of the bench before rising to their feet. "I am *not* getting squeezed in the Frog Truck. Smith, the middle seat is all yours."

Jade guided them both towards the exit, all three blending themselves into the casual in-out flow of cigarette smokers. Saying goodbye to anyone felt too big for Smith. They made it all the way to the middle of the parking lot before their legs froze up.

"Smith?" Jade tugged their hand.

"See her, about to go inside?" Smith pointed. The full moon's glow made it easy to spot a woman in a puffy down jacket, holding her ID for A-Bomb to inspect. "I was her, one night. That's Andy's sister, Ellesandra. She was Levi's ex, too, so she must've been at his funeral. Do you think they talked? Are they about to? She—"

"Whatever!" Jade torqued Smith's wrist, dragging them to the Frog Truck. "You had their bodies. Let them have their lives. It's fucking cold out here; let's go."

As Selene held the passenger door, Smith buckled into the middle seat of the Frog Truck. They blew hot breaths through their fingers while the engine warmed itself, still blasting cold air through the vents. Jade steered for the main road. Selene unraveled a charging cord and plugged their phone into the cigarette lighter. Smith wiped condensation off the inside of the windshield with the cloak of Tom's costume.

Block after block, the city thinned. Shops, trees, lots, and apartment buildings gave way to the bare green shoulders of a wider turnpike. A sweeping exit ramp sent the truck up a smooth, two-lane parkway with no streetlamps or driveways, only steep downward hills and late autumn forests.

"Where are we going?" Smith asked, only after the city vanished in the passenger mirror. Selene pointed to Jade, who stared at the road ahead. Smith trusted her well enough. The truck entered a tunnel carved through the rough mountain stone. At its opposite end, the headlights caught a sign for a narrow turnoff. Jade slowed the truck and cruised to a stop in a small lot alongside the roadway. She killed the engine. The headlights faded, and the parking space overlooked a valley of darkness below. Over the truck's hood, Smith tried to distinguish the shapes of the distant mountains. "Why here?"

"Shh," Selene hushed them. They pulled a lever to recline their seatback, which included Smith's middle seat. Jade unbuckled her seatbelt. She spoke in a whisper, but no other noise challenged her.

"When I came out to Ember, the summer after high school, I said I *knew* what came next." She took a deep breath and held it. Smith held theirs too, until Jade let hers go. "I told him the rest of my life would be chaotic, loud, and short. That's how it was headed, between getting kicked out, losing jobs, and relying on *bad* people. The whole country started screaming that I'm *wrong*, like, for even existing. I barely remember parts of that summer, but I do remember the night Ember picked my ass up and drove me here, in his parents' minivan. You can't see shit from this overlook at night, cause Lewesboro is behind the ridgeline. If you wait long enough, though, look *up*. Away from the city, the stars shine brighter. You're starting to see 'em now, right? Ember told me some of those are the oldest or farthest in the universe, fresh from the Big Bang. He said it in his way, you know. He said, 'those are the stars that remember *true* chaos, all the nuclear explosions that made our atoms.' He told me that what I felt, the pressure and fear and uncertainty of coming into *being* is what those stars felt, casting their first light. Everything they are bursts from them in every wavelength, reaching across the dark to bring even the tiniest *pinpoint* of a rainbow." Jade's voice grew hoarse, almost cracking. Her darting eyes sewed imaginary constellations on the patchwork of emerging glimmers in the black. "Ember said, 'the stars are afraid until we see them.' And to show them what we see, he said, to shine *back* at them, Ember said that's why we put the rainbow on a flag. We have to wave it for the young stars and hope they see they're not alone."

Until the stars melted, Smith didn't notice themself crying. "I see them," they told Jade. "I see them all."

"That means you're one of us." She sniffed. Jade wiped her eyes and opened her arms. "Is it okay if I give you a hug?"

It was, so she did.

"C'mon, save some for me." Selene sat up and joined the embrace.

Jade unfolded the blanket from behind her seat, promising Smith that she washed their puke off it. She, Selene, and Smith shared its woolen heft. Waiting for more stars to arrive, they took turns telling each other everything they could: the stories, the names of strangers, and the nights they forgot or missed at Arcana. Smith fell asleep, curled in the middle seat, neither needing nor caring to dream.

On the first morning of their life, Smith awoke when their pupils contracted. Warm rainbows of tremendous new starlight flooded the Frog Truck's cabin. Glassy droplets beaded inside the windows and trailed rivers down their fogged surfaces. Dehydrated, delirious, and still draped in Tom's ghost costume, Smith reached over the dashboard and wiped the dewy inside of the windshield. A miraculous sunbeam unveiled the expanse ahead. Smooth mountain ridges swam across the land like a pod of giant whales. Dawn mist crested off their backs like sea spray into the cloudless peach sky.

The world was bigger than Arcana, bigger than Smith feared, and bigger than the people they hoped to call friends. They considered waking up Jade or Selene, but they didn't dare to break the quiet. Smith tucked their arms back under the blanket and closed their eyes. Soon enough, Smith would quench their thirst. For now, they could live off the dream of one more day.

RAISE YOUR GLASS

Cheers to Mif Rodriguez for designing and creating twenty-two magnificent chapter illustrations, representing the trumps of Jade's New American Arcana. Cheers to the talented authors of Phoenix Fire Writing Guild, St. Marks Place Creative Writing Meetup, NYC Book Writing Meetup Group, Writing Under the Influence, and Brooklyn Novel Workshop for their constructive insights and camaraderie. Cheers to my family, friends, and partners who have listened to many ramblings about this project and provided feedback on its drafts. Cheers in particular to Bren for lending tarot knowledge and to Ceci for providing brutal critiques. Cheers to Nicragomi for checking my Eastern Band Cherokee translation. Cheers to Brooklyn, New York's Turtles All The Way Down for lending table space as the backdrop for the photograph on this book's jacket. Cheers to Hillary, who once told me that *when some people drink, they're basically haunted*. Cheers to Priscilla Chambers for asking me an important question. Cheers to the faithful owners, bartenders, barbacks, entertainers, and bouncers of Asheville, North Carolina's 27 Club, for reasons completely, definitely, absolutely unrelated to this book.

ABOUT THE AUTHOR

S.C. Giedzinski is a Brooklyn-based electrical engineer who designs solar farms throughout the United States. She periodically carries cumbersome objects across the city, creates open-source 3D-printing projects, and dances for hours at a time. Giedzinski graduated from the University of Maryland in 2021 with a B.S. in mechanical engineering and a creative writing minor. She is proudly transgender.

ABOUT THE ILLUSTRATOR

Mif Rodriguez is a New York City-based creative who enjoys their time tattooing, crafting, and drawing. They are a local punk, with a battle jacket and—at time of publication—spikes to boot. They are most likely seen during the evening hours and are seldom punctual. Though rarely found, inquiring parties may seek them on Instagram @skunk.riot.